Thank you and I hope you

MW00893958

Copyrights

ISBN 978-1-7324852-0-4

INTRODUCTION

CIA HEADQUARTERS

CIA Director Lynn Bancroft picked up the file on the top of the stack and slowly sat down at her desk. "FOR DIRECTOR OF CIA EYES ONLY" was stamped in red on the front of the folder emblazoned with the CIA seal. "WARNING: UNAUTHORIZED DISCLOSURE WILL RESULT IN 20 YEARS IMPRISONMENT AND/OR FINE OF $100,000." Bancroft felt her blood run cold when she read the first line of the classified document: SUBJ: Missing Five Portable Prototype Nuclear Devices.

Her worst nightmare had just become a horrific reality. She clearly recalled being informed that those prototypes had been recovered and destroyed. The possibility of who had lied to her was unthinkable. The fact that five portable Nukes were missing was even more unthinkable. Bancroft knew that there was one person she could trust. She opened the top desk drawer and pulled out another file, "OPERATION KNIGHTHOOD." The pilot program she had created to produce the best-trained counterterrorist agents was a glimmer of hope in the darkness of the rapidly approaching storm. She could feel her heart pounding as she took a deep breath, picked up her phone and speed dialed Special Agent Jack Connor.

SITE 23, RUSSIAN SPACE COMMAND
URAL MOUNTAINS

Viper ignored the cold numbness in his lower body as he lay prone in the trench he had methodically crafted the day before. Cloaked by a NASA lightweight thermo blanket and wearing a ghillie suit specially designed for the snow, he blended into the winter terrain. He had painstakingly coated his Light Woodland Camouflage Chandler Sniper M40 rifle barrel with flat white gun metal paint to prevent any reflections off the icy surfaces. Since his ghillie suit covered the base of the man-of-war rifle, only the barrel needed to blend into the landscape and virtually disappear. His target stood a thousand yards from his firing position.

Viper knew that a millimeter of movement in his scope at this distance meant at least ten feet of variance in the bullet's path.

1

Frost had accumulated on his eyebrows, but he fought off the urge to blink as he rotated the weapon on the attached bipod and slowly acquired his target.

Two Russian officers stood outside the entrance to the restricted Site 23 of the Russian Space Command, a secret fortress burrowed into a hillside in the Beloretsk area of the Southern Ural Mountains. Their nostrils flared as they exhaled plumes of smoke into the frigid air and scanned the landscape.

"Comrade Colonel, this assassin must be stopped at all costs and brought to me before the winter's end! He is an enemy of Mother Russia and our new world order!" Vice Defense Minister of Russia's Space and Technology Program Igor Ivanovich barked. He struck an imposing figure in a tailored extreme cold-weather military overcoat that hid the rank on his uniform.

Colonel Vladimir Alexandrov, a high-ranking officer of the Federal Security Service of the Russian Federation (FSB) stared intently at the vice minister and paused before he replied.

Viper maintained a controlled breathing rhythm as he slowly began to squeeze the trigger, the target centered perfectly in his crosshairs. He subconsciously calculated the path of the .388 cal. round as he slightly increased the pressure on the trigger. Suddenly, blurred white-and-black stripes appeared in his visual field. He eased his finger off the trigger and squinted into the scope. A massive Siberian tiger turned its head in Viper's direction and momentarily froze. The tiger tensed into a crouch and it sniffed the air as its bright eyes searched for any sign of prey.

"Comrade Minister, I will brief my team and I assure you, we will track him down," Colonel Alexandrov crisply replied.

"You must keep this operation secret. Tell no one. I will explain the importance of this mission later tonight. Is that understood?" the vice minister demanded. As a former KGB officer, the minister inspired fear, but commanded respect. He had handpicked the colonel because he knew his reputation and was confident the colonel would complete the mission, no questions asked.

"Yes sir!"

Unable to sense movement or scent, the tiger moved cautiously down the snowy slope, leaving a silent trail of ominous paw tracks. Viper slowly adjusted the elevation on the 15x50 NXS scope and resumed his firing sequence as he reacquired the target.

"Comrade Col...Ahhh!" The vice minister choked on his scream, as he jolted backwards and slammed onto the icy floor.

"Guards! Guards!" The colonel yelled toward the security post as he wiped bone fragments and brain matter off his face and stared at the minister's blood-drenched body. Colonel Alexandrov took a deep breath and clenched his hands together in a tight fist to stop the shaking. He stood motionless in the eerie silence, stunned by the swift action of violence.

Viper imagined the sharp whipping motion of the minister's face through his NXS scope as the bullet made impact. He knew that with this caliber, range, and velocity, death was a mathematical certainty. He slithered through the snow into the tree line leaving no trace. One of the last few individuals to pose a threat to Viper's identity...*terminated.*

CIA HEADQUARTERS, LANGLEY, VA

"Ma'am, please check Merlin. It's a Code Red B-1 hit from the Moscow Station Chief," the duty officer spoke abruptly from his computer screen in the operation center at CIA headquarters.

"Okay," Director Lynn Bancroft responded as she swiveled her chair around and hit the Enter key on her laptop. Merlin was the CIA's code word for its classified e-mail system. Code Red B-1 meant that a friendly or neutral high-ranking foreign government official had been assassinated.

Bancroft scanned the e-mail from the agency's top official in Moscow and considered the implications of the assassination. She grabbed the red titanium phone and instantly connected to a secure line to Jordan Zif, the National Security Adviser.

"Yeah."

Bancroft immediately recognized the distinctive growl in his voice. "It's Lynn. We've got a problem. Vice Defense Minister Ivanovich was just assassinated at Site 23 in the Ural Mountains. That's all we got for now, but I think it was Viper. We tracked him to Colombia, but we later developed intel that he had suddenly returned to Russia for a mission."

"Russians catch the bastard?"

"No."

"Why do you suspect Viper? He's gone rogue now, and freelances for the cartel, right? You think the cartel had the minister killed? Why would they do that?" Zif replied in disbelief.

"Viper is the only assassin we know who has the knowledge and experience to pull this off. My gut tells me that the Bogotá Cartel had nothing to do with this, and that's what's truly disturbing. If it was Viper, it means he's also working for someone else, maybe someone inside the Russian government. Right now you know as much as I do. I'll get back in a few hours with an update."

"Thanks. I have a meeting with the President in ten minutes and I'll fill him in."

The top five assassins known to the CIA popped up on Bancroft's Merlin screen as fast as she typed the word assassins. Her eyes only focused on one name- *Viper. Identity unknown. Suspected Russian Special Forces. Freelance. Suspected association-Bogotá Cartel.*

Bancroft got up and walked to her window, oblivious to the peaceful Virginia countryside. Her mind raced and she felt a rising sense of apprehension. The agency's highest ranking spy in Russia had just been murdered. Why?

CHAPTER 1

REDWOOD SHORES, CA

Jack Connor glanced at his Ironman watch as he ran, breathing harder than normal. In a split second, his head turned at the whining sound of a V-6 engine and his feet came to an abrupt halt. He nearly fell as he pulled back to avoid running directly into the SUV as it briefly slowed at the intersection before turning right in front of him.

He caught a glimpse of the woman reaching into the backseat toward a baby in a car seat as her SUV rolled through the turn. She was clearly oblivious to how close she had come to hitting him.

Killed running, not in the Marines, CIA, or DEA but by a soccer mom, Connor grimaced, his heart pounding as he stood at the edge of the curb. His iPhone vibrated, and he recognized the caller.

"Good morning, Jack." The CIA Director's face appeared on his 2085 Dpi resolution screen.

"Morning, ma'am."

"How is that prototype satellite iPhone 10x working out?" Bancroft established eye contact on the crystal clear screen.

"Excellent." Connor appreciated the director's zeal for procuring the most advanced technology. The Apple prototype looked like the new iPhone, but it had both standard cell site coverage and satellite capability with several unique, classified features.

"Good, remember there are only three of those and we have two of them, at $10,000 a whack, so be careful with it. Listen, there have been some disturbing developments. A sniper just killed Russia's Vice Defense Minister and I have a hunch it was Viper, that assassin I told you about. Second, we traced the terrorist you've been tracking to cell sites in the 6-5-0 area code, specifically between Menlo Park and Redwood City. Who knows, they might be your neighbors in the Shores. Last night we got two intercepts between the cartel and the terrorist cell."

"Just what I want to hear, terrorist neighbors. Something to remember next time I start my car," Connor groaned.

"Gets even better. The top cartel financier in Bangkok just defected. Seems he has developed a conscience about cocaine trafficking. Who knows, maybe he can provide a connection between the cell and the cartel. I want you to debrief him as soon as possible. I know that DEA will jump all over this after I throw your name out, so be prepared to travel to Quantico. Time is running out. We have to establish a link between the cartel and the terrorists and stop this cell!"

The iPhone went silent and the screen dark. Connor took a deep breath and tried to process his conflicting and complex assignments. He took off down the path. Maintaining a seven-minute mile pace was much more difficult now than it had been during his earlier years in the Marine Corps.

BOGOTÁ, COLOMBIA

Three men stood together on the ornate black-and-white Italian marble balcony overlooking a deep, mountainous gorge. Waterfalls sprayed the lush green vegetation nearby. Years ago, Paez Indians had cultivated the same vegetation on secluded ridges in the San Jorge Valley in the department of Cauca in southwest Colombia. Here, it grew in wild profusion, a profitable cash crop for the three brothers who approvingly surveyed their family business, coca. Like the Paez, they carefully selected small grow-sites to make aerial detection more difficult.

The Spanish-style hacienda, which they arrogantly named The Palace, was home to Joaquin Gusto. He and his younger brothers, Julio and Jorge, headed the Bogotá Cartel. They processed and shipped over a hundred tons of cocaine to the United States each year.

"I want Juan Sanchez dead now! I want his family beheaded, every one of them! We will hang their rotting skulls at the marketplace in Bogotá for all to see! No one on my council betrays me to the Americans!" Spit from Joaquin's mouth sprayed on his brother's shirt as he stomped on the balcony. Joaquin's tone was venomous, his eyes full of hatred.

"Has the *asesino* signaled us?" Julio asked, using the Spanish word for assassin.

"No," he replied, "something interfered and he had to return to Russia. We are to blame! Sanchez, a man I loved like my own brother betrayed me like a common thief! We were fools to trust him! He was born to a peasant whore! Viper must deliver our revenge and we will make an example of Juan Sanchez. Contact Raven. Order him to find out everything about this bastard!" Joaquin ranted in a fit of rage.

"We must not inflame the people. They will revolt," Jorge added cautiously, reluctant to fuel his brother's fury, but even more reluctant to cause an uprising among the peasants who harvested the crops. Sanchez had risen from their ranks to join the Gustos' inner circle and the peasants were loyal to him.

"Then they will die with him. Let us share wine my brothers." Joaquin's eyes glinted as he put his arms around their shoulders and led them into *The Palace*.

CIA HEADQUARTERS

"How long are you going to keep Jack Connor in his present assignment?" Emma Brown, Bancroft's executive assistant nervously asked her boss.

"Until we dismantle this terrorist cell, or until DEA figures out we have one of our own CIA officer's undercover in their agency," Bancroft replied with a sigh.

Director's Eyes Only the folder read. Bancroft opened Connor's file to log her latest entry. "And until we find that damn FBI mole," the director grumbled to herself.

"Ma'am I'm worried about your undercover program that places our top officers covertly into other agencies, especially DEA."

"I appreciate the concern Emma, I do. There are a lot of government agencies that fight terrorists. We spend billions of dollars trying to find just a handful of them. We have all types of theories and massive egos, but yet a few terrorists continue to cripple our country and its economy. Not to mention the constant attempts to detonate a nuclear weapon on U.S. soil. Our government is too bifurcated and has too much overlap. One person can make a difference, as we have learned from our terrorism scholars. We fight fire with fire, we cut through the red tape... Emma, don't worry so much! You know my two favorite mottos."

"Yes ma'am. *Who Dares Wins and Keep it Simple Stupid*...the Brits SAS commandos' and Marine Corps' mottos."

"That's right Emma, besides, the President agrees with me. If you wanna worry about something, worry about what happens if we don't win because we've made it too complicated."

Brown didn't respond and walked back to her office. Bancroft appreciated and valued Brown's counsel and candor. There weren't many Columbia University Ph.D. Rhodes scholars in international relations among the government elite cabinet level appointees or senior executive service ranks, let alone executive staff.

REDWOOD SHORES, CA

One of the officers recognized the long stride of the dark-haired, lean, six-foot tall runner as he approached the crime scene.

Jack Connor struggled to maintain his pace as he rounded the corner, then automatically slowed down at the sight of red, amber, and blue lights flashing in the parking lot of the large office complex.

The paramedics stared from the back of their ambulance as the cops rolled bright yellow crime scene tape around a clump of bushes. Connor was taken aback at the sight of the lifeless body of a young woman in jeans with a torn white tank top, her face bruised and swollen.

"Hey, Jack! What are you doing up this early in the morning? You Feds always sleep late," a voice called out from a group of uniformed officers standing near the running path.

Connor recognized Redwood City police officer Randy Hernandez. Hernandez helped DEA a couple months earlier, when a last minute target of opportunity thrust Hernandez into the role of undercover officer. He was the spitting image of a Bogotá Cartel transportation lieutenant and Hernandez' efforts helped DEA seize 1,000 kilograms of cocaine.

Hernandez had played his undercover role so well that the main target asked him to be the best man at his wedding. That was where an army of DEA agents busted them. They went ballistic when Hernandez pulled out a half-dozen pairs of flex cuffs and started arresting people. As he was being wrestled to the ground, the main target kept yelling, *"DEAA, DEAA, DEAA!"* traffickers Spanish slang for DEA, and *"Man, you can't trust nobody!"* The DEA agents later presented Hernandez with a shirt with *"DEAA,*

8

you can't trust NOBODY!" embossed across the back, which he wore proudly under his bulletproof vest.

"What happened?" Connor asked over the voices in the background.

"Man, it's strange, a Cessna pilot on his final approach to the San Carlos airport saw a guy exit a van and drag that young girl's body over there. The pilot was low on fuel and couldn't abort the landing to follow the guy, so he radioed the tower and they called dispatch. I was in the area and responded within five minutes, but the asshole was gone. It's the first murder in Redwood Shores. Hey, maybe your wife will be assigned the case."

"Possibly, but she's new to the homicide unit. Damn, I wish I'd been a few minutes earlier," Connor responded shaking his head. His wife Barrett was a Deputy District Attorney for the San Mateo County. She had been assigned to the homicide unit one month earlier.

"You might have caught him, but you wouldn't have saved her life. I overheard one of the medics say she was probably strangled somewhere else and dumped here. I've got to get back to work. News crews will be here shortly, and it will be a real zoo," Hernandez added as he ducked back under the crime scene tape.

Connor flew the last mile home. He got to his stairs in six and a half minutes flat and was out of breath when he walked into the bedroom. Barrett was standing in front of the floor-length mirror, unbuttoning her cream silk blouse and taking off her black suit jacket. She was five foot seven inches tall, but looked taller in her Italian heels. Her eyes were steel blue and she had long, thick blonde hair pulled back into a knot at the nape of her neck. She glanced at him as he stood there and stared at her while he caught his breath.

"Well, I'm glad I leave you panting for air, but don't get any ideas. These clothes have to come off for purely business reasons. I just got a call from the DA's office. There's been a homicide in the Shores and they want me to respond to the crime scene."

"I know, I ran into ten Redwood City cops on the running path near the slough. Somebody murdered a young woman and dumped her body near the marshy area."

"I've got to coordinate the investigation with the police. My first homicide!" Barrett was eager to get to the scene.

"You'll do fine. Randy is on the scene now. He said he hoped you'd get the case. Sounded like they don't have much to go on."

"That's why forensics will be so important."

"Barrett, maybe we should start running together after work."

"A great idea except for one simple fact. You usually work late and are not here when I go for my run. We've had this discussion before Jack, you work for the government and have a dangerous job. I'm okay with it. I can't stand it when you tell me not to do something because you think it's dangerous. You sound like my dad!"

"Ok, ok, I got it." Connor knew not to remind Barrett of her dad.

She gave him a quick kiss on the cheek then headed for the door.

"Hey, not so fast," he grabbed her and kissed her hard on the lips.

"Don't worry, I'll see you later."

"Damn attorneys. You can't tell them anything!" he yelled after her.

He still vividly remembered the first time that he saw her. He was following a lead on campus. She was a third-year law student at Boalt Hall, UC Berkeley. She was chasing a guy twice her size, yelling at him to stop. The guy, a thief, who had just stolen a fellow law student's backpack, ran directly into Connor because he kept looking over his shoulder at the screaming woman running after him. Barrett yanked the backpack out of the guy's hands and slugged him with it as she loudly berated him, "You no good piece of shit!" It was love at first sight for him. It took her a while longer. He still felt a rush when he saw her. He couldn't believe they would soon celebrate their first wedding anniversary.

Connor slipped his high-rise leather holster onto his belt that fit firmly against his hip. A quick compression check ensured that his government-issued Sig Sauer P228 9mm handgun was hot. Satisfied, he slid the weapon snugly into the holster, which blended seamlessly under his casual shirt, and headed to his car.

Like most federal agents, he had an assigned government vehicle, fondly referred to as "G-rides" by the agents. DEA was one of the few agencies…like the CIA…that boasted an impressive fleet of cars. Many were high-end sports or luxury cars that had been seized from cash-heavy drug dealers. All DEA vehicles underwent a thorough retrofit in which they got upgraded suspensions, a security system with remote-activated start-up, emergency pursuit electronics with wigwag lights, and Motorola UHF and VHF radios. Right now, he was driving a Ford Mustang GT with a 5.0 coyote engine. It wasn't as flashy as the BMW he had just turned in, but the Mustang had a V-8 engine that rocked, thanks to his unauthorized purchase of a few Shelby performance parts. They boosted horsepower by thirty percent to 525 hp, without a supercharger, which meant the car was lighter in the front-end for better handling. Anyone who knew Connor knew that he was obsessed with muscle cars, especially Mustangs. The horsepower was entirely wasted as he slowly merged into northbound traffic on Highway 101.

"Damn," he muttered in frustration, irritated that he would be late for an 8:30 a.m. meeting with his boss and the Special Agent in Charge or SAC, as commonly referred to by DEA personnel.

R&B TOWING, MENLO PARK, CA

"Assad! Where have you been?" the receptionist demanded. "Hakeem has been asking about you every 10 minutes!"

"I went out to Starbucks for coffee and something to eat."

"Hakeem needs your help!" *May Allah forgive your soul*, the receptionist mumbled as Assad walked past her toward the secure area at the far side of the towing warehouse.

Hakeem turned around at the sound of footsteps. "Finally, you are back, Assad. Any problems with the body?" Hakeem asked in a hushed tone.

"No."

"Next time we will not use outsiders for anything. We cannot expect Americans to follow Allah's path…I just received this, do you think you can make this device?" Hakeem abruptly changed the subject and handed Assad a diagram.

"With a little time, yes," Assad responded submissively.

"Good. Start immediately," Hakeem ordered, then quickly walked out of the security area.

Assad stared intently at the diagram, then walked into a small storage room and reached for two plastic containers full of a chemical compound.

CHAPTER 2

SAN FRANCISCO

Christ, it's 8:45 a.m. and I'm 15 minutes late for my meeting with the SAC, Connor thought as he rushed through the closing doors of the Federal Building elevator. The elevator jerked slowly toward the 14th floor where the DEA offices were located. *Come on, come on*, Connor grew impatient. He could never understand why the elevators didn't work when the government spent fifty-million-dollars to renovate the relic building.

"Connor, you're late," a voice echoed down the hall.

"I know boss, I tried calling but you've been on the phone."

"That's how it is when you're a GS son, you're always on the damn phone. Officer Hernandez called and said there had been a murder in Redwood Shores. Did you see anything?" Group Supervisor (GS) Bill Cartwright asked curiously.

"No sir."

"Well tell Barrett to be careful, that's a little too close to home," Cartwright added.

"Tell me about it!"

Cartwright was a piranha, real old-school, a former Chicago police officer, tough as nails, who almost broke every bone in his body in the line of duty, not as a DEA agent, but as a Chicago police officer.

"The SAC wants us in his office now! The administrator called, there's a new development on the Gusto investigation," Cartwright said. The Gusto investigation targeted the Bogotá Cartel cocaine trafficking organization and Connor was the case agent. No one in DEA knew that Connor was actually a CIA agent. His undercover DEA assignment had been covertly arranged by the director of the CIA.

"Let me grab my case file," Connor replied and headed into his group's squad bay.

"Hurry up, I don't want to keep the SAC waiting!" Cartwright barked, never one for mincing words.

The large open bay housed the fifteen agents in Group Two, the cocaine group. Connor's desk was near the front and his phone was ringing. Voicemail didn't kick in on the fifth ring because it was overloaded with messages. Connor ignored the incessant ringing.

13

"Hey Jack, what's the deal? Someone was murdered in Redwood Shores. Man, no fucking place is safe," one of the agents greeted him as he approached Connor's desk.

"You got that right!" Connor was amazed how fast the word had spread around the office.

Connor grabbed the case file on his desk with big bold print, *"Level One Investigation, Bogotá Cartel-Gusto Brothers"* which meant that DEA headquarters in Washington, DC gave it the highest priority for staffing and resources. It was definitely a priority investigation, however, the CIA's version of priority was vastly different from DEA's.

Connor tried not to focus on the dilemma of his dual identity in both his personal and professional life. He was trying not to second guess his decision to take this assignment. He felt like he was violating the trust of the agents he worked with in DEA by concealing the fact that he was actually a covert CIA case officer.

Connor remembered his first day in training at "the farm", the CIA's Academy, when a senior instructor said, "Gentlemen, in the CIA there are no friendlies." Connor had to constantly remind himself of that phrase. The director was adamant that his undercover mission was essential to national security, but that didn't make it any easier.

His dilemma was magnified by the fact that he was not yet authorized to disclose his status as a CIA agent to his new bride. Given Barrett's temperament and her hatred for the CIA, which she had never fully explained, he dreaded thinking about how she would react to that news. He hoped that in time, as their relationship cemented, he would finally be allowed to tell her.

"Connor! SAC's office, now!" Cartwright yelled into the squad bay.

"On the way."

BOGOTÁ, COLOMBIA

The thunderstorm hit Bogotá hard. Rain pelted the streets, sending alley rats scurrying for cover between rusting and overflowing garbage cans clustered beside dilapidated brick buildings. Outside Bogotá, occasional bolts of lightning illuminated the rain-drenched mansion on the hillside. Inside *The Palace*, in a spacious and ornately decorated room, logs crackled in the fireplace as four men sat around an austere, highly polished antique table, in 17th century tapestry-covered chairs from Spain.

Joaquin Gusto had convened an emergency meeting of the senior members of his council. They were three powerful men, carefully chosen by Joaquin to assist him in the administration and management of the most profitable drug enterprise in Colombia's history. Seven of the eleven chairs were vacant.

"Where is Enrique?" Joaquin demanded impatiently. Enrique Molina was responsible for distribution in Asia, not a volume buyer like the United States, but a loyal one whose appetite was growing.

No one answered.

"We will wait," he said as he nodded to a woman dressed in a black-and-white uniform who stood by a table at the other end of the room. She immediately picked up a silver pitcher and began pouring freshly brewed coffee into white china cups, monogrammed with a silver "G" on one side and a gold engraved likeness of *The Palace* on the other.

Joaquin had taken Maria and her son into his house and given her a job after her husband, a trusted lieutenant who had worked for him for five years, was killed in downtown Bogotá by a car bomb meant for Joaquin. She was a beautiful woman in her late twenties, petite, with dark, thick hair that hung to her waist. None of the men openly acknowledged her presence as she moved from place to place around the table because Joaquin had made it clear that Maria was strictly off-limits, a level of respect that few women in the Gusto household were afforded.

Joaquin surveyed the table and wondered if any other member of his trusted Council intended to betray him. His brother Jorge was loyal, dedicated and hardworking; his name meant "farmer" in Spanish. He coordinated distribution to the United States and Canada. Joaquin could not imagine that Jorge would betray him.

Their younger brother, Julio, was aptly named, for Julio meant "youth." He was content to follow in the footsteps of his brothers. He coordinated distribution to the low-volume buyers… the former Soviet Union and a few Eastern European countries. Julio would not betray him because betrayal would require work and Julio was permanently afflicted with laziness.

Roberto Fuerte, the chief security officer, kept his eyes on the door as he sipped his coffee. He diligently protected the Gustos. He knew that they had many enemies.

When they were young men, Joaquin had saved his life. Joaquin remembered that day many years ago. An old rival cartel ambushed them at one of the Gustos' processing plants. Roberto fell to the ground after a bullet struck him in the back. Joaquin ran into the open through a barrage of bullets and pulled him inside the plant. They escaped through underground tunnels. Joaquin carried Roberto on his back to a doctor and stayed with him for a week until he was well enough to return home. Roberto's loyalty was fierce. Joaquin was certain that his loyalty could never be questioned, but he was beginning to wonder if he could really trust the other seven members of his council. Joaquin only truly trusted his brothers and Roberto.

The men sipped their coffee in respectful silence, nervous at the calling of this meeting and the unstable temperament of their leader. The silence was interrupted when the great doors swung open and Enrique Molina entered the room.

"Enrique, I know that your name means 'rules the house,' but I remind you that this is the house of *Gusto*, not the house of Molina," Joaquin scolded, and then smiled. Everyone laughed. They knew Joaquin judged a man by what his name meant in Spanish and would often shout at them to either live up to their names or live them down.

"I apologize, Jefe," he replied sheepishly.

"Where is Franco Ramirez?"

"He is on his way," Enrique replied reluctantly. Joaquin had ordered him to bring Ramirez, one of the cartel's accountants to the meeting. "He has been unexpectedly delayed. He had to take an urgent phone call concerning one of the Asian accounts."

"We will begin without him. Have we calculated the losses caused by Juan Sanchez' treason?" Joaquin asked the senior council members.

"Yes. The loss is minimal. Fortunately, Enrique discovered Sanchez' slush fund after he disappeared, but before he stole the Asian accounts. I convinced the Swiss to reverse the transfer of funds and to freeze Sanchez out of our accounts," Roberto replied.

"How did you do that, Roberto?" Joaquin asked in awe.

"I taught them simple mathematics...addition, subtraction, multiplication, and division." He paused. "I told them if they added the total amount of money in Gusto accounts, subtracted that amount from their deposits, multiplied that amount by one hundred percent...our projected profits for this year...and divided by the number of deaths of their mothers, they would arrive at the solution." The men burst into laughter and Joaquin slapped him on the back.

"Well done, Roberto, well done! We need to clean up the mess, now. Have you received any communications from Viper?" Joaquin continued.

"Not yet. When we last communicated, he said he was finishing a winter vacation. But I am certain that he will contact us as soon as he has completed the mission. He will hunt Juan Sanchez down and kill him like a filthy dog," Roberto's tone was murderous.

Only Roberto and the Gusto brothers knew Viper's identity. Roberto met Viper years ago when Roberto was a lieutenant in the Black Tigers...a secret unit within the Colombian army that provided protection to Colombia's conservative party president. The period was known as *la violencia*, where party membership was sufficient reason to kill. Conservative party leadership was the target of a liberal third-party political group, the Revolutionary Armed Forces of Colombia (*Fuerzas Armadas Revolucionarias de Colombia...FARC*), the guerrilla arm of the pro-Soviet Communist Party of Colombia. It employed terrorist tactics...torture, kidnapping, extortion, and murder...to intimidate voters into supporting candidates with Marxism-Leninism ideologies. *FARC* continues its campaign of terror against the Colombian government, but now with the support of the invisible hand of the Bogotá Cartel.

Ironically, the Special Forces of the GRU, the Russian military intelligence organization, secretly trained the Black Tigers after the fall in the Soviet Union. Roberto met Lieutenant Ivan Volkov...now Viper...a young officer of a Spetsnaz platoon, part of an anti-VIP brigade in Russia. An anti-VIP platoon's mission is to identify, find, and kill enemy political and military leaders. All of the soldiers assigned to the small "sabotage" companies were Olympic-caliber athletes.

Lieutenant Volkov and his highly trained sniper team taught professional assassination techniques, including penetration into and withdrawal from enemy territory without detection. Roberto learned to stalk a prey for days before a kill in order to memorize the terrain in the kill zone and to learn the prey's daily routine. He developed the skill of becoming one with his surroundings, becoming invisible in the desert, the jungle, the woods, the urban sprawl of cities, the dirty streets of slums, the glamorous ballrooms of the wealthy, and the shopping malls of the middle class. Volkov once told him, "The hunted can find no safe place." Roberto had never felt safe since.

Volkov left the Soviet Union shortly after it began to fall apart. He knew that professional soldiers could find work anywhere in the world. He rose out of the ashes of his crumbling country like a phoenix, self-reincarnated as Viper, assassin-for-hire.

"There is some good news, from Raven," the cartel's most secretive American informant, Roberto continued, "He has learned that Juan Sanchez has not yet been debriefed, the word the Americans use to describe their Gestapo-like interrogation tactics. The CIA's lead interrogator is in Japan, completing the debriefing of an individual who was part of a newly formed terrorist cell. Raven is unsure, but he thinks the CIA is waiting for him to complete this interrogation before they debrief Sanchez," Roberto explained.

"Why wouldn't the DEA debrief him?" Joaquin asked.

"Jefe, the CIA wants to control everything," Roberto responded.

"Stupid Americans. Their agencies squabble like school boys fighting over a sweet young girl," Joaquin scoffed.

"While I'm thinking of it, I want to give Raven a bonus for his assistance in this matter. The information he provided was exceptional. What do you think, Roberto?"

"I think you are too generous, but it is a wise investment. A bonus will motivate Raven in the future. How much would you like me to pay him?"

"Fifty thousand dollars. With this information, and a little luck, Viper should have three more days to stop Juan Sanchez before the CIA begins his debriefing."

"Perhaps Viper will silence Juan Sanchez as we speak," Roberto replied.

"We must make sure that the CIA interrogator does not leave Tokyo. Watch his every movement. Kidnap him if possible. Kill him if he gets within five miles of Tokyo International. We must delay their interrogation of Sanchez. What is the American saying, 'A dead man carries no tales'?" Joaquin growled.

"Jefe, the CIA agent is at the American Embassy," Julio cautioned, mindful that embassy security was the most difficult to breach.

Joaquin slammed his fist onto the table, rattling the fine china and startling the group.

"Where he is staying is of no concern to me. He must *not leave* Tokyo until Sanchez is dead. Do you understand me?" His powerful voice boomed as his piercing eyes scanned the room.

Julio lowered his head deciding not to challenge his brother.

There was a soft knock at the door, followed by Joaquin's invitation to enter. Franco Ramirez stood awkwardly in the doorway, his damp hair plastered against his head, raindrops dripping from his coat onto the hardwood floor.

"Maria!" Joaquin bellowed.

Ramirez, visibly startled, stammered an apology, "Please forgive my tardiness, Señor Gusto. The rain is heavy and the road was blocked by fallen trees."

Maria hurried into the room and took Ramirez' coat, nervously eyeing the water on the floor.

"Sit down, Franco," Joaquin directed, motioning to the empty chair between Julio and Roberto. "I have told the Council many good things about you. You have done well…for a Peruvian," Joaquin added, sarcastically.

"I have lived in Colombia for fifteen years, señor. That is longer than I lived in Peru as a child. Colombia is my country now," he replied defensively.

"I hired you because Juan Sanchez told me that you were a *brilliant* financier. Are you brilliant, Franco?"

"I have invested millions of your dollars, which have made many more millions. If you measure a man's mind by his ability to make money, then I am a smart man."

"I have decided to promote you, Franco. You will be the senior financial manager for all Asian accounts," Joaquin announced in a congratulatory tone.

Ramirez, clearly relieved, smiled gratefully, placed both hands on the table and started to stand. "Señor Gusto, I am honored…"

Before he could finish the sentence, Roberto plunged a thirteenth-century Peruvian dagger through the top of one of Ramirez' hands, pinning it to the table. Ramirez' shrill scream echoed through the cavernous room but was abruptly silenced when Roberto slit his throat from ear to ear in one expert stroke. Ramirez slumped back against Roberto, his eyes wide, fixed on the specter of his own dark red blood dripping from the jagged edge of the knife blade Roberto now pointed at his face.

Joaquin stood, slowly leaned across the table, and stared into Ramirez' eyes and inhaled the smell of fear. "Today you will meet your wife and son in hell," Joaquin spoke slowly and deliberately.

"You will hear them calling your name, asking you *Franco, Franco, what have you done?*" Joaquin taunted, his voice rising. "Tell them that your name means weak. Tell them that you were a fool to protect Juan Sanchez and tell them that *no one* betrays the Gustos!" he roared. His face contorted in rage, the veins on his neck bulged, and his hands clenched into fists, and beat the table.

Roberto released Ramirez. His lifeless form slumped to the floor as drops of blood mingled with drops of rainwater and began to pool around his head. Each of them sat frozen in silence as Joaquin glared at Ramirez, as if waiting for him to rise from the dead so that he could continue the tirade against him.

Joaquin struggled to quell the rage that had festered inside him for days. Killing Ramirez had not satisfied him. Ramirez was a pathetic substitute for the king of traitors. It was Juan Sanchez' blood that he wanted to spill onto the floor for Maria to soak up with filthy rags.

Joaquin turned and faced the Council. "Ramirez was loyal only to Juan Sanchez. He knew that Sanchez intended to betray us. He lied about the transfer of money to cover up for him and he tried to warn him that Roberto was on his way to Tokyo. We do not know if he planned to join Juan Sanchez in Lisbon, or if he planned to remain with us. It does not matter. Betrayal is betrayal and has no degrees."

"Tonight, Ramirez's wife, son and brother will die. Tell your people the fate of traitors. I will kill any traitor's entire family. Be certain that they understand! Do you understand what I am saying?" he asked in a low, ominous voice full of threat as he pointed his finger directly at each man at the table.

"Yes, Jefe," they all replied, their eyes wide as they watched Roberto wipe the blood off the dagger with a white linen napkin.

Silence filled the room like smoke from a fire. "If everyone will excuse me, I'm tired."

"Roberto," Joaquin called.

Joaquin's two brothers also stopped but continued as Roberto nodded for them to proceed. Both brothers understood Joaquin's mood and gladly obliged.

Roberto waited a few seconds before closing the door. At the other end of the room, the door to Joaquin's private study opened slowly and one of the deadliest and sought after individuals in the world, Mohammed Abdul, the leader of Jihad-7, entered. Dressed in a long brown djellaba, his face covered by the shadows of his long dark beard and the pointed hood that draped over his forehead, he initiated eye contact with Joaquin.

"Is there any doubt we will succeed?"

"No, there isn't, my brother," Mohammed responded, having observed the entire meeting from a video in Joaquin's study.

"Our alliance will remain secret and we will be able to deliver the package as promised." Joaquin confidently noted. "Please sit with me, I have some fresh Indian Chai tea that was flown in from Bombay yesterday."

"It would be my honor my brother," Mohammed responded with a simple short bow of his head.

Mohammed inhaled the hot vapors. "This tea is magnificent, it's my favorite." Mohammed sighed, closed his eyes, and breathed in the fragrant aroma.

"Mohammed, time has come to join forces, to bring the infidels to their knees and teach them respect. My men will carry out their mission and deliver my gift to you safely."

"Joaquin I've come to respect and honor your word. May Allah's peace be upon you and grant you safe passage. Our meetings must be limited in the future. We need to be extremely careful of the devils of the sky and to what we speak." Mohammed hated the CIA's unmanned predators and their missiles.

"I agree Mohammed, but in my home we can speak freely without worry of the infidel ears. One of my sources in America has provided me with new technology, an anti-reflective titanium based paint, which the Americans have secretly developed that prevents satellites from eavesdropping through buildings and walls. I assure you that it works. They use it at the White House and if it's good enough for the President of the United States, it's good enough for us. There are some advantages to being rich! My brothers and I call this our Coca Hut," Joaquin laughed.

"Allah is truly with you my brother," Mohammed responded as both men laughed out loud. For the next half hour the men quietly discussed their joint operation.

"Roberto, would you please ensure that our guest has a safe departure?" Joaquin directed.

Within two hours, Roberto returned to *the Palace*. "Are you sure we want to do this, Joaquin? I know we acquired this device by luck and by our good fortune, but…"

"Roberto, I've had it with the Americans!" Joaquin's voice elevated interrupting Roberto. "They think the world is their empire. They force their will on anyone they choose. They invade countries, assassinate heads of state…I've had it with their arrogance. These pigs must be stopped!"

"If we're not extremely careful they will eliminate us. We're not high on their list right now, but in time we could be, especially if your plan backfires," Roberto warned.

"Eliminate us! They made that device. It's time to make them pay! We just need a little help from Allah," Joaquin laughed.

DEA, SAN FRANCISCO, CA

Cartwright and Connor walked into the executive office of George Melconi, the Special Agent in Charge. His face was pitted and scarred by acne from his youth. At forty-seven, 5'7", Melconi maintained a rigid fitness routine in order to endure the cracks about his height and his appearance which only intensify his short man complex. The rank and file nicknamed him 'Scarface', but no one dared call him that to his face.

"Sir," Connor greeted him as they entered the office.

"Jack, Bill, have a seat," Melconi gestured toward the two leather chairs in front of his desk.

Connor sat in the comfortable, high-backed leather chair and his feet sank into the deep, plush crimson carpet. The walls were covered with expensively framed photographs of Melconi posing with an assortment of VIPs, including one in which he was shaking hands with former President George W. Bush on the steps of the White House. Connor didn't care too much for these "hero walls" but about half of the senior administrators in DEA had them. Some administrators covered every square inch of the four walls in their office with outdated diplomas, awards, and certificates, scattered among faded photographs of much younger versions of themselves standing beside war trophies, tall stacks of plastic wrapped kilos, or sour faced suspects in handcuffs. This was in sharp contrast to CIA senior officials, who rarely displayed anything on their office walls because they didn't want to admit they were anywhere.

Connor didn't care much for Melconi, for the simple fact that he was out for himself. Connor had run into bureaucrats like him in both the agency and DEA. Their top priorities were self-promotion and power, which in most cases spelled disaster for field agents. Connor had one simple rule and that was to stay away from this moron as much as possible and let his supervisor have all the contact.

"I got an interesting call from the DEA Administrator this morning. It seems that the CIA Director wants us, and mentioned your name Jack, to debrief the Bogotá Cartel financier, Juan Sanchez, who turned himself into the CIA in Tokyo. You didn't call the CIA, did you Jack?" Melconi asked jokingly.

"Hell no sir!" Connor snapped back.

"Didn't think so. At least we know they read our reports and we got their attention." Connor never really knew what Melconi thought of him and he didn't care.

"Anyway, the CIA must have an angle. I don't see them giving up the interrogation of a high-profile target like Sanchez for nothing. But at this point, I don't fucking care what their deal is. They've got him at some secret location in Quantico called Charlie Barracks. This is a great opportunity for us. Jack, check the flights to DC and get there ASAP! Debrief that bastard before the CIA changes their mind and report back to me immediately."

"Yes sir."

"Any new intel from your informant in Bogotá?"

"No sir. I expect to hear from him any day now," Connor replied.

"Sir, the administrator's office is on the line," the SAC's secretary said as she opened the office door, interrupting his conversation.

"Jack, get going. Bill stay. Oh, Jack, ask Sanchez why he didn't turn himself into DEA… maybe the CIA lied to him and he refused to talk to them. Something's up with this. I would sure like to find out the real reason the CIA wants us to debrief him. The CIA has an agenda here, believe me and it's not in our best interest," Melconi added.

"Yes sir," Connor replied as he left the office.

There are no friendlies, there are no friendlies, focus on the mission, Connor kept telling himself, not wanting to think what Melconi might do if he found out that he was CIA.

Connor's group had left for an early surveillance. He sat down at his desk and heard a growl in his stomach. He opened his drawer and grabbed his last Stabilyze chocolate mint nutrition bar, a recent find from Costco, when his phone rang.

"Connor."

"Jack?" asked a familiar voice on the other end of the line.

"Hey babe, what's up?"

"I got assigned to that homicide as the lead prosecutor. The other senior homicide prosecutors are swamped, so it's my case." Barrett's voice was upbeat with enthusiasm.

"That's great!" He knew how badly she wanted to be a homicide prosecutor.

"This could be the break I've been waiting for. Sorry about this morning. I'll take you up on that run if you get home tonight."

Connor hesitated, "Sorry Barrett, something critical just came up on my case, and I have to fly to DC right now to debrief an informant."

"Ah shit, Jack! I thought we could at least have dinner together. I hardly ever see you anymore. Fine… I'll go out with my team!"

"Barrett, I'm sorry I'll…"

"I've got to go, I'm busy!" Barrett hung up before he finished his sentence.

"Shit!" Connor swore through clenched teeth. Barrett had a stubborn streak that often frustrated him, but she had a point. The phone rang again and Connor angrily snatched it to his ear. "Connor!"

"Jack, you have a message on the undercover phone," one of the tech agents advised.

"I'll be down in ten minutes. I've got to make a quick flight reservation."

The Technical Operations group was located on a separate floor, which housed all of the field division's sophisticated electronic equipment, undercover telephones, and computers. They routinely monitored all undercover voicemails and e-mails 24/7 to ensure that all case agents never missed any important communications from informants or agents in the field during critical operations.

Tech agents were called "buggers" because they set up court-ordered wiretaps in the homes and offices of unsuspecting criminal targets. The street agents secured the area while the buggers wired the phones and installed an array of electronic eavesdropping equipment. They could capture a twenty-by-twenty foot room with a lens smaller than a bird seed, concealed in an array of various types of wireless devices. Connor was glad they were around because he was not a techie.

Connor listened intently to the message. He immediately recognized his informant, Carlos' voice. The CIA covertly arranged for Connor to sign Carlos as a DEA informant. In most DEA cases, whoever developed an informant was the case agent, which was the reason Connor was in charge of the Gusto investigation.

"Jack, my friends will be in the Monterey area in one week. They got a new car. Will call you when they arrive. Say hi to Nancy for me. The next time I'm up there, let's have a toast of champagne. I have seven bottles of Dom Perignon to celebrate."

Connor recognized their prearranged code words. Unlike the typical confidential informant (CI), Carlos was educated in Bogotá, Colombia where he had received a bachelor's degree. He had suggested "Nancy" as a code word for cocaine, because former first lady Nancy Reagan was famous for the *Just Say No* crusade against drugs. New car was code for the new submarine that the Gustos were using to smuggle loads of cocaine into U.S. waters. *Seven bottles* was code for the amount of cocaine, seven tons. *At least there's some good news*, Connor told himself.

It took Connor a few minutes to brief Cartwright. His thoughts were preoccupied with what he needed on the trip and getting to the airport. He was halfway out the office when he heard his boss call after him. He turned around, annoyed.

"Connor, I almost forgot to tell you, you're the proud father of a new partner. He graduates in a week from Quantico." Cartwright smiled as he enjoyed the look on Connor's face, which changed from one of grim determination to visible irritation.

"What?"

"Hey, you know the new policy. They skipped over you the last two times. You're overdue, my boy."

"Boss, I am too busy right now to break in a new agent."

"No buts, Connor. Anyway, you can use the help. Introduce yourself to him when you get there. Maximize your time while you're there, Jack, and save the taxpayers some money and get your butt back here to cover that load," Cartwright said, smiling.

Connor thought about it for a few seconds and then decided not to object. He knew that Congress had recently appropriated funds to hire two hundred additional DEA agents. The funds would be re-appropriated if they didn't hire the new agents and get them through the academy during the designated time period. He quickly resigned himself to the fact that he would have to suck it up.

"No problem," Connor managed.

"I love it when you agree with me," Cartwright dead panned, knowing full well that the Field Training Agent program was a pain in the ass for the FTAs who were assigned to the new agents.

"Good morning," Assistant U.S. Attorney Jason Steiner greeted the receptionist through the bulletproof glass window of the DEA San Francisco Field Office.

"Good morning, sir," the receptionist responded the moment she recognized him. "Is he expecting you this morning?"

"No, court is in recess and I thought I'd stop by," Steiner replied.

"Let me track him down for you." She dialed Group Supervisor Cartwright's extension.

"Excuse me, could you hold the door for a second?" Steiner immediately side stepped to open the door, noticing that the USPS worker had a huge load on his cart.

"Thank you," the worker replied as he pushed the loaded cart into the reception area.

Steiner noticed a few U.S. Marshal Inspection stamps on various sections of the packages, indicating they had been opened…a routine security measure to prevent explosives and illegal firearms and other contraband from entering the Federal Building.

God knows what drug traffickers or terrorists might want to send to DEA. No place is safe from bombs anymore, Steiner thought. The receptionist buzzed the door and waved him in.

"He's in his office waiting for you."

"Thanks."

"Hey, Bill. How are you doing?" Steiner asked as he entered Cartwright's office.

Steiner knew all too well about Cartwright's reputation. Steiner felt a chill run down his spine. He shuddered to think what Cartwright would do if he found out what his son in-law really thought of his daughter. Steiner looked at the framed photo on the expensive credenza behind Cartwright's desk. It captured Cartwright's daughter being sworn in by the United States Attorney General as an Assistant U.S. Attorney for the Southern District of Miami. The proud father was in the background. Mary Cartwright had been one of two AUSAs prosecuting a major Colombian cartel ring that Cartwright's group in Miami was investigating. There was some confusion as to who the letter bomb was actually addressed to, but Mary was the one who had opened it. Cartwright, who was the lead DEA supervisor at the time in Miami, blamed himself and would never get over his daughter's untimely death.

Cartwright noticed Steiner staring at the photograph. "You know it's been four years today since the bombing. It seems like only yesterday, doesn't it?"

"It does. I can still see her in her wedding dress. I even remember the vows we said that day, every word. The three years I was with her were the best years of my life."

Steiner always played the sentimental card on Cartwright because he knew how much he loved his daughter. His daughter's memory was Cartwright's only weak spot. Steiner had never loved the skinny bitch. He only married her to get ahead. Her death had been a major inconvenience, but there were some perks, like the life insurance policy and his lucrative association with the Bogotá Cartel.

"What's the latest on the Bogotá connection?" Steiner changed the subject after ensuring that he had opened the old wound.

"You know that cartel defector I told you about who turned himself into the American Embassy in Japan that the CIA got?"

"Yeah," Steiner responded, nodded curiously.

"Our case agent will be doing the debriefing tomorrow," Cartwright replied.

"Great. I wish the FBI could get a break like that on our wire case.

"How's that going?" Cartwright asked.

"Slow. I don't think we have a chance in hell of locating that terrorist cell. I'm starting to wonder if it really exits." At that moment Steiner's cell phone vibrated and he glanced at the screen.

"Hey, I've got to go back upstairs to court."

"Maybe you can come over next week for dinner?"

"I'll call you back later, and let you know," Steiner muttered distractedly as he left the office.

SAN FRANCISCO INTERNATIONAL AIRPORT

"Hey Barrett! You're a nice surprise," Connor smiled at the unexpected sight of his wife. "How'd you get past security?"

"I called Cartwright and he pulled some strings. I don't like the idea of you leaving on a bad note. It's not my idea of a romantic dinner, but I do love eating with you any time of the day. I'm sorry I was so abrupt over the phone earlier. I just thought we'd celebrate my first homicide case, as moronic as that sounds."

"That's very thoughtful of you. I'm sorry I've been working so much lately. Let's grab lunch. I bet we can still order pancakes!"

Barrett smiled. Pancakes were one of their favorite comfort foods. Connor motioned toward one of the restaurants in the terminal.

They were seated next to a window overlooking the runway. Fog shrouded San Francisco in the distance.

Connors' phone rang just as their food arrived.

"Yeah, okay, thanks." Connor frowned.

28

"What?" Barrett asked.

"That was Bill. I'm being assigned a new partner from the academy."

"God, like you've got time to be an FTA!"

"Exactly, that's the last thing I need. I don't want to babysit anybody right now. Even if he turns out to be great, it still won't be the same as it was with my last partner."

"Well, you'll always have one partner who never changes," she smiled seductively and reached under the table to stroke his thigh.

"Maybe I'll cancel this trip and stay here so you can talk dirty to me," he replied as he stopped her traveling hand a few inches away from his zipper.

"Hey, we've got an hour before your plane leaves. Maybe we can find a deserted maintenance closet," she lowered her voice and nodded her head in the direction of a door in the corner of the restaurant.

Connor laughed and placed his hand on her thigh, "I'm game if you are. I can always take the red eye."

"Don't test me," she challenged him as she started to get out of her seat, her eyes dancing with laughter.

"Okay, okay, you win."

"Don't I always? Eat your pancakes! I know you have a healthy appetite," she grinned.

"Any developments in your homicide case?" Connor asked.

"No, nothing right now, they're still going over the evidence. What a shame, she was a young college student, only 19 years old. Hopefully they will develop a lead in the next few days. What's up with your case, why do you need to go to DC so quickly?"

"A top level cartel member turned himself into the CIA at the American Embassy in Tokyo the other day. Turns out he's been moved to a safe house in DC and they want me to interview him because of my case on the cartel. DEA wants this done ASAP. Could be a big break for our case." Connor was always cautious when he brought up the CIA in conversation because he never knew how Barrett would respond.

"You know Jack I wasn't going to mention this, but you know what today is?"

"No hon, what?" Connor was cautious in his response.

"Today is the day that the CIA told me my dad died. Remember when we first met? I told you I didn't mind if you were a government agent as long as it wasn't with the CIA?"

Connor squinted tensely, fearing that the only secret he kept from his wife was going to be exposed.

"My dad was killed because he worked for them. My mom and I never knew it until after his death. My dad was telling me one thing and doing the opposite. They never produced his body. They said it was unavailable. What type of fucking outfit won't let you tell your family who you work for or have a proper funeral? I hate those lying bastards! I'm convinced that my mom died from the shock and stress of all of that bullshit! If you'd told me you were working for them, I wouldn't have married you." Barrett's voice cracked and her eyes brimmed with tears that did not spill.

Connor noticed her hands trembling and felt her tension and anger. He stared at his wife, not knowing how to respond.

"You work for DEA and you have a dangerous job, but at least I know about it. I'm okay with it, but I can't stand it when you tell me not to do something I enjoy because it's dangerous, when you do dangerous things every day, just like my dad. It reminds me too much of him. I'm sorry I never told you before, but I was ordered not to tell anyone. I don't care what they think anymore. Plus, you're my husband and you can't testify against me. Spousal privilege, you know," Barrett managed a weak smile. "So now you know why I hate the CIA."

"That's terrible, Barrett...I'm so sorry," Connor made up his mind and took a deep breath, "Hon ..."

"Attention passengers on United Flight 765 to Washington DC, please report to gate 23, last call." The voice over the intercom abruptly interrupted before Connor could finish his sentence.

"Barrett, I have to go," he said softly as they left the restaurant and walked to the departing gate. He leaned over and kissed her as they paused at the boarding area. They made eye contact and she stood on her tiptoes to kiss him hard on the lips.

"I'm gonna miss you Jack. Have a good trip and I will be careful if I run at night."

He held her tightly for a few moments and took a deep breath of her perfume. It was his favorite scent in the world. It was French and smelled like gardenias.

"I'll give you a call when I land," he reluctantly walked away and boarded the aircraft. He was seconds away from telling her that he worked for the CIA, but the timing sucked.

Connor leaned back in his seat as the 757 lifted off the ground. His body jerked upwards as a small pocket of air jolted the aircraft as it made its steep ascent. He took a deep breath and exhaled slowly. Flying was not his preferred method of travel.

Seated in a row by himself, Connor did not feel the first vibration of his iPhone but felt the second silent buzz. Among many technological advances, this prototype was designed not to interfere with any of the cockpit electronics or flight instrumentation. Connor punched in his code and a classified e-mail from the CIA appeared.

"Sir, would you like a snack?" the flight attendant asked.

At the sound of her voice he rotated his hand to conceal his iPhone screen. "No thanks." He reached in his pocket with his other hand and pulled out another Stabilyze mint bar. He hated airline food.

CHAPTER 3

CHARLIE BARRACKS, U.S. MARINE CORPS BASE QUANTICO, VA

On a hillside near Charlie Barracks, a prone figure lay motionless in the shadows under a cluster of Virginia pine trees and brush. Viper had been watching the safe house for the past four hours, a restful task considering the arduous flight it took to arrive at this base. The warm wooden stock of the modified Remington 700 sniper rifle rested lightly against his cheek. Ironically, this was the same weapon Marine snipers used in the field. The customized Marine version was referred to as the M40A1. He was, for all practical purposes, invisible. His face was concealed behind lightweight mesh netting in green, brown, and gold hues. His dark brown eyes, under thick brows, were cold and mechanical as he stared down the metal barrel through the crosshairs of his Nightforce NXS scope. He slowly moved it left to right and right to left as he scanned the terrain he had now memorized. He waited patiently for the perfect split second to arrive.

A gust of wind swept orange and yellow leaves across the sprawling grounds at the Marine Corps Command and Education Center, Marine Corps Base, Quantico, VA. Located off exit 49 on I-95, Quantico is also the home to the U.S. Marine Corps Officer Candidate School and the FBI and DEA training academies. The officers' training prepares them for military warfare. The agents' training prepares them for street warfare. Anyone who thinks that the term "street warfare" is a macho exaggeration needs to spend half a day watching the agents, dressed in black or tan SWAT-style BDUs (Basic Battle Dress/Duty Uniforms), go through simunition training, repelling down walls with submachine guns strapped to their backs. All three groups pride themselves on their rosters of the most highly skilled marksmen in the world. FBI and DEA agents who score 100 percent on their range tests have their names memorialized on a bronze plaque, distinguishing them as members of the *Possible Club.*

Another group resides anonymously near the back of the immense compound. Charlie Barracks is one of five top-secret witness protection facilities in the United States. A small, elite group of Marines, composed of three officers and twenty enlisted men, assist the U.S. Marshals Service Witness Protection Unit as it provides a safe house to the United States' most valuable "assets," foreign and domestic. Most of the assets are government informants who don't stay there long…usually just long enough for the government to process the paperwork for their new identities and finance their relocation.

Charlie Barracks is the most secure location of the five. The safe house isn't actually a barracks. It is a fully contained housing unit with two master bedroom suites, two full baths, a small cardio and weight room, a recreation room, a dining room, and a kitchen. The security detail monitors the safe house twenty-four hours a day from the attached operations room, equipped with the latest surveillance and electronic equipment from Westinghouse Space and Technology Division.

The safe house is rigged with audio and video access so sensitive that the sound waves generated by a sneeze can be displayed on a video screen. Electronic sensors, used by NASA's satellite program, are concealed from view in the walls and ceiling. The weight of a single cockroach could trigger an alarm, followed by a real-time video display of the tiny intruder's location and speed, an often welcome diversion for the night shift detail.

Outside, sensors are deployed every twenty-five yards around the barracks. However, they are adjusted for wildlife, so that they do not activate every time a raccoon or squirrel comes close to the building. A small forest of maple trees naturally insulates the distant perimeter. Marine sentries secure all entrances and exits, and no one gets on the compound without authorization. Security has never been breached.

Charlie Barracks Marines rotate shifts at the safe house. When they are not on duty, they train weekly in close-quarter battle tactics, designed to perfect their skills in hand-to-hand combat situations. Although range training is scheduled twice a month, most of them go to the range at least twice a week. Even when they are decked out in their dress blues, you can catch a whiff of Break Free gun solvent if you stand close enough.

Staff Sergeant Tom Baker reported to the operations room. He exemplified a Charlie Barracks Marine. His hair was closely cropped, shaved on the side, short on the top, the distinctive Marine Corps *high and tight*. He was tall and rock solid from hours of weight training in the base gym, where dozens of sweaty Marines bench press twice their weight while their buddies spot them. He wore his freshly pressed, immaculate, Marine Corps digital cammies like a modern day warrior in a recruiting poster.

After relieving the sergeant who had worked the previous shift, Baker keyed his radio mic and instructed Sergeants Devon Jones and Ray Smith to pick up the witness.

"On the way," Jones responded.

Baker walked into the spacious living room that had been professionally furnished in southwestern décor; a blooming cactus plant provided a splash of color from a terra cotta planter that matched the tile floor.

"Let's go," Baker said to the short, overweight man sitting on the sofa and staring at the 50-inch Samsung Smart TV where a re-run of *Cops* cut to a commercial. "It's time for dinner."

The only Deputy U.S. Marshal on duty was in the next room preparing for the short trip to the mess hall. The marshals assigned to the witness protection unit were highly trained professionals, specially selected for assignment to Charlie Barracks. He double-checked his .40 cal Glock 23, and then picked up what looked like ordinary gym bags and headed into the living room. The Eagle Industries black nylon bags cleverly concealed H&K 9mm submachine guns, required hardware for field trips.

A federal witness would not normally be required to leave the safe house for food, but due to a grease fire, the kitchen had been demolished and was in the process of being remodeled. For the next few weeks, all meals would be served in a reserved section of the Officers' Club.

"Sir, the facility is about a half-mile down the road. Check in with the Staff NCO and he will direct you." The Marine sentry was precise in his instructions. After observing Connor's name on the authorized visitors list, he returned Connor's government identification. Connor's nonstop flight arrived early due to a tail wind, so he decided to go straight to Charlie Barracks. The road became pitch dark within seconds after Connor passed the illuminated sentry shack in his rental vehicle. Although he knew he was on the Marine base he had an eerie feeling of isolation as he drove on.

Viper silently watched from the hillside. He activated the stopwatch on his G-Shock watch as the forest-green Chevrolet Suburban pulled into the driveway.

"How long are we going to be babysitting this one Devon?" Sergeant Ray Smith asked Jones as they pulled into the driveway in front of the safe house.

"It's going to be a long one. This guy is some kind of big deal drug cartel money roller, can you believe that? If he's really a millionaire, he must be pretty pissed that he's got to eat mess hall grub," Sergeant Jones grinned.

"No way he's a millionaire! Dude, all he does is watch old TV shows. You know, the really bad ones, like Gomer Pyle!" Sgt Smith replied as he killed the engine.

Hey! I love that show, it's about Marines!" Jones mocked as they got out of the SUV.

Viper followed the movements of one of the Marine sergeants through the scope and admired his erect posture as he walked purposefully toward the safe house. Viper stopped his watch. It took the sergeant exactly twenty-three seconds to enter the building. He loved the Marines' efficiency. The members of the witness protection security team operated like an experienced military drill team. Their routines never varied, nor did the timing. Predictability is a wonderful quality, he thought. *Right on time*, he checked his watch, it was exactly 8:00 p.m. or 2000 military time.

Viper slowly rolled his rifle to his side and peered through his Minolta 200mm 8x50 binoculars at the two familiar figures. *Come on, Marines, bore me with your routine.*

"Juan, your ride is here, it's time for dinner...you ready to go?" Staff Sergeant Baker called, as he walked out of the operation room into the living room.

Juan Sanchez sat silently on the oversized sofa, staring intently at the television's blank screen.

"You know, that TV gets a lot better reception if you actually turn it on," Baker tried to change Sanchez's mood. He knew how difficult it was for some of the protected witnesses to adjust to a safe house's isolation.

Still no reply.

"Juan, what's wrong?" Baker asked, worried. Sanchez had been getting weirder as the hours wore on. He had stopped watching

TV and would barely speak unless spoken to. He paced the living room most of the night and had developed dark circles under his eyes from lack of sleep.

"Juan, what is wrong with you?" he repeated loudly as the deputy marshal came into the operations room to see what was going on.

Sanchez ignored the two men standing near the doorway and sighed dejectedly. "I'm not hungry."

"What's bothering you? Speak up Juan." Baker was starting to get annoyed.

"You do not understand how powerful these people are," Sanchez's voice was barely audible.

"They will hunt me down like an animal. The longer I stay in one place, the closer I get to my death. What is taking so long? Why has no one talked to me? I do not know what is happening!"

"Juan, listen to me," the marshal interrupted the Colombian's increasingly desperate plea. "I have worked witness protection for fifteen years and no one...I mean *no one*...has ever been hurt on our watch. This is a Marine base, for God's sake. At any given time of the day or night, five guys are close enough to hear you fart. A friggin' army of killer Marines surrounds you. Nothing is going to happen to you, nothing. Except, of course, you may get bored to death," the marshal smiled and patted Sanchez on the back.

Sanchez stared at the floor and shook his head. *"You do not know Joaquin Gusto,"* he whispered.

"Quit mumbling, what did you say!" Staff Sergeant Baker commanded. The marshals could coddle these witnesses, but Baker didn't have the patience to appease these criminal bastards.

"I said you don't know *JOAQUIN GUSTO!*" Sanchez yelled back.

"Mr. Sanchez, I give you my word as a MARINE...we will protect you! Do you know the Marine Corps creed *Semper Fi*? It's Latin for *Always Faithful*. That is what we are, faithful to our mission and to our country. Right now, our mission is keeping you safe. We are going to do that or die trying." Baker spoke with such conviction, Sanchez allowed a half-hearted smile.

Baker had grown up in the Bronx. He'd had joined the Marines when he was eighteen years old, starting out as a grunt in the Second Marine Division in Camp Lejeune, North Carolina. From there, he went to the 26th Marine Expeditionary Unit (MEU), Special Operations Capable (SOC), and worked his way up to Force Recon First Platoon, their motto, Swift, Silent and Deadly.

Baker was no stranger to combat. He won the Navy's Silver Star medal for valor and heroism in Iraq. He wasn't going to let anyone harm this pencil neck accountant who was afraid of his own shadow on his Marine base.

After a few moments Baker broke the silence. "Let's go, Mr. Sanchez. Your dinner is getting cold. Mr. Sanchez hold on one second," Baker paused after hearing a radio transmission in his ear piece.

"Looks like the federal agent who is going to debrief you has arrived early. Your debriefing might start tonight."

Viper shifted his scope to the new set of headlights as it approached Charlie Barracks. Viper tracked the visitor in the crosshairs as he entered the facility.

"Lieutenant Connor, how the hell are you?"

"Sergeant Tom Baker?" Connor asked in surprise. "They didn't tell me you were the Staff NCO."

"It's staff sergeant now, Special Agent Connor."

"It's great to see you staff sergeant," Connor shook hands with the junior enlisted Marines, but gave his combat buddy a hug.

"Believe me, I was just as surprised to see you on the authorization list. Sir, you just caught us as we are making a chow hall run for your witness. I was expecting you tomorrow, do you want to interview him tonight?"

"It's up to him, I came in early, so I thought I would drop by and check out the place."

"Sir, you can join him for chow if you like."

"Tom, stop the sir, I'm not in the Marines anymore, it's Jack. I'll chill here if that's okay. I need to go over my notes. I'll see him when he gets back."

"Affirm, if you need anything the weapons locker is right here." Baker opened the door to the vault type room next to them displaying a cache of weapons and tactical equipment.

Connor smiled appreciatively as he observed several H&K 9mm sub-machine guns, Marine issue M-4 assault rifles hanging on the wall in a locked rack, night vision goggles, and a crate containing flash bangs and various other combat gear. "I do miss the Marines Tom. I use my pen and phone more than my weapon."

"Oorah!" Baker grunted. "Corporal, Special Agent Connor will stay here while we take the witness to the chow hall. If he needs anything, make sure he gets it," Baker ordered.

"Yes staff sergeant!"

Baker introduced his team of Marines to Connor, who stayed focused on their respective tasks, as they briefly acknowledged his presence.

Viper was careful not to compromise his position. Snipers call it minimization. Viper was curious about the arrival of the visitor, but he did not alter his course of action. He adjusted his shooting platform so that he lay flat against the ground. Darkness did not necessarily prevent detection. Exposed skin would reflect moonlight and streetlight. He was very careful to cover every inch of his skin, because some of the Marines were snipers and, like Viper, they constantly searched the darkness for any sign of life. He wore a customized camouflage mesh hood embedded with foliage on his face and a light pair of camouflage gloves on his hands. His ghillie suit was designed for military snipers in wooded terrain. He had threaded leaves and small branches from the surrounding brush into the mesh material that covered the suit. Even a Marine sniper would be unable to detect him at this distance. He was positioned on a crest, approximately 75 yards from the front entrance of the safe house. A longer distance shot was negated due to the location and terrain of Charlie Barracks.

Viper's mind was his own time piece now. The Marines were five minutes behind schedule. *Are you going to surprise me after all?* His muscles tensed, and his heart rate increased ever so slightly as he felt the cold euphoric rush of adrenaline. It was an intensely sexual feeling, the raw desire to feel his finger wrap around the trigger. The sniper rifle was more familiar in his hands than any woman. He knew that it would thrust into his shoulder as the rounds discharged. He loved the thrilling satisfaction of dropping an unsuspecting target to his knees. As always, he would have to fight the urge to stay and watch, to press his body into the cold dirt and watch them scurry around like manic ants. He wet his lips and continued to wait. Viper held the Remington firmly, the crosshairs of his scope on a fixed location. He had rehearsed the scene many times and knew the exact number of steps from the door to the kill zone.

"Staff Sergeant Baker, the Suburban is ready," Sgt. Jones reported as he walked into the living room.

"Alpha One to Control, we are exiting the building," Jones radioed.

"10-4."

Sergeant Smith monitored the radio traffic as he sat in the Suburban and watched the door, as he waited for the team to come outside. The entrance opened up onto an L-shaped sidewalk that led to the driveway where the Suburban was parked. The Suburban was no more than twenty yards from the door.

Sergeant Jones turned off the interior lights before he opened the safe house door, to avoid silhouetting the team in the doorway. He and Baker checked video cameras one and three, and the team moved into a standard diamond formation around Sanchez. Security protocol called for a diamond formation for high priority witness protectees, even in the secure environment of the Marine Base.

Three, four, five, six. Viper counted silently as he trained his weapon on Juan Sanchez. He recognized the familiar hunched posture and the shuffling gait. *There you are.*

"Juan, it's cool out tonight. Do you want me to get you a heavier coat?" the marshal offered.

"No thank you, marshal." The arrival of the federal agent had helped him overcome his anxiety. He took a deep breath of crisp, fall air and felt an unexpected pang of hunger, as he imagined a juicy steak.

Twelve, thirteen, fourteen, fifteen. Viper continued his silent countdown. He began to pull the slack out of the Remington's trigger as he carefully controlled his breathing and waited for the target to cross into the circular magnifying glass of his scope.

Staff Sergeant Baker scanned the surroundings as they walked outside. His trained eyes searched the dark terrain in the distance. Nothing moved.

Eighteen, nineteen. Viper counted, focusing all of his energy on the image now materializing in the crosshairs.

Twenty. His finger smoothly pulled the curved trigger as far back as it would go, its slight click muffled by the custom-built Israeli silencer that quietly enveloped the speeding projectile as it launched from the rifle's barrel. The silent movie in Viper's scope unfolded in a split second as Juan Sanchez slumped to the ground and one of the security team members stumbled into him, caught off guard by the fall. Viper savored the moment when their confidence turned into confusion and confusion turned into panic.

Baker felt a warm spray of blood and chunks of tiny bone chips hit the side of his face and immediately realized that Sanchez had been shot.

"Code Blue! Code Blue! Move target to the vehicle!" Baker instantly radioed the designated distress signal to the operations room while the Marines pulled Sanchez toward the Suburban. The marshal drew his weapon and pointed into the darkness as the Marines positioned their bodies around Sanchez to form a moving, human shield.

"Shit!" The operations room sergeant swore as he hit the red alarm switch, activating perimeter flood lights that lit up an area as big as a football stadium around Charlie Barracks.

"It's a sniper hit!" Baker radioed as they dragged Sanchez to the Suburban. "Did anybody see muzzle blast?"

"No," came the immediate reply.

"Open the…" Baker was interrupted by a loud popping noise that sounded like a cherry bomb firecracker coupled with a blinding electric flash.

"Fuck me!" Baker screamed. The floodlights went out and Charlie Barracks lost all electrical power. The lights flickered as the emergency generator came online, and then went dead after another short burst of the peculiar noise. Communications were severed. The team inside the dark operations room blindly scrambled for emergency flashlights.

Startled, Connor's body jerked for a second as he anticipated the worst after hearing Baker's radio transmission from the operations room. From memory, Connor knew exactly where and what he wanted as he rushed into the weapons locker and grabbed a pair of the night vision goggles. Connor ignored all the confusion and ran straight outside.

"Tom you got hit by an e-blast! All your power is gone…comm, cells, everything. Where did the shot come from?" Connor called out.

"I think straight in front of us over the hill!"

40

"I'm going after him." Connor darted into the darkness, not waiting for a response.

The e-blast blocked the electronic emergency signal that should have been sent to the Military Police headquarters. The entire contingent of Marines scrambled into the dark room, grabbed rifles and shotguns from the weapons locker and rushed out of the building, breaking up into pre-designated teams.

"Sergeant, take a fire team of Marines. Track that fucker down! Get another fire team in Humvees and start patrolling the perimeter roads. We need to contain that bastard! All of our comm is down. Get someone over to the MPs now and have them secure the base. Move!" Baker shouted.

"Affirm!" the sergeant responded, sprinting back to the barracks.

Viper smiled, knowing the effects of his single shot and e-blast. He shoved his military grade tactical Samsung 8.4 PRO Tablet into his pack. He imagined the chaos that had seized the highly trained security team. He loved the perverse irony of their predicament: Marine snipers pinned down less than one mile from their world-renowned sniper school, their top-secret, high-tech safe house's elaborate communications and security systems completely disabled. He reluctantly gave up the view in his night scope and quickly packed out, leaving the Marines scrambling.

The Marine fire teams waited fifteen seconds after the popping noise stopped before making their move, concerned that there would be another volley of shots. The first fire team charged the hill, following Connor as the second fire team started to deploy in Humvees.

"Let's go! Let's go!" Baker ordered as the team piled into the Suburban.

Sanchez lay on the back seat, his head saturated with blood that was already beginning to coagulate into a thick black gel. His eyes were wide open, seemingly fixed on something in the distance that only he could see. Baker put his hand to Sanchez' throat to check for a carotid pulse, knowing it was futile. He knelt in front of the seat and kept the body from rolling off as the driver slammed the big four-by-four into reverse, straightened it out, and floored it. Baker felt physically sick…not because he still had Sanchez' skull fragments on his face, but because he kept hearing the echo of his own words to Sanchez: *I give you my word as a Marine...we will protect you...Simper Fi, always faithful...our mission is keeping you safe...we are going to do that, or die trying.*

"Damn!" One of the corporals yelled inside the operations room as he tried to get the base radio to operate. He grabbed his M4 5.56mm carbine, a shortened version of the M16A2 combat rifle, and ran outside to join the other Marines, as the Suburban screeched onto the road, leaving an acrid smell of burning rubber. It was deathly quiet. Nothing moved, and the only sound was the roar of the big Chevy and Humvees' engines with their blue lights flashing as they sped away from the scene.

Flashlights cast long shadows in the operations room as the rest of the security detail feverishly worked on the electrical control panel and video monitors, attempting to restore power.

"Whoever blew this knew exactly what he was doing." One of the sergeants stated the obvious.

"How long until we're back on line?" another asked.

"It's gonna be awhile. You smell that shit?"

"Yeah, what is that?"

"Fuck if I know! If my guess is correct, this high-tech operator hit us with an e-bomb that burned out all of our electronics, computers and communication systems, instead of blowing 'em," he replied. He knew that they were going to have some serious explaining to do.

The adrenaline in Connor's body vaulted him to the top of the first hill, but he was out of breath. He quickly looked behind him and saw some of the Marines rapidly approaching. He waved them on and continued running as his eyes scanned for anything that moved.

The Marines didn't stop at the top and kept running toward Connor.

"Tripwire! Cover!" One of the Marines yelled as he launched through the air.

The first blast, a concussion grenade, was deafening followed by a bright flash that would have stunned most personnel. Connor and the other Marines took cover behind the trees as the second blast from a grenade sent metal fragments through the air piercing into nearby tree trunks.

42

Within a split-second of the first blast Connor thought he saw a shadow running about 50 yards ahead. Connor turned toward the Marines who were closer to the blast. He saw one Marine signal for him to continue. Connor grabbed his iPhone and pressed the pre-designated number in the satellite mode. Connor hoped that his prototype technology was one step ahead of the e-blast emission.

"Center." The voice from CIA headquarters operations command was clear and direct.

"This is Arrowhead." Connor used his field operational code name. "I have a priority five immediate tasking, my operation code is One, Alpha, 006, Delta Red, over," Connor spoke quietly and slowly.

"Standby," the duty officer replied as he confirmed the authorization code. This type of emergency request was normally reserved for the assistant director or station chief level with the exception of five undercover field agents.

"Go ahead Arrowhead," the duty officer responded after a brief pause to confirm the code.

"Track the GPS on my phone. I need a half-mile radius satellite coverage of any single person running within my GPS. Enemy action at Quantico Marine Corps base, a hostile killed a protected witness and is trying to escape. Hostile probably going for a vehicle, we need to ID him and the vehicle. Hostile carrying a long rifle. Focus north of my GPS location," Connor directed as he glanced at the compass reading on his iPhone.

"10-4, standby."

Connor placed a miniature earpiece in his ear, pushed himself away from the tree and started running in the direction of the shadow.

Viper heard the tripwire explosions and wasn't surprised, but he became more acutely aware of his timing as he ran down the opposite side of the incline and made it back to his staging location in a nearby tree line. He got up on one knee, careful not to silhouette himself, then slipped out of his ghillie suit. He placed it into a camouflaged utility bag and changed his clothes. He methodically dismantled the wooden stock from the barrel of the Remington and packed the weapon into a backpack with the barrel slightly protruding.

He checked his stopwatch. It had taken him three minutes to get to the first station. He was thirty seconds ahead of schedule. He knew that every second counted. The weakest link in his operation was getting off of the Marine base. The first 15 minutes were crucial to his successful escape. He slipped the backpack over his shoulder and moved out. The next staging point was a half mile away and he planned to cover the distance in five minutes. He had practiced the run the previous night and with any luck, he could beat that.

He saw flashes of blinking blue lights in the distance as he ran through the trees, carefully sidestepping the uneven areas he had marked with branches. His circular path led him to a point in the road south of the safe house. Satisfied that all traffic had passed, he darted cross the road, two minutes away from his next destination.

Colonel William Hacker, the base Provost Marshal at the Marine base, finished his steak and refilled his glass of wine.

"Honey, would you like another glass?" he asked his wife as she got up to clear the table.

"No, thanks, you know that two is my limit," she replied as the phone rang in the living room.

"I'll get it," Hacker called as he walked into the other room.

"Colonel Hacker," he answered in his usual crisp, military greeting.

"Sir, this is Staff Sergeant Baker, Staff NCO at Charlie Barracks. We have a critical situation involving the U.S. Marshals' protected government witness," he began.

"Staff Sergeant, that witness isn't my problem, is he?" the colonel interrupted, as he tried to recall the details of the recent classified memo he got from the marshals. He usually didn't pay too much attention to the marshals' memos, because Charlie Barracks witnesses were Special Operations and fell under a different chain of command.

"Sir, it is a base problem right now, because five minutes ago a sniper hit our protectee just outside Charlie Barracks and is still at large. He cut power and disabled our op center."

"What!" Hacker barked in disbelief.

"Sir, we request that you order an immediate base lock down and order a search of every vehicle and ID all personnel leaving the base. All Charlie Barracks security teams have been dispatched."

"Done. I'll mobilize every Marine on base. We've got to move quickly or that bastard will escape," the colonel replied abruptly, knowing in reality that it would actually take 15 to 20 minutes to affect a complete lockdown. "What is your location, Staff Sergeant?"

"Sir, we're at the base dispensary. The witness died before we got here. Half his face was blown off. We're heading out now. All our communications, including our portable comm sets were fried. We're trying to get new ones now."

"Have you notified your CO?" Baker's commanding officer was a full bird colonel and was also the executive officer of the Marine Base at Quantico.

"I am going to do that now sir," he replied as they hung up.

Baker knew that he had violated the chain of command by contacting the Provost Marshal directly, but he also knew that every second was critical if they had any chance of catching the sniper.

Viper was breathing hard when he reached his second checkpoint in four minutes and 40 seconds. He carefully surveyed the area for any movement.

Baker waited as the duty officer connected him to the CO, the phone call he dreaded most of all. The CO was one gung-ho, oorah, Marine, with a short son-of-a-bitch temper. He roared angrily into the phone like he had just been yanked out of bed with a Playboy playmate of the year.

"What is it Baker?" he demanded impatiently.

"Sir, a sniper hit our witness in front of Charlie Barracks when we were on the way to the mess hall. Single shot to the head, silencer. The witness didn't make it. All comm went down in the ops room immediately after the hit. Base lock-down procedures have been initiated, and all details have been dispatched," Baker reported.

"Enemy action at Quantico? You gotta be shitting me, Baker! Tell me you're shitting me son!"

"No, sir," Baker nervously replied.

"Chesty Puller is rolling over in his grave. You get those Marines *on it*! Do you hear me Baker?" he yelled like a drill sergeant at a boot recruit.

"Yes sir!"

45

"I'm going to my office to get a comm set. I'll raise you when I get there."

"Yes, sir," Baker replied to a dial tone.

Connor stopped for a second and surveyed the terrain through his night vision goggles. *How does he plan to get off the base?* Think, think, Connor kept telling himself. *If he stashed a vehicle at some point it could be stopped, how else...*

"Arrowhead, this is center." Connor's earpiece came to life.

"Go ahead," Connor whispered.

"We have a live satellite feed. Nobody to your north, but we do have a single individual approaching what looks like a compound to your direct south. There are multiple military Humvees in your area patrolling, but minimal civilian vehicle traffic."

Shit, Connor thought. "He must have doubled back on us, that's gotta be him. Can you send the live feed to my iPhone."

"10-4, standby, give it 20 seconds," a duty officer replied.

"Sir, do you see something? Do you have live comm?" the lead Marine asked Connor in a loud whisper as he tried to slow down his breathing.

"No, I was trying to get my phone back on line. It's not totally dead. I'm going back, the suspect might have doubled back on us. You Marines continue forward in case I'm wrong," Connor commanded.

"Affirm sir but take one of us. You don't want to be mistaken for the sniper in the dark."

"Ok, let's go Marine," Connor tapped one of the Marines on his shoulder.

"Corporal, make a quick run over to the MP headquarters and pick up at least half a dozen handhelds. All of these radios are dead, and they can't be fixed. We need comm now!" The sergeant barked the order.

The corporal grabbed his M-4 and flashlight, exited the rear of Charlie Barracks and ran to the vacant motor pool area toward the remaining Humvee. He opened the driver's side door and put his weapon down on the passenger seat. He paused for a second when he heard footsteps. He turned and reached for his sidearm, but the cold muzzle of a silenced 9mm pistol made contact with the side of his head.

POP! POP! A bright flash was the last thing the corporal saw.

Viper reached down and took the keys out of the corporal's pocket, dragged him 15 yards, then rolled the body to the edge of the parking lot and down the steep ravine. Viper froze for a few seconds. The only faint sound came from the barracks. He climbed into the Humvee and drove out of the motor pool past Charlie Barracks. Within a few minutes, he approached the Charlie Barracks sentry with his blue lights flashing. He slowed with one hand on the steering wheel and the other hand holding his H&K P7 9mm in his lap. He nodded to the sentry, who signaled him on.

"Arrowhead."

"Go," Connor spoke softly as he slowed his pace and listened to the CIA duty officer.

"We have a bad feed, complete satellite disruption. Possible hostile action at the compound, believe suspected hostile just left in a military vehicle," the duty officer reported.

"How much further till I get to the compound?" Connor asked.

"Are you with another friendly?" the duty officer asked.

"Affirm."

"Ok, we got you, you're about 50 yards from the compound."

Connor took longer strides and increased his pace as he descended down the slope towards Charlie Barracks. Just as Connor realized he was going too fast, he lost his balance and fell to the ground on his backside. He slid another 10 yards down the steep slope onto the road behind Charlie Barracks.

"Sir, are you okay?" the Marine asked as Connor started to stand.

"Yeah. Listen, be careful, go cover that corner of the building, make sure we don't get ambushed. Then go inside the barracks and tell them the suspect may be in the area. Search the area! I'm going to drive to the guard shack and check in with the sentry. Go Marine!" Connor ordered. The Marine was off and running before Connor finished his sentence.

Connor brushed the dirt off his pants and out of his hair, ran to his rental car, and called in.

"This is Arrowhead, what's the status of the hostile?"

"Standby…Arrowhead, hostile vehicle is on the west perimeter road heading toward the south base exit."

"Copy. I'm en route," Connor replied as he approached a guard shack.

The sentry recognized Connor's vehicle and waved him through.

"Center patch me through to the base dispensary." Connor concentrated and willed himself to slow his breathing and concentrate as he accelerated. If he was going to stop the shooter, he had to act fast.

"Dispensary," a woman's voice answered.

"This is DEA Special Agent Jack Connor. We just had a shooting at Charlie Barracks. Is Staff Sergeant Baker there?"

"No sir," the operator responded. "But his phone is back on line, do you want me to patch you through?"

"Affirm."

"Tom, I'm in my car. Is that south rear gate that merges with I-95 still open at night?"

"Yeah."

"I think the sniper doubled back on us and made it back to Charlie Barracks. He may be in one of your Humvees. Call the sentries and tell them not to let any Charlie Barracks Humvees off base. He's probably in a Marine uniform. I'm headed to the south gate now."

"On it, I'm en route!" Baker hit his brakes, made a violent U-turn, flipped on his blue light bar, and sped towards the south gate. He kept one eye on the road and the other on his phone as he tapped numbers onto the screen.

Viper watched a civilian vehicle being searched ahead as he approached the last guard shack at one of the remote base exits. He knew the most dangerous part of his plan was approximately 50 feet ahead and time was running out. He dimmed his headlights, but kept his blue lights flashing. His pulse increased. He kept his 9mm under his right thigh as a pretty young blond woman stepped out of the Honda in front of him. Her toddler watched from the back seat. Viper watched intently to see how the Marines reacted to her.

The Marine sergeant noticed the blue military identification sticker on the bumper of her car. Experience told him that in all probability she was a Marine officer's wife and not the suspect they were after. The sergeant who spoke with her was extremely formal, addressing her as "ma'am" throughout his intense questioning. Another Marine corporal methodically and efficiently searched her car.

"Excuse me ma'am." The sergeant turned away and walked toward the Humvee approaching the checkpoint.

"Anything suspicious?" Viper spoke with calm authority. The sergeant immediately noticed the Charlie Barracks sticker on the Humvee's bumper.

"No Staff Sergeant," he replied as he made eye contact with the driver, dressed in duty utilities, one rank his superior.

The phone rang inside the guard shack.

"We think this may be another drill," the sergeant added.

The phone continued to ring, but the sergeant ignored it.

"That's a negative, this is real world. Our comm is out at the barracks. Be on the lookout, report anything suspicious and don't let anybody through until cleared by the base. We are starting to patrol the outside of the base."

"South gate, please stand by," the sergeant answered, then placed his hand over the receiver.

"NO! …This is Staff Sergeant Baker Staff NCO Charlie Barracks! Enemy hostile force is wearing a Marine uniform driving one of our Charlie Barracks Humvees! Use of deadly force authorized, stop and apprehend hostile! Copy that!" Baker yelled into the phone.

"Where is the target vehicle now?" Connor asked, speed approaching 100 miles per hour toward the south gate."

"The target vehicle has stopped at the gate," the CIA duty officer reported.

"Driver, halt! Put your hands outside the window!" The sergeant yelled, drawing his weapon from his holster.

Pop! Pop! Pop! Pop! Viper's 9mm rounds ripped through the sergeant's head and corporal's chest. Both Marines dropped to the ground and blood gushed from their wounds.

The young woman screamed and stumbled as she grabbed her child. Viper fired two shots in her direction. He glanced in his rearview mirror and saw two bright headlights rapidly approaching. He reached into his pack and pulled out a small square chunk of something that looked like white clay…C-4. He took out a small

49

remote timing device wrapped in detcord and molded the C-4 around it. With a flick of his wrist, he tossed the device into the guard shack and sped toward the I-95 on-ramp.

"Shots fired! He's on the move again."

Connor heard the anxiety in the voice from his earpiece as he saw the Humvee's taillights speeding past the guard shack.

A bright flash erupted in front of Connor's windshield and he instinctively veered to the side. The force of the explosion and debris momentarily blinded him, and he crashed into the right embankment. His air bag exploded into his face and chest.

Connor felt pinned down and disoriented as he tried to move his arms and legs. He looked over to the passenger side of the vehicle and saw a steel rod lodged in the passenger seat that had penetrated the windshield like a projectile.

"Jack, you okay?" Baker asked, out of breath, as he pulled open the door and cut the deflated airbag away from Connor's face with this duty knife.

Connor felt the heat from the flames of the explosion as the fresh air hit his face. "Yeah."

"Go, go, he's got about two minutes on you, he's in one of our Humvees, on I-95 now!" Baker yelled at the two military police vehicles that skidded to a stop behind them.

Connor gingerly crawled out the car, surveyed the carnage, then stared at Baker in grim disbelief. They knew the shooter had escaped.

CHAPTER 4

SAN MATEO COUNTY DA's OFFICE
REDWOOD CITY, CA

Barrett was reading the police and crime scene reports from the homicide investigation. It was 5 a.m. and she was already on her second cup of coffee in her office at the San Mateo County's District Attorney's office. She subconsciously tapped her fingers on her desk, engrossed in the reports.

The phone rang, and she immediately thought of her husband. "Jack, I'm sorry I didn't call you last night."

"Ms. Connor this is Admid Shiriff, Simi's father. I didn't think you'd be in so early. I was going to leave you a voice message."

"Sir, its 5:00 a.m. in the morning. How did you get my name and number?" Barrett asked.

"Ms. Connor, I overheard one of the police officers mention your name yesterday and I know the DA. My company helped him on his last campaign. He told me how to contact you."

"How can I help you sir?" she politely replied.

"I found some notes and papers that belonged to my daughter. I thought that they might be relevant, and I wanted to give them to you. I can come now or later this morning. My wife and I couldn't sleep last night. We want to do everything in our power to catch the people responsible for murdering our daughter," his voice cracked as he struggled to maintain his composure.

"Sir, our building opens at 6:30 a.m. I'll meet you at the front entrance." When the conversation ended, Barrett pulled up the office telephone roster on her laptop. She focused on the first name on the list and dialed the District Attorney's home phone.

CHARLIE BARRACKS, MARINE CORPS BASE
QUANTICO, VA

The sentry recognized the familiar, military green four-door Chevrolet sedan with a small obscure Charlie Barracks bumper sticker, as it approached his post.

"Sir, your ID please?"

Connor handed over his ID. The Marine sentry examined the ID thoroughly and looked twice at Connor's photo. The base was on high alert after the previous night's shootings.

"Thank you sir," he returned the ID and waved Connor through.

Connor felt wide awake, despite the fact he had been sucker punched by his airbag, scraped half the hair off his ass, and had gotten less than three hours of sleep. He had spent most of the night briefing Cartwright, the DEA SAC and the CIA Director.

As Connor approached Charlie Barracks, he noticed how different the terrain looked in daylight. He glanced over at the gravelly hillside and grimaced as he felt a stab of pain in his leg from his downhill slide.

"Jack, we got a real shit storm here," Staff Sergeant Baker greeted. "Let's go inside."

Connor saw the dark blood stains inside the chalk outline where Sanchez's body had collapsed onto the floor. He ducked under the yellow crime scene tape and entered Charlie Barracks.

"Everybody but the President has already been here this morning; the Marine Corps Commandant, Director of the U.S. Marshals Service just to name a couple. After you left this morning, we found the missing corporal...dead. Two shots in the head. Looks like he was ambushed near his Humvee. We found him down in the ravine behind the barracks," Baker grimly continued. "The sniper killed Sanchez and three good Marines. Miraculously, a Marine officer's wife and baby somehow survived the blast at the guard shack with fairly minor injuries."

"Yeah, I saw her duck and roll under her car just before the explosion. I can't believe she made it!" Connor shook his head.

"A few hours ago, the MPs found the Humvee abandoned off-base. No sign of the sniper. Fuck me Jack! We train for this shit! I thought we were good. I can't believe Sanchez was killed on my watch." Baker's lips formed a thin, tight line of frustration.

"I'll tell you one thing, he's Special Forces trained. How the hell did he get on the base with a sniper rifle and pull off a kill shot on a witness in the middle of a Charlie Company protection detail?" Connor's jaw clenched as he considered the sniper's extraordinary skills.

"That's exactly what I think. Maybe Russian? Nothing but total stealth. Just like we train. It doesn't surprise me that he was wearing Marine utilities when he went through the rear gate."

"If I had just been one minute faster…" Connor felt like shit.

"I was in charge of the protection detail, it's on me." Baker looked down at the ground, then continued, "He flat-out vanished. I'll never underestimate the cartel again. If you get within a hundred miles of this asshole, call me ASAP. I don't care where I am, I'll be there within 24 hours, even if I have to go AWOL."

There was no doubt in Connor's mind that Baker would be a valuable resource in the investigation. Baker was a decorated combat veteran of several armed conflicts, with ten plus years of military service. They had served together in Iraq and Connor had recommended him for the Navy Cross. The brass had downgraded his recommendation to a Silver Star and that had never set well with Connor.

"Tom, if I have any say in the matter, you'll be right there with me."

"That's good enough for me. Jack, there's nothing left for you here except wasting your time. You don't want to get sucked into the red tape that will be going down here for the next two days. You must have other important things to do, including hunting down this asshole," Baker shot Connor a wry smile.

"Yeah right, lots of important things, like returning my rental car and filling out a shitload of paperwork explaining why the airbag is sticking out of the steering wheel like a giant limp garbage bag and why it needs a new paint job," Connor grinned. "I do have to meet my new partner who's finishing basic training at Quantico. He'll be joining me next week in San Francisco."

"Good luck with that bro!" Baker gave him a bear hug and laughed when Connor winced in pain. "Take care of yourself man!"

"Keep me posted on any new leads on your end Tom."

"Roger that."

Connor headed back to the FBI Academy. It had been good to see Baker, but he doubted that they would be joining forces any time soon. It wasn't often that the Marines and DEA combined forces in the streets of San Francisco. God knows he could use the backup.

U.S. ATTORNEY'S OFFICE, SAN FRANCISCO

"Mr. Steiner please, Barrett Connor, San Mateo County District Attorney's Office." Barrett spoke to the receptionist through the bullet-proof enclosure. It had been a while, but Barrett was always impressed with the inlaid marble and the thick carpet in the reception area. It was in stark contrast to the dingy walls and linoleum tile floors in the San Mateo County District Attorney's Office. Barrett glanced at the framed pictures of the President and the U.S. Attorney General.

"Ma'am, here's your visitors badge. Mr. Steiner's office is down the hall on the right. He's expecting you." The buzzer sounded as Barrett walked through the secured door. Barrett enjoyed looking at the San Francisco skyline as she walked down the hall staring through the glass office walls at the city's picturesque views.

The attorney stood up from his desk as he saw the visitor approach his door. "Barrett, Jason Steiner, I'm glad to finally meet you! Bill Cartwright speaks very highly of you, please have a seat."

"Thanks," Barrett noticed his impeccable suit and tie and his self-assured demeanor. "As I mentioned when we spoke earlier, a college student was murdered yesterday in Redwood Shores. Her father contacted me early this morning. He told me that his daughter, a second-year student, dropped out of college about six months ago after meeting a new boyfriend. She began acting strange and stopped communicating with her parents. The father knows nothing about the boyfriend, except that he is Muslim. They initially didn't give it too much thought because they are non-practicing Muslims, themselves. They thought she was going through a phase and wanted to give her some space. They're American citizens and are very wealthy. Her father owns a successful semiconductor company in Silicon Valley."

"Interesting," Steiner listened intently.

Barrett leaned forward and continued, "Turns out the father found a hidden envelope in his daughter's apartment. It contained a couple of coded letters and a few pages from the Quran. The lab is processing for trace evidence now. The PD ran a check on the boyfriend and found out he's a person of interest in a FBI terrorist investigation."

"Where's your investigation going?" he asked curiously.

"One of the Redwood City PD detectives told me that you and the Bureau have a wire up, targeting a couple of individuals who may be linked to a terrorist cell in Washington, DC. It's probably a long shot, but we were wondering if you could check your wire intercepts to see if there is any connection between our victim or her boyfriend and your target." Barrett handed him a folder containing a copy of the case file, photos, and other relevant evidence reports, including phone numbers for the victim, her boyfriend and a phone log of numbers they called. Steiner opened the envelope and thumbed through the documents. "I'll take a look at it. As you probably know, I can't discuss the contents of a federal court wiretap with you until you've read the affidavit and received a minimization briefing. But, I'll call the wire room to see if one of these numbers came up," Steiner scanned the list, picked up his phone and read off the two main numbers.

Barrett looked out the window while they waited. A couple of minutes later Steiner's phone rang.

"The San Mateo County DA's office has an ongoing homicide investigation that might be related to our case. Deputy District Attorney Barrett Connor will be minimized today, and I would appreciate it if you could brief her on our case and show her the line sheets related to the numbers in her case. Thank you." Steiner nodded at her as he spoke into his phone.

"Looks like there's a connection. Do you have time to be briefed in?" Steiner asked.

"Absolutely!" Barrett responded, excited at the possibility of a lead in the homicide case.

"Good." Steiner dialed his secretary and asked her to draft a minimization memo for Barrett.

"Do you know what line sheets are?" Steiner asked.

"Yeah, they're a short synopsis of pertinent information from conversations captured on the wiretap, right? I went to a three-day, state wiretap training course. But, I haven't worked a state wire yet. Our county doesn't work wires as much as the feds, but we do have one or two a year. About six of us are wire certified," Barrett explained.

"Good, your minimization should take about 20 minutes. Contact this number after it's completed, and you can go to the FBI wire room and review the line sheets. I can tell you that this is the first I have heard anything about this particular phone number. I suspect it's of minimal significance in our investigation. But, you're welcome to review all the information to develop whatever leads that may pertain to your case. Be aware that you must clear any potential evidence with me, before you discuss it with anyone else. Including your supervisors, except for those who have been minimized," he emphasized the last point.

"Understood."

"Sir, here's the minimization memo," the administrative assistant interrupted as she entered his office.

Both Steiner and Barrett jumped up in surprise when the assistant tripped and fell to the floor. "Are you okay," they asked at the same time.

"I'm fine. It's these new heels, they keep catching on the carpet," the assistant explained, clearly embarrassed.

Steiner's smart phone and a few other items flew off his desk and landed at Barrett's feet. Barrett reached down to pick up the phone and noticed it was vibrating and saw the text.

R- thanks for information it was helpful-R.

Barrett tried to hide the fact that she had read the message as she handed the phone back to Steiner.

"Thanks, all you need to do now is read and sign the affidavit. Then you can call the wire room," Steiner gave her a broad smile.

"Thanks for your help, I'll contact you if I develop any leads," Barrett replied as she looked down and tucked her files back into her leather folder.

Steiner glanced at his phone and subconsciously gritted his teeth as he read the message. He immediately deleted it as he stared at Barrett's vanishing silhouette.

BOEING 747, DULLES TO LONDON

The Boeing 747's first-class cabin was very spacious, affording ample leg room. The non-stop red-eye flight from Dulles to London was unusually empty at this time of year. The five passengers were fortunate to have the undivided attention of the tall, strikingly beautiful flight attendant. Her tailored navy uniform emphasized her shapely, yet slender lines. Her glossy jet black hair fell softly around her shoulders.

Tara Parks was twenty-four years old and worked as a flight attendant to supplement the sporadic income she received from various modeling jobs. She had just been offered two generous modeling contracts. She signed with Victoria's Secret and said c'est la vie, to the mile-high soda-and-pretzel routine, her resignation effective in one week.

Tara had a reputation for being a master manipulator. She often told her friends that she wanted a lifestyle like the rich and famous and she planned to do just about anything to get it. In fact, she made a point of introducing herself to carefully selected first-class passengers and slipped them gold engraved business cards that advertised her availability for modeling or acting. In fact, both contract offers arose from smitten male passengers.

On today's flight, she had set her sights on seat 4B. She scanned the passenger list. His name was Jacques Devinuer. He was elegantly dressed in a lightweight gray Armani suit and crisp white dress shirt with French cuffs. Black alligator shoes and belt perfectly accented the ensemble. She caught a glimpse of an 18-carat gold Patek Philippe watch under his cuff. He noticed her assessing him and smiled. He expected attention from women. Enough of them had complimented his rugged, handsome and tall, muscular frame.

Tara smiled back at him as he stood up and put his expensive leather briefcase in the overhead bin. However, she was slightly disappointed when he sat down and immediately turned his attention to the New York Times. She was unaccustomed to being ignored by men.

Let's see who flinches first, she wrote in her little notebook and smiled as she fastened her seat belt and prepared for take-off.

He folded the newspaper and tucked it into the seat-back in front of him as the plane's engines roared into full gear and they ran out of runway and lifted off. He stared out the window as they climbed to cruising altitude. The flickering lights on the ground below became faint and eventually disappeared in the low cloud cover. The Virginia countryside below would still be crawling with federal, state, and military authorities. He went over the operation in his head and mentally critiqued his every move. Everything had gone exactly as he had planned, except for a few minor operational adaptations. He was impressed with the accuracy of the Gustos' intelligence, especially the last minute update.

In a few hours he would be in London. He relished the idea of informing Roberto that the mission had been accomplished. He smelled the fragrance of expensive French perfume seconds before the flight attendant lightly brushed against his arm. She sported a hundred-watt smile as she leaned over to give him an optimal view of her cleavage even though it was snugly concealed in her uniform. The gesture was not lost on him and he allowed his gaze to linger on her nametag and the area below it. He knew she wouldn't mind.

"Monsieur Devinuer, may I offer you some champagne before we begin our late dinner service?" she asked in a hushed tone that conveyed the possibility of other offers.

"That would be very nice, mademoiselle," he replied in an accent she did not quite recognize. It was a hybrid...the type of voice inflections acquired by those whose wealth provided the luxury of expensive education and international travel. She smiled. She could recognize money at any altitude and he reeked of it.

She expertly filled the champagne flute, reached across his lap, and pulled his tray table from the arm console in a single graceful movement. The sheer proximity of her arm to his crotch aroused the early stages of an erection. He watched her ass with renewed interest as she bent over to serve the passenger in the seat in front of him.

He had seen dozens of women just like her. They knew they were beautiful and they used their beauty with as much skill as a sniper, carefully identifying their target, then drawing the target into range. He did not mind being in her crosshairs. He took a sip of the ice cold champagne and closed his eyes. He was tempted to relax and enjoy the whole glass, but he did not want to celebrate prematurely. He would wait until he had landed and reported to Roberto. When he was sure of victory, he would then toast himself and enjoy a glass of champagne.

Tara glanced back, confident that she would find the heated gaze of Mr. Devinuer upon her. To her complete dismay, his eyes were closed, and he appeared to be napping.

This may require a more direct approach, she wrote in her notebook as she contemplated the fact that a straight male had never ignored her in her entire life. Tara had a habit of writing notes to herself as a mental exercise to force her will.

R&B TOWING, MENLO PARK, CA

"Ahhh! Get the cleaning materials and turn on the ventilation fans!" Assad yelled.

"What happened?" Hakeem was frantic when he saw the sharp broken glass edges and liquid substance dripping over the work bench onto the floor.

Hakeem's eyes widened in fear when he saw a thin layer of vapors rising from the floor. "Is that contaminated?" Hakeem croaked.

"No, not yet. Get me those cleaning supplies now...before it's too late!" Assad's voice was loud and booming.

Hakeem called out to two other workers as they ran back into the room with the supplies.

"Put these on now!" Assad tossed thick rubber gloves and heavy, white hazmat suits to the two workers.

"What is it?" Hakeem asked, visibly irritated at the receptionist, who nervously looked past Hakeem at the workers.

"There are two firemen in the lobby. They're here for a fire inspection of the building," she whispered.

"Allah!" Hakeem raised his head and held his hands in the air and looked toward the ceiling. "Assad, get this cleaned up now!" he hissed.

"Ouch!" The receptionist cried out, as Hakeem spun around and knocked her off-balance.

"Shut up, you're okay, go back to the reception area and tell them I'll be there in a few minutes!" Hakeem steadied her as he gripped her shoulders.

"Assad, how long will it take to clean up this mess?"

"Less than five minutes." Both workers had pulled on their mask and hazmat gear and were frantically mopping up the acrid liquid.

Hakeem walked over to one of the tow-trucks, started the engine and let it idle.

The receptionist tried not to look nervous after she returned to the reception desk and offered the firemen cold bottled water. They politely refused. The door opened, and Hakeem walked in.

"Gentlemen, my name is Hakeem and I'm the owner. I apologize for making you wait, but one of our trucks had an engine problem. Is there a problem?"

"No sir, we're here for a routine fire inspection. We need to check your fire sprinkler system and your fire extinguishers."

"Please follow me and I'll show you around." Hakeem spent a few minutes showing them the front reception and lobby area before entering the warehouse.

"Open the bay door," Hakeem ordered one of the workers, who was standing at the rear of the warehouse.

"Be careful of those diesel fumes. You should keep your vent fan on and the doors open when you have a vehicle engine running," one of the firemen frowned.

"Thank you, we usually do."

The firemen split up and started their inspection.

"What's in that room over there?" one of the firemen asked.

"That's our tire room. We use it for repairs," Hakeem answered as they walked toward the closed door.

"Assad, the fire department is here to conduct a routine inspection," Hakeem called out. Assad turned off the small blowtorch and turned to acknowledge their presence.

"What's that smell?" The firemen asked as he observed various rows of tires stacked along the wall and saw Assad standing at the work bench.

Hakeem was positioned behind the fireman and frowned at Assad.

"I was repairing some truck tires…burning rubber smells bad," Assad replied. Sweat dripped down his back onto the 9mm pistol which was tucked in the back of his pants under his shirt.

"Is the ventilation in this room code compliant?" fireman asked Hakeem.

"Yes. We installed an additional vent fan last year."

The fireman slowly looked around the room. "Where's the ventilation switch?"

"It's in the storage closet over there," Hakeem replied.

One of the workers stood motionless inside the closet, a rubberized bag on the floor at his feet. He had a hard time breathing through the heavy mask and he felt his heart racing.

The fireman started to walk toward the closet door. Hakeem locked eyes with Assad and silently nodded as the fireman approached the door. Assad slowly reached behind his back, pulled out his 9mm handgun from his waistband, but kept it concealed under the lower portion of the workshop bench. The fireman sniffed as he detected a slight increase in the unfamiliar odor.

Hakeem nodded to Assad as he took a few steps back and peered through the door frame to check the location of the other fireman.

"Hey Roland!" the fireman near the lobby yelled, his voice amplified by the acoustics in the warehouse.

All the men were startled for second. Assad almost jerked the trigger of his weapon, as his eyes locked on the other fireman standing four feet away.

"We got to go now! There's a three-alarm fire down by the harbor and they want all units to respond." His voice grew louder as he walked into the warehouse.

"Thank you sir," the fireman nodded at Hakeem as he turned away from the closet, "Everything looks fine here."

"Thank you, feel free to come by any time," Hakeem replied as the firemen hurriedly left the building.

"Did you find anything?" he asked his partner.

"No, the sprinkler system is old, but it will pass. There was an odd smell in that room and it wasn't from burned tires. I've never smelled anything like that before."

"Roland, this is a tow shop, there's all kinds of weird smells in the place, it's nothing.

We've got to get back to the station ASAP. One of the restaurants at Pete's Harbor is up in flames. They're concerned about the fire spreading to the boat docks and the private yachts. They want all units to rollout as a precautionary measure."

Assad tucked the 9mm back into his waistband and opened the closet door. The worker stepped out slowly, unzipped the top portion of the hazmat suit, ripped off his mask, and gasped for fresh air.

BOEING 747 FLIGHT

The 747 hit a pocket of turbulence as the flight attendants made their way down the narrow aisles, pushing the food service carts. Tara expertly controlled her cart so that it didn't hit the side of the seat where a ten-year-old passenger sat with his earphones in place, watching images of explosions and speeding police cars on the small monitor in front of him. He flashed her a smile as she

61

reached across his tray table and picked up the empty bowl that had held his second serving of ice cream. She was glad that the meal service was finally over. The other passengers were either sleeping or reading and she now had time to devote her undivided attention to Mr. Devinuer.

Although he had seemed distracted at the beginning of the flight, he later praised her culinary skills and proclaimed her to be the loveliest chef to ever prepare a filet to *frightfully rare perfection*. In fact, he had asked for another portion and she made sure that he got the largest prime cut on board. She smiled at how the pilot had sulked when he had to settle for the salmon, but it wasn't her fault that the food vendors had shorted them a steak.

"Is there anything else I can get for you, Mr. Devinuer?" she asked quietly as she knelt next to his seat.

"I am quite satiated, thank you. I am also embarrassed. I do not usually eat two steaks at one meal," he replied in a conspiratorial tone as he leaned toward her.

"I like a man with a healthy appetite, and besides, you seem very fit to me," she whispered with a grin.

"I consider that a great compliment coming from you, because I could not help noticing that you appear very fit as well. Perhaps you will tell me about your fitness regime if you have time?"

"I'd be delighted to! Let me get a glass of something cold to drink, my throat is parched. May I refresh your wine?"

"No, but I would love a café."

She stood up and smoothed her skirt into place as she glanced around the cabin and satisfied herself that the other passengers were occupied. It was time to turn up the charm meter.

He stood and stretched. His arms and legs were slightly sore from all the hours he had crawled around Charlie Barracks terrain with a sniper rifle during the past few days. A small price to pay for such a handsome reward, for what he loved to do best...hunt. Although he was tired and would have preferred sleep to conversation, he had to admit that the flight attendant intrigued him. He had watched her as she had conversed with the other passengers and was impressed by her ability to discuss software with the balding executive who had been glued to his laptop throughout the flight and by her caring attention toward the small boy traveling

62

alone. She was like a chameleon, instantly altering her personality to mirror those of the passengers. The way she subtly changed her voice to a low, throaty whisper when she spoke to him created a hint of mystery, but the look in her eyes was not a mystery. She stared at him exactly the way he stared at her…as prey.

She almost startled him when she returned with a steaming cup of espresso, interrupting his vivid daydream of her naked body.

"Are you sure you want company? Everyone else is sleeping," she asked politely.

"A man can sleep anytime. He must not resist an opportunity to speak to an interesting and beautiful woman," he replied smoothly.

"So, what you are saying is that you find me irresistible?" she teased.

"Quite!" he laughingly exclaimed.

"I must admit that you intrigue me. You don't really fit any of the passenger profiles in our flight attendant code book."

"What are the categories?" he asked, amused to play along.

"Well, let's see," she paused. "There's the computer geek. You know the guy with the laptop. Flight attendants hate them because they are never satisfied, never sleep, and make constant demands during the entire flight because they're uptight workaholics. There are the old money millionaires. They are the worst. They call us "stewardesses," like we are waitresses at greasy-spoon dives along the freeway."

"What is this greasy spoon?" he asked with a warm smile.

"It is a low class restaurant that serves greasy food on tacky dishes."

"Oh, I see. That is an insult, no?"

"Definitely! Then, there is the trust-fund baby. He orders a $400 bottle of champagne just to impress me and spends half the flight trying to stare down my blouse or up my skirt. He acts mortally wounded when I won't give him my phone number, then later calls our corporate office and leaves messages for me telling me of his undying love. Some of the flight attendants go out with the cute ones, but I avoid them at all costs," she continued, maintaining eye contact to gauge his attention.

"But why, Tara? Perhaps one of your trust-fund men will be so bewitched by your beauty and charm, he will spend all the money in his bank on extravagant gifts for you," he said in a low tone as he watched a smile slowly form on her lips.

"I am perfectly capable of earning my own money and buying my own extravagant gifts, thank you very much. And I don't need to compete for attention with his rich papa who pulls the purse strings. Those men are destined to marry the snobby, pale, plain-looking daughters born to the country club crowd," she said with such forceful emotion that he immediately suspected that she had learned this lesson through personal experience.

"I am happy to tell you that I have no trust fund. Am I still a candidate?"

"A candidate for what?" she asked with an innocent smile.

"For dinner, in London."

"Well, that depends. First, you must tell me about yourself. I should know what I am getting into, don't you agree?"

"I will be delighted to tell you my humble and short story, but only after I have heard yours. You have told me nothing of yourself. I am certain that you are a woman with many accomplishments and perhaps a few secrets. Won't you please share them with a weary traveler? You are a delightful storyteller," he coaxed.

"Well, since you asked, I will tell you that I have a Victoria's Secret…" she paused for effect, then added, "swimsuit photo shoot in Mexico coming up soon. If I make the grade, you'll see me in next summer's catalog."

"I am certain that they will dedicate many pages to you," he replied smoothly.

"I have done some modeling, but I never made much money until I found my new agent. He has a lot of contacts in the business and is definitely keeping me booked during my down time. I play tennis and snow ski. I love poker, especially five-card stud. My brothers taught me. I used to have a black cat, but the little tramp left me for a big Tom. I guess I was on the road or in the air too much for her taste. Enough about me, Mr. Devinuer, tell me about you," she implored.

"I cannot. I cannot until you agree to call me Jacques," he teased.

"Alright then, Jacques," she laughed.

"My life is not glamorous. I have no agent and no portfolio. I must confess, I do not like to be in photographs."

"I find it hard to believe that you lead a boring life and I am amazed that you don't like pictures. You are quite handsome, but then, I suspect you've heard *that* before."

He smiled and ignored her last comment. "My life is quite boring. I am an investor, what you call a silent partner in various businesses."

"That sounds very mysterious. What types of businesses are we talking about?" she asked in a playful, yet sly tone.

"Ah, I see, you wish to confirm that I am not one of the computer geeks," he smiled, and then added, "My latest venture involves a new line of designer fashions. I am on my way to London to meet with the principals."

"Really?" she exclaimed. "Who is the designer, maybe I know their label." She sounded overly enthusiastic and his eyes narrowed as he assessed the success of the lie.

Women are so gullible, he thought as he saw how easy it was going to be to seduce her.

"I cannot divulge a company secret before the premiere, but if we keep in touch…" he invited a reply.

Silent partner, my ass. I'll go along for the ride, she thought cynically.

"Well, I've heard enough to agree to dinner, but I warn you, I'll have to know more about you before I give up my phone number." She knew that he would immediately lose interest if she appeared too eager or acquiesced too early. The problem was, he knew that was exactly what she was thinking.

"It is settled, then. Where are you staying?"

"The Landmark hotel," Tara replied.

"I know it well. I will meet you in the lobby at 6:00 p.m. tomorrow night. I will make our dinner reservations. Do you like French food? I desperately hope that you do, because the British do not know how to cook," he replied with a dark smile as he lifted her hand and lightly brushed her fingers against his lips.

"On that, we agree. French food is my favorite." She let her hand linger in his for a moment. She stood as the pilot's voice came over the intercom and announced their impending arrival.

Viper spent the last twenty minutes of the flight thinking about business. The flight attendant never crossed his mind.

The 747 lumbered onto the runway in a bumpy landing at Heathrow International. Tara, continuing her first-class service and made sure that Mr. Devinuer was the first passenger off the plane.

Within an hour, he had checked into his hotel and had begun to prepare his communiqué to Roberto. Standard operating procedure dictated that Viper avoid all hard wire communications because of the possibility of interception by the vast network of governmental intelligence agencies. He avoided face-to-face meetings, because his clientele was often under surveillance. The method he preferred was coded written instructions and replies exchanged by mail or dead drops. The KGB and its two current successors, FSB (Federal Security Service of the Russian Federation) and SVR (Foreign Intelligence Service of the Russian Federation) have used dead drops effectively for over 40 years as a standard method of communication in the espionage world. He had perfected this technique in the military and it had served him well.

He remembered how he and Roberto had met as he navigated through heavy London traffic toward the Federal Express office. It seemed so long ago that he had been lieutenant of the anti-VIP Spetsnaz unit and trained Roberto's unit of the Colombian Army's Black Tigers. Roberto had proved to be a formidable Special Forces operator. They had formed a brotherhood born of bloodshed.

They had kept in contact after their first training session and maintained their friendship through correspondence and occasional visits, both official and unofficial. After a couple of years, Roberto left the Colombian army and joined his close friend Joaquin Gusto, the leader of the Bogotá Cartel. At first, Viper could not comprehend why Roberto would leave the prestigious and powerful Black Tigers to work for a drug dealer. However, he soon realized that the cartel was more powerful than the governments of most small countries, including Colombia. Roberto's position as the security chief was roughly equivalent to being in charge of the old KGB or the new FSB, with perhaps a few more perks.

Viper was shaken from his thoughts when a red Peugeot cut in front of him and forced him to brake sharply. He gave the driver a murderous stare as he pulled in front of her and let her close in before he suddenly braked and turned right without signaling. He glanced into his rearview mirror and saw the initial flash of fear in her eyes turn to rage. He laughed when her red lips formed the word *merde* and her tires screamed the high-pitched cry of rubber burning onto asphalt. He looked over his shoulder in time to see her vulgar hand salute as she drove away. He was still smiling when he pulled into the parking lot of the Federal Express office on Sheraton Street to mail the letter.

CHAPTER 5

QUANTICO, VA

Connor had a problem staying fully alert after he returned from the rental car agency with another car. He had given them a sanitized version of the deployed airbag mishap the night before and they reluctantly rented him a Jeep Cherokee. Maybe the Jeep would be a little more durable. Connor was now fully capable of pursuing suspects off-road. He enjoyed the scenic drive back to Quantico watching thick tree canopies shed colorful autumn leaves that floated into the wind. This was Connor's home away from home. Between the Marines and DEA, he had spent a lot of time at Quantico. He had actually spent more time training at Quantico than at Camp Peary, the CIA's Academy. It amazed him how much the FBI Academy at Quantico had expanded in recent years.

In 1985, the DEA Academy had been relocated and it shared the same facility at the FBI Academy. That caused a little overcrowding, rivalry and led to a fair share of ego clashes. In 1999, the DEA built a separate academy on one hundred acres donated by the Marine Corps, adjacent to the FBI Academy.

The back story to this was that the Bureau was a little pissed over DEA's acquisition and the fact that DEA was going to have its own stand-alone academy that arguably, some day may rival the prestige of the FBI Academy. Connor surmised that this opinion was probably not held by a majority within the Bureau, but rather by some top FBI bureaucrats whose only claim to fame was writing at a desk and had never experienced the hard knocks of investigative work. Connor also knew that the Bureau did not have a patent on this type of individual, and unfortunately, they existed in both DEA and CIA. To the chagrin of many DEA agents, the academy was initially called *The U. S. Department of Justice Training Center, Drug Enforcement Administration.*

Connor loved the DEA approach to bureaucratic ego boxing. Within a year of completing the academy, the black ops section of DEA management somehow bypassed the FBI's spies at GSA, the General Services Administration, and got new GSA signs approved and installed. One morning, to the Bureau's complete surprise, a new bronze sign appeared at the facility that simply read, *DEA*

ACADEMY. The sibling rivalry between the two enforcement bureaucracies continues to this day.

When Connor checked in, the DEA Academy was full due to overlapping classes and in-service training and as a result he was assigned a room at the FBI Academy. Although Connor would not openly admit it to his DEA counterparts, he preferred staying at the FBI Academy. It was where Connor had received his training as a DEA agent. The FBI Academy was an outstanding complex, with more facilities, better food and a great gym, including the diversity of all types of federal, state, local, and international law enforcement agencies present. It is the premier law enforcement university of the world, so unlike the CIA's Academy…The Farm…which was predominately a closed training environment.

Connor got back to his room about 10 o'clock in the morning and was feeling sluggish so he decided to take a quick two mile run to bring life back to his body. The morning sun made his eyes squint. The first half-mile was always the toughest. After that, the jetlag and the effects from the Charlie Barracks incident dissipated, as the endorphins kicked in like clockwork and he finished his run with a kick at the end. After a shower at the gym, he changed into the uniform of the day at the FBI Academy, a pair of 5.11 tactical cargo pants and a polo shirt. Back in the day those exact pants were made by Royal Robbins, the original badge of honor before being sold to the 5.11 brand. Connor still owned a few pair of those coveted durable tactical pants. Feeling invigorated, Connor made his way to the cafeteria so that he could beat the lunch crowd.

Past echoes of memory filtered through Connor's mind. When he went through DEA basic training, the FBI associate director of the academy had instituted a policy that strictly forbade anyone from wearing jeans after hours on academy grounds. That associate director was long gone and so was that lame policy.

As he walked down the hallways, he was reminded of why the place was called the Gerbil Cage. The academy was essentially a cluster of small buildings joined by suspended walkways encased in glass. From a point above the buildings, the place looked just like a gerbil cage, with various walkways and glass rectangle tubes connecting the buildings.

As he started up the stairs, he heard loud music coming from the Boardroom, a little Irish pub adjacent to the cafeteria that served hamburgers, pizza, and sandwiches during lunch, dinner and beer after hours. It was the only game in town at the academy. Instructors, administrators, students, and support staff hung out there and as always, it was jam-packed at the end of the day when classes were over.

He got in line in the cafeteria and recognized two guys wearing the distinctive bright yellow shirts that signified that they were DEA firearm instructors.

"Hey, aren't you one of the firearms instructors from San Francisco?" one of the instructors asked.

"Yeah, Jack Connor," he replied. Acting as a firearms instructor was only one of Connor's collateral duties.

"What brings you here?" the instructor asked after they introduced themselves.

"I'm an FTA and I'm here to meet my new Basic Agent Trainee, Alex Ryker. You guys know him?"

"Oh, yeah. Ryker is the tall Hispanic kid, the movie star look-a-like. The guys call him Number One. You know, the First Officer on *Star Trek...the Next Generation*," the instructor added as he rolled his eyes.

"Oh please! Where do they come up with these names?" Connor shook his head.

"Ryker was a little cocky at first, but his counselor stepped on him pretty hard and he's doing fine now," the instructor said as he washed down his sandwich with black coffee.

"Tell you what, the kid is a damn good shot! He's in the group of BATs we call the *Hollywood boys*...they're all clean-cut, cocky, and crack shooters," the other instructor chimed in.

"Oh great, just what we need. A bunch of wannabe TV feds," Connor groaned.

"Connor, if you have time tomorrow, come by and help us on the firing line. We have a new class and tomorrow's their first day at the range. We need all the help we can get," the first instructor said as he got up to leave.

"I'll see what they have for me and call you later."

Connor surveyed all the young agent trainees as he walked out. He was only in his thirties, but it felt like decades ago that he had been here as one of them. He had been clean-cut, cocky, and a crack shot too. *Maybe I'll get along with Number One.*

LONDON

A gunmetal gray, four-door Bentley Continental Flying Spur pulled alongside the curb at the Landmark London Hotel in downtown London. The bellman greeted the driver by name,

"Hello Henry, who are you picking up tonight? Anyone I know?"

"Ms. Tara Parks," he replied as he got out and walked around to the front of the car so that he could keep an eye on the entrance.

"You lucky bloke! You scored the winning ticket tonight! Have you seen Ms. Parks? She's quite something!" the bellman enthused.

Within seconds, she appeared in the lobby, illuminated by the bright lights. A silky black sheath dress clung to her hourglass figure. It had a plunging neckline and a single slit that stopped high on her slender thigh. Both men stared appreciatively as she took long, poised strides toward them, oblivious to the admiring glances from men around her and the envious glares from the women with them.

"Good evening, Ms. Parks," the bellman greeted her with a slight bow as he opened the limo's rear door.

"Good evening," she replied with a coy smile, flattered that he remembered her name.

"Your chariot has arrived," he smiled as he gestured toward the impressively appointed limo.

"May I introduce myself, madam? I am Mr. Devinuer's driver, Henry. He had some unexpected business that required his immediate attention and he requested that I express his deepest regrets that he was unable to personally greet you. However, he awaits your arrival at the restaurant," the driver explained reassuringly as he placed his hand on her arm and assisted her into the back seat. He surreptitiously peered down the front of her dress, and then shot a wink at the bellman.

"Which restaurant are we going to?" she asked as she settled into the velvet comfort of the seat and crossed her legs, fully aware that the driver was enjoying staring at her in the rearview mirror.

"I am sure that Mr. Devinuer has reserved the best table at the Princess Ship."

"I'm impressed. Mr. Devinuer certainly knows where to find fine food." She smiled as she pressed the button to raise the privacy panel between them. The Princess Ship was the hottest place in town and it was practically impossible to get reservations. She couldn't wait to tell the snobby pilots that she had managed to get in.

"Ms. Parks," the driver called as he lowered the privacy panel a few inches. "Would you care for a glass of champagne?"

"That would be lovely, thank you," she exclaimed in delight.

The driver poured the chilled sparkling wine into a Waterford flute and placed it on a silver tray with a tiny crystal bowl of Russian caviar and delicate pastries.

"Henry, I feel like a princess," she said as she lifted the glass in a small salute. "Dom Perignon, I would expect no less. What sterling service!"

"You are Mr. Devinuer's special guest, Ms. Parks," he replied respectfully, being careful not to be too obvious about his admiration. He regretted that he had caused her to feel uncomfortable enough to raise the privacy panel. He hoped that she wouldn't criticize him to Mr. Devinuer.

"Please call me Tara. I'll be sure to tell Mr. Devinuer that you certainly made me feel special," she replied.

Viper waited near the front entrance of the restaurant. He checked at his watch and scanned the driveway as limousines pulled in and dropped off the restaurant's elite clientele. It was 7:55 p.m. and he knew that the driver would be prompt. He overheard someone say that Sir Elton John was in the lounge area. Although the snobs tried to be discreet, everyone who entered craned their necks to get a glimpse of him. Viper had paid 500 Euros for a private booth in the most remote corner of the restaurant. The added distraction of the flamboyant rock star and his entourage ensured that he and Tara would have a quiet evening, free from prying eyes. Concealing his identity was a full-time concern. Once he reached Paris, he would not use the name Jacques Devinuer again.

At precisely 8:00 p.m., Viper saw the distinctive body style of the Flying Spur as it pulled in front of the main entrance. He watched from a distance as the driver crisply opened the rear passenger door and offered his arm to the stunning woman with exquisitely long, lean legs. This was the first time that Viper had seen her out of her airline uniform and he was surprised at how elegant and graceful she appeared. He was amused at the crowd's reaction to her. Several men stopped in mid-sentence and gawked at her as she walked up the entranceway.

Tara's electric blue eyes searched the faces in the crowd expectantly. Viper stepped out, took her arm, and fell in step beside her. Her face lit up with a brilliant smile. The crowd parted to let them through. So much for not attracting attention.

QUANTICO, VA

"Jack, I'm sorry I haven't called, but wait till you hear this," Barrett's voice was animated.

"What is it?" Connor replied enthusiastically. He was happy to hear her voice.

"I met the victim's dad this morning. He called me at the office at 5:00 a.m.! Can you believe that? He told me that the victim cut off ties with her family about six months ago after she hooked up with a new boyfriend, a Muslim guy. The dad found a couple of weird letters and some passages from the Quran hidden in her apartment. Turns out, the boyfriend's cell phone number popped up on a wiretap that the FBI has going on a terrorist group that has connections to Washington, DC and to the bay area. I already met the AUSA on the case."

"Wow, this is turning into some case Barrett."

"No shit Sherlock. I was minimized today and I'm in the FBI wire room right now reviewing the line sheets. There has got to be some connection to my homicide. My first homicide might be connected to a terrorist plot, can you friggin believe that!" She could barely contain her excitement.

"No, I can't," Connor responded cautiously and tried to keep his concern out of his voice.

"Anyway, how was your flight? Have you interviewed your witness yet?"

"No, in fact, we're gonna need a motivated attorney like you," Connor sighed.

"What do you mean?"

"Our witness was shot and killed last night by a sniper, right outside the witness protection safe house."

"Oh my god! Where were you when this happened?" Barrett asked, clearly alarmed. She had told him more than once that he was a magnet for dangerous operations.

"Well, it was at night and I was indoors when it happened. The sniper made a clean getaway and vanished," Connor replied, careful not to fully disclose his involvement.

"What's going to happen now?"

"Well there are a whole lot of people asking how a sniper infiltrated a Marine base and killed a protected witness at a secure location. Fortunately, it's not my problem so there's nothing for me to do here. I'm at the DEA Academy now to meet my new BAT."

"Thank God honey. Hey, some people just came into the wire room, I've got to go, call you later, love you," Barrett's whisper made him wish he was in San Francisco with her.

ARLINGTON, VA

The U.S. Attorney General and the National Security Advisor waited to be seated at the Carlyle Grand Café in Arlington, Virginia.

"Jordan, how did you find this place?" Hank Henderson asked as he watched the hostess seat another party ahead of them.

"My wife discovered it and we've been hooked on it for over a year. The lunch menu is the same as the dinner menu. Lots of great choices. The thing I like most is that it is not on the DC lunch circuit, so the wait isn't too bad," Jordan Zif replied.

"Any word on Viper?"

"Unfortunately, nothing yet."

"This guy worries me, Hank. If the cartel ever really had a hard-on for the President, well, I don't want to think about it. We've got to find him soon. I remember another assassin with a similar MO, very much like Viper's. It was several years ago when I was assigned to the Israeli Army. His code name was El Aguirre, *The Snake*. Who makes up these names anyway?"

"Who knows, it's probably a spy thing," Henderson shrugged.

"He wasn't a terrorist. In fact, he was a good soldier who just happened to work for the wrong side. He took out a heavily guarded Israeli general. He also killed a cabinet minister a few months later.

They caught him by chance. God knows how much damage he might have done. He was top notch, a security nightmare."

Hank noticed the worried look and deep wrinkles in Zif's forehead. Zif had a reputation as a fearless military officer and an effective politician. He had undoubtedly dealt with his share of terrorists and assassins just as deadly as Viper.

"The thing that concerns me the most is that I think Viper is much more dangerous than the Snake," Zif paused as the hostess seated them at a window table. The waitress set a basket of warm biscuits and a pitcher of ice water on the table.

"He's an instinctive and methodical killer. It's hard to believe he penetrated the Marine barracks," Henderson replied, as he picked up a biscuit and took a bite.

"I have read all the reports on the last two hits and both read like special ops plans. He does his homework and executes the hits with military precision and expertise. He poses a serious threat. If he could assassinate a witness in our protection, he could assassinate the President. There is no doubt in my mind," Zif spoke quietly, mindful of the diners seated nearby.

"You tell me, what are we going to do about the situation?" Henderson leaned forward.

"I'll talk to Bancroft again. She feels the same as I do and I know she is doing all she can do to stop him. I believe he's abroad somewhere, probably Europe."

"I agree. We need to commit every available resource to finding out who he is and who he works for!" Henderson replied, more loudly than he should have.

"I know, Hank. That's why I wanted to discuss the issue with you personally. The President has always been good to me and I respect him more than any other politician in Washington," Zif said with conviction. Zif was acutely aware of the close personal relationship between the President and the Attorney General that dated back to their college days.

"I'm meeting with the FBI Director tomorrow and we're discussing domestic terrorism. I'll talk to him and see if there have been any new leads. I'll let you know if there are," Henderson assured him.

The waitress brought their lunches and for the next ten minutes, they sat in silence, enjoying the food. Zif looked at his smart phone as it busily vibrated.

"Well, I've had thirty minutes without an interruption. That should be a record for this week. It looks like I have to return to the office. You ready?" asked Zif.

They paid cash, left a generous tip and slipped out of the restaurant under the watchful eye of their security details. Their black Suburbans quietly merged into the afternoon traffic.

LONDON

"Mademoiselle, your loveliness is breathtaking, but I must confess that I have a weakness for you in your prim and proper uniform," Viper whispered as he led Tara toward the entrance.

"Really?" Tara smiled and raised a skeptical eyebrow as she glanced at him.

"Yes. It is true. I have a lifelong fascination with women in uniform," he replied in a conspiratorial tone as he led her into the restaurant.

"We will have to explore this topic. It worries me," she responded, playfully.

The maitre d' greeted them immediately and led them to the booth Viper had reserved. Tara was enthralled by the tasteful and artistic design of the restaurant. Although it was crowded, the tables and booths were spaced far enough apart to give the diners privacy.

She smiled at him without speaking. He sensed that she was not a woman who cluttered a conversation with nervous, idle chatter. She was letting him take the lead. He liked that.

"Would you like to choose our wine for the evening?" he asked politely, fully expecting her to decline.

"I would be happy to, Mr. Devinuer," she replied in a confident tone as she studied the extensive wine list.

The waiter articulately described the dinner specials to the powerful couple.

"The scallops sound luscious," Tara replied as she glanced up from the wine list.

"I'll have the lobster," Viper waved him away to give her more time to study the list.

76

"Jacques, what do you think about a 1994 Batard-Montrachet Verget?"

"That is an excellent choice!"

"Don't sound so surprised, Mr. Devinuer. The French aren't the only people on earth who know about wine," her tone was playful, yet self-assured.

"Apparently not. I am certain that you have many talents I have yet to learn and explore. Where did you acquire your vast knowledge of wine? Are you an heiress to a winery?" he asked as he placed his hand on top of hers.

"I haven't decided to share all of my talents with you. And I may be an heiress…or not." Her laugh had a deep throaty sound that he found extremely alluring. This woman intrigued him much more than he had anticipated.

He let her do most of the talking. She was extremely well read and discussed international politics intelligently. Clearly, she did more during her international travels than model and shop. However, she was the most animated when discussing her recent modeling opportunities.

Whenever she attempted to steer the conversation to him, he expertly maneuvered the focus back to her, although it had been hard to divert her away from questions about his clothing line. He regretted that he had chosen that ruse. She was much too informed for him to bluff her. He fell back upon the tried and true role of the international investor with varied financial interests throughout Europe. He spoke in convincing detail about an upcoming trip to Germany where he planned to negotiate a real estate deal for a shopping center in Bern.

He was impressed by her responses. She listened carefully to his explanations and asked insightful questions. She repeatedly attempted to redirect the conversation so that he was talking about topics of interest to him. He was slightly taken aback when she placed both of her hands on top of his, leaned across the table toward him, and spoke in a serious and hushed tone.

"Jacques, I sense that you want me to do all the talking. Don't get me wrong, I find that very flattering, and believe me, it is a pleasant change of pace. But, I must admit, the more you duck my questions, the more mysterious you become. Is that the effect you're going for? Because if so, it is really working." Her gaze intensified as she awaited his response.

He paused for a few seconds. His eyes locked with hers as a slow smile tugged at the corners of his mouth. He turned his hands over so that their palms were touching, then grasped her wrists, and pulled her toward him. His touch was electric.

"In that case, I will not change anything." He leaned across the table and lightly kissed her lips. She gave him a delightfully coy smile. He could hardly wait until the meal was over.

Tara was extremely pleased with the way the evening was unfolding. She would have preferred to develop more specific information about Mr. Devinuer. He was definitely secure, confident and rich. Most importantly, he seemed to respect her. Not many men would trust a woman to choose the wine. She was happy that she had paid attention during culinary classes at the two-week luxury spa retreat she took last summer in the heart of the wine country in Sonoma, California. And, that her reading of the dozen or so discarded wine magazines during the tedious international flights was not in vain.

"Tara, I hope you have enjoyed this evening. You are a most delightful companion. I would very much like to see you again the next time I am in the United States."

"It would be my pleasure." Her voice was as smooth as melted caramel.

"It is such a beautiful night. Would you like to take a walk before we return to your hotel?"

"That sounds great after all that rich, wonderful food."

Viper waited until she left the table for the ladies room before he paid the bill in cash. Cash was not fashionable in this day and age of plastic and he did not want to make her more suspicious than she already was.

He waited for her at the entrance so that he could watch as she walked across the room. She saw him and quickened her pace.

"Do you realize that everyone watches you when you enter a room?" he asked, slightly amused.

"Do you?" she shot back.

"I am invisible when I am not with you," he replied.

"Jacques, the very last thing you are is invisible," she answered pointedly. He laughed as they walked hand in hand out of the restaurant.

DEA ACADEMY, QUANTICO, VA

"Hi, I'm Jack Connor from San Francisco." He walked into an office located in the east wing of the DEA Academy where the DEA training staff was located.

"Hi, Jack. I'm Frances Hunt, class coordinator for Basic Agent Class 230," Hunt replied in a formal, almost stern tone as she stood up from her desk and extended her hand.

"Is this your first time back as an FTA?" This time the harsh coldness in her tone was all too clear.

"No, Frances. I've done this a few times," *Oh no*, Connor thought as he watched her size him up.

"Good. Please sit down. I need to go over some policy issues with you and brief you on your basic agent trainee."

He dreaded what was coming next. *Policy issues. I'm in trouble now.* He took a seat and gave her a forced smile.

"First of all, you should know that I run a tight ship around here and I expect to be notified immediately of any misconduct. The special agent in charge of training has made it quite clear that all trainers, as well as staff, will be on their best behavior while at the academy."

I wonder if this person has ever made an arrest, Connor thought as she continued to talk in her arrogant monotone.

"So far, we have had only had one minor incident. We had to reprimand one of the trainees for abusive language to an FBI senior instructor. The SAC has personally informed me of his approval of the performance of this class."

Connor nodded his head in agreement, all the while thinking that this agent wouldn't last two minutes on the street.

"Let me see, your trainee is Alex Ryker. He's a bit too cocky for me, but his counselor has cooled his heels and he should graduate with the rest of the group. I want your opinion on him after you have had a chance to study him. As you are well aware, it is never too late to terminate a trainee."

"I'll watch him closely and if I detect any excessive cockiness or think he's not measuring up to academy standards, you'll be the first to know."

"I expect you to do so. Teamwork is key."

"I couldn't agree more, Frances." He managed to keep his tone supportive and professional, despite the fact that he considered her a pencil-necked, bean-counting bureaucrat who couldn't hit a hard target at ten feet.

"What's the class doing today?" He broke the silence as she stared at him.

"This is the second day of their final field exercise. They were out all last night doing a round-up. Search warrants will be executed later today. The command center for this operation is located on the third floor of the classroom area. Why don't I give you a tour?" She stood up and started to walk around her desk.

"You know, Frances, I'm sure you must be busy, especially with graduation less than a week away," he replied. He got out of his chair and moved toward the door as quickly as he could, trying hard not to look like a fleeing felon. "I'm sure I can find my way up there. I'll call you if anything comes up," he was already halfway out the door.

"You're right. A lot of people around here don't realize how much work needs to be done at graduation." She gave him a stiff smile and smoothed the front of her polyester skirt as she sat back down at her desk.

Thank God I'm not assigned here. Connor rolled his eyes and headed to the classroom.

LONDON

Viper and Tara walked arm in arm down the deserted sidewalk. He liked the fact that her voice had a pleasant, lilting tone, and in contrast to the way he felt with most women, he enjoyed listening to her talk. She was animated as she told him about her upcoming photo shoot for Victoria's Secret. Viper carefully surveyed their surroundings as they continued walking. He had an uneasy feeling that he couldn't quite shake. Although there was not another soul in sight, he definitely sensed that someone was watching or following them.

He had a deadly accurate sixth sense that alerted him when he was being watched. He focused his attention on a narrow alley that intersected the sidewalk a few feet in front of them. He took Tara's elbow and began to guide her toward the other side of the street, but before he could tell her what he was doing, someone rushed out of the alley and charged toward them. Viper gripped her arm tightly and stopped dead in his tracks. Tara froze and her face blanched in panic and fear.

Viper could see him clearly as he stood directly in front of them, pointing a vintage seven-inch, switchblade knife directly at Tara's chest. The assailant was a little over six feet tall, with a bulky frame and completely shaved head. A small, crescent-shaped scar near his upper lip created a disfiguring sneer that complimented his harshly whispered command.

"Your wallet and purse, mates! Over here…move!" He motioned toward the alley.

Another figure appeared behind the man in the darkness, similar in appearance. He didn't say a word, but Viper caught a glimmer of light as it reflected off the blade of the knife in his hand.

"I said *now*, chap!" The knife-wielding assailant stabbed the air in front of Viper to make his point.

"We don't want any trouble. We'll give you what you want," Viper feigned a nervous tone as he pretended to fumble for his wallet in his back pocket. "Please don't hurt us," he implored as he clumsily dropped his wallet on the ground and then reached down to retrieve it while he moved away from Tara.

"Just give me the bloody wallet," the attacker hissed as he tried to grab it from Viper's hand. That was his first and last mistake. In one smooth movement, Viper grabbed his hand and applied a wristlock, instantly breaking several of the small bones, which gave way with small popping sounds. The searing pain caused the assailant to loosen his grip on the knife. Viper wrenched it from his grasp, plunged it deep into his neck, and twisted it counterclockwise as he pulled it out to insure that he had severed the carotid artery.

The rear attacker had no idea what was happening because he had directed his attention to Tara. He lunged toward her to grab her purse. She instinctively withdrew and broke her frozen silence with a shrill scream as she lost her balance and fell backward onto the sidewalk. Her attacker stopped momentarily and then bent down, reaching for her purse. Viper leapt in between the two of them with a sharp kick to her attacker's knee. The force of the kick caused the knee to bow inward with a loud crack, turning the leg into a distorted semi-circle that collapsed on impact. Their attacker screamed in pain as he grabbed his knee and rolled on the sidewalk, shouting obscenities and ordering his partner to kill them. But his angry commands went unanswered as the prostrate form beside him was surrounded by a dark, liquid shadow.

Viper assessed the situation around the deserted street and pulled Tara to her feet. "Run across the street and wait for me on the other side," he instructed in a forceful, yet calm tone. Her eyes were wide with fright, but she instantly obeyed him.

Viper dropped to his knees directly behind the writhing attacker and gripped him around the neck in a paralyzing chokehold. The two men struggled wildly and Viper did not feel the knife blade as it glazed his shoulder. In a single violent movement, Viper wrenched the man's neck against his body with such force that he dropped the knife onto the pavement shouting obscenities. Viper kicked it into the gutter.

The shouts, suddenly silenced, were replaced by sputtering gasps and the sound of the attacker's hands slapping the sidewalk as he tried to swing at Viper. It took almost a minute for him to die. His neck was thick and muscular. Crushing his windpipe took all of Viper's strength. He pinned his arm against the attacker's throat for another minute after he felt the hyoid bone collapse. By then, all movement had stopped. Viper let the body slump back onto the sidewalk. He instinctively checked for a carotid pulse and respiration. When he was satisfied that the assailant was dead, he stood up and brushed the dirt off his trousers. He carefully avoided stepping in the blood that was fanning out around the body of the other man and crossed the street toward Tara.

Viper looked back across the street uneasily and carefully scanned the area. DNA...his blood was on the knife. Viper ran back and retrieved the one piece of evidence that could link him to the crime scene.

Tara was motionless, staring at the dark forms on the other side of the street in horrified disbelief. Entrenched in fear she did not respond when he called her name.

"Tara, everything is going to be all right. We must go now," Viper said in a low, soothing tone as he put his arm around her shoulder.

She didn't move or acknowledge him. He recognized the shock and put both of his hands on her shoulders as he forced her to look into his eyes.

"Tara. We are safe now. I am going to take you back to my hotel. We must leave here now. Do you understand?" he asked in a slow, deliberate tone.

Her eyes filled with tears and he put his arms around her and held her close for a few seconds to give her time to compose herself.

"What happened? Are they dead?" she asked in disbelief.

"No, but we've got to get out of here now! Before the police arrive. The hotel is only a few blocks away and we will be there in minutes." He replied in a reassuring tone as he firmly took her arm and began walking at a brisk pace away from the alley. He regretted that she had now become a liability.

Tara kept looking over her shoulder, her eyes full of fear. She tripped on an uneven stone in the sidewalk and Viper reached out to keep her from falling. He winced in pain when she grabbed his arm.

"You're hurt!" she whispered in alarm as he recoiled, and she touched the wet fabric on his jacket sleeve.

He quickly pulled off his jacket and inspected his arm but did not slow down as they continued to distance themselves from the alley. His white shirt sleeve was saturated around the three-inch cut in the fabric, and the wound was still bleeding. He took off his jacket and wrapped it tightly around his arm. He was sure that he could make it through the hotel lobby without drawing attention to his injury.

"Do not worry, *ma cherie*, it is a very small cut," he lied. He knew that he would need stitches to close the gash in his forearm.

"You've lost a lot of blood. Are you sure?" she asked in alarm when she saw the dark stain on his sleeve.

"Believe me, it is nothing. When we get to the hotel, I will phone a detective I know. He is a good friend of mine and he will handle this discreetly. Promise me that you will say nothing."

"What?"

"Please, Tara, media coverage of this may delay a pending business transaction and cost me and my shareholders millions of dollars. Do you understand me?"

"Yes, I guess," she replied hesitantly as they approached the hotel entrance.

"Good! I assure you that I will take care of everything. There is no need for your trip to be delayed because of this. You have been through quite enough," he said as he put his arm around her shoulder.

"I need a good, stiff drink." She tried to stop trembling as he pulled her close.

"Stiff drinks are my specialty. We are safe now, don't worry," he whispered reassuringly as he leaned his head down against hers and led her through the hotel lobby.

DEA ACADEMY, QUANTICO, VA

"Jack Connor, FTA from San Francisco," Connor introduced himself to the head of the Tactics and Practical Unit who was standing in the training operations room.

Connor looked around the operations room. There were four agent trainees in the room, so engrossed in the exercise that they hadn't noticed Connor enter.

"Who's your trainee?" the supervisor asked.

"Alex Ryker."

"Ryker's young, but I think he'll make a fine agent."

"Where is he now?" Connor asked.

"Let me see," he paused as he picked up an operations plan. "He's over in Hogan's Alley at the FBI Academy. He's in charge of the arrest team for one of the main defendants in the exercise. If you want, you can take my G-ride, it's right outside. Go watch your boy in action," the supervisor offered as he tossed the keys in the air.

"Thanks!"

Connor parked the car about two blocks from the designated arrest location, behind a large black truck. He had an unobstructed view of the hotel's parking lot, yet the trainees could not see him. If they did, they would recognize him as an instructor because of his attire. He went in a side door and walked into an adjacent observation room. Several instructors were reviewing the op plan.

They looked up as he entered the room. He introduced himself. None of them were familiar faces.

The only thing worse than FTA duty is counselor duty, if you are a field agent. For each Basic Agent class of forty to fifty recruits, four field agents are designated as counselors. Their job is to assist in the training and development of the recruits, bridging the gap between the students and academy staff.

"You made it just in time, Jack. We're going to have the big round-up in about half an hour. I'm the counselor for your trainee, Alex Ryker. He's the arrest team leader on today's practical," the agent counselor said.

"Surveillance-One to Arrest-One."

"Go ahead, S-One," Ryker replied to his call sign.

"I think the suspect just passed me in a red four-door Chrysler Sebring."

"10-4. We'll be on the lookout for it. Let's stay on our toes and don't just focus on the primary. Remember what happened on the last exercise. Nothing is as it seems, so be prepared," Ryker's voice echoed over the airwaves. He was confident in his team members, but he knew that the exercise was designed to be misleading, just like real-life scenarios.

"We have the suspect in the hotel parking lot. He's parking on the southeast corner, next to the pickup. It's Mr. Red," one of the BATs reported.

"10-4. One of you guys use the repeater radio channel and advise the control room that the principal has arrived. Tell them to send the UC to the meet location."

"Copy that." Approximately a minute later, one of the trainees radioed the arrest team that the *UC*, undercover agent was on his way.

"A-one to S-two, if anyone else shows up on scene, they're your responsibility," Ryker transmitted.

"Copy that."

Mr. Red, Connor remembered. *Some things never change.* The trainees still used code words to describe the staff who participated in the training exercises. Mr. Red, in this case, had red hair.

"We're going to throw a monkey wrench into this one. It will be interesting to see how they handle the unexpected," one of the instructors told Connor in the situation room.

"The UC just pulled into the lot next to Mr. Red," one of the BATS transmitted.

"10-4. Okay, guys, heads up. It's showtime," Ryker responded as he watched the UC agent get out of his car and walk over to Mr. Red, who remained seated in the Chrysler Sebring.

"Ryker! We got a vehicle with two males heading your way, the passenger, white male, black hair, approximately 40-years old, has a gun in his hand," blurted one of the surveillance agents over the radio.

"Copy. Try to cut them off before they reach the meet location," Ryker shouted back.

"The UC just gave the bust signal!" one of the trainees radioed excitedly.

"Let's go, go, go!"

The arrest team charged out of the hotel room, running toward Mr. Red's car. Caught up in the excitement, one of the trainees tripped over his own foot and fell to the ground. His weapon, flew out of his hand, skidded toward the arrest vehicle, and almost caused another agent to trip. Oblivious to the fallen student, the remaining team members approached from the rear, converging on the vehicle within seconds and yelling commands at the driver. At the same time, two of the surveillance teams cut off the second vehicle and detained the other suspects as they approached the parking lot.

The instructors watched the chain of events unfold and several of them laughed as they watched the trainees experience the adrenaline of the simulated tactical situation.

Ryker had positioned himself against the hotel wall, so that he could observe his team and the surveillance team. Everything appeared to be under control. He purposely did not participate in the arrest, so that he would be ready for any surprises the instructors planned. He scanned around the area and didn't observe anything suspicious. He was just about to holster his weapon and return to his team when he felt the door next to him slowly start to open. Everybody else was focused on the arrest and no one was looking in his direction. The door continued to open.

Ryker stood very still as he raised his weapon and trained it on the door. He watched as a gun appeared in the doorframe. It was pointed directly at the arrest team.

"Freeze!" Ryker ordered in a loud voice as he pointed his weapon at the suspect's head. The suspect stopped moving for a second and both men rigidly held their weapons, trained on different targets. Suddenly, the suspect turned toward Ryker, who reacted instantly and fired two simunition rounds at the suspect.

"Not bad. The fourth suspect usually gets a few shots off at the arrest team, and sometimes takes a hostage. Not today. Speed, surprise and violence of action are what we teach these trainees. Looks like your boy might actually get it," the instructor told Connor as the other instructors headed out to the arrest location to critique the exercise.

"Violence of action," Connor mumbled, as he thought about the Charlie Barracks' victims.

LONDON

Tara was still in semi-shock as she entered the suite. Viper led her to the sofa and she sank down into its luxurious cushions. He maintained his grip on the jacket wrapped tightly around his arm while he poured scotch into two shot glasses from the wet bar. He downed his and handed one to Tara. Fire burned his throat as he gulped another hit of scotch to dull the acute throbbing pain as he walked into the bedroom. He gingerly unwrapped the jacket from around his arm and managed to dislodge the dress shirt that had become fused to his skin with sticky, clotted blood. The steady stream of cold water turned to dark red and stung as it coursed over his arm and drained into the white porcelain sink. He surveyed the three-inch gash on his arm. The edges were jagged, but it was fairly shallow. He fished a medic kit out of his bag and pulled out a bottle of Betadine. He winced as he flushed the wound with the stinging antiseptic.

Tara coughed as she drank the scotch, she still felt cold. She took a deep breath and tried to slow her breathing. She could not stop the horrifying images swirling around in her mind. Nothing had prepared her for the visceral and harshly brutal images. She closed her eyes and remembered the glint of the knife as it slashed in the air, only inches in front of her face. She tried not to think about the look she had seen in Jacques's eyes. Its cold hardness had frightened her more than the threat of the knife. She wondered what kind of man he was. A sliver of fear made her open her eyes.

She eased herself out of the chair and quietly walked to the bar and poured herself another shot. She downed it and felt its burning heat. *Just relax, everything is going to be okay*, she silently reassured herself.

She walked into the bedroom and stood silently in the doorway of the bathroom, watching him tend to his arm. She felt a wave of dizziness when she saw the bloody jacket lying on the floor at his feet. He was intent and focused and did not look up when he spoke.

"I am not hurt. I told you it was nothing," he replied quietly, trying to hide his irritation. She immediately felt sorry for him. He was trying to reassure her when he was the one who needed reassuring. She crossed the tile floor in two steps and put her arms around his waist. She leaned against his back. She felt his smooth, olive skin. His arms and torso were extremely muscular and his waist was tapered, accentuating his broad shoulders. He was still wearing his finely tailored slacks. His body was tense and she felt him pull away from her.

She wrapped herself closer around him and whispered, "You saved my life tonight. Thank you."

He caught a whiff of the slightly floral fragrance she was wearing and slowly relaxed, leaning back against her. He paused for a moment before he reached out and turned off the water. He wrapped a clean towel around his arm and turned to face her. He brushed his lips against her forehead, taking in the worried expression in her eyes.

"Everything is going to be all right, *ma cherie*," he said in a reassuring tone.

"Then why do I feel so scared?" she asked in a soft voice.

He bent his head toward hers and gently kissed her lips. He felt her quiver as he pulled her close. He immediately forgot the throbbing pain in his arms as they began to kiss. The taste and smell of her aroused him. He was surprised when she responded eagerly and aggressively. They hurriedly stripped off their clothes and he lifted her into a sitting position on the tile countertop beside the sink. She wrapped her legs around his waist and pulled herself into position so that he could enter her. She cried out when he thrust inside her. He covertly watched their coupling in the mirror, a voyeur to his own pleasure. She mashed into him, urging him to hold her tighter, to push harder. It took intense concentration for him to delay the inevitable. When he heard her breath coming in short gasps and felt her contract around him, he plunged deeper inside of her, taking her as hard and deep as he could. She answered every stroke with her own thrusting as they finished together in a grand finale of frantic motion.

Their bodies suddenly became very still, their breathing came in quiet gasps. As he leaned against her, he felt a warm trickle going down his arm. The towel had fallen to the floor and the gash was bright red with fresh blood. He hurriedly covered his arm so that she would not become alarmed again.

"*Ma cherie*, you are magnificent," he exclaimed in a husky whisper as he lifted her and gently stood her in front of him.

She brushed her hair out of her eyes and smiled at him as she leaned against him for support. She could not remember ever feeling this exhausted and sexually spent. They stood in the embrace for several seconds without speaking.

"May I ask for your kind assistance?" he whispered, his eyes soft and imploring. She nodded. "Would you please visit the shop in the lobby and bring back a small bottle of hydrogen peroxide? There is cash in my wallet, it's in my jacket in the living room." He motioned with his uninjured arm.

"Of course," she replied immediately, embarrassed that she had forgotten the fact that his arm was cut and bleeding, as she quickly dressed.

He went to the bed, pulled his suitcase from underneath, and took out a suture kit. He had used this before in the field with his Spetsnaz unit, in far less desirable circumstances, and with far worse lacerations.

Tara scanned the living room and spotted his jacket on the table at the end of the sofa. She reached into the inside right breast pocket and pulled out an expensive black leather wallet. She jerked it open and dislodged some credit cards which fell onto the carpet. As she placed them back into the wallet, she noticed that one of the cards was a German driver's license. Devinuer's picture was on the license, but the name on the license was Hans Studgard, a German citizen.

"Did you find the money?" he called from the bedroom.

"Yes." Startled, she removed a Euro 20 note and quickly put the German driver's license in the wallet and back into his jacket.

She took a deep breath and contemplated her next move. She didn't want him to know what she had seen. She walked down the hallway toward the bedroom. Her footsteps were silent as they sank into the plush rug. She peeked into the room and saw him opening a packet of what appeared to be thread.

"I found the money, I...I took a twenty. What's that?" she stammered, nodding toward the object in his hands.

"It is a first aid kit that I am going to use to repair my arm."

"I'll be right back." She nervously grabbed her purse and jacket on the way out the door.

He changed towels and noticed that the bleeding had stopped. Still naked, he walked with the suture kit back into the bathroom where the light was more intense.

Outside the room, Tara frantically pushed the elevator call button, wishing that the doors would hurry and open. She couldn't decide which frightened her more, the fact that she had just seen two people possibly die during a violent crime, or that she had just had sex with a man who had different identities. She didn't want to feel afraid of Jacques, or whoever he was, but a little voice in her head was telling her to leave...right now.

Maybe there is some perfectly logical explanation, she told herself as the elevator slowly descended. *Maybe he is some kind of government agent, from France or Germany. Maybe he's with the CIA. That would explain the dual identity. Agents would need to know how to defend themselves and use a suture kit. Maybe he is a criminal or terrorist. Hell, maybe he has three wives!* She didn't really know what to think. Part of her desperately wanted to believe that there was a reasonable explanation. The other part sent chills ricocheting up and down her spine. Her hands were cold as ice.

The loud ring from the electronic elevator bell startled her and the doors opened. She hurried across the lobby and was relieved to find that the hotel shop was still open. She purchased the item he had requested and instructed the clerk to have it delivered to his room with a penned note, which read, *Jacques, I know that we are both exhausted and that your arm must be killing you. I decided to return to my hotel so that you can get some rest. I hope your arm is okay. Thank you for dinner. Maybe we'll run into each other the next time you're in the States. Take care of yourself. Tara.*

She left the shop and hurried outside, rushed past the bellman and got into the back of a waiting taxi.

"Please take me to my hotel, I need to get there right away," she implored in a soft voice.

The driver nodded as she gave him the address.

"Americans!" The bellman shook his head as he picked up the phone and called another cab for the hotel guests waiting impatiently in the lobby.

Viper heard a knock at the door and a voice called out, "Housekeeping."

He frowned as he interrupted a stitch and re-wrapped the towel around his arm. He pulled on the white terrycloth robe hanging on the back of the bathroom door and went into the living room.

"Yes?" he asked observing the uniformed bellman through the peephole standing patiently and holding a white bag.

"Sir, I have a delivery from the lobby store," he replied.

"Moment please," he called as he walked to the sofa and took his wallet out of his jacket to retrieve money for a tip. He paused. His German license was clearly visible, not hidden in the back behind his credit cards.

He handed the bellman a few Euros and took the bag. A note was neatly folded and taped to the bottle. He read it, then tore it into pieces and dropped it in the trash.

"Fuck!"

His mind started to race, but he forced himself to focus. He immediately ruled out killing her tonight. In fact, he decided that he would not kill her in London. It would be too easy for the authorities to identify him as a suspect from the flight manifest. He did not think that she would go to the police. She was clearly afraid and would not want to explain why she hadn't reported the crime. She didn't seem like the type who would want to explain why she had fled a scene where two people had been killed, or why she had gone to a hotel with the man who had killed them. She would have a difficult time explaining why she had sex with him, a virtual

91

stranger, and failed to call the police. He would deal with this loose end later. Right now, he needed to finish sewing up his arm.

He was sure that she was frightened and would not want to get involved as a witness, especially since a scandal could thwart her modeling career. He would have to track her down in the States and that wasn't going to be easy. He didn't really know much about her, but he had his sources.

Tara could barely think as she paid the taxi driver. She had ruled out contacting the police, the guys deserved what they got. *Hell, if Devinuer hadn't been there, they probably would have raped me.* She wasn't sure if she was rationalizing the whole thing or even worse, if she cared for the mysterious Mr. Devinuer.

She was still shaking when she arrived in her hotel room. She grabbed her things and cleared out of the room in two minutes. Right now, she wanted to get as far away from London as possible. She moved quickly through the mezzanine and scanned the faces, frightened at the prospect of seeing Devinuer.

"I need a taxi to the airport," she abruptly interrupted the bellhop as he was putting luggage on a cart.

"Right away, madame," he replied with a smile and motioned to a waiting taxi. He hurried behind her and opened the taxi door. She slid into the back seat and took a deep breath. She had never felt this unnerved in her life.

CHAPTER 6

LANGLEY, VA

The phone rang at the South Gate of CIA Headquarters and a guard answered.

"This is Emma Brown from the director's office. The ANSA will be arriving shortly to meet with the director. Please notify us immediately upon his arrival." Brown was always specific when she referred to the National Security Advisor as ANSA, Assistant to the President for National Security Affairs, as opposed to the NSA, which was more commonly associated with National Security Agency.

"Yes, ma'am," he crisply replied.

A few minutes later, a black Suburban approached the gate. The guard snapped to attention as the car stopped.

"Good morning, sir. Can I help you?" he asked.

"We have an appointment with the director. The National Security Advisor is on board," the driver replied.

"ID, please."

The driver had already anticipated this request and handed the guard their ID cards. The guard ran each card through a magnetic reader. The verification process took seconds. The computer screen displayed two color photographs and the names and titles of the cardholders. The guard bent down and stared through the bulletproof glass of the side rear window and recognized the ANSA. He returned the ID cards, activated a floor switch that caused the large black gate to retract and waved the car through. He phoned the office of the director and reported the arrival.

"Good morning, Lynn." Zif greeted the Director of the Central Intelligence Agency as he would have an old friend. "I think this is the first time I've been here since you took office."

"Quite right, Jordan. How are you?" Bancroft warmly replied.

"I like the way you've redecorated. Where did you get the oil painting of Big Ben?" Jordan asked.

"In Cambridge, when I was working on my doctoral dissertation."

"Very impressive, as are the other paintings." Her office décor was scholarly and majestic, an accurate reflection of her style and demeanor.

"What brings you to my office that we can't talk about over the STE phone (the U.S. government's encrypted telephone communications system)?"

"It's about the assassin, Viper. Have your people developed any leads yet?"

"No, not yet. I had the case officer in Bogotá make contact with his source inside the cartel to determine if they could get any leads, but I haven't heard anything yet. I have the crisis team and my top analysts working on identifying him."

"I am concerned that he could be a threat to the President. If DEA is successful in interrupting the cartel's pipeline of cocaine into the United States, the Gusto brothers may exact revenge. They are known for brutally murdering people who interfere with their business."

"Jordan, are you sure you aren't overreacting? There are probably half a dozen world leaders, not to mention God knows how many terrorists, who would like to get to the President, for nothing other than to make a statement. We have the world's most advanced electronic and satellite capabilities, not to mention the Secret Service and the FBI. They've already foiled two plots this year."

Zif rose out of his chair, walked over and placed both hands on her desk, and leaned toward her. "Listen, Lynn. I know all of that. I'm telling you right now this guy is dangerous. He is one of the most effective snipers I have ever investigated. How did he get past the Marines at Charlie Barracks? Where did he get his information? How did he get on and off a military base without raising a hint of suspicion? If he is sent to kill the President, how do you know that all of our safeguards and agencies won't fail again?"

Bancroft knew Zif's reputation, both on the battlefield and in the minefield of politics. She leaned back in her chair, somewhat taken aback by what he was telling her.

"Lynn, I once encountered an assassin like Viper who took out two top Israeli officials in their own backyards when they were under the protection of Shin Bet and under the watchful eye of Mossad. It took them months to track him down and end it. There's no doubt in my mind that Viper is a more skillful and dangerous assassin," he spoke with conviction.

Bancroft noticed the veins standing out on his forehead and on the back of his hands. She was silent for a moment.

"An assassin like him comes along once in a lifetime and it is too bad that he came along during ours."

"Jordan, you've got my attention. What do you think I do around here? You're not the only one who has sleepless nights!" she snapped. "What do you want me to do?" She leaned forward and stared straight into his eyes.

"Right now, we need the agency to keep as many agents and analysts as possible on the case. Use every intelligence resource we have. We need to find out who he is, where he's from, and where he is right now," Zif responded calmly, not overreacting to the director's comment.

"Should we notify the President?"

"That's a double edged sword. For now, I don't think so. There is no need to alarm the White House or Secret Service until we know who we are dealing with. There is no direct threat and no reason to think otherwise. God knows there are already enough threats against the President to keep them on their toes. The main purpose of my visit was to let you know how seriously I take this and to be sure you and your team give it the highest priority. If you get any leads, contact me immediately, day or night. Let's keep each other in the loop on this one."

"All right, Jordan, I understand your position. You've made your point and I'll convey it to the crisis team."

"Thank you, Lynn. I knew you would understand the situation. We can stop this killer, but only if we work together."

After he left, Bancroft sat at her desk for a few moments, deep in thought. Zif had made his point. He didn't tell the director anything that she didn't know or suspect. She pressed the intercom button for her secretary.

"Emma, please go down to the Middle East section and bring up the closed file on the assassinations of Interior Minister Kellman in Tel Aviv and General Tamir, I think that's what his name was, in Jerusalem, both in 2011. Don't make a big deal over this request. It is just a routine file audit, okay? Also get Stevens up here," Bancroft directed.

"Yes ma'am."

Bancroft knew the significance of Zif's warning and was worried that history could repeat itself.

"Go ahead, she's waiting for you," Brown advised as she briefly glanced at his level 5 security badge. She continued staring at her computer screen while she edited the director's itinerary for the Senate intelligence subcommittee meeting tomorrow.

Greg Stevens, the senior intelligence analyst and crisis team leader didn't break his stride as he continued straight into the director's office and closed the door behind him. A red privacy light blinked above the door. They wouldn't be interrupted.

"Thanks for coming down so quickly Greg. Anything new on my three least favorite topics: the terrorist cell in San Francisco, the Charlie Barracks shooting, or our FBI mole?"

"Not much ma'am. We're getting closer to the terrorists' location based on the recent cell activity. We have nothing more on Viper or the FBI mole. However, I do believe ma'am, if you allow me to contact the FBI and enlist their help, we might find the traitor more quickly."

"Really Greg? The last time the FBI had a mole, he was the fucking leader of their crisis team. Remember? Former Agent Jansen? The leak is someone way up the organizational chart, not some mid-level team leader. We can't risk bringing them in, not yet. In the long run, this decision could delay our efforts to nail this asshole and could cost more lives but bringing them in too soon could tip off the terrorist with even worse results." They were quiet for a few moments as they contemplated the implications.

Bancroft broke the silence, "I just had a visit from the National Security Advisor. He spent an hour in traffic for a two-minute conversation with me. He is emphatic that Viper is a national security threat. I know you're doing everything you can Greg but know that this assassin has more than the NSA's ear. I think that all three of your targets are related, either directly or indirectly. That makes your job even more difficult. It would not surprise me if the information about where Sanchez was being held was leaked by the rat in the FBI.

"Okay ma'am, I've got the message, loud and clear," Stevens replied in grim determination.

BOGOTÁ, COLOMBIA

The cold war and the threat of global communism were pretty much a fading memory for the CIA and its agents stationed all over the world. But for every international threat put to rest, another of equal or greater intensity arises. Hugh Heist, a veteran case officer of the cold war, knew that all too well in his current official assignment as the Agricultural Attaché for the American Ambassador in Bogotá. His real assignment was the assistant CIA station chief in Bogotá.

Heist had legendary status within the agency for his great success recruiting top Kremlin officials. The current station chief in Bogotá specifically requested Heist for his extraordinary talents as a case officer. Normally the assistant station chief would not be relegated to this duty, but he was assigned to this top priority investigation. Heist was the control agent for the most coveted undercover operative within the Bogotá Cartel, Joaquin Gusto's personal housekeeper, Maria, code name...Striker.

Heist practiced his trade better than anyone in the business. He had just serviced a dead drop at a farmers market in downtown Bogotá and left the appropriate signal as he headed back to his apartment with a bag of fresh fruit and vegetables. He knew that Striker made a daily trip to the farmers' market every morning and she would look for his message.

"Good morning, señorita. Do you want some fresh bananas today? Come, try one."

"Gracias, señor. I do not need bananas today," she replied to the fruit vendor. The coded communication meant that she had a message waiting for her. She smiled and walked into the restroom. She reached behind the base of the toilet in last stall and pulled off a note that had been taped to the back. She could feel her heart pounding as she unfolded the note. No matter how many times she had done this, she always felt nervous and afraid. She knew the consequences all too well.

The note read: *Striker, find out anything you can about the name Viper. Anything, no matter how small or insignificant the information may seem. Contact me the usual way as soon as you get anything. Match.*

She tore up the note, flushed it down the toilet, and left the restaurant. She squinted as she walked into the bright sunshine and put on her sunglasses. She had the strangest feeling that she had heard the name Viper. She just couldn't remember where.

FBI ACADEMY, QUANTICO, VA

Connor was gazing out his dormitory window on the eighth floor overlooking the tree-lined grounds at Quantico when the phone rang.

"Hello?" Connor grabbed the phone on the second ring.

"Jack, Ron Williams. How are things going?" Williams was Connor's DEA counterpart case agent for the Bogotá Cartel's cell, operating in the Washington, DC area.

"Hot as hell back here, Ron. I was going to call you tomorrow. What's up?"

"Well, I need a big favor."

"You name it."

"We have a UC meet tonight with one of Gusto's top lieutenants. It's a big break for us but I've got a problem. Our new surveillance van, the one with the latest monitoring equipment, is parked behind the tech building at the academy. One of the guys in my group was going to switch it out this afternoon with one of our old vans, but something came up and he couldn't make the switch. I was wondering if you…"

Connor interrupted, "Sorry, Ron, I can't tonight. We have a mandatory meeting at six to meet our trainees and take them out to dinner. I've got dinner reservations in less than an hour and I was just on my way out to pick up my trainee."

"Listen, we really need this van. Why don't you just bring him with you? You can bond in furtherance of this investigation. All you'll have to do is switch the vans. You'll be back in no time or take him out to dinner in D.C."

Connor paused and considered it for a few seconds. "All right."

"Thanks, Jack. You're a lifesaver. I already called tech and had them leave the key to the van at the front desk. It's under your name."

"Okay, where do we meet?"

"At the rear of the Washington Monument in one hour. If anything comes up, you can reach me on channel four or reach me on the Nextel, there's one in the van. You've got the number, right?"

98

The older agents still referred to the push-to-talk, *walkie talkie* radio style phones as Nextels even though Sprint bought the rights to the Nextel technology.

"Yeah, I've got it. See you in an hour." Connor glanced at his watch as he hung up and phoned Ryker. He explained the change of plans and told him where to meet.

Connor was impressed that Ryker was waiting for him as he approached the loading dock.

"Hello, sir," Ryker greeted him.

"Knock off the 'sir.' We are going to be partners in less than a week, so call me Jack, or hey you, but not 'sir.' Okay?"

"You're the boss."

"Not yet. I'm just your partner. In the meantime, we've got to shuttle this van to the Washington Field Office for an agent working on a joint case we're working with DC and SF. You'll be involved once you get to SF."

"Are we going to help them out on surveillance tonight?" Ryker asked, a hint of excited anticipation in his voice.

"No. You don't have a badge or creds yet. Trust me, you'll get more than you can handle after you get to San Francisco." Connor grinned at his enthusiasm. He remembered how anxious he was to hit the streets when he was a new agent.

"Damn, it would be great to get some real OJT."

"Well, there's this thing called liability. We don't want any of that, believe me. I hear they call you Number One. Don't tell me you're a Trekkie or Trekkor or whatever you geeks call yourselves."

"Not me, captain. I have only watched the show a couple of times," Ryker replied in mock seriousness, then raised his hand and flashed him the Vulcan, split-finger greeting and said, "Live long and prosper." They both laughed.

Connor liked the kid's sense of humor. Ryker's demeanor conveyed confidence, not cockiness. That was always a good sign in a new agent. Lack of confidence or overconfidence could get him killed.

"Alex, I hear you're single. Seeing anyone special?"

"All of them are special, Jack. I'm still looking for the ideal woman."

"The only looking you're going to have time for in the next couple of months will be from one of these surveillance vans. So, what is your idea of the ideal woman?"

"The ideal woman...let me think. She is smart, professional, athletic, likes the outdoors and guns, is a good shot, is independently wealthy, and built like a brick shithouse. You know, the usual."

"That sounds just like my wife, Barrett. But, she is already taken,"...*or at least she was the last time I checked*, he thought. Connor knew he couldn't keep his real job a secret from her much longer. The longer he waited, the worse she was going to take it.

"Man, I can't wait to meet her!" Ryker whistled like a construction worker watching a pretty woman walking away.

"She's a prosecutor. We'll have to see if she can get some of her single friends to come over for dinner sometime so that you can meet some people in the area," he added.

"That sounds great. I want you to know that I am really looking forward to working with you in San Francisco. I don't care how many hours we have to work or what kind of grunt work I have to do. I know it sounds kinda corny, but I really am just happy to be here. It's something I have always wanted to do."

"I don't think that's corny, that's a great attitude to have." *This kid has potential*, Connor thought.

"What do you think about your DEA training so far?"

"For the most part, it's been great, but we definitely have had some screw-ups in the group," Ryker replied.

"Every class does. Believe me, my basic agent class had some real winners too. What do you think of the staff?"

"Is this a loaded question? I don't want to seem like a rat, or worse, a complainer," Ryker paused before continuing.

"Listen Alex, we're going to be partners. I don't want the company line or the academy answer. We need to be straight with each other, right from the start," Connor replied with conviction.

"Okay, well, most of the instructors and counselors are great, but the class coordinator, how do I put this...she's fucked up and way too full of herself!" Ryker was pointedly blunt.

"Well, I'm glad to see you aren't holding back your true feelings," Connor laughed."I know what you mean. I had the same reaction the first time I met her. The only question I have is, how long did it take you to figure her out?"

"After she introduced herself to the class."

"You must be a slow learner," Connor cracked a smile.

Connor exited off I-95 and they saw the Washington Monument lit up in the distance. When he pulled up to the area, he saw Williams talking with a small cluster of agents. He immediately sensed that something was wrong.

"Hey Ron, what's going on?"

"We've got another friggin problem! One of the guys in my group got involved in a wreck in the van about thirty minutes ago over on I-495. The other driver lost control and sideswiped him, possibly a drunk driver. Everybody's okay, but the agent and the van are out of commission tonight. I've paged a couple of other agents, but they are at least sixty minutes out. That is no help because the meeting is in thirty. We do not have the option of rescheduling the meet. The bottom line, Jack, is I need you to work the surveillance van tonight. I've only got four agents to cover the meet."

"No problem, Ron, except I have Ryker with me, remember?"

"I can work this van in my sleep. I've already had a week in it," Ryker interjected enthusiastically.

Connor stared at him and raised his hand, palm forward, in the universal sign for stop, which Ryker did immediately.

"Do you know what would happen to both of us if anything went wrong tonight, Ron?" Connor asked.

"I hear you, but it's just a surveillance. All we have to do is cover a brief UC meet. Jack, we can't miss this meeting and we need to record it. You know how important the case is to both of us," Williams voice gave away his apprehension.

Connor paused a few seconds. "Okay, but nobody knows about this except us."

"Agreed!"

Ryker was so jacked up, he wanted to high-five Williams but decided against it.

"And you, Junior. Not a word of this to anyone. I better not hear a single rumor at the academy. Understood?" There was no mistaking the intensity in Connor's voice.

"Yes, sir! I'm perfectly clear on the concept."

"Okay, we're going to brief in ten minutes in the Marriott parking lot on Connecticut Street," Williams said as he turned to his car.

"I know where it is. We'll meet you there." Connor watched as Ryker immediately jumped into the captain's chair in the back of the van and started to power up the equipment. A smile crossed his face as he remembered what it felt like to get that first real adrenaline rush.

"Alex, stay in the van and be quiet while the briefing is going on. I don't want the other agents to see you out here. You should be able to hear the plan and I will fill you in on anything you miss."

"10-4, boss," he replied with a grin as he continued to power up the equipment.

Connor pulled into the back parking lot where three agents were standing next to a white Range Rover. Williams pulled in behind Connor.

"Okay, we all know the routine. Jose Mendoza, Gusto's lieutenant on the East Coast wants to meet tonight to go over the delivery details for the next shipment. Our confidential informant will be driving Big Dog, our local target, to the restaurant where the meeting is scheduled to go down. The CI is already wearing the wire and with any luck, we should hear what's being said and we'll know when the meeting is about to break up."

"This is Jack Connor the case agent from San Francisco," Williams introduced him to the surveillance team. "We're light on manpower tonight, so he'll be operating the van and taking pictures by himself." Connor and Williams briefly exchanged eye contact as Williams continued.

"I think we all know the Old Ebbitt Grill, it's on Fifteenth between F and G Streets. The meeting shouldn't last more than an hour. The van will be on point outside the restaurant and two agents will go inside to cover the meet. The rest of us will keep it loose outside and hopefully we will get more help before the meeting is over. Here are some photos of the players. Everyone take another look so we remember who's who. Jack, keep these in the van and I'll collect them after the meet."

"What's the plan for after the meet?" an agent asked.

"I want a loose tail on our target, Big Dog and the CI. Nothing on Mendoza, he's too paranoid, we need more manpower for him. We don't want to take a chance and spook him. I will hook up briefly with Jack and get the recording of the UC meeting and then Jack and I will debrief the CI after he drops off Big Dog."

"You guys inside, try to leave the restaurant a little before the UC meeting ends and help out with surveillance. We'll only have three cars on Big Dog and the CI when they leave the restaurant," Williams added.

They nodded in agreement.

"If more agents come we'll reassess. Also, if anybody needs medical attention, we'll go to George Washington Hospital; it's ten blocks from here on Pennsylvania Avenue. Jack, why don't you go in first and park as close to the restaurant as possible. Guys, we need to bring our A game tonight," Williams emphasized the point.

"Ron, I forgot to tell you, the SAC might drop by tonight and join in the surveillance," one of the agents volunteered.

Connor stopped in his tracks, turned to Williams, and glared at him.

"That's fucking great Ron!" Connor lowered his voice so that no one else could hear him.

"Relax, Jack. He comes out every once in a while. His wife is a doctor, they don't have kids and he gets bored when she's working the night rotation. He's a good guy, probably won't stay long, if he even shows up."

Great, I'm in the middle of an undercover meet, waiting for the DC SAC to drop by and visit. I've got a trainee with no badge, no gun, no creds... no friggin' problem! Jack thought sourly as he headed back to the van.

"You get all that, Number One?" Connor asked as he opened the van door and saw Ryker sitting in the captain's chair expertly operating the controls on the panel.

"Aye aye, captain," Ryker grinned and reached for the photos in Connor's hand.

On the first pass by the restaurant, Connor found an ideal place to park about half a block from the restaurant on the same side of the street.

"DC-111, this is SF-211," Connor transmitted.

"Go ahead 211."

103

"We're in position about half a block from the restaurant. Targets not yet sighted," Connor radioed.

"10-4," Williams acknowledged as he scanned the streets and got into position.

"The wire equipment is working, so we should hear them when they get close enough," Ryker told Connor, as he marveled at all of the tech equipment in the van. "Hey, Jack, mind if I ask you a question?"

"Sure."

"Why do you carry two phones…an iPhone and a government phone?"

"I like to keep my personal numbers separate on my iPhone. Plus, the iPhone has a great GPS system that I can use anywhere."

"I've seen some agents carry two phones, but it seems it's mostly work-related. I figured one of those phones was dedicated for headquarters in case the DEA Administrator wanted to contact you."

"Sorry, Alex, I'm not that important. Some agents carry a UC phone, but my iPhone is for my personal use, that's all." Connor smiled, he knew it wasn't the DEA Administrator, but rather the CIA Director who would be calling. Ryker was sharp, no doubt about it.

The agents were silent for a few minutes as they watched the streets for traffic. Pedestrians walked on the sidewalks, oblivious to their presence. About ten minutes passed before the wire monitor started to crackle.

"Jack, I think our boys are on the way," Ryker's tone was professional, but his enthusiasm was apparent. Connor grinned at him in the rearview mirror.

"SF-211 to surveillance, we expect contact within the next few minutes. The wire is going active."

The sound of music came across the monitor as clearly as if it were playing on the van's radio.

"We have contact," Ryker called to Connor as he adjusted the volume on the unit.

The sound of voices became pronounced as the music faded, "Dude, just keep your mouth shut tonight and listen to me and the main man and you might learn something."

"I'm cool, Big Dog," the confidential informant's voice did not reveal a hint of anxiety.

Ryker was surprised that the voices came in so clearly over the background music, unmistakably rap. The new equipment was designed to enhance conversation and minimize other noises. He peered out of the van's tinted windows and saw a dark green Volvo S80 drive past them with two black male occupants.

"Jack, check out that green Volvo. Is that them?" Ryker asked. "I only got a partial plate, November three four nine," he added.

"SF-211 to DC-111."

"Go ahead."

"A dark green Volvo, Virginia license plate number November three four nine lima two one arriving on scene."

"Affirmative, that's them."

Man, Connor is quick, Ryker thought as the Volvo headed westbound onto 15th and turned left at F Street.

"This is DC-115, I've got 'em. They parked in a spot on F Street. They're out of the car and headed toward the restaurant."

At this point, the wire was picking up clear conversation and the sophisticated equipment in the surveillance van was recording all of it. As they turned the corner, Ryker strained to get a look at a real criminal. Big Dog looked exactly like he did in his photograph. He was wearing a long, black leather coat, black silk shirt and black pants.

Ryker was surprised at the gangster attire. It was very similar to what the instructors wore when they played the roles of crooks during the undercover and surveillance exercises. He always imagined they overdressed during their role-playing to exaggerate for dramatic effect. He couldn't help thinking that it was a shame he couldn't tell his buddies back at Quantico about real life on the streets. He had never felt so excited in his life.

"The CI and Big Dog just went into the restaurant. Surveillance team, go in now. The main target should not be that far behind," Connor radioed.

Two of the agents responded and walked toward the entrance to the restaurant.

"Well, what do you think? Your first surveillance living up to your expectations?" Connor asked.

"It's a whole different feeling than training exercises. I don't know how to describe it, it feels more exciting, but it also feels more real."

"You're doing just fine. Some of this just takes a lot of practice. Let's see if we can ID Mendoza's car when he arrives," Connor replied in a supportive tone.

"Yeah. I see a single male, possibly Hispanic, about a block away and coming toward us," Ryker replied. They turned their attention in that direction. Ryker turned down the volume on the wire to concentrate on the suspect, who walked toward the van, then crossed the street.

"10-4. I've got him. Yep, that's him," Williams radioed the group.

Ryker turned up the volume on the wire and the sound of voices rose over the static and background noise inside the restaurant. They listened intently as they heard a voice begin.

"Welcome to Washington, my friend. How was the trip?" The deep voice clearly belonged to Big Dog.

"No problems," Mendoza had a thick Spanish accent and he was direct and to the point.

"SF-211 to surveillance, we have contact in the restaurant and are getting good wire."

The next hour went by quickly as the team stayed in place. The digital recording captured the conversation although some of it was inaudible because of excessive background noise in the restaurant. Connor was always amused at what dealers talked about. As a general rule, they spent fairly little time talking about dope, and a lot of time talking about women they had sex with or wanted to have sex with, sports, or in this case, the size of the waitress's breasts.

"Jack, I think Mendoza just got an incoming phone call and he may have left the table," Ryker advised holding his right hand to this head set trying separate the static from the voices.

"I have to take this call, I'll be back in a second. I need to get…" the next few words were inaudible.

"Cool dude," Big Dog replied.

FBI WIRE ROOM, SAN FRANCISCO

The four walls of the rectangular wireroom were plastered with two separate organizational charts of suspected terrorist cells, with photographs and cell phone numbers in San Francisco and Washington, DC. At the top of the chart for San Francisco, was an empty box with only a question mark inside, with the word *Engineer*, printed below it. There were both horizontal and diagonal lines connecting various boxes on the charts which represented telephone contact between the suspected terrorists. The FBI's goal in this investigation was to identify and locate the *Engineer*. So far, they didn't know his real name or associated cell phone numbers.

Along both sides of the room were five monitoring stations, each capable of monitoring ten cell phones at one time. This investigation had five phone lines that were being intercepted.

Barrett hardly took any breaks as she read all the daily summary sheets for the last month, as well as the detailed individual "line sheets," or transcripts of each telephone call. After the first few hours, she had a good working knowledge of how the wire room operated.

Barrett looked up when she heard the three second humming tone of one of the DVR machines, followed immediately by the digital dial tone. That meant that someone using one of the target cell numbers was making a call.

This particular phone number was being monitored by an Arabic translator, who picked up a headset and waited for the conversation to begin.

"Do you have the device yet?" a voice asked in English.

"No, I'm meeting them now in a restaurant. I should have it soon," the other voice replied.

"Good, we need it as soon as possible. Are you sure she won't cause any problems?" the first caller asked.

"No, she's family. I trust her, nothing will go wrong."

"Great, I'll see you in a few days," the first caller replied.

"Okay." The line went dead.

Since English was the only conversation being intercepted, the monitor allowed all four individuals inside the wire room, including Barrett to listen. Normally, if more than one conversation was being intercepted at once, the monitors would listen to the conversations through their respective headsets.

"Today, we identified Jose Mendoza and he is going to receive the device. We know that he has ties to the Columbian Bogotá Cartel. It looks likes the terrorists and the cartel are working together. Hopefully, we can establish the connection soon," the FBI agent assigned to the shift explained to Barrett, then reached for the telephone.

"Jason Steiner," the Assistant U.S. Attorney answered and pressed pause on his TV remote. Steiner had a reputation for being very *FBI friendly* and as result, agents informed him about any significant leads that developed in the wire room, day or night. Steiner loved being kept in the loop.

"Jason, it's Agent Michelle Logan in the wire room. We just had an intercept. The targets are planning to deliver *a device* within the next couple of days."

"What type of device?" Steiner asked.

"Don't know. I called the case agent in DC and they're trying to GPS the target's phone."

"Good. How many of you are working tonight?"

"I'm here with two monitors and the DA."

"The DA! What is she still doing there!" Steiner demanded. He didn't sound pleased.

Barrett didn't flinch. She tried to appear engrossed in reading the transcripts so that the FBI agent didn't pick up on the fact that she was straining to hear their conversation.

"We are all fine here, I'll call you if there's any further developments," the FBI agent replied coolly and deliberately ignored the tone in Steiner voice.

"Call me if they locate him. Thanks for the call." Steiner swore to himself. *Why is the DA still in the wire room this time of night?* He immediately walked to his closet, pulled out a change of clothes and was in route to the office within minutes.

WASHINGTON, DC

"Jack, check it out!

A black 5-Series BMW parked behind them. A stunning woman got out. She was in her mid-twenties, a tall, top-heavy brunette wearing a short black skirt and revealing top. Ryker's stare wasn't completely work-related. *Some things never change on surveillance,* Connor thought.

"What do you think, Alex?" Connor asked with a knowing smile.

"Well, she could be a high-class hooker, but she looks a little too sophisticated for that. Plus, she has too nice a ride. Frankly, I'd rather ride in that Bimmer than this van, whether she's in it or not," Ryker grinned. He noticed that she was carrying a briefcase. *That's weird*, he thought, but before he could say anything he was distracted by the voices on the wire.

"Listen, it sounds like the boys inside are expecting somebody else to join the party," Connor transmitted.

"Thanks for bringing this. We're just about to leave," Mendoza's voice cracked over the wire.

"No problem, I was going out anyway. See you soon," a female voice responded.

"Heads up, we've got a female suspect inside the restaurant who brought something. Sounds like the meeting is finishing up," Connor transmitted.

"10-4. Surveillance teams prepare to follow Mendoza," Williams radioed.

"The undercover surveillance team is out," Connor replied.

"Jack! A guy's trying to break into the BMW with a slim-jim," Ryker exclaimed, causing Connor to glance back toward the movement.

"Damn! Whatever happens, Alex, stay in the van. Got that!" Connor replied in frustration. He radioed the situation to the rest of the surveillance team as he kept an eye on the stocky male wearing a baseball cap who was in the process of jamming a long narrow strip of metal into the driver's side window of the BMW.

"SF-211, I'm moving closer to your position. Surveillance team, focus on the entrance until the targets emerge," Williams directed.

As they watched, the would-be car thief kicked the front tire and started walking away. They split their attention between him, the front of the restaurant, and the conversation coming across the wire.

"SF-211 to surveillance, the main target is outside carrying a briefcase. He is westbound on 15th Street. Big Dog and the CI are still inside, waiting for change. They'll be out shortly."

"Jack! The car thief is coming back. He is walking toward the BMW with something in his hand." Ryker focused the zoom lens of the camera and snapped a photograph.

"SF-211 to surveillance, the guy by the BMW is holding an unknown object. Standby."

"I'll stay with the van until the primary leaves the area, all of you stay on plan," Williams radioed as he headed around the block to Connor's location.

"Need any help?" one of the agents asked.

"No, stick to the op plan."

"Here comes our boy," Ryker said as the target, Mendoza, passed the van. Ryker immediately recognized the briefcase.

"Jack! The woman in the BMW is connected to Mendoza."

"What?" Connor was confused.

"Yeah, she had a briefcase. She's probably the one who met him in the restaurant. It looks like Mendoza's carrying that same briefcase!" Ryker exclaimed.

Connor alternated watching Mendoza, the restaurant entrance and the BMW. The guy who had tried to break into the BMW was back. He waited until Mendoza was at the intersection before he began approaching the BMW.

"I can't tell what the guy is holding, Connor. It may be some sort of burglary tool, but I'm not sure," Ryker said as he came within an arm's length of the BMW.

"What's the status on the inside?" Connor asked.

"Sounds like they're still paying the bill. They're talking to the hostess. Wait, I think they're walking around," Ryker reported.

"DC-115 to DC-111, we set up on Big Dog's car and are ready for a take away."

"10-4." Williams responded.

"Jack, the female is walking back toward the Bimmer," the tension in Ryker's voice was rising.

"Damn! Remember, whatever happens, Alex, stay in the van! Got that?" Connor ordered.

"Ron, this situation might get interesting any second. The BMW driver is coming back this way. We think that she passed Mendoza a briefcase inside the restaurant. She went in with it, but he came out with it. You'd better get over here. Everybody else, stay put," Connor radioed.

"10-4," Williams replied.

"Jack, he sees the woman coming and he's hiding behind our van," Ryker's concern was obvious from his hushed tone.

What is going on? Connor thought, as he moved close to the van's back door and saw the figure crouched outside.

"Ron, where are you?" Connor whispered, torn between jumping out of the van and attacking the guy now or waiting for Williams.

"Give me thirty seconds, Jack."

"Might not have it." Connor sensed the predator's instinct to pounce on the unsuspecting woman.

"Jack, she's headed your way," Ryker whispered excitedly as she passed in the front of the van.

The crouched figure poised to strike. Connor didn't hesitate. He swung the van's back door open and struck the would-be attacker as he jumped toward the woman. The van door threw him off balance but did not hit him with enough force to knock him to the ground. Connor sprang out of the van and squared off in a fighting stance.

Anger replaced surprise as the thief swung but missed as Connor instinctively lowered his body and moved out of striking range. A second later, Connor connected with a direct kick to the shin and immediately followed with a straight-line elbow strike to the chin that sent him crashing to the sidewalk. Connor quickly flipped the suspect onto his stomach to apply handcuffs but he bolted back to life and struck back. The woman screamed, then took off running, but it was the sound of screeching tires from another direction that caught Ryker off guard. He turned toward the front window. He saw Williams' vehicle closing the distance in a hurry, but what caught his eye was a shadow running directly toward Connor.

Ryker had no time to think as he jumped out and ran around the front toward the sidewalk. He didn't have a plan, but his instincts told him to intercept. Like a defensive back, he hit the speeding figure full force, t-boning him from the side. The impact sent the runner flying into the wall. Ryker started to roll him over to handcuff him, realizing at that moment that he did not have any cuffs with him.

"Ryker, I got him," Williams rushed in between him and the prone figure, grabbed the suspect's arm, twisted it behind his back and began cuffing him as the man struggled and swore.

"Get back in the van and stay down!"

Ryker's first instinct had been to punch Williams, but only because he hadn't seen him coming.

"Okay, okay!" he replied as he ran back to his van and got in.

"Jack, you all right?" Williams called as he secured the cuffs.

"Yeah, I'm fine, he's a little tougher than he looks," Connor replied as he tightened the cuffs on the man face down on the pavement, still focusing his attention on the assailant.

The loud blare of sirens abruptly halted as a police cruiser skidded to a stop at the scene as the two patrol officers jumped out.

"Looks like you guys don't need much help here," one of the police officers drawled.

"DEA!" Williams announced as he turned toward them so that they could see the badge hanging on the dog-tag chain around his neck.

"Yeah, we know. One of your surveillance agents called it into dispatch and requested backup."

"Well, well, lookie who we have here! Hey Jamal, hey Richie," one of the police officers taunted the handcuffed men. "Y'all ready for your ride downtown?"

"Fuck you!" one of them spit the words at the officers.

"Everybody all right here?" Special Agent in Charge Lucas Crenshaw asked as he approached.

"Yeah, it's under control," Williams replied as he pushed one of the suspects toward the cruiser.

"Boss, meet Jack Connor, the San Francisco case agent I told you about who is at Quantico for a week. Jack delivered the new van from Quantico for us. We came up shorthanded at the last minute and he agreed to help us out tonight." Williams hoped that his SAC had not just witnessed the incident. He would never be able to explain what Ryker was doing in the mix.

"Glad to meet you, Jack. Good work."

"Thank you, sir."

"Dawg, check it out!" the CI exclaimed as he pointed in the direction of the police cruisers gathering at the scene.

"Damn fools, the 14th street gang got caught trying to rip off another car. Why they gone try that shit up in here? Man, ain't no safe place to park," Big Dog shook his head in disbelief as he walked in the opposite direction and tried to stay under the radar.

Crenshaw was engrossed in a conversation with the two police officers who had first arrived on the scene. After they had safely secured the suspects in the back of the squad car, Williams and Connor walked back to the van.

"What the hell was that about?" Connor asked as he looked at the patrol car.

"I don't know. Sounds like those guys are regulars with the locals. I'll check it out with them later," Williams replied.

"Ron, you made it just in time," Connor said appreciatively.

"Not exactly, Jack."

"What do you mean?"

"It wasn't me. Your new partner cold-cocked that second guy."

"What!" Connor exclaimed in exasperation, realizing he'd been oblivious to Ryker's actions.

"That's right. What a tackle! I saw the whole thing. That hit could have made the Top Ten on Sports Center highlights."

"Where is he now?"

"In the van. Don't worry, nobody else saw him," Williams replied under his breath as Crenshaw approached them.

"Okay guys. You better get going. Ron, you'll need to make a statement tomorrow down at the station. You don't have to do it now, they know we're on a surveillance," the SAC directed as he surveyed the van.

"So, this is our new van?" Crenshaw leaned toward the rear window in an attempt to look inside. Connor braced for the worst. If the SAC opened the door, he'd find Ryker inside and they would be in a world of shit. Crenshaw paused for a moment and then turned around and started walking away.

"I'll see you in the morning, Ron. Glad to meet you, Jack. Good work, tonight." he said with a wry smile.

"Yeah, see you later," Williams replied as he glanced at Connor.

"He's your SAC?" Connor asked incredulously.

"Oh yeah, in the flesh. He's a pretty good guy. He remembers what it's like to be a field agent."

"Thank God he didn't open the van door."

"It's not like you've got naked women in there, Jack. Nothing wrong with a little on-the-job training, right?" He grinned and slapped Connor on the back.

"Yeah, right. The next time you're an FTA, I'll be sure to call and get you to bring a couple of basic agent trainees by for a little buy-bust experience," Connor replied facetiously.

"No, thanks. This is as close as I want to get."

They walked over to the van and Connor opened the driver's side door.

"Well, what did you think of the field training exercise, Number One?" Connor asked.

"Man, it was amazingly." Ryker grinned from ear-to-ear.

"What you just did is the best example of your training…speed, surprise and violence of action. I would have preferred that this all went down after your graduation, but you did well, Number One."

"Thank you, captain!"

"Hungry?"

"I'm starved!"

"Funny how a good bust will work up an appetite," Connor smiled.

"Hey, Ron. Want to get something to eat?" Connor called out of his window.

"No thanks, Jack. I've gotta catch up with the rest of the troops. You guys go ahead. Thanks again for helping out!"

"Ron, try to keep me out of this mess if possible. It would be great if I could avoid having to testify about this arrest. It's a huge waste of time and my supervisor will be pissed off if I have to travel back here to testify in a local case," Connor sighed.

"I get it, don't worry."

"I recorded the whole thing, except for the last part showing my involvement. I turned it off when I jumped out of the van," Ryker interjected.

Connor and Williams made eye contact with one another and both thought, *the kid's a winner.*

"Hey Alex, ever thought of working in DC?" Williams volunteered.

"Not a chance, buddy! I trained this kid. He's mine!" Connor protested

Ryker looked at them, sheepishly handed the digital recording to Williams, secured the van's rear door, and climbed back into the passenger's seat.

"Jack, take the van back to Quantico. I will have someone pick it up tomorrow. I need to go catch up with the surveillance team," Williams called as he walked back to his car.

"Number One, what are you hungry for?" Connor asked as he got back into the van.

"A big, juicy steak."

"Yeah! Me too, I'm buying."

"Alex, one more thing, what I'm about to tell you stays in this van and you tell no one, copy? It's related to my ongoing case in San Francisco."

"Sure." Ryker was all ears.

"Here's another example of how a bad guy can use the tactics of speed, surprise and violence of action against us. Connor briefed him on the sniper attack at Charlie Barracks. Ryker listened intently, his expression a mixture of disbelief and surprise. Connor locked eyes with him and his message was clear...never again.

FBI WIRE ROOM, SAN FRANCISCO

"Deputy DA Connor, you're burning the midnight oil. Have you found anything interesting that I missed?" Steiner asked. As he walked into the wire room, he noticed how good Barrett looked in her tailored suit.

"Not yet, interesting case though," Barrett replied as she caught his appraising glance.

"Let me know if you have any questions or comments. It's always good to get a fresh take on the wire intercepts."

Barrett nodded as Steiner walked past her toward the FBI duty agent.

"Are these the line sheets from tonight, Agent Logan?" Steiner asked as he picked up the clipboard containing the written synopsis of the conversations recorded in the last four hours.

"Yes, we haven't heard anything from our counterparts in WFO," the FBI agent replied, referring to the FBI Washington Field Office.

Steiner sat quietly for the next 10 minutes as he read the line sheets.

"Ms. Connor, care to join me for a quick cup of coffee downstairs. I'm interested in your thoughts."

"No thanks, I'm in court in the morning and have to argue a motion. I have to review it tonight. I'm on my way out."

"Isn't your husband out of town on a case? I seem to remember that Bill Cartwright told me he was in DC this week. Come on, have some coffee before you drive home, ten minutes tops."

Agent Michelle Logan looked up from reading the transcripts and shot him a look of disgust.

"No, I don't have time, and frankly its none of your business where my husband is," Barrett snapped and got everybody in the wire room's attention.

"I meant no disrespect," Steiner replied, clearly chagrined. There was an uneasy silence for a few minutes while Steiner pretended to read the transcripts.

"I'm calling it a night. Agent Logan, call me if we get any other calls on the device, and make sure you pass that along to the midnight crew as well." Logan only nodded in response as Steiner left the room.

"Unbelievable!" Logan whispered to Barrett as she gathered her things to leave.

"Yeah!" Barrett mouthed her reply.

CHAPTER 7
BOGOTÁ, COLOMBIA

Maria's heart was pounding like a jackhammer as she stood inside the doorway to Joaquin Gusto's office. She was seldom in the office by herself. Joaquin would be gone for at least two hours, so this was an ideal time to search through his desk to see if there was any information on Viper. She held Joaquin's key chain in her hand. She had taken them from the spot in his bedroom where he kept them hidden. Joaquin was a very organized individual and she knew that if he kept anything on Viper, it would be in his locked desk. Maria looked at the desk, a huge English flattop with intricate, hand-carved designs on each end. Joaquin collected art and antique furnishings and every piece of it was expensive.

She tried two of the smallest keys and the desk drawer opened on her second try. Every item in the drawer was neatly organized. There were two separate folders in the middle of the drawer. She picked them up and placed them on top of the desk. She opened the folder that had a small square of yellow paper stuck to it that read *TO BE FILED*. She stared at each document carefully for anything that might be related to Viper. Her eyes caught a letter that was torn in four sections. She reconstructed the letter on the desk. It began with the letter *R* and ended with the letter *V*

As she read the letter, she recognized that it might be important. She rubbed her hands together to stop them from shaking. *Someone* died and V had sent a dozen roses. Could the initials be names? V for Viper and R for Roberto, Joaquin's security director?

She pulled out the high-tech miniature camera device her CIA control agent had given her and took photographs of the letter and everything else in the folder. There were ten documents. She pressed an icon on the tiny screen which automatically e-mailed the photos to the encrypted computer server at CIA headquarters. She set the camera on the desk and put the documents back in order. Suddenly, she heard voices and footsteps rapidly approaching the entrance to the office.

No! She silently screamed as she crammed the papers into the folder and placed both folders back into the desk drawer. One of the pages flew out of her hand and sailed across the floor. The voices grew louder as they approached the office door. She frantically searched for a place to hide, but it was too late. The door swung open.

"Maybe someday, I will have an office like this one," Pedro, a security guard, bragged to the other guard.

"I do not think so. You, my friend, are not smart enough to have an office like Señor Joaquin."

Maria's heart was beating so loudly she was sure it echoed through the room from her hiding place under the desk. She could see the piece of paper in the corner on the carpet only a few feet from where they were standing.

"Check out the view. Very nice," Pedro said appreciatively as the two men walked closer toward the window.

Oh my God, the keys! Maria held her breath. The keys lay on the desktop only inches above her head.

"Amigo, how do you think I would look sitting behind this desk?" Maria watched their feet get closer and closer to the desk. She closed her eyes and trembled uncontrollably. She felt faint from holding her breath.

"Like a fool, Pedro. A dead fool if El Jefe catches us in here."

"El Jefe is not here, is he?" His voice was full of false bravado.

NO! NO! NO! Marie wanted to scream as their feet drew closer and closer to the desk. A loud, static-filled radio transmission erupted into the room and startled her so badly she nearly lost control of her bladder.

"Control to Pedro, over."

The guards stopped in their tracks and stared at each other.

"Go ahead, control."

"Where are you?" the speaker's accusatory tone was unmistakable.

"We are walking patrol in the residence," Pedro replied unevenly, a knot forming in his stomach as he spoke.

"El Jefe has returned. Get back to your post immediately," came the clipped response.

"Yes, on the way."

"He has returned early," Pedro hissed in a loud whisper as they briskly walked out of the office and quickly closed the door behind them.

Maria waited for a few seconds until she heard their footsteps fade. She did not want to risk leaving the office while they were still in the hallway. Her heart was in her throat as she slipped out from under the desk. The keys were gone…an overwhelming sense of panic engulfed her.

"Where are they?" she whispered out loud in a state of near hysteria. Her hand bumped into the front of the desk and she felt a sharp jab. Glancing down, she saw that the keys were hanging from the lock in the top desk drawer. She walked over to the corner and picked up the piece of paper that had landed on the floor and put it back into the folder. Relief flooded over her as she locked the desk and put the keys back in her pocket.

She cautiously peeked through the window and she saw Joaquin's motorcade enter the courtyard. She tried to focus as she left the office and hurried to Joaquin's bedroom where she quickly replaced the keys in the hidden compartment in his jewelry box on the dresser. She momentarily froze as she closed the door and reached into her apron pockets and fumbled desperately. They were empty.

The camera! Where is the camera?

She rushed downstairs toward the office with a sense of dread mingled with abject fear. The tiny camera was literally the difference between her life and her death. She heard the entourage enter the residence as she turned the knob on the office door.

The camera sat on the desktop exactly where she had left it. *Please, God,* she prayed as she slid it into her pocket. At that moment, the door flew open and Joaquin's voice boomed into the room.

"Maria!" Joaquin shouted before he was all the way into the room. He did not see Maria jump as he slammed the door. When he did see her, she was standing by the window, calmly wiping a dust cloth across the cool panes of glass.

"Señor Joaquin! What happened to you?" she managed in a normal tone of voice.

"We had a flat tire and locked ourselves out of the vehicle for a bit. I had to stand in the rain while they changed it. Go to my

119

room and lay out dry clothing. I must change at once!" He barely noticed her at all as he emptied his pockets onto the top of the desk.

"Yes, Señor Joaquin," she replied and hurried out of the office. She stopped when she reached the top of the stairway and stood motionless for a few seconds. The last time she had felt this afraid and alone was when her husband had been killed. She thought about a time before that, when he was alive. For few brief moments she remembered feeling his strong arms around her. If only she could feel safe again.

DEA ACADEMY, QUANTICO, VA

Connor hit the stop button on his Ironman after he finished his six mile run and noted that the digital read-out was just under forty eight minutes. His heavy breathing was intensified by lack of sleep and the pound of steak he had eaten late last night. It felt like lead weight in his stomach. He walked around and tried to cool down before he headed back to the gym to shower and change. He had gotten up early so that he could tie up some loose ends at the DEA Academy before his flight back to San Francisco. He heard his phone ring and fished it out of his nylon sports bag.

"Jack? Ron. Thanks again for the help last night."

"Interesting night Ron," Connor replied as he wearily sat down on the gym bench.

"Just want to give you an update. You won't believe this. We checked the video and it turns out that Mendoza did get that briefcase from the unknown female. The surveillance agents completely missed it. Who, what, where, why, is a mystery to us. Also, Big Dog and our CI are missing."

"What?" Connor perked up.

"Yeah, no clue where they are, both disappeared. The guy who Ryker decked had a loaded thirty-eight on him. The ballistics matched a drive-by shooting in the same area two weeks ago," Williams added then paused. "It gets more interesting. The FBI came by after you left and took custody of one of those pricks. Turns out they're involved in some sort of terrorist investigation. The guy Ryker nailed is an FBI suspect and the guy you tackled is an FBI informant...It gets better. The FBI target is Mendoza. Not for drugs, but terrorism! Big Dog is somehow involved too. The BMW is registered to a female, one of Mendoza's cousins. It's a little confusing now and way above my pay grade. Our SAC is meeting with the FBI SAC. As of right now, we are continuing our investigation, but the Bureau is the lead agency. We need to keep a lid on the FBI involvement…direct order from our SAC. You believe this shit? Our case is tangled up with terrorists. Fuck me! Street dealers and terrorists!"

"Nothing surprises me anymore," Connor replied cautiously. "Keep me in the loop, Ron."

"I will."

"I am so glad the kid didn't mix it up with the guy. They would have had our asses in a sling!" Connor grimaced at the thought of what kind of clusterfuck there would have been if Ryker had been shot or had shot someone as a trainee.

"Well, it all turned out. I wish I had a junior partner who saved my butt just before he got his badge," Williams added.

"Ryker and I talked about the surveillance while we were driving back to Quantico. I must admit, he is really mature for his age, especially in light of the fact that he doesn't have any prior law enforcement or military experience. He's fluent in Spanish too! Can you imagine him undercover?"

"Hey, did you hear that Sanchez was killed at a safe house at Quantico the other night? I forgot to ask you, but weren't you supposed to debrief him? Did you get a chance to talk to him?"

"No," Connor grimly replied.

"Shit man, what is going down on our investigation. Well, you were a Marine. You go figure out how he did it."

"I might do just that."

"Hey Jack, I got an incoming call from the SAC's office, got to run. I'll get back to you."

Connor was glad when the phone went dead. He immediately dialed Bancroft's private line.

"Hi Jack, wait one second please." Bancroft excused herself from the group and walked to a corner down the hallway.

"Go ahead."

"Ma'am, I just got information that the Bureau is working a terrorist investigation in DC that is connected to one of our targets, Jose Mendoza."

121

"Don't worry about him, Jack. Our intel tells us that Mendoza is nobody. We told the Bureau that, but as usual they didn't listen to us. Anything else?"

"No".

"Okay, call me if anything comes up." Connor could tell that the director was busy. After the conversation, he tried to recall the details of the classified, top-secret document the SAC had shown him just before he left for Quantico. He still couldn't believe that an assassin had infiltrated the Marine base and executed one of the Gustos' top lieutenants under the government's highest level of informant protection. The whole idea sounded impossible. He wondered where Viper had hidden while he plotted and planned the cold-blooded murder.

MICHOACÁN, MEXICO

The silhouette of a man was discernible for only a second before he disappeared into the dense vegetation of a remote hillside in the Michoacán Valley in Mexico. Although the night was clear, the air was warm and humid.

"Carlos, where are you?" Francisco Felix spoke into his hand-held radio.

Carlos and his men were at the end of the runway. He was thinking about his next contact with Connor and he did not hear Francisco's first transmission.

"Carlos! I said, *where are you?*" Francisco barked. The harsh irritation in the disembodied voice jarred Carlos back to reality.

"Sorry, Francisco. We are in position at the south end of the runway. We haven't heard anything yet," Carlos replied.

"That's good. Be alert. Remember, the cartel will be unmerciful if we screw up." Francisco's organization was the transportation cell for the Gustos' west coast cocaine distribution into the United States.

Francisco admired his new Oyster Perpetual Submariner two-tone, stainless-steel-and-18-carat-gold Rolex watch. The luminous dial glowed in the dark. He felt a pinprick of pain on his wrist and adjusted the watchband. The glow from the dial revealed that a large mosquito was the source of his discomfort. He slapped his wrist and crushed the intruder. As he wiped away the tiny blood spot, he swore under his breath. He would have his men light up the airfield in approximately ten minutes. He wanted to get this over with so that he could return to the air-conditioned comfort of his hacienda, but he would not rush. He would wait until after they established radio contact with the pilot before he gave the order to turn on the runway lights. He stared at his radio, expecting to hear the pilot's voice at any moment.

What Francisco did not expect lay in wait on the west side of the runway. Ricardo Felix, the cousin he hated and had fought with all his life had set up an ambush. Ricardo and fifteen of his men crouched in the heavy brush. They were split into two groups. They wore camouflage utilities and were heavily armed with automatic weapons, assault rifles, and two ancient M203 grenade launchers which at close range were quite effective.

"Remember, stay down. Whatever happens, don't start shooting until the aircraft has off-loaded and left the runway. Nothing must happen to the pilot or the plane. I'll kill anyone who disobeys me!" Ricardo radioed his men in a hoarse whisper. He did not want to start a bloodbath with the Bogotá Cartel by killing one of their sacred pilots.

"Okay," one of Ricardo's men radioed. The men were keenly aware of the feud between the two Felix families that had begun long before their births. No one was sure what had started it, but their grandfathers had killed each other, and their sons had extracted revenge on each other for years. His hands trembled slightly on the steering wheel while he led the second half of Ricardo's team in a convoy of three worn-down trucks, slowly down the path, headlights off, approximately one quarter mile north of the runway.

"Once the attack begins, focus on the suitcases. The five million is more important than the five tons of cocaine."

Unfortunately, the five tons of cocaine on the aircraft would be of little use to Ricardo because he did not have the contacts to distribute the fine, white powder. He found that aspect of the mission bitterly disappointing.

I will learn this business once Francisco is dead and out of my way, he thought in anticipation. Francisco had robbed him of many opportunities during his lifetime. *I am El Jefe this night,"* he whispered under his breath.

Francisco transmitted the prearranged signal to the pilot to let him know that the landing site was secure. The cartel had insisted on this precaution to ensure their plane and pilot's safety. The slightest deviation from the coded message would cause the pilot to break off contact, abort the landing, and return to Colombia.

"Night Rider, I am five miles out and will be landing from the north," the pilot broke radio silence.

"Roger. We are turning on the runway lights now...copy?" Francisco gave the signal to light the runway and within seconds, parallel strings of blue strobe lights created a welcoming corridor of high visibility for the approaching aircraft.

"Copy. Looks like a blue Christmas from up here."

Ricardo's men saw the runway lights flash on and knew that the plane would land in less than five minutes. Ricardo's lieutenant saw Francisco's men, silhouetted by the lights near the perimeter of the northern end of the airstrip. He could make out five new SUVs and approximately twenty men around the airstrip. Only two of the men were in their vicinity. It would be simple to take the men out because their attention was directed toward the approaching aircraft and they were not expecting visitors.

"Night Rider, I have you in sight. I'm beginning my approach...over."

"Roger. Standing by."

Francisco heard the sound of the plane's engines in the distance but could not yet see it over the ridge. After several seconds, he saw the plane's running lights and watched it touch down, then taxi along the runway.

The lieutenant keyed his radio three times slowly to signal Ricardo that the plane was on the ground.

Ricardo clicked four times slowly to signal that he wanted his men to move closer to the airfield. The trucks maintained lights out as they slowly moved into position. The drivers adjusted their night vision goggles to accommodate for the light radiating from the plane and the other vehicles near the runway. The sound of the plane's engines masked that of the trucks as they crept closer and closer.

Francisco scanned the airstrip and saw that his men were fully deployed. He was close enough to see Posadus, his second-in-command, give him a thumbs-up sign.

"Carlos," Francisco spoke into the hand-held, "we're starting the off-load. Keep your eyes open."

"Si señor."

Francisco walked briskly toward the aircraft as the pilot climbed out. "Welcome, Alejandro," Francisco shouted over the noise of the aircraft's engines. Alejandro was one of the best fliers in the elite group that worked exclusively for the cartel. They referred to themselves as the Bogotá Cartel Air Corps, a moniker that greatly amused the Council.

"My good friend! Is this the new Russian plane you told me about?" Francisco's voice boomed in welcome as he slapped the pilot on the back.

"Francisco, old friend! It is good to see you! This is my new lady. She is beautiful, no?" Alejandro replied as he pointed appreciatively at the plane.

"You told me you did not like Russian women!" Francisco declared in mock surprise as he smiled at his friend.

"That was before I met this one. She is an Xian MA-60 turboprop, the latest in Sino-Russian design. She is one of the fastest, heavy-payload turbo props in the business and the most advanced. Although she is fully loaded, she maneuvers better than an American stripper…the next best thing to sex!" The pilot roared as both men laughed.

The sound of their laughter filled the air. The sound of two short clicks went unnoticed as Ricardo keyed his radio to determine whether his men were in position. A single return click signaled that they were ready. He estimated that it would take between fifteen and twenty minutes to off-load the plane. In the meantime, they would wait. He smelled the smoky fumes from the plane's exhaust. He did not know what was more pleasing, that he would take Francisco's money or his life.

"Did you bring any packages for me?" Francisco asked as he motioned his men toward the plane.

"No, Francisco, not this trip," Alejandro replied with a straight face.

"What?" Francisco exclaimed and caused Alejandro to burst out laughing.

"You lying bastard! Let my men finish this work so that they can get back to their whores!" Francisco signaled them to begin the off-load as he keyed his radio. "Carlos, security report?"

"All clear," came the immediate reply.

125

"Francisco, help me with your luggage," the pilot directed as he walked up the rear cargo ramp into the rear of the plane, retrieved two medium sized mental briefcases, and passed them to Francisco.

"There are two more," Alejandro added as Francisco turned and briskly walked to his Suburban. He wanted to secure the cases as soon as possible.

"Shoot anyone who touches this luggage," Francisco ordered the driver as he handed him the two bags.

"Si, señor," he responded crisply as he loaded the cases into the back of the vehicle.

After Alejandro completed his pre-flight inspection of the aircraft and refueled, he helped the men as they unloaded the last dozen pallets. He knew the physical exertion would help keep him awake for the long flight back.

"Have a safe flight home, my friend," Francisco replied as he stepped back from the plane and Alejandro fired up the turbo prop. The high-pitched whine of the engines was deafening against the quiet backdrop of the jungle. Francisco covered his ears and turned to walk to the edge of the runway to escape the noise and acrid odor of jet exhaust as the plane picked up
speed and headed toward the north end of the runway for take-off.

Francisco glanced down at his Rolex. The entire off-load, from start to finish, had taken less than thirty minutes. He was pleased. His men were becoming more and more efficient. The bonus program appeared to be working. He grinned as he thought about how he would spend his $5 million cut. *Not bad for a hard night's work,* he thought as he saw the plane lift off the dirt runway and fade into the night. He watched for a few minutes until the sound of the engines became a faint drone in the distance.

Ricardo's lieutenant keyed his radio: *click, click, click, click, click.* Ricardo responded with five clicks.

Francisco saw a single blinding flash before he heard the explosions. The concussion from the blast hurled him into the air and he landed on the runway with a hard thud. Ricardo's bandits got off their first volley of fire, catching Francisco's men off guard. The two M203 grenade launchers were deadly accurate as they slammed ordinance into the lead and rear Suburbans. The lumbering vehicles instantly burst into flames, guaranteeing a jarring, fiery death for the unwitting occupants.

Francisco's motorcade came to an abrupt halt as the remaining SUVs careened into one another. Chaos reigned for a few moments. Some of the men shouted as they frantically reached for their weapons while the drivers struggled to maneuver around the burning wreckage.

Ricardo's primary attack force charged out of hiding toward the temporarily disabled motorcade. Ricardo stood in the truck bed of the lead vehicle, his muscular arms vibrated as he aimed the cab mounted M60 machine gun and sprayed 7.62mm rounds at the moving vehicles. He stood like a modern day Ben Hur leading a charge, his jaw clenched, and his feet rooted in place as the truck bounced onto the road and lunged closer to the flaming trucks up ahead.

Francisco's remaining men recovered quickly and began to return fire with an assortment of military-grade assault weapons. They overcame their initial disorientation and began to repel their attackers with deadly accurate aim.

Ricardo's secondary force readied to fire a volley from the M-203s in order to finish off the convoy. The shooters knelt and stabilized the heavy weapons, taking careful aim as they began to squeeze the slack from the triggers.

Carlos and his men launched into their counterattack when they heard the blasts from their position of cover. The sound of their approach was muffled by the exchange of gunfire. Ricardo and his men didn't see them coming. They rushed them from the rear and fired round after round point blank at the shooters. Blood and flecks of brain matter sprayed into the air as the shooters fell face first into the dirt. Ricardo's team had been neutralized before they could turn around to defend themselves. It would have been a brilliant military maneuver, but given the circumstances, it was merely a massacre.

Time was running out as Carlos ran to the edge of the runway. The lights from the runway and from the moving vehicles barely illuminated the area. He could see Francisco staggering to his feet approximately ten yards in front of the disabled motorcade. Carlos grabbed a light anti-tank weapon system rocket, fully extended the tube, swung it onto his shoulder and zeroed in on Ricardo's lead vehicle as it bore down on the motorcade, firing a hail of rounds from an M-60 machine gun. Francisco was in the direct line of fire and Carlos could not tell whether the fierce volley

127

of machine-gun fire had hit him. He unshouldered the LAW for a moment and sidestepped to the right so that he could get a clear shot at Ricardo without risking blowing off Francisco's head. The next split second, Ricardo's truck moved into his field of vision and Carlos watched the trailing flames of the rocket as it hit its mark. Francisco dropped to the ground a second before the deadly projectile cut through the air above him. The force of the explosion shook the ground when the rocket detonated and slammed into the front of the lead truck. The sheer force of the impact flipped it over and sent it flying into the rapidly approaching truck behind it.

The sound of gunfire melted into the deafening roar of the explosion as Carlos' men advanced on the attacking force, taking full advantage of the cover of the billowing, black smoke. Francisco's sharpshooters picked off the drivers of the second and third trucks in the speeding procession. The trucks veered out of control and slammed into the mass of burning metal that blocked the road.

A few of Ricardo's men jumped from the rear truck, rolled onto the ground, and tucked their weapons into shooting positions, as they shouted profanities in anger and pain. Francisco's men, now on foot, raced toward them, firing round after round, effectively silencing the return fire within seconds.

Francisco's ears rang from the thunderous explosion as he struggled to regain his composure. He winced as he tried to pull himself off the ground and felt a wave of nausea as he inhaled the toxic fumes of gasoline, gunpowder, burning rubber and felt the hot vapor suffocating him.

"Francisco, are you okay?" Carlos yelled from a distance, his voice muffled by the roar of the flames in the burning vehicles.

Francisco couldn't speak but lifted his hand in a weak wave as he dragged himself to the side of the road and collapsed in a fit of convulsive coughing. The ringing in his ears throbbed in agonizing waves of pure pain. He vomited on the ground, then rolled onto his side and tried to fight the dizziness that gripped him.

Carlos ran across the road and reached his side in seconds. "Francisco, are you hit?" he exclaimed as he rolled him onto his back to check for entry wounds. Francisco stared at him numbly, unable to comprehend the question or respond.

"Francisco!" Carlos yelled again.

Francisco heard his name over the din of loud ringing in his head and struggled to focus.

"Francisco, you haven't been shot. I do not see any blood. Let me help you stand." Carlos encouraged him and struggled to help Francisco to his feet. They surveyed the carnage around them. Their eyes burned, and they coughed as the thick, acrid smoke blew into their faces.

"I'm okay. Get us out of here now, Carlos," Francisco croaked as he regained his balance and gingerly touched his neck where a bright red burn mark throbbed with pain.

One of Carlos' men ran over to them and shouted, "It was Ricardo! He and his men attacked us!"

"Ricardo?" Francisco roared. "That bastard! Where is he?"

"Burning in hell," the man pointed at a pile of burning debris that had once been a truck. "He was leading them, Señor Francisco."

When Francisco reached the burning vehicle, he ran around it and peered inside as if searching for someone still living, someone he could pull out and kill with his bare hands. He recognized Ricardo's charred remains and spit at the blackened corpse. His screams echoed across the runway, "May your mother rot in hell with you, you dog born of a bitch!"

"Francisco, we must leave here now!" Carlos commanded as he assessed all the carnage.

"Where is the money? Where is the cocaine?" Francisco shouted as he turned away from what was now Ricardo's funeral pyre and stared around at the other burning vehicles littering the road.

"There, I see three of the cases." Carlos pointed to a couple of charred silver alloy cases lying on the ground a few feet away from one of the burning Suburbans.

"Where is the other one?" Francisco shouted in anger and frustration.

"I do not know," Carlos shouted his reply. He was alarmed about the possible loss of the cocaine and money, but he was more concerned for their safety. They had to leave now. There was no time to waste.

"Over here!" One of Carlos' men called out from the side of the U-Haul type truck as he held the fourth case above his head. The men inspected the four containers. Except for assorted dents and superficial charring, they appeared to be intact.

"It pays to buy quality," Francisco wryly observed as he stared at the Halliburton cases. He glanced down at his wrist. His Rolex wasn't even scratched.

"Francisco, we have lost four men including Posadus. Three have minor wounds, but do not require immediate medical attention. We lost two Suburbans and another one requires repair. Both of the transport trucks were damaged, but the cargo is secure. We are changing the tires on one of the trucks. We should be ready to pull out of here in ten minutes." One of the men gave the damage report as the others hurriedly attended to the disabled vehicles.

"We must get out of here before sunrise! Move, move, move!" Francisco shouted. He buried his face in his hands and attempted to wipe away the salty taste of his own sweat and the grime from the smoke and fumes. His eyes burned, and his head felt as though it was going to split wide open.

"Francisco, are you all right?" Carlos implored as he rested his hand on Francisco's shoulder.

"The ringing in my ears is deafening, Carlos. I cannot stand this pounding inside my head.

Tell me what happened," he demanded.

Carlos briefed him on the attack.

"Ah, so that is why my head feels that it is about to explode and my neck is burning," Francisco stared at him intently, then laughed out loud and grabbed him in a tight bear hug, lifting him off the ground. "You were a true warrior, today. This day, you saved my life and you saved the lives of many of my men. I am in your debt," he continued in a quavering voice.

Carlos was initially startled by Francisco's uncharacteristic display of affection, but as the two men stared at each other, he realized that he had gained Francisco's complete trust. With a slight pang of guilt, he dropped his eyes and replied, "It is my honor to protect and serve you, Francisco." Francisco returned to his men and Carlos headed to his SUV.

Later that afternoon, Carlos sat in his car in the parking lot of the restaurant and dozed off as he waited for it to open for happy hour. His had a splitting headache from the aftermath of the scene at the airstrip. He roused when he heard the kitchen staff clanging pots and pans. He ducked into the back entrance and found a pay phone outside the men's room. He dialed Connor's secure line and left a quick message. As he turned to leave, Francisco barreled around the corner and bumped into him.

"Carlos! Why didn't you tell me you were coming here when you left the airfield? Where are you sitting?" Francisco asked in surprise.

"I just came in," Carlos instinctively recoiled with a sharp intake of breath. He hoped his nervousness wasn't too obvious.

"Please, join me at my table. I insist." Francisco pointed to a table near the back. "I'll be back in a few minutes," he added as he entered the bathroom.

Carlos looked cautiously around the crowded bar. The noise level was high and he was fairly certain that Francisco could not have overheard him leave the voicemail for Connor. He didn't detect anything in Francisco's demeanor that concerned him.

He was relieved he hadn't been on the phone for very long. Francisco would surely have seen him using the phone if he had taken time to talk to Connor about the fiasco at the airstrip in detail. Carlos knew that Connor would have had a heart attack if he knew everything that had happened. There were certain things that were better left unsaid in the CI world.

"Carlos, are you hungry tonight?" Francisco asked as he returned to the table. "They serve excellent steaks here, they bring them in fresh from Texas every day."

"I will have the New York steak."

"Waiter, two New Yorks…rare," Francisco raised his voice to catch the server's attention.

"That's just the way I like it."

"I've been thinking, Carlos. We have much in common. I need someone like you. Someone who I can trust. You showed me many things at the airstrip. You were calm and acted decisively under fire. Can I trust you, amigo? That is the question. I need your answer tonight." Francisco looked him straight in the eyes.

"Of course, amigo, but can I trust you?" Carlos lowered his voice and stared at Francisco intently.

"Yes, you can trust me, Carlos, because I have bigger and better plans for you. Are you interested?"

REDWOOD CITY, CA

"This is the captain. We will be landing in fifteen minutes. Please be seated. Flight attendants, please prepare the cabin for landing," came the announcement, rousing Connor out of a light sleep.

Even though the trip had only been four days, Connor was anxious to see Barrett and be back home. He knew the next month was going to be busy, so he wanted to spend as much time with her as possible. Traffic was light and he made it home twenty minutes after landing.

He called her name as soon as he got through the door. There was no answer.

"Barrett?" Connor called her again as he walked down the hallway.

The bedrooms were empty. He walked into the living room, picked up the newspaper on top of the piano, and saw a note next to it. It had been written few minutes earlier, according to the time written at the top corner. *Welcome home, good lookin'. I'm out for a quick run. Come join me if you get here in time. I can't wait to see you. Hope you're not too tired. Love you!*

He quickly changed into his running gear and headed out the door. *She only has a two-minute head start. If I haul ass, I can catch up with her.* He started his stopwatch and took off at a pace he usually reserved for the sprint at the end of a run.

SAN FRANCISCO, CA

A tall, distinguished looking man with impeccably styled thick black hair stood impatiently at the Nordstrom's counter in the men's department while the sales associate rung up another customer. He cleared his throat and glared at the associate.

"May I help you, sir?"

"Yes, I'd like to buy this tie."

"This new Italian designer line is one of our hottest sellers. May I show you a shirt to go with it?"

"No, thank you." He paid in cash and tucked the Nordstrom's bag under his arm as he left the store and walked outside to the second level parking lot. Raven blended into the crowd with all the other shoppers.

Yesterday, he had received a letter with a set of car keys and instructions. The letter, as usual, was short and to the point. He was instructed to be at "top level"...a parking garage across the street from Westfield San Francisco Center shopping mall...at precisely 1:12 p.m., where he would find a dark blue Accord parked in the northeast side of the structure closest to Nordstroms.

The Colombians were true professionals. He knew he had to be on time. Three minutes late and they would abort the meeting. He made it a point to always arrive early. He was surprised to hear from the cartel so soon. It had only been a few days since he had provided them with the intelligence on Sanchez.

He looked around the parking lot and quickly spotted the dark blue Accord. He approached the trunk of the car, clutching the keys in his right hand. His breathing was quick and shallow and he felt his heart race. His hands trembled slightly as he opened the trunk and saw the black attaché case. He reached in and grabbed it, barely able to contain his excitement. He hated all the cloak-and-dagger stuff, but the Colombians had insisted. The seriousness of what he was doing was not lost on the Colombians or on him.

He dialed the numbers on the lock to 3-9-9. The case popped open to reveal neat stacks of cash and a letter. He quickly retrieved the letter, closed the attaché case, and walked quickly to his car. He opened the letter and read it.

R.

YOUR INFORMATION WAS EXCEPTIONALLY VALUABLE THIS TIME. WE THOUGHT YOU DESERVED A BONUS. WE APPRECIATE YOUR ASSISTANCE. KEEP UP THE GOOD WORK.

R.

He felt exhilarated as he pulled into the parking lot of an upscale grocery store. He ordered a lobster roll from the deli, then walked outside and sat alone at one of the bistro tables. It was a particularly sunny afternoon and he felt completely relaxed in the shade. The lunch crowd had come and gone so he had the place to himself. He wished he had time for a bottle of wine.

Raven wasn't stupid. He had done extensive research on traitors in recent history, including FBI counterintelligence agent Jansen. All of them had vices that had led to their arrests. Raven had no vices. He maintained a modest lifestyle and paid cash for expensive items, primarily vacations and entertainment. He regarded himself as a financial advisor planning for his own early retirement.

He knew what type of financial transactions raised suspicion at the IRS and was careful not to spend more than $10,000 at a time. He invested his money conservatively, always aware that he could become the subject of a routine inquiry. Raven also knew that the FBI and CIA were concerned primarily with terrorism and industrial espionage. DEA was overwhelmed and understaffed as a result of the recent surge in heroin and methamphetamine related cases. In the past few years, the Mexican cartels had moved into markets traditionally controlled by the Colombians and they were now equally formidable.

He was determined not to become too greedy. He felt that if he adhered to the strict tradecraft of a spy, the probability of detection was low. Given the handsome payoffs, the rewards outweighed the risks, at least for now.

He secured the attaché case full of money at a safe location, then returned to work. After he parked in his reserved spot, he took the stairs two at a time. He smiled broadly as he greeted the U.S. Marshals manning the metal detector.

MICHOACÁN, MEXICO

It was 1:00 a.m. Francisco and Carlos were still in the restaurant drinking tequila. Francisco had had twice as many drinks as Carlos…who was trying not to get drunk…and he was well on his way to total inebriation.

"Carlos, in six months, I will have made enough money to start purchasing my own cocaine paste from Bogotá. I have established enough good connections in Los Angeles to start my own distribution network. Within one year, I will be able to net five times what I do now. My plan is to rival the cartels in Mexico and believe me, I can do it. I need a loyal man like you to be my new security chief, to assist me, to protect the operation," he exclaimed as he pounded his fist on the table and continued, "Posadus failed in his job as my security chief. He deserved to die on that airfield!"

Carlos seized the opportunity to cement his relationship with Francisco, aided by a little acting and the warm buzz of the alcohol. He stood up from his chair, held his shot glass in a salute and raised his voice, "I'm with you my brother, 'til death." He downed the tequila and slumped back into his chair.

"Amigo, I hope I have not made the wrong choice. You cannot stand on your own two feet!" Francisco threw back his head, roared in drunken laughter, then reached for the bottle to pour another shot.

WASHINGTON, DC

The phone's loud ring shattered the silence in the well-appointed home office and momentarily startled Jordan Zif.

"Jordan, it's Hank. Sorry to bother you so late. I tried to reach you this afternoon, but you were out of the office. We got our first lead on the sniper," the Attorney General reported.

"Really? What do you have?" Zif greeted Henderson enthusiastically.

"It's not much, but at least it's a start. We recovered the stolen Humvee, burned to the metal chassis."

"What else do we know?"

"The only evidence we've been able to recover so far is the remnants of a stolen, and charred, temporary FBI parking pass from the National Academy Class. The bad news is that we didn't find any latent prints on the pass and it's unlikely that we're going to recover significant forensics, given the condition of the vehicle. The Bureau has a whole team working on it, including the assistant lab director."

"At least it's a start, Hank. Tell Huntington and the boys they're doing good work and to keep on digging. Thanks for the call. Keep me posted on any developments."

"You got it," Henderson hung up the phone and stared out the window at the full moon. He wondered if Viper could see the moon from whatever hiding place he was holed up in.

CHAPTER 8

CIA HEADQUARTERS

"Good morning, Emma. How are you this morning?" CIA analyst Greg Stevens spoke into the phone.

"Just fine, Greg, what can I do for you?" the executive secretary replied.

"Is the director in?"

"Yes, she's going over her weekly briefing reports in preparation for a meeting with the President."

"When she has time, would you tell her we received some information last night on Operation Black Knight?" Black Knight was the CIA's unclassified code phrase for the operation to identify and capture Viper.

"Greg, would you hold for a second?"

She didn't have to look at her hit list of current top-priority operations to know that the director wanted to be immediately informed on this one. Stevens was glad he was on Emma's good side because he and everyone else in the agency knew her reputation. She was an extremely intelligent and efficient office manager and she was keenly aware of her 'Iron Lady' status. She guarded her boss's time and scrutinized every request and intrusion so that she could help the director manage more things in ten hours than most people managed in twenty-four.

"Greg, can you be here in fifteen minutes?"

"Sure, Emma, thanks!"

Stevens got there five minutes early and Emma escorted him into the director's office.

"Good morning, Ma'am."

"Good morning, Greg. What have you got?"

"An e-mail from Hugh Heist. Striker was able to get our first intel on Viper."

"Excellent!" Bancroft placed the briefing papers on her desk and stared intently at Stevens.

"In a nutshell, Striker found a letter written in code."

"Coded?" Bancroft asked curiously.

"Our analysts think they worked out the code. They think that the note is from Viper to Roberto Fuerte, Joaquin Gusto's security chief confirming the hit on Juan Sanchez. It's not much, but at least it's a start. Plus, it may give us a sample of Viper's handwriting. Striker was able to get some bank account information, but we don't yet know if it's related to Viper. We'll have to wait for more intelligence to confirm this."

"Any new information on Viper's profile?"

"Not yet."

"Like you said, it's a start. Keep me posted. The Bureau found the stolen Hummer Viper used in his escape from Quantico. It was almost destroyed in a fire. Contact their assistant lab director if you want to see it," Bancroft added as Stevens reached the door.

"You bet I want to see it. I'll call him today. Oh yeah, we stepped up our electronic and satellite coverage, but nothing yet. I know it's expensive, but we might want to set up a separate satellite once we get any actionable leads in Bogotá."

"You might be right. I'll think about it. Anything new on the terrorist cell in San Francisco?"

"Not exactly, but something interesting happened last night. Remember Mendoza?"

"Yeah, the Bureau was working him last night in DC."

Stevens paused, "I don't know if you heard about this but, there was an altercation last night involving one of Mendoza's female cousins. Turns out the trunk of the BMW she was driving tested positive for trace radioactivity."

Bancroft frowned in concern and locked eyes with him.

"The Bureau is very tight lipped about this since we told them that Mendoza is a nobody," Stevens cautiously replied.

"Shit! How do you intend to get more intel?"

"Maybe if we told them that we suspect a mole within their ranks and that we are tracking a secret cell in San Francisco, they would be more cooperative."

"I don't think so Greg, we already had this conversation. This stays in-house...understood?" Bancroft did not wait for a response, "Using them could severely compromise the investigation. We can't afford to lose any more agents or assets. Trust me Greg, do what you can to squeeze more information out of them. Use whatever resources you feel necessary."

"Yes ma'am."

CABO SAN LUCAS

The view from the five-bedroom luxury villa was panoramic. The morning sunlight filtered through the tree branches and cast shadows across the well-manicured grounds of the seaside sanctuary of the Palmilla resort, located on the tip of San Jose del Cabo. The exclusive resort was ten miles west of Cabo San Lucas, isolated from the popular tourist haunts favored in that part of Mexico. Francisco Felix walked out onto the main balcony of the master bedroom suite overlooking the calm, crystal clear waters of the Sea of Cortez.

"Good morning, Carlos," Francisco greeted his newly appointed security chief, Carlos Padilla.

"What a beautiful morning it is," Carlos beamed.

"Make sure the men are up. Have them outside to provide security. Our guests will be arriving this morning. I want to keep this low key."

"Sí, señor." Carlos gazed at the sun reflecting like liquid gold off the water and wished that he were here simply to enjoy the million dollar views.

The two cartel members arrived in a full sized rental sedan with two bodyguards. Francisco's security team instantly recognized them. The phone in the spacious living room rang and Carlos picked it up on the first ring.

"Francisco our guests have arrived."

"Right on time."

Two pretty maids wearing black uniforms with crisp white aprons put finishing touches on orchid centerpiece arrangements. The elegant linen covered tables on the deck were loaded with colorful platters of food and fruit. Ocean waves lapped on the sandy beaches in the background.

Francisco grew impatient as they fussed over the flowers. He curtly dismissed them, poured a glass of champagne and stared at his watch. Things were going exactly as planned.

"Señor Garcia, it is a pleasure to see you again," Francisco greeted him warmly as he opened the front door to his villa.

"Francisco! I am very happy to see you." Pedro Garcia, director of transportation for the Bogotá Cartel, opened his arms and the men embraced.

"Francisco, I would like to introduce Jorge Gusto, Joaquin's brother. He is in charge of North American operations."

Francisco was stunned for a second, but he quickly composed himself. "Señor Gusto, it is a pleasure to meet you," he replied as he extended a firm handshake.

"My brother and I have heard many good things about you, Francisco."

"Your words honor me. Please come in."

Francisco gestured toward the living room and added, "This is Carlos Padilla, he's in charge of my security."

"It is an honor to meet you," Carlos bowed his head as he replied, never making eye contact with the two cartel members.

"I hope you are hungry. I have prepared a feast!" Francisco pointed in the direction of an elegant table of artfully displayed food.

"Yes. I am a man of great appetites," Pedro roared as he slapped his generous stomach and laughed.

"As am I," added Jorge.

"Please be seated. The staff will serve you." Francisco nodded and Carlos walked to the door and motioned a young woman into the room. She began preparing the dining table and pouring wine.

"Excuse me, Francisco. I need to check outside," Carlos interjected as the men talked among themselves.

They drank expensive wine and took hearty portions of the many delicacies as if they hadn't eaten in days. The conversation was light and inconsequential. A cool sea breeze stirred the fresh orchids and tropical flowers in the centerpiece. After a leisurely meal, the expert staff cleared the table in minutes, leaving crystal bowls of Italian gelato and fresh berries.

"Francisco, how is the loading operation proceeding?" Pedro officially initiated the true purpose of their visit.

"Everything is on schedule. Loading should be completed by tomorrow night. Would you and Señor Gusto like to inspect any of the loading operation?" he added.

"No, we trust your judgment," Pedro replied.

"This new program is very important to our family, Francisco. You are the only individual we are allowing to use the new sub and we are not interested in expanding its use at this time," Jorge spoke in a hushed tone.

"I am honored, Señor Gusto. I will not disappoint you."

"We do not think that you will. We want to change your contact instructions. If anything goes wrong, call this number," Pedro gave Francisco a slip of paper.

"It's a 24-hour number. Tell the person who answers that you cannot attend the birthday party and that you want to talk to Chico. I will call you as soon as I can and make arrangements to meet you. Remember, never use the words 'sub' or 'submarine' over the phone." Pedro stared intently as he gave the instructions and assessed Francisco's expression.

"I understand."

The front door opened. Carlos reentered the suite and exchanged glances with Francisco. "Francisco, we are impressed with your hard work and you have been loyal to us. Did you know that demand is high, especially from our best customers in the United States? We will increase our production by ten percent over the next few months."

"That is good, señor. That is very good."

"Could you handle your own distribution network?" Jorge looked him directly in the eye and watched his response.

"Yes, without any doubt. I have been developing my own network for the past year and was going to suggest this to your family...at the appropriate time," Francisco replied, clearly pleased.

"One more favor, Francisco."

"Yes, señor?"

"My brother wants a separate package delivered on the sub. It is very important, and nothing must happen to it."

"Sí, señor. Where is it? I will protect it myself."

"That's not necessary right now." Jorge leaned toward Francisco and whispered his final instructions.

"You have my word. It will be taken care of, señor!" Francisco snapped to attention.

"Great minds think alike, my friend." Jorge reached for a glass of champagne.

"A toast!" Pedro raised his glass to theirs and the sound of the crystal flutes touching sounded like glass on the verge of breaking.

"To wealth and the American way," Jorge proclaimed, his words slightly slurred. A lazy smile crossed his face. A single bead of sweat formed on his brow. The breeze had stilled, and the tide had retreated, leaving a broad shoreline of white, hot sand.

Approximately fifty yards from Francisco's villa, the entrance door of a nearby villa opened and a very fit Colombian entered the living room area.

"Señor Fuerte, everything is quiet," the security man announced.

"Thank you, Luis."

Roberto Fuerte, head of security for the Bogotá Cartel, sat in a wicker chair in the living room, surveying the grounds of the villa where the mini-conference was taking place. By his and Joaquin's design, every time one of the cartel members traveled, a minimum of six cartel bodyguards accompanied their personal bodyguards. Francisco and his security team were unaware that Roberto and the advance team of six men had arrived the previous day to provide protection for the arrival of Pedro and Jorge.

Travel to Mexico and within South America was relatively safe, but Roberto came along when it involved the security of any member of the cartel. The cartel maintained the highest government contacts in Mexico; it allowed them safe travel within the country. This particular visit was unannounced because of its short duration.

Roberto took a long draw on his Cuban cigar as he marveled at the azure blue of the ocean and the manicured grounds of the resort. A hint of a warm breeze blew the smoke from his cigar into the living room. Evening fell over Cabo San Lucas and the last rays of sunlight faded as a gust of wind kicked up a sand devil on the shore.

Roberto stood alone in the lobby of the new Westin Regina Resort, designed by the world-famous Mexican architect Javier Sordo Madaleno, and admired the massive cascading water wall with its bright splashes of color. He looked at his watch: 6:45 p.m. The meeting would start in fifteen minutes. He tried to fight off nervousness.

He had almost come to blows with his two personal bodyguards when he had instructed them to wait for him back at the Palmilla resort after they dropped him off. They didn't think it was safe. He knew it was. Roberto drank an icy margarita. He knew that today's meeting had been a success and that Pedro and Jorge were on their way back to Colombia in their private jet. Overall, it had been an excellent day.

"Señor, I believe you have a telephone call on the house phone," a bellman interrupted his thoughts and pointed to the phone by the outside bar.

"*Hola, amigo,* where are you?" Roberto was happy to hear the voice on the other end of the line.

"You'll find out soon enough. Put that margarita down and wait for me outside the front entrance of the hotel," the caller directed, hanging up before Roberto could reply.

He took one last sip of his drink, then walked briskly through the lobby and stood outside the hotel entrance.

"Señor, would you like to take a cab?" the doorman asked.

"No, thank you."

About five minutes later, he saw two headlights approach the driveway. As the Grand Cherokee passed him, the passenger door swung open.

"Get in," the driver ordered.

Roberto got into the Jeep and shook the hand of his longtime friend. They drove out of the resort and merged into light traffic.

"Ivan, my friend, you look remarkable! I would not have recognized you, if I had not heard your voice. Do you think your doctor could give me a new face? He did such an impressive job with you, I am tempted to go under the knife." Roberto could not stop staring.

"I am afraid he cannot help you. You see, he is no longer with us. He died in a tragic car accident shortly after my full recovery. Such a shame, not wearing his seat belt, a snapped neck they said." Viper kept his eyes on the road.

"Did his neck snap before or after the unfortunate accident?"

"I am sure we will never know," Viper turned to him and gave a tight smile through hard, calculating eyes. "Anyway, my name is not Ivan, it is Karl Hanns. I don't use my Russian name anymore, especially with employment with your family. It's too risky. You should know that since you and Joaquin paid for my new face and name. Here in Mexico, I am using the name Alfred Herman."

"I cannot remember all of your aliases. It's easier just to call you Viper. I like the sound of that better," Roberto replied.

142

"No! You must never call me that. The Americans hear too much with their satellites and wiretaps. We do not know when or where they are intercepting our communication, even now!" he replied harshly.

"You are right, my friend and smart to be cautious," Roberto replied, chastened. "It's been almost two years since our last visit. How have you been?" Roberto asked with genuine interest.

"Nothing has changed. Work consumes much of my time. I find time to travel and take pleasure with women when I can. And you?"

"My life is too much work, work at every turn, twenty-four hours a day. I am not complaining, there are perks to this lifestyle, but I envy you and your freedom."

"You must find freedom, it will not find you."

They passed through the gates of the Presidential Hotel and drove past the main entrance to a private driveway leading up to the resort's exclusive villas. Viper's suite was impressive. Floor-to-ceiling windows lined the wall that faced the ocean.

"What can I get you to drink?"

"I will have sparkling water tonight. I need all my senses about me when I speak with you," Roberto replied.

Viper took a chilled bottle of water from the refrigerator and tossed it to Roberto.

"I see that you still have good reflexes, comrade," he said as Roberto snatched the bottle in mid-air.

"Not as good as they were when we were in the unit, but I manage."

Roberto pulled an envelope from inside his jacket and handed it to Viper.

"I know this is short notice, but we need this job completed in less than seven days," Roberto explained as Viper opened the envelope.

"I know of this individual." Viper examined the photographs.

"I thought you might."

"I wish I had known about this assignment last week. I could have spared myself a trip."

"This is an interesting case. We recently found out that our friend will be traveling to the Far East for a meeting with our

143

competitors. We do not want them to establish an alliance, it would be bad for our business. Can it be done?"

Viper analyzed the contents of the envelope and rubbed his chin before he replied, "Yes, I'll have to leave tomorrow and I will need more intel on the location, but I can do it."

"If you complete the assignment in our time frame, there will be a $250,000 bonus."

"That's a pleasant incentive." Viper took a long drink of water from the frosted bottle.

They walked out onto the balcony. A group of people on the beach laughed and talked around a bonfire. The faint smell of burning driftwood filled the air.

"The clock starts now. I'll take you back shortly and I will begin working on the project tonight." Viper finished the bottle of water in a single swallow.

Viper drove Roberto back to his hotel and was back in less than 15 minutes. He went directly to the bedroom and retrieved the envelope from its hiding place. He returned to the living room, helped himself to a plate of fresh fruit, and opened the new file. He took out photographs of a nondescript Hispanic male, Diego Cuevas…one of the most powerful business tycoons in Mexico. He stared at the photos for a few minutes and started writing a list on a notepad.

REDWOOD SHORES, CA

A rooster crowed loudly outside, but Connor was already awake. It was a little before 6:00 a.m. on Saturday morning. He was still on East Coast time and his conversation last night with Barrett about her father and the CIA had kept him up all night. Not telling her about his employment with the agency had clearly been a mistake. The real dilemma was whether it was a bigger mistake to tell her now.

"I wish someone would shoot those damn roosters!" Barrett rolled over and pulled the covers over her head. "Just one morning, just one, I would like to sleep past 6 o'clock." she moaned in exasperation.

Actually, Connor liked the roosters. They added a touch of farmland to the suburban sprawl of condos and tract homes. The roosters had been left behind in the 1980s, when *Marine World*

Africa USA relocated from Redwood Shores to nearby Vallejo. During the move, some of the birds had escaped and nested in landscaped yards and still made quite a mess in some places. Barrett was one of a large group of urban-minded locals who wanted to get rid of the noisy intruders. Connor secretly rooted for the roosters to win the battle.

Connor lay in bed and watched her. Barrett's blonde hair spilled out from under the covers she had pulled over her face. His cell phone vibrated on the bed side table. Connor grabbed it and slipped out of the room. He hated to wake her…weekend mornings were precious to her since she had to leave for work at 6:00 a.m. during the week to beat the wall-to-wall traffic.

"Hello," Connor tried to speak quietly as he trotted down the hallway into the living room.

"Jack, it's Ron Williams. Sorry to call so early. Hope I didn't wake you, I know you are an early riser."

"No problem Ron, I need to get my ass in gear for a self-defense class I've got in an hour."

"Do you ever rest?"

"Yeah, when I'm sleeping. What's up?"

"A couple of quick things. First, Big Dog and our CI are still missing. It doesn't look good. It's all hush hush over here on the FBI side regarding their terrorist wire. We were told to lay off Mendoza. The word in our office is that the San Francisco FBI office has the wire on the terrorist investigation. You got any intel on that?" Williams asked.

"Not really, I heard they were up on a wire, but I have no information," Connor replied.

"We probably have a better chance of identifying a terrorist cell than they do. Any word from your CI on the next cartel shipment?"

"I got a voice mail from him last night. Nothing new, the shipment is due in less than a week," Connor added.

"Okay, keep in touch."

Connor hung up the phone and hurriedly threw on his workout clothes. He went to his morning Hapkido workout with several buddies who were also law enforcement officers. The workout only lasted forty-five minutes.

He stopped on the way home and picked up a blueberry bagel and light cream cheese, Barrett's favorite. She was warming up on the doorstep when he got home, already in full running gear, ready to go.

"How about I give you a five-minute head start, so you don't have to worry about keeping up with me," she teased.

"Don't be funny or I'll give you an elbow strike right now."

"Okay. I give up, Grand Master, I give up. I want my bagel."

"Don't go anywhere. I'll be right back," he said as he tossed the bagel to her and went to change into his running shorts.

They kept a brisk pace on the five-mile run. They didn't try to chat as they sometimes did. They concentrated on improving their time.

They were back in forty minutes, relaxing on their deck. Connor took in a deep breath, enjoying the aroma of the toasted bagel.

"Hey hon, I'd like to continue our conversation about your dad," Connor said.

"Sorry I went off on you about my dad and the CIA the other day. I don't know why I can't just get over it."

"I can see that it really bothers you and I don't want to keep anything …"

"Don't worry about it," Barrett interrupted him as she pulled herself out of her chair and kissed him gently on the lips. Connor pulled her into his arms. He had to tell her.

"Have you ever worked a wire case with the FBI?" she abruptly changed the subject.

"No, why."

"This is my first federal wire case. I've read their affidavit and gone over all of the daily summary sheets. Maybe the laws are different in federal court or in terrorist investigations, because I can't believe a judge found probable cause to let them go up on this wire."

"Did you find any leads to your case?"

"No, not yet, but there may be a connection to one of the phone numbers in my case."

"It's funny you mentioned that case. The other night I was helping DEA agents in DC surveil a UC meeting with a top Colombian cartel lieutenant named Mendoza. Long story short, we a

146

had minor altercation at the end of the meeting. This morning I got a call from the DEA case agent and he told me that Mendoza may be the target of a FBI terrorist related wiretap being conducted out of the FBI's San Francisco office."

"Holy shit!" Barrett's mouth dropped wide open as she stared at Connor. "I'm not supposed to talk about it with anyone not briefed on this case without permission from AUSA Steiner, who, by the way is an arrogant dick. But since you brought it up..."

"Let's compare notes," Connor's internal radar was on full alert.

CABO SAN LUCAS

Carlos wiped sweat off his forehead. It was early morning and it was already stifling hot in Cabo San Lucas.

"Amigo, it's going to be hot today," Francisco stated the obvious as he greeted Carlos.

"Sí, the sun will show no mercy. I wish I was going on this trip. I love the sea."

"Carlos, I need you with me. My timetable is about to change and we are soon going to be very busy."

Carlos could smell the odor of decaying fish from the nearby pier. Francisco owned a fleet of fishing boats and two repair facilities in this small fishing town about five kilometers from Cabo San Lucas. Inside the covered repair facility at the end of the pier, the crew was loading the cocaine. Four men worked feverishly in the heat, loading boxes full of tightly wrapped bricks.

"They should be done in less than an hour," Francisco glanced at his Rolex.

"Do you want to go down and see how the loading is going?" Carlos asked.

"Yes, perhaps it is cooler on the water."

Armed security manned the fishing trawlers anchored nearby, all equipped with hidden machine guns. They stood guard over the pier in case of uninvited guests. When Francisco and Carlos entered the facility, it took a minute for their eyes to adjust to the shaded space. Everyone was working quietly and efficiently.

"Señor Francisco, we will be done in less than an hour. Everything is going well. The modifications to the sub should make

147

the trip easier and a little quicker this time," the loadmaster greeted them.

"Good! Where's the crew?" Francisco asked.

"Two are over there, by the sub," the load master pointed. "Lester, Lester," he yelled over the noise and motioned to them. The men hurried over.

"Señor Francisco," Lester, one of the most trusted senior workers, greeted them.

"Are you ready for this ride?"

"Sí, señor. We will leave tonight. The weather forecast is good. We should return within seven days depending on the weather."

"I need a special favor. I have a package that I will give you later, to be delivered on the sub. Don't let anything happen to it," he directed as he handed him a folded note. "When you arrive in Monterey, contact this person on this radio frequency. He will arrive in a small boat, 30 minutes before the main off-load at the same location. He will identify himself to you as Robert and he will give you one-half of a U.S. $100 bill. This is the matching half. If anyone else tries to take the package, kill them. Do you understand?"

"Yes señor!" the man confidently replied as he tucked the note and partial bill into his pocket.

"Good. I know I can rely on you."

"Carlos," one of the security guards called out as he approached the group.

"What is it?" The guard whispered something to Carlos.

"Francisco, Capitán Mora is here to see you," Carlos turned to Francisco.

"Excellent! It is time to formally introduce him to you, my new security chief."

"Francisco, what's in the package?" Carlos asked curiously.

"I don't know. Señor Jorge gave it to me and told me it was extremely important to Señor Joaquin. He told me to guarantee delivery. Let's go meet the good Capitán Mora."

They walked back to the modest office building on the pier where Francisco conducted his legitimate business.

"El Capitán, it is good to see you again," Francisco welcomed him with open arms. "This is my new security chief,

148

Carlos Padilla. I believe you two have met before." Francisco put his arm around Carlos' shoulders.

"I am happy to see you, El Capitán," Carlos extended his hand.

"Sí," replied Mora, a cigarette dangled from the side of his mouth.

The first time the two men had met, Carlos had disliked Mora instantly and today was no exception. Mora was an overweight man in his mid-forties. His police uniform was dirty and he smelled of sweat and stale smoke. His eyes looked cold and cunning. Carlos had no doubt that he was as ruthless as he was filthy.

"El Capitán, I have something for you. Please come inside to my office," Francisco waved him inside.

They followed Francisco into the foyer of the office and watched as he walked to the back of the office and returned with a manila envelope. He handed it to Mora and he opened it and greedily thumbed through the cash. Fifty thousand dollars was more than twice his annual salary.

"*Mis amigos,* if there is anything I can do for you, do not hesitate to contact me," he offered with a half-smile, his yellowed teeth coated in plaque. Ashes from his cigarette fell to the floor.

"I am thinking of hosting a big dinner next week. Do you think you will be able to join me, El Capitán?" Francisco asked. He knew that Mora would be bloated with self-importance at such an invitation.

"Of course, amigo. I am never far from fine food and drink. Will there be women to keep me company?"

"Many women."

His eyes narrowed at the prospect. He dropped his cigarette butt on the floor and stuffed the envelope into his waist band and lazily walked back to his patrol car. Carlos watched in disgust.

"I hope you do not leave cash in your office, Francisco. I fear that El Capitán may be tempted to visit here at night," Carlos warned when they were alone.

"Carlos? You don't approve of El Capitán?" Francisco feigned surprise. "He is not an educated man, but he is not an ignorant one. He will follow instructions as long as he is on my payroll."

"I hope that you are right."

The loadmaster walked into the office. "Señor Francisco, the loading is complete. We will be ready to launch tonight."

"Very good. Thank you," Francisco turned and dismissed the loadmaster.

"Carlos, let's go back to the hotel and get something to eat before the launch."

Dinner had been brief. On the drive back, Carlos tried to think of a way to phone Connor and pass along all the information he had obtained. He broke his burner phone. Connor always warned him not to use his personal cell for security reasons. Francisco had seldom left his side and it would be risky to try to make a phone call at this point, so he decided to send a short coded text.

The car was warm inside, even with air conditioning, and Francisco dozed in the passenger seat. *You know, this isn't a bad job after all,* Carlos thought. *The pay is great. I have power and I am good at this. I could face a much worse fate, especially if Francisco were to find out that I am a DEA informant.*

Carlos remembered what his father had told him just a few days before his death: *Carlos, someone must stand up for what is right or else our people…you, your sons, and their sons…will be doomed* Carlos' eyes hardened. His father had been an honest Colombian General and they had killed him. A car bomb had exploded when he was driving to a narcotics raid on one of the cartels. Carlos had loved his father more than anyone. He swallowed hard. He had sworn on his father's grave that he would exact revenge against the cartels, even if it meant giving up his own life. He wiped the sweat from his brow with his shirtsleeve as Francisco snored, oblivious to the heat.

REDWOOD SHORES, CA

Connor and Barrett had just returned from shopping at Barrett's two favorite stores, Ann Taylor and Neiman Marcus. She was on her way upstairs when Connor's iPhone rang.

"Morning Jack, shop much?" Bancroft joked when she saw the shopping bags hanging on Connor's shoulder on her high-definition prototype iPhone.

"Hey, I'm *fashion-forward*, Ma'am." Connor saw Bancroft's smile on his iPhone screen.

"Looks like it! Sorry I missed your call earlier. What's up?"

"It's about the FBI's wire case and Mendoza. My wife Barrett has been briefed on it because a homicide case she's working may be connected to the terrorist cell. She was in the wire room a couple of nights ago when she heard an intercept between one of the terrorist targets in San Francisco and Mendoza in DC. The target asked Mendoza if he had picked up the device yet. I was covering that meet with the DC DEA office when Mendoza took that call. The DC DEA target and their CI are both missing after their meet with Mendoza. Rumor has it that Mendoza picked up a device and may be planning to deliver it to his contact in San Francisco."

"Jack, I know your assignment is complicated. Don't worry about Mendoza. That device is a decoy. It's our attempt to flush out the FBI mole. Nobody knows about this except me and two other people, including you. Don't get distracted by Mendoza. Stay on course with the cartel and I will feed you accurate intel as I receive it. Sorry, gotta go. I have an important meeting with the Chairman of the Senate Intelligence Committee and I'm running late."

"Yes ma'am." Connor placed his phone into his pocket with a stunned look on his face. *My God! Talk about the right hand not knowing what the left hand is doing.* A nagging sense of dread hung over him. Telling Barrett about it was not an option. It was just one more thing on his shit-list of non-disclosure.

CHAPTER 9

UNITED FLIGHT TO SAN FRANCISCO

"Jack. It's Alex. How you doing? You still want to pick me up tonight?" Ryker tried to speak over the noise at Dulles airport.

"Absolutely. Barrett and I have been expecting your call. The spare room is all made up. No partner of mine is going to stay at a hotel!"

"I really appreciate what you're doing."

"I have your flight info. We'll be curbside outside baggage claim. Have a good flight and get a lot of rest on the plane, because you're going to be very busy starting Monday morning."

"Hey, I'm ready now! See you tonight."

Ryker had arrived at the airport early. This was his first time flying with a firearm. He wasn't familiar with the Dulles' policy regarding carrying concealed weapons, so he allowed plenty of time to check in.

He was surprised that it was no big deal. He showed his creds, filled out a form, and that was it. He passed through security and walked around the terminal with an hour and fifteen minutes to kill. He hung out at the newsstand and glanced over the magazines and books, but he mainly watched the crowds.

What would happen if a terrorist penetrated the security checkpoint and attempted to hijack the plane? Well, if I had a clear shot I would double-tap him in the head. Ryker adjusted the Glock 23 in his high-rise hip holster.

"DEA AGENT THWARTS TERRORIST HIJACKING ATTEMPT AT DULLES," Ryker envisioned the Washington Post and USA Today headlines. *Geez, I've got to get a grip. I'm a friggin' rookie, not the airport police or a U.S. Marshal. With my luck, I'd shoot an innocent passenger, get taken as a hostage, or get sued. I have got to get my mind back in the real world.* He wondered if all new agents had adrenalin-fueled day dreams the first time they flew with a weapon. He felt ridiculous.

He pretended to read a book as he stood near the boarding gate, but in reality he was checking out everyone in the area, especially the ones who looked suspicious. The problem was now everyone looked suspicious, even the moms with babies. Baby strollers were an ideal place to conceal a bomb. As much as he hated to admit it, he suspected there's probably a little *James Bond wannabe* in all freshly minted federal agents.

"Hi, how are you today?" Ryker politely greeted the ticket attendant as he introduced himself.

"Mr. Ryker, here's your new boarding pass. Your seat assignment is now 7A. We'll be boarding first class passengers soon. Be sure to identify yourself to the flight attendant so the captain knows where you are seated."

"There must be some mistake, I'm in coach."

"Let's see," she paused as she brought up his name on her computer screen, "You've been upgraded to first class, according to the computer."

"I don't think so."

"Well," she paused again and scanned the screen. "There is something in the special comments section. Okay, let me see…" She opened the drawer and searched through a folder until she found an envelope with Ryker's name on it.

"This is for you," she handed him the envelope and watched curiously as he read it.

Thanks for your help on the DC case. This is your graduation present. Remember, if you get tired of Connor, call me. Good luck and always keep a spare magazine with you. Ron

Ryker was absolutely stunned. He had never flown first class and had no idea that federal agents had those kinds of connections. *I love this job*, he thought as he handed her the ticket.

"Thanks, ma'am, you're right, I do have a first-class ticket. I just didn't know it."

"Lucky you."

Within minutes, the boarding announcement had been made and Ryker was seated in the first class section of the Boeing 747. About one quarter of the seats were filled in the first class cabin and only half in business class. He stretched his legs, taking advantage of the generous space between seats. *I could get used to this.*

"Hello. May I get you something to drink?" the flight attendant flashed a brilliant smile as she greeted him.

"Diet Pepsi, if you have it please," he returned her smile. He settled back in his seat and tried to adjust his Glock. Wearing a gun made sitting back against the seat uncomfortable. He didn't want to expose the gun, but he definitely had to readjust it, it was digging a hole in his kidney.

"Hey Tara, check out 7A. He's hot," the flight attendant whispered as she returned to the first class station and began placing drinks on a tray. They both peeked around the corner to get a look. He had his head down and seemed to be fidgeting with something under his jacket. They watched as he discreetly unbuckled his pants belt and tried to take it off, but it seemed stuck.

"What is he doing?" they whispered at the exact same time, then laughed.

"Maybe he's taking his pants off. Hey, a girl can dream," Joan sighed.

"Wow, he's smoking hot, I'll give you that," Tara grudgingly admitted, then added, "Where's the manifest?"

"As they say on the Sopranos, *forget about it*. He's a LEO…as in law enforcement officer, which means he has no money. The only traveling you would do with him is from jump seats and red-eye standby flights from hell. With overtime, we probably make just as much money as he does," she whispered in a conspiratorial tone, keeping her voice low so that the passengers in the nearest row couldn't hear their conversation.

"What did he order?"

"A diet Pepsi. See, he's a boy scout, not your type at all."

Tara picked up a can and a glass of ice and put them on her tray.

"He's in my section," Joan exclaimed.

"You're married, I'm not. And money isn't the only thing that matters. Come on, lighten up, he's cute!" She pushed past her friend and headed down the aisle.

"Oh please," Joan rolled her eyes and put a few more drinks on her tray.

About halfway down the aisle, Tara made eye contact with him. She wanted to be friendly, but not too friendly. He was probably used to having women throw themselves at him.

"Here's your drink, you ordered a diet Pepsi, right?"

"Yes, thank you," he briefly glanced up at her.

"Can I get you anything else?"

"No, thank you." His tone was polite but detached. He was clearly not a flirt.

154

She tried not to openly stare at him as she served beverages to the other first-class passengers, but she couldn't stop herself. He was distracted and seemed uncomfortable in the seat. He had her full attention. When she returned to the serving station, Joan greeted her.

"Well, did you ask him for his financial portfolio yet?"

"Would you knock it off? Look at the guy. He's gorgeous. Such a sweet smile and dark brown eyes," she sighed wistfully.

"Earth to Tara, he's broke. Earth to Tara, you are not a cop's wife type. You have to admit that girlfriend."

"Would you quit calling him a cop? He's a federal agent, maybe FBI. How sexy is that anyway? Don't you watch TV?"

"Yeah, ever heard of crime lab and spy scandals? I got your FBI right here!" She made a rude gesture and Tara frowned at her.

"Would you please shut up!" Tara brushed past her.

The 747 ascended to cruising altitude. Ryker observed the wing slicing through the clouds. Four months ago, he was a catering manager for Marriott, and now he was a special agent flying first class to his new assignment in San Francisco. He had finally gotten comfortable after repositioning his holster closer to his side.

It took over an hour for the flight attendants to finish cabin service and Tara finally had time to take a break. She sat in a jump seat and pulled a paperback crime thriller out of her bag. Her eyes kept straying to 7A. He was on his laptop. She wondered if he liked James Patterson's books. The one she was reading was just getting interesting.

"Excuse me?"

Tara looked up from her book and smiled at him.

"Sorry to bother you on your break, but I'm thirsty. Think I could get a refill?" His smile was disarming.

"Sure," she stood up and he stepped aside to let her pass into the service area.

Ryker's eyes followed her as she opened a can and filled a fresh glass with ice. Her nails were tastefully manicured and she wasn't wearing any rings.

"I could get used to first class."

"Your first time?"

"Excuse me?"

"In first class…your first time?"

"Oh…yeah, first time in first class," he stammered, his face flushed.

"How do you like it so far?" She smiled at his obvious discomfort.

"Great! You guys do such a great job…and the seats, man they are comfortable, not like the cattle-call in coach."

"Are you comfortable? I was a little worried about you when we took off, you seemed to have a problem with your seat."

"I just needed a little readjustment. I'm not used to all that space." Ryker wondered if she had seen his weapon.

"Traveling armed can be uncomfortable," Tara stated nonchalantly.

"It takes some getting used to," Ryker whispered and felt a little awkward talking about his weapon. "I haven't flown armed before and I didn't count on having my duty weapon wedged between my back and the seat. It took me a while to figure out where to wear it so that it wasn't stabbing me in the back," he added sheepishly.

"A lot of the agents wear ankle holsters, don't they?"

"I don't know. I haven't talked to other agents about that. That makes sense, but I don't think I'd be able to pull my gun as accurately from an ankle holster." Ryker silently cursed himself for discussing tactics with a complete stranger. *She must think I'm an idiot.*

"Which agency do you work for?"

"U.S. Department of Justice," he tried to be technically truthful, without actually disclosing that he was a DEA agent.

"Department of Justice, is that code for FBI?" she whispered as she learned toward him.

"No, FBI agents never speak in code. They always want you to know who they work for." He gave her a dead-serious look, but his eyes twinkled.

"But you? You want to keep it a secret?"

"Well, let's just say it's on a need-to-know basis." There was a light in his eyes.

"In case you *need-to-know*, my name is Tara and I am specially trained to protect the identities of all LEOs on the flight." She kept her voice low and looked knowingly around the cabin.

He frowned at her with a quizzical expression on his face. She added, "*LEO,* you know, law enforcement officer? Let me guess, you're new, huh?"

"God, I am so lame. Is it that obvious?" He felt his face flush under her appraising gaze.

"No, not at all. You look like a seasoned, weathered old guy with years of experience in the field," she said with a straight face.

"That's not right," he stifled a laugh.

"Let me think …okay, you're flying out of Dulles, so maybe you just finished training somewhere in DC? Am I close?"

"Yeah, I just finished the academy at Quantico. San Francisco will be my first duty station."

"What exactly do Department of Justice agents do? Agent …?"

"Ryker, Alex Ryker. I'm sorry, I should have introduced myself earlier. You got me all confused and distracted. All us old weathered guys can't handle attractive women giving us a hard time," he grinned as he watched her face light up from the compliment.

"Oh, I'm sure that never happens to you, Agent Ryker."

"You can call me Alex, and no, it doesn't. I'm usually the one giving the hard time, not getting it."

"So it's like that? You can give me grief, but not the other way around?"

"Okay, okay, truce?" Ryker replied, enjoying the banter.

"I'll think about it," she said as she closed her book and put it back into her bag.

"Tara, how long have you worked for the airlines?"

"About two years, but this is my final voyage." She liked the fact that he called her by name.

"What's next, modeling or acting?" he asked, half kidding.

She smiled at him and paused a moment before answering. She didn't want to sound vain or snobby.

"Good guess. Modeling. I have a shoot with an online catalog in the next few weeks. I hope I'll be able to find other modeling jobs after that."

"You aren't one of those online brides, are you?" he feigned shock.

"Excuse me!"

"Well, you said online catalog. That's hardly descriptive. I mean, you can imagine how my mind is racing about what product you might be selling."

"It's on a *need-to-know* basis."

They both laughed. She stood up and took a glass from another passenger who had approached the galley. He watched the gracious way she interacted with the passenger. She patiently answered questions and offered a magazine to read. She made the rounds through the cabin and returned with a tray full of empty glasses. He waited for her. He was tired of sitting and the galley was big enough to let him walk around a little.

"Are you still here? Don't you have some bad guys to arrest or something?" Her tone was playful.

"Look, don't try to get out of telling me about the catalog. Maybe I can boost their sales by ordering some stuff. Come on, you can trust me. I'm a federal agent. You know, one of the good guys," he implored with a sly smile.

"Okay. It's Victoria's Secret. And just because they take my picture doesn't mean they are going to use it in one of *their catalogs*. Satisfied?"

"Whew! I'd better get you to autograph something before you run off and get famous."

"Look pal, or Alex, or whatever your name is, if you don't knock it off, I'm not going to show you around San Francisco." She gave him a playful punch on the arm.

"I'll be a perfect gentleman, I promise. I would love for you to show me around the city. I don't know anyone there yet and it would be nice to have a friend nearby," he said sincerely as he cupped her elbow with his hand.

"Deal. Now, I've got to get back to work or my partner is going to kill me," she looked around him and saw Joan glaring at her as she came up the aisle.

"Let's exchange phone numbers after we land," he whispered.

She watched him as he walked back to his seat and noticed that a couple of the female passengers did the same. A woman in her forties winked at her and waved her hand, palm down, back and forth, making the international sign for *he's hot*. Tara laughed and put one finger across her lips in a silent signal.

"Looks like James Bond is looking for Pussy Galore. I seriously thought you two were going to join the Mile High Club right here in the galley! Talk about your proverbial sexual tension! I could feel it ten rows away. I don't know about you, but I need a shower." Joan wiped imaginary sweat from her forehead.

"God, Joan, you are bad!"

"So, you gave him your phone number?"

"Not your business, thank you very much."

"Come on, I'm joking, okay? Hey, it's hard for us boring old married women to watch you bachelorette beauties snag all the hot guys."

"You don't think I should go out with him, right? You think he's just a cop who doesn't make any money."

"I didn't say don't go out with him. By all means, go out with him, screw his brains out, then tell me every juicy detail. I said don't marry him. Big difference."

"God, you kill me. He really seems like a nice guy."

"I cannot believe my ears. Who are you and what have you done with my friend Tara? She was into big, I mean huge, financial portfolios the last time I flew with her."

"I have my own portfolio. Now let's get back to work." Tara realized that for the first time she wasn't thinking about a man's bank account. The awful experience in London a few days ago had changed her. She'd never felt so freaked out in her life. She figured she could take a chance on Alex. She sensed something special about him. *Or, it could just be his ass, but hey, why not? I'll give it a shot,* she thought and began formulating a plan, as the time passed quickly.

"Ladies and gentlemen, this is the captain. We will be landing at SFO in approximately twenty minutes. Please return to your seats and fasten your seat belts. Flight crew prepare the cabin for landing."

Ryker put away his laptop and buckled up. When Tara passed him, she slipped him a piece of paper that had her telephone number carefully written in neat, precise handwriting. His face lit up when he read it and she felt silly for being so gleeful at his response. Embarrassed that her face was probably beet red, she quickly turned around and headed back to the galley.

As Joan locked the beverage cart into place, she noticed the red warning light flashing on the control panel above her. Alarmed, she looked to see where Tara was.

"Tara!" Joan called in alarm.

Ryker looked up and saw the panicked expression on the flight attendant's face. *Something's wrong*, he thought, one second before a violent jolt almost ejected him out of his seat.

The 747 started to shake and lurch. A loud roar echoed through the cabin and air rushed in. The aircraft went into a nose dive and all hell broke loose. Passengers started screaming as oxygen masks dropped from the overheads. Ryker looked around and saw Tara crawling on the floor. He unfastened his seat belt, lunged toward her and managed to grab her ankles. It took all his strength to pull her towards him. The whirling air flow had changed directions and it felt like a wind tunnel, furiously sucking them in. She struggled as she pulled herself into a kneeling position and held onto one of the aisle armrests. Wind whipped around them, objects flew past their heads, and papers and magazines stirred up a small storm inside the aircraft. Ryker yelled to her, but he couldn't hear his own voice over the deafening roar. He grabbed her around her waist and tried to pull her out of the aisle into his row.

The tremendous sucking force pulled her away. The *fasten seat belt signs* were flashing and oxygen masks whipped back and forth, slapping his head and face. Someone was speaking over the intercom in a broken jumble of static.

"Hold on!" Ryker yelled over the noise, "Pull yourself towards me."

He felt short of breath and his lungs burned. He had to get to his oxygen mask, but he wouldn't let go of her.

"Don't let go!" Tara screamed as she clung to the armrest and desperately pulled herself toward him.

He reached up with one hand, grabbed a swinging mask, and pulled it over his nose. He took a few deep breaths to fight the dizziness he felt coming on. The rapid descent continued and the roar grew louder by the second. He saw her face, blanched with fear. He braced his feet on the seat post in front of him and grabbed her around her shoulders. He pulled with full force as she struggled to launch herself toward him.

"Come on! Come on!" he shouted encouragement.

"Don't let go!" He could barely hear her scream.

"I won't! Pull! Pull!" She mustered all her strength and lunged forward, her dark hair plastered against her scalp by the sheer force of the wind.

Ryker roughly pulled her across his lap into the middle seat and together they fought the flying metal buckles of her seat belt until they finally secured it.

Ryker grabbed one of the flailing oxygen masks and held it tightly over her nose and face. She breathed the oxygen in long, heaving draws. He felt the aircraft leveling off. The deafening roar was clearly coming from the front of the cabin. He could see some type of opening on the left side of the plane. Everything in the area was gone and articles of clothing, purses, and a baseball hat flew out of the opening as if being sucked into a mammoth vacuum.

"Joan, where's Joan?" Tara shouted as she strained in her seat to see the other passengers.

Ryker didn't answer. The last time he had seen the other woman she had been standing directly in front of the gaping hole.

"Alex, did you see her?"

"I don't know. Maybe she made it to a seat."

"The plane is leveling off. They've descended and pulled out of the dive," her voice was becoming hoarse as she tried to speak over the noise.

The other passengers had stopped screaming, but they gripped their armrests and gasped oxygen through the masks like petrified and unwilling patients in an ICU. All eyes were transfixed on the gaping opening in the front of the cabin. A seat belt flapped against the wall where the jump seat used to be.

"This is the captain. We have the aircraft under control and are going to land in approximately fifteen minutes. Stay in your seats with your seat belts fastened. Emergency crews on the ground are waiting to assist those passengers who need medical attention."

Ryker breathed a sigh of relief and squeezed Tara's arm. She had composed herself and appeared calm. She looked around the cabin, hoping to see her friend. Ryker knew that was unlikely, but he kept that to himself.

The plane touched down in a fairly smooth landing and the passengers cheered in relief after the aircraft came to a complete stop.

Tara helped the emergency ground crew evacuate the injured. Miraculously, there didn't seem to be any serious injuries, only a few people with cuts or bruises from flying debris. Joan was nowhere in sight.

"Joan, Joan?" Tara called out anxiously as she walked the aisles and opened the bathroom doors. There was no sign of her. Anything that wasn't bolted to the frame had been sucked out of the aircraft. A few of the passengers looked around for the missing flight attendant. Some shook their heads in disbelief and other's eyes filled with tears.

Tara waited until all of the passengers were off the plane before she returned to Ryker. He had stayed in his seat, waiting for her. When she walked toward him, he stood up and held out his arms. She embraced him and started to silently cry. He held her for a few moments as the gravity of the situation settled upon them.

"You saved my life," she kept her face pressed against his chest.

"You got some pretty strong arms. You work out?" He tried to coax a smile from her.

She looked up and tried to smile through tear filled eyes. He tightened his arms around her, crushed her to his chest for another few seconds, and then reluctantly let her go.

"Tara, let's get the hell off this plane."

"Follow me," she took his hand.

Once inside the terminal, they clustered in small groups with the rest of the flight crew and gave statements to FAA inspectors. Tara introduced Ryker to the pilots, who were very interested in his observations of what had happened inside the cabin. All anyone knew was that the exit door next to the galley had blown off. It was not yet clear what type of malfunction had occurred. So far as anyone knew, there was no evidence of an explosion. The emergency crew confirmed that Joan was not on the plane. Several of the flight attendants wiped tears from their swollen, red eyes.

The group stood, transfixed as Tara told them how Ryker had pulled her into a seat and kept her from being sucked out of the aircraft. Her voice broke a few times as she recalled feeling faint from the lack of oxygen. He told the story another way.

"Look, I was scared shitless. Oxygen masks were flying around like bats with rabies, trying to knock my head off. I pulled her into my row so she could save me, not the other way around!" The group erupted in laughter, a brief reprieve from the intensity they all felt.

"Agent Ryker, you can fly with us anytime!" The captain shook his hand.

Ryker looked over the captain's shoulder and saw a familiar face approaching.

"Alex, are you alright?" Connor called out to him.

"Yeah, but my first time in first class fell a little below my expectations." Ryker tried not to look as freaked out as he felt.

"So I heard. I badged my way through once I heard there was problem." Connor nodded to the rest of the group.

"Captain, this is my senior partner, DEA Agent Jack Connor. Jack, this is the flight crew and the pilots who saved our lives."

"Agent Connor, we've made Alex an honorary member of our crew. He helped keep one of our crew onboard when an exit door blew off. Tragically, we lost one of our best flight attendants, but the passengers made it through all right." The pilot's voice quavered, but he maintained his calm professionalism.

"How about the rest of you, is the flight crew okay?" Connor asked in concern.

"Yeah, other than a few cuts and bruises, we all seem to be fine. Tara had the worst of it. She was standing in the aisle when the door blew and the vacuum nearly pulled her out. Agent Ryker hung onto her and managed to get her into a seat. That's pretty remarkable given the extreme conditions inside the cabin. Maybe we should make you a sky marshal Alex."

"No thanks captain, I'm staying on the ground for quite a while."

The crew slowly dispersed. Ryker followed Tara after she walked away from the crew, then stopped her.

"Are you gonna be okay tonight?"

"Yeah. I'll be fine. Thanks Alex. You really did save my life you know."

"You saved yourself. I just helped out a little. Do you still feel like apartment hunting with me?"

"Absolutely! Call me. It'll take my mind off this." She looked up at him, tears threatened to spill over. He put his hand on her shoulder and they were silent for a few seconds.

163

"Bye." they said it at the same time.

He watched for a few moments as she walked away, then turned and headed back toward Connor.

"You all right?"

"Yeah," he sighed in relief and suddenly felt exhausted.

"Fuckin' planes! Welcome to San Francisco. My wife's waiting for us at curbside, let's get out of here."

CHAPTER 10

CABO SAN LUCAS

Carlos glanced at his watch: 10:45 p.m. He and Francisco watched from a mountain ridge overlooking the Sea of Cortez.

"They are leaving now," Carlos replied as he looked through the Nikon 8x50 binoculars. He could see the two fishing trawlers, side by side with the submarine in the middle, being escorted from the harbor to the open sea.

"It is a perfect night for a launch."

"Yes, it is," Carlos wholeheartedly agreed.

The streamlined sub glided through the calm waters, disrupting the reflection of the moonlight shining on the surface, barely visible. The two men stood and conducted surveillance on the ridge for a half hour until the trawlers were out of sight, then returned to their hotel.

"Francisco, I am going to the lobby to buy a newspaper and get something to eat. Do you need anything?" Carlos asked.

"No, I am going to take a shower. I will meet you in twenty minutes. We can eat then," Francisco replied from the bathroom.

"Twenty minutes."

Carlos hurried out of the room. He had made up his mind that he would call Connor and leave a message. He looked around the lobby. It was deserted, except for the staff behind the desk. He walked to the pay phones off the rear of the lobby, in a hallway leading to conference rooms. Carlos was cautioned only to use his cell phone in extreme emergencies to avoid any compromise. He quickly dialed an international calling card number that Connor had given him and left a brief, coded message. He was on the phone for less than one minute. The hallway was still deserted when he hung up.

He walked back through the lobby area into the nightclub. It was dark and smoky and was already getting crowded. He made his way to the bar and ordered a margarita. He tried to shake off his uneasiness.

Carlos saw Francisco come into the bar. As he made his way through the crowd, he stopped and whispered something to an exotic looking young woman, with long, silky dark hair. The woman motioned across the table to her equally stunning friend and they linked their arms with Francisco and headed toward the bar. Francisco wore them like glittery ornaments as the crowd parted and let them pass. The flashing laser lights above the dance floor made their approach appear choppy and in slow motion. Carlos swallowed hard and felt the tequila burn his throat on the way down. It was going to be a long night.

BOGOTÁ, COLOMBIA

The night was stiflingly hot and humid in Bogotá. A different type of nightlife chirped and croaked throughout the compound grounds. The guards frequently interrupted their patrol to get cold bottles of water from the small refrigerators in the guard shacks. The guard dogs' tongues hung out of their mouths and they lapped up water from metal bowls as if they hadn't had water in days. Inside *The Palace,* the temperature was a comfortable 68 degrees. Joaquin refused to sweat inside his house.

He and his brothers Jorge and Julio lazed across leather sofas in the cigar room, laughing as they watched the latest American blockbuster action film. The movie had not yet been released in the United States.

"I hope you paid your source in Hollywood a good price for this movie, my brother. It is excellent!" Joaquin congratulated him.

"My source will be rewarded. I only pay if we like the film."

"Excellent business strategy."

Maria came into the room. She was on duty whenever the brothers were awake.

"Señor Gusto, may I get you anything?"

"Yes Maria, please get us a bottle of Russian cognac, and bring another glass. Roberto will arrive soon," Joaquin answered, never taking his eye off the screen.

"Sí, señor."

The phone next to Joaquin's chair rang, interrupting an action scene.

"Who is it? Yes, send him up…Roberto is on his way!"

The brothers groaned, and then erupted in laughter at the action on the screen.

When Roberto entered the room, Joaquin abruptly pressed the pause button on the remote.

"Joaquin! Turn the movie back on, business can wait," Julio implored.

"I agree, Joaquin, the film is near the end," Jorge joined in.

"I want to hear from Roberto first." His tone left no room for debate. "Did Viper accept the assignment?"

"Yes. He asked us to supply the things on this list." Roberto pulled out a piece of paper, unfolded it and handed it to Joaquin.

Joaquin read it, then passed it to his brothers.

"We can deliver these in three days. Do you agree?" Joaquin deferred to his brothers.

"I will get the Jeep," Julio replied.

"I will get the rest," Roberto volunteered.

"Discuss this with no one. We are the only ones to know of this," Joaquin made eye contact with each of them. They nodded in agreement.

"Diego Cuevas is an ambitious man who wants to be the most powerful man in South America. He has to go through me to achieve that!"

"That will never happen, Joaquin! You too are an intelligent man and are more cunning. He is no match for you," Jorge interjected.

"Do not overestimate me my brother, nor underestimate Cuevas. I am concerned about his meeting with General Sun next month. Cuevas must never leave Mexico to meet the General. I have studied Cuevas for two years. I have watched how he does business. He plans five years in advance for when he wants to make a move."

"Not one of our informants has been able to determine the purpose of their meeting. They make their own heroin. I do not think that General Sun is planning to buy coffee from Cuevas," Joaquin replied skeptically.

"What do you suspect?" Julio asked.

"The only thing we know is that Cuevas called the meeting with General Sun, but we do not know where the meeting will take place. The General has not left Thailand for the last twenty years. I do not think he will leave now. We must anticipate Cuevas' moves. I suspect that the meeting may be about us. We must not be complacent! We must protect our position as leaders. Viper will protect our interests."

"Joaquin, do you think Cuevas will challenge us?" Julio asked in disbelief.

"I remind you, brother, the mighty General Sun himself tried to challenge us in the Far East three years ago. Our strike against the general's chief of staff put things back in order." Joaquin stopped to think for a second and stared at the ceiling.

"Perhaps this is how General Sun will strike back at us. He may devise a rivalry between Cuevas and our family. Whatever he is planning, will not be in our best interest," Joaquin added after a long pause.

"The hit must not come back to us in any way. We cannot afford to have a war with them. Because we do so much business with Cuevas, his people will not suspect us," Jorge added

"That is true."

"We will continue to do business with the Cuevas organization, but we will not let him deceive us or gain an advantage."

They stopped talking when Maria entered the room with a bottle of cognac and a tray of glasses. As she handed a glass to Roberto, she saw Julio surreptitiously slip a folded piece of paper into one of the desk drawers.

Joaquin raised his glass. "A toast...to the French who distilled this cognac and to our success." Joaquin picked up the remote and the sound of gunshots echoed through the surround-sound system as the movie resumed. Startled, Maria steadied the tray and set it down on the marble coffee table, then silently slipped out of the room.

Two hours later, she returned to the empty cigar room. The gold anniversary clock on the desk showed the time: 1:15 a.m. She walked over to the sitting area and started to pick up the empty glasses. As she bent down, she looked toward the door to be sure that she was alone. She opened the desk drawer and found the piece of paper that she had seen Julio place there earlier.

Her heart raced as she scanned the paper. She pressed it flat against the desktop and smoothed the creases with her hand, then reached into her pocket, took out the small camera, and took three pictures, which were simultaneously transferred via secure e-mail to the CIA operations rooms at the U.S. Embassy in Bogota and CIA HQ. She put the camera back in her pocket, refolded the paper and placed it back into the drawer, exactly as she had found it. When she stood, she paused for a few seconds. Her nerves were raw. She picked up the tray of dirty glasses and headed into the hallway.

"Señor Roberto!" Maria exclaimed with a quick intake of breath as he walked in the room at the same moment she was walking out.

"Maria, you startled me! What are you doing?"

"I cleaned the room, señor," she replied, glancing down at the tray of glasses in her hands.

"I left some papers in the room."

"Sí Señor Roberto. Do you need anything else?"

"No, Maria. It is late. You should get your rest."

"Sí."

Her hands started to tremble as she walked down the hall. When she heard the delicate tinkling of the glasses, she willed her hands to be still.

SAN FRANCISCO

Traffic was light on Interstate 101 just south of San Francisco.

"This commute hasn't been bad so far, Jack." Alex Ryker was eager to begin his first day on the job as a federal agent.

"It's 6:45 in the morning Alex, but if you leave much later than this it will take you an hour plus to travel twenty-two miles."

"I guess I am going to have to try and transform into a morning person. Man, that is not going to be easy."

"You and Barrett…both night owls!" Connor replied in exasperation.

"She is so cool. She stayed up late and watched *Clear and Present Danger* with me because she knew I was too jacked up to sleep."

"Vintage Tom Clancy. I heard you guys laughing. She was one tired camper this morning, but she has no one to blame but herself."

Connor enjoyed seeing the awe on Ryker's face as he took in the San Francisco skyline. It never failed to inspire. They listened to sports and traffic reports on KNBR as they passed through the Tenderloin district on the way to the federal building. Connor braked at an intersection as a homeless man ignored the traffic light

169

and pushed his overloaded shopping cart into the street, flipping them off as he crossed.

"Nice," Ryker said sarcastically as he gave Connor an incredulous look and shook his head.

As they turned into the Federal Building underground parking lot, another homeless man was relieving himself on the sidewalk. Steam rose from the pale urine as it streamed down the ramp. He flashed them a drunken grin and tried to piss on their car as they passed.

"Welcome to the neighborhood Alex."

"You've got to be shitting me!" Ryker craned his neck around and continued to watch in disbelief.

Connor drove past the security guard and parked in an assigned spot in the basement parking lot and they walked up a flight of stairs to the main lobby and took the elevator to the DEA offices on the 14th floor.

"Welcome to the San Francisco Field Office, Alex." Bill Cartwright stood up from his desk and waved them into his office.

"Thank you, sir. Everyone is making me feel right at home." Ryker shook hands and he and Connor took a seat. Framed diplomas, awards and plaques covered the wall behind the desk.

"I'm sure that Jack has probably filled you in on the way we work around here. If you have any questions, problems, whatever, tell Jack and listen to what he says. He's one of our top agents and he knows what he's doing."

"Yes sir."

Connor watched Ryker. He was deferential...good start.

"You are very fortunate, Alex, because you are going to be involved in one of DEA's biggest investigations. We brief the DEA Administrator weekly and we brief the SAC every day."

"I'm looking forward to doing whatever I can to assist. I don't care if I have to work 24-7."

"Believe me, you will, but that's a good attitude. I hope you keep it. You're single, right?" Cartwright continued.

"Yes."

"Good, because I don't want to be the cause of another divorce around here...we've had a few lately. You'll be logging in late hours on this one, son. I reviewed your file from the academy and you did an outstanding job. Keep up that kind of performance and you'll do fine here." He leaned toward Ryker and lowered his voice. "There is no room for screw-ups on this one. Understand?"

"I do, absolutely." Ryker replied earnestly.

"Good!"

"Jack, any news from Carlos?"

"Not yet. I'm going to check the messages on the UC line after we're done here. We should hear something soon."

"Before you do that, the SAC wants to meet Alex and welcome him aboard."

"Go right in, he's expecting you," the SAC's secretary greeted the three men as they walked into the executive office area.

"Sir, this is Alex Ryker, the new agent from Quantico," Cartwright introduced him.

"Good morning! Have a seat, gentlemen," Special Agent in Charge George Melconi gestured toward the tasteful leather chairs in front of his desk.

"Alex, I just got off the phone with the CEO of United Airlines. Saving a flight attendant from an air disaster en route to your first duty station is a good way to start your career."

"I didn't look at it as a career move at the time, sir," Ryker replied cautiously.

"Shit happens fast, doesn't it?"

"In the blink of an eye."

"What happened up there? They aren't saying much on the news, just that the cause of the *malfunction* is under investigation. Don't you love how they spin it, a door blows off a commercial aircraft, one of the flight crew is sucked out and disappears, and they call it a *malfunction*?"

"To be honest, I don't know what happened. I heard a loud noise, not an explosion, but something very jarring and the next thing I know, it's a wind tunnel in there, sucking everything out a hole where the door used to be," Ryker replied and described the chain of events.

"You acted decisively up there and that is a good sign. You have to think quickly on your feet in this job, people's lives depend on it," Melconi nodded approvingly.

"Yes sir."

"Anyway… welcome," Melconi went into his standard *welcome-aboard* speech. "You're lucky to be paired up with Jack.

171

He's got one hell of a case going on. Speaking of the case, any news yet from your CI?" Melconi turned his attention to Connor.

"Not yet, but I think we'll hear something soon."

"Good, keep me posted."

The intercom line rang. "Mr. Melconi, headquarters is on the line. Do you want me to tell them you'll call them back?"

"No Mary, tell them I'll be with them in a second. Alex, I have an open-door policy around here. Feel free to come and see me if you need to, okay?" He stood up, signaling the end of the meeting and they began to file out.

"Glad to meet you sir," Ryker called over his shoulder.

After they walked out of the SAC's office, Cartwright spoke. "Alex, I have an open-door policy as well, but if you've got a problem, take it to Jack first and if he can't handle it, or if he's not around, then bring it to me. I don't want to see you in the SAC's office unless you have my permission. Is that clear?" Cartwright sounded like a drill instructor on the first day of boot camp.

"Yes sir."

Connor enjoyed the deer-in-the-headlights look Ryker got after that little directive. *The kid probably hasn't said this many 'yes sirs' since he was in grade school.*

"Don't piss him off. He can either be the best boss ever or the boss from hell. I love the guy, but I make it a point not to get in his way," Connor said quietly as they walked down the hall.

"Trust me, I will not piss him off."

Connor couldn't suppress a smile as he clapped Ryker on the back. "You'll do fine."

"Hey Jack, you got a message on the UC line," one of the tech agents called out as he passed them in the hallway.

"Thanks, I'll check it out."

They walked into the tech room and went straight to the monitoring table where several digital recorders were already in use. This was Ryker's first time inside a real tech room. The front portion of the room looked like a typical office space with several desks. The adjoining work area was enclosed in a steel cage that housed DEA's sophisticated electronic and audio equipment.

Ryker was clearly impressed by various devices and electronic equipment stacked neatly on shelves along the wall.

Connor walked to one of the digital recorders and depressed the play button. A man's heavily accented voice filled the room.

"Amigo, it's Carlos. I have to keep this short. I will not be able to visit you next week. I have to stay here. I have been promoted to chief security officer and I cannot leave the area. Two friends of mine left tonight and should arrive in Monterey in a few days. I hope you will be able to see them. They will not stay long. I am working at a new location where it is harder for me to get to a secure phone. Also…"

"Hey Jack, could you give me a hand?" One of the tech agents yelled from a secured cage located in the tech room. Connor hit the pause button.

"Alex, would you mind helping him?" Ryker gave a thumbs-up signal and walked over to the cage.

"…there's a separate package being delivered to a different person. Francisco said he does not know what it is, but it was given to him by the Gustos and it is very important. That is all I know. I must go. See you soon *amigo.*" Connor could hear the stress in Carlos' voice. The news about the additional package concerned him and he wondered if this new development had anything to do with the terrorist cell.

"Shit," the tech agent yelled. "Jack did you finish listening to the message from your CI?"

"Yeah, why?"

"I just hit the master delete button by mistake and erased all the incoming calls on that UC line for the last 24 hours."

"Don't worry I think I got it all."

"Hey, did I miss anything? Any problems?" Ryker asked as he rejoined Connor.

"Hard to say. You got most of it, but the plot has thickened. Seems our CI got a promotion, or they suspect something and want to keep closer tabs on him. Either way, he's not coming with the shipment."

Connor walked back to Cartwright's office and found him sitting behind his desk reading the morning e-mail traffic.

"News?" Cartwright asked enthusiastically, happy for a break from the tedium of reading the daily intelligence reports from DEA headquarters.

"Yeah, Carlos left a brief message. The load will arrive in Monterey in a few days, depending on the weather." Connor decided to keep the information about the separate package to himself.

"Good."

"Carlos has been promoted to chief security officer and will be even closer to Francisco."

"That's really good news."

"Right, I'll contact JTF-5 and Monterey so we can start getting ready for the load," Connor replied.

"I just got off the phone with the SAC from the Washington Field Office. He was impressed with the way you helped out his agents on the Gusto investigation and surveillance. He was especially pleased with the way you handled yourself with those suspects outside the restaurant that seems to be connected to the FBI's terrorist wire."

Connor held his breath. He couldn't tell whether Cartwright suspected Ryker's involvement or not.

"I know you didn't particularly want to go to Quantico, or get stuck with a junior partner right now, but I know you will be a good role model as an FTA. I also know you wouldn't do anything to jeopardize your role, right?" Cartwright looked him straight in the eyes.

Shit, he knows, about Ryker! Connor thought, "No sir."

"I like the kid and so does the SAC. He'll be a good asset to our group. Whatever you need, just let me know."

"Okay boss, thanks." Connor turned around and walked out of the office as fast as he could.

CIA HEADQUARTERS

"Emma, this is Greg. The director in?" Stevens greeted her.

"Not yet. She had to go over to the White House this morning. There was some new activity in Afghanistan last night and she had to brief the President," the executive secretary replied.

"I'm here all day. Tell her that we got some good news on Black Knight when she comes in."

"I'll tell her."

She stared at her watch. It wasn't even 9:00 a.m. and the CIA Director already had twenty-two messages.

NICE, FRANCE

The sun was starting to set over the French countryside where the Marcel family vineyard had been cultivated for four generations.

"Francois, Heinz's auto is outside. I fear my hearing is older than my sixty years. I did not hear him arrive. Did you?" Jules, the matriarch of the Marcel family, asked her husband.

"I did not hear an auto, *ma cherie*, are you sure it is Heinz?" Francois replied as he brought her a cup of strong French roast coffee and joined her on the veranda of their hillside villa and looked out over the sweeping views of the French Riviera.

"Oh yes. See there?" She pointed to the mini coupe.

"We have not seen him for many months. Perhaps he will join us for dinner."

The Marcels had met Heinz Von Berg five years ago when he stopped at the scene of an auto crash. Their son had driven off the road in pouring rain, less than two miles from the vineyard. He had been killed instantly and if not for Mr. Von Berg, their only grandson and sole heir would also be dead. Von Berg had pulled the child from the wreckage only moments before it had burst into flames.

They were eternally grateful to him and showed their gratitude by befriending him. They allowed him to stay in a small cottage on their vineyard, hidden behind rows and rows of grape vines. Their son had loved the cottage. They never knew when to expect Mr. Von Berg. He never announced his presence, or departure for that matter.

The man they knew as Heinz Von Berg was already in the cellar of the cottage, inspecting a modified Remington. He was preparing it for shipment to Venezuela for his next assignment. He lightly cleaned the barrel with a specially treated cloth, then placed it in the shipping container, carefully concealing it among sections of metal pipe.

The Marcels never came to the cabin. They knew he insisted on complete privacy and they respected his wishes. He felt at ease working on his equipment. He stored some of his professional tools in hidden compartments which he had meticulously built into the cellar's walls and floor. It was a perfect, isolated location and an ideal safe house. He had stumbled upon it by chance. It had no direct connections to any of his identities.

He retrieved seven special 7.62mm rounds from a concealed compartment in a wall wine rack. The rounds had been specifically designed for his weapon and would be perfectly suited to this particular mission. He carefully inspected all seven rounds, selected five, and put the remaining two back in the hidden compartment. He then slipped the rounds, one by one, into a metal pipe and placed it in the shipping container next to the rifle barrel. Tonight, he would get a good night's sleep. He would drive back to Paris in the morning and ship the crate to a secure drop-off location in Venezuela.

He walked up the cellar stairs and out onto the rustic limestone patio. A full moon rose low over the vineyard as he walked onto the narrow dirt path that led to the main house. His stomach growled when he smelled fresh baked bread.

CIA HEADQUARTERS

"Greg, she's back and will see you in fifteen minutes."

Greg Stevens was in the executive office in ten.

"Good morning, Emma. Busy day?" Stevens flashed her a smile.

"I get more done when she's out of the office. She's off the phone, you can go in."

"What do you have, Greg?" The CIA Director glanced up from her computer screen.

"It looks like Viper's got a new assignment. Striker photographed a handwritten note, a list, she found at the cartel's residence in Bogotá." He handed her the photograph.

"A picture truly is worth a thousand words," Bancroft replied as she studied the note.

R

These are things I need from you
--Jeep Grand Cherokee, deliver to PIA
--traveler's itinerary for 14 days
--1/8 kilo C-4
--local security info
--topo map
I have everything else

V

"Dear God! C-4? What do you make of it, Greg?" Bancroft exhaled in frustration.

"I think the list is from Viper to Roberto, Gusto's security chief. We'll be able to confirm that after we compare the handwriting with the first sample. Looks like a shopping list for a professional hit. He wants a vehicle, the target or traveler's itinerary, explosives, and details about the hit location. *PIA* could be Panama International airport. I suspect the hit will be somewhere in Central or South America. My guess...Central America."

"Why?"

"The Gustos control South America so they could do a job there by themselves. Plus, I don't think Viper would want to cross the border into Panama from Colombia in a vehicle. I think it's Mexico. I'm going to contact our office at the Embassy in Bogotá and see if Roberto has traveled in the last two weeks. I think Viper personally delivered the list to Roberto. Wherever the two met and exchanged the note is probably where the hit will occur."

"Why do you think that Greg?"

"Because of all the rampant violence in Mexico lately. There's total chaos in that country and it has poor security."

"Makes sense."

"We'll contact every station chief in Central America to determine if there are any important meetings coming up within the next two weeks. The C-4 is a serious problem. That could mean multiple targets, a car bomb, hard to know," Stevens frowned as he looked at the list.

"It's not much to go on. Do you think we can stop it?"

"Hard to say right now. Hopefully we'll have more answers in the next few days."

"Good, let me know when you get something more definite."

"One more thing, ma'am."

"Yes?"

"The list contains items that Viper could easily get himself. He usually works alone, so this is out of character for him. Unfortunately, we don't know what to make of it yet," Stevens admitted.

"That's a mystery to me too," Bancroft replied.

"I'm purely speculating now, but maybe the Gustos need to rush this hit and that's why Viper doesn't have time to acquire the items himself. If they're in a hurry to get the job done, he would need their help."

"Do you think it's political or business-related?"

"Unclear. The only thing we can be fairly certain about is that they want it done soon."

"You and your team have your work cut out for you."

"That's why we get paid the big bucks." He gave her a grim smile as he got up to leave.

"Greg, one more thing, any more phone calls between the Gustos and the terrorist cell on the west coast?"

"No ma'am, nothing, just the two recent phone calls…that's it."

"Thanks, Greg." Bancroft thought about the new intelligence from Connor's CI concerning the separate package being delivered. She reached for her secure phone and pressed the pre-programmed number for the direct line to Derek Schmidt, the Director of NEST, the Nuclear Emergency Support Team.

JOINT TASK FORCE FIVE (JTF-5) COAST GUARD ISLAND, ALAMEDA, CA

Connor pulled into the parking lot. Ryker observed that there were no markings on the outside of the two JTF-5 five buildings, except for the numbers 101 and 102. As they entered the reception area, Ryker noticed the large JTF-5 insignia on the wall. The insignia was cryptic, it contained a ship, plane, satellite, and the silhouette of a person.

"Good morning gentlemen. Mr. Franklin will be out in a few minutes," the receptionist greeted them as she handed them visitor's badges.

JTF-5 was established in 1989 as a result of the Reagan and Bush era war on drugs. It was comprised of representatives from all five branches of the military, and various federal law enforcement agencies, including DEA, FBI, and U.S. Immigration and Customs Enforcement. JTF-5's mission is to combat drug-related transnational organized crime, reduce threats to the Pacific region, protect national security and promote regional stability. The purpose was for the military to provide logistical and intelligence support to federal law enforcement agencies in international interdiction efforts. The key word was support…the military is strictly prohibited from engaging in any narcotics investigations within the U.S.

"Welcome back, Jack."

"Thanks. Alex, this is Tony Franklin, our DEA JTF-5 representative."

"Glad to meet you, sir."

"I briefed Alex on how you fit in and how the military supports our missions."

"Good. Follow me to my office. What have you got for me, Jack?" Franklin asked.

"The sub left yesterday and should arrive in Monterey in a couple of days," Connor reported.

"Last time we got lucky and spotted it earlier. I'll alert the Coast Guard and the Navy today. Maybe we'll get lucky again. At least we know it's coming to Monterey."

"My CI won't be with it this time, but we do know where their home port is."

"That's a bonus!"

"Yeah, all we need to do now is coordinate a military air strike and take out their operation," Ryker interjected.

"It's not quite that simple," Connor replied as he and Franklin exchanged a knowing smile. It wasn't so long ago when they were new on the job and were under the mistaken impression that the real world mirrored the movies.

"We'll go to Monterey and link up with the agents down there for the surveillance," Connor continued.

"Are you going with the shipment or with us to follow the sub back?"

"I'll go with the sub and Ryker will go with the load."

"Here's the list of the military personnel that will assist you. They will be waiting for you when you get down there."

"Thanks."

"Alex, would you like a ten-minute tour of our facility?" Franklin asked.

"That would be great, if we have the time," Ryker replied eagerly as he looked at Connor for approval. Connor nodded.

Franklin picked up the phone and pressed the intercom button, "Chief, can you arrange a tour for one of the agents?"

When Ryker left, Franklin continued. "When you get down there, contact Joe Hatfield. He's a SEAL. His team is ready and they have been training for the mission. Hopefully, we'll spot the sub and put the tracking device on it."

He paused and then added, "I made a trip back to Washington while you were gone. We have a new prototype tracking device with a self-destruct mode. They say that it works like a charm. We got authorization to be the first to use it on a live op. Hopefully, this time we won't have a problem with the tracking device. I like how your new partner thinks. He's got the right idea, just the wrong method. These guys fresh out of the academy think we can order up drone strikes like take-out pizza." Both men laughed.

"Yeah."

"It should be interesting to see how our new prototype works on their new sub. Fucking carbon fiber sub, go figure. The thing is 90 feet long, virtually undetectable with a seven ton payload and no underwater signature. It was a miracle that NOOC, the Navy Oceanography Operational Command, was able to detect the sub in the first place, and from right here at Fleet Numerical, the Meteorology Oceanographic Center in Monterey. There is justice after all, but I'm told that their tracking capabilities are hit and miss and consequently, not reliable. It's no wonder the Navy wants to blow the damn thing up. Can you imagine what could be smuggled into the country…forget drugs…anything. God help us if terrorists get ahold of one of these."

"No shit."

"I can only imagine what the DARPA boys have on the drawing board on the black side of the world. There are other U.S. elements working on how they manufactured and funded it. How ironic that the U.S. government is trying to steal stealth sub technology from the cartel. Anyway, this is highly classified and is way above our pay grades. The call has been made to blow up the damn thing."

Franklin paused, "Jack, only a handful of people know this part of the operation--the administrator and us. He wants us to keep it that way, clear?"

"Crystal."

FAIRFAX, VA

National Security Advisor Jordan Zif looked through the tinted window of the Suburban as his driver approached the gated entrance. He was on his way to see CIA Director Lynn Bancroft in her affluent Fairfax County community. Zif had been in a marathon nine-hour meeting with the Israeli Defense Minister. It was 8:30 p.m. when he arrived at her residence.

"Thanks for coming by. Would you like anything to drink, Jordan?" Bancroft was unfailingly gracious, despite the late hour.

"A glass of wine would be wonderful, Lynn."

"I have a Merlot you might like."

"Excellent. I apologize for the late hour, but the meeting went far longer than we expected. With everything going on in Israel right now, there are hardly enough hours in the day to react to the latest crisis."

"The amount of intel is staggering. It sometimes takes me an hour just to get through all the e-mails for a single day. That's why I wanted to speak with you tonight. We finally got some intel on the assassin." She poured a taste of wine into a glass and offered it to him. He took a sip, nodded his approval and she filled the glass.

"Well Lynn, what do you have?" Zif asked.

"We think he's going to execute a hit somewhere in Central America in the next two weeks."

"Is the intel reliable?"

"Yes, we think so. A highly placed source intercepted a handwritten note from Viper to Roberto Fuerte, the Bogotá Cartel head of security. Here's a copy." Bancroft handed it to him.

Zif scanned the list and took a sip of wine, lost in thought for a few moments.

"We compared the handwriting with the first note, so we know it's authentic, or at least that the same person wrote both," she added.

"He wants C-4 and a Jeep delivered to PIA? This should make it easier to ID him, don't you think?"

"We think PIA is Panama International airport. We don't have an official office in Panama, but we do have some undercover agents stationed there in a storefront operation. I have already

181

contacted the station chief in Costa Rica and he'll have an entire team at the airport. I'm also sending a team from here to help out. The problem is that we don't know what day or time…a two-week time span is difficult to cover. And, one thing puzzles me, C-4 is not Viper's MO," Bancroft added with a worried look on her face.

"Anything big going on down there in the next few weeks?"

"The only thing…" she paused as she considered the possibilities.

"The certification conference!" Zif blurted, interrupting her before she could finish her sentence.

"Exactly! The one you and the AG are attending."

"I doubt we're the targets," Zif quickly dismissed her suggestion.

"I agree, but we still need to be careful."

"The situation has been problematic since the State Department declared the Mexican government hostile regarding drug enforcement and has started enforcing economic sanctions against them. We are meeting with the President to determine how to get them off the hit list. The Gusto's know we are not effectively thwarting their trafficking activities through Mexico, so the meeting, or its outcome for that matter, would be meaningless to him," Zif contemplated the implications.

"Yeah, that's my take on it too."

"So, who is the target? What is Viper up to?" His frustration was apparent.

"That is the million-dollar question. Frankly, we don't have enough intelligence to hazard a guess. The plan is to ID him at the airport and put him under surveillance," Bancroft added.

"What's the plan if we don't identify him?"

"Any ideas, Jordan? I'm listening."

CHAPTER 11

SAN FRANCISCO

Ryker had just walked out of the Federal Building onto Turk Street when he saw the red convertible Nissan 370Z pull up in the loading zone. Tara smiled at him as he maneuvered his long legs into the passenger seat and shut the door.

"It's great to see you." She gave him a friendly hug before nudging the Nissan into traffic.

"I appreciate you helping me find an apartment," Ryker replied as cars boxed them in on all sides in the slow-moving street traffic of San Francisco.

"Helping you find an apartment is such a small favor after what you did for me on the plane, I mean, I can't stop thinking about it. Joan, she…" her voice wavered.

"I know that she was your friend, Tara. I'm so sorry about what happened to her, but I'm glad that you're okay." He put his hand over hers as it rested on the gear shift knob.

"Yeah, I'm glad you're okay too. I promise, I am not going to be morose today. We are going to find you an apartment." She tried to shake off the solemn mood with an upbeat, determined tone. "Anyway, it's the least I can do for my government. You do still work for the government, don't you *Special Agent?"*

"Yes ma'am, I do."

"I'm glad that's settled. I found four places from online apartment rental sites." She handed him the printout of descriptions and photos.

"Impressive! You didn't tell me you were a realtor too!"

"I have a marketable skill-set of business abilities. First, we're going to look at one-bedrooms. Two are located in Noe Valley, one is in the upper Richmond and the other one is near Cow Hollow, around the corner from me."

Ryker admired the quaint streets of row houses as Tara circled around the block searching for a parking place. The apartments, however, were less impressive. They were downright cramped and decrepit. The hardwood floors creaked so loudly when he walked across them, he was afraid he was going to crash into the downstairs unit. The asking rent was a little too rich for his blood, but he wasn't about to admit that to her. The first thing he had learned in the academy was that women fell hard for the "government agent" mystique, but they got up and ran when they found out what entry level GS-7s took to the bank.

He liked the way she drove…an aggressive driver, who skillfully darted in and out of slow-moving lanes. *This woman definitely has spunk,* Ryker thought, as she downshifted, then accelerated to overtake a cable car.

"We'll go to the Richmond address next and then to the area where I live," she raised her voice over the road noise as the wind whipped her dark hair around her face. He admired her long, lean lines in her form-fitting jeans and white T-shirt. She looked casual, yet elegant. Her only piece of jewelry was a stainless steel Tag Heuer watch. With the sun shining off of her face, almost devoid of makeup, it was apparent why she was pursuing a modeling career…she was one of the most naturally beautiful women he had ever seen. He was glad she was driving, then maybe she wouldn't notice how much he was staring at her.

They looked at apartments for a couple of hours and he was shocked by the rental prices. He was relieved that she also thought the places they looked at were overpriced dumps.

"Where are we?" he asked, staring at the large mansions as they passed Filbert Street. He had heard about the city's steep streets, but he never imagined it would feel like he was reaching the top of the world's highest roller coaster.

"This is Pacific Heights, the tony section of the city where the socialites dwell. It's also one of the streets they filmed *Bullitt* on." She grinned at the tone of incredulity in his voice as she power shifted through the intersection causing the front end of the Nissan to lift as it sped down the steep street.

"Oh," Ryker was taken by surprise and didn't want to appear off guard as he felt his stomach jump at the sudden change of speed and descent continued, "Socialites, huh? Maybe one of them will rent me a room. Wow, what a view!" He took in the Golden Gate Bridge and Alcatraz in the distance.

Tara smiled to herself as she downshifted as they continued down the street.

He loved the apartment in Cow Hollow, the neighborhood at the base of Pacific Heights, but then who wouldn't? Figuring out how he was going to afford the rent was another problem altogether.

184

"My place isn't too far from here. Do you mind if we drop by there? I'm expecting a package from FedEx. Afterwards, we can catch an early dinner, if you have time. One of my favorite restaurants is on Chestnut Street, just a few blocks from here."

"Sounds good to me."

Within minutes, the red Nissan pulled into a driveway.

"You live here?" he asked in subdued surprise as he tried to reveal less intimidation than he felt.

"Yep, but it's a long story."

As they walked up the front steps, Ryker saw the FedEx package. Tara picked up the familiar white-and-blue box and handed it to him while she opened her purse and got out her keys. He noticed that the sender was Victoria's Secret.

As soon as they entered the house, the phone rang. Tara darted across the room and caught it on the last ring. The house was old, probably built in the 40s, but it was in excellent shape. Crown molding graced the rooms and the subdued eggshell-white paint gave off a warm, light glow. The furniture was predominately Mission-style…not reproductions, but classic, original pieces that were tasteful and expensive. *She has got to be from old money,* he told himself, a little worried that she might be way out of his league.

"It's a seven-day shoot in Mexico!" Tara couldn't contain the excitement in her voice as she hung up. She slipped off her ballet flats and left them on a small Persian carpet in the entryway.

"Your place is very impressive," he said with conviction.

"Thank you, Alex. I got lucky. Let's go into the kitchen, because I want to show you a few more rental ads on my tablet."

"Tara, I don't want to waste any more of your time. Don't get me wrong, I greatly appreciate your help, but to be honest, I can't afford something like this on my salary. As it is, I'm probably going to have to find a roommate to share expenses, at first. I haven't had a chance to check that out. Maybe there are other single agents in the same boat."

He felt uncomfortable bringing up his salary, but he didn't want to give her the impression that he could afford her lifestyle. He definitely could not and the sooner she knew that, the better. To his surprise, she looked up and flashed him a hundred-watt smile.

"Listen, you saved my life for Christ's sake. Tell you what, why don't you rent a room from me? I'm going to be gone a lot the next few months. There's no lease involved if you stay with me, so if you find something else you like, you can snap it up. What do you say to six hundred a month? You'd have your own bathroom, bedroom, and a garage space for your car, a premium commodity in this city, believe me. It would almost be like having your own place," Tara spoke quickly, running her sentences together as she moved around the kitchen, opening and closing cabinet doors.

He was momentarily speechless. When he didn't immediately reply, she turned to face him, holding a couple of glasses.

"There's been a rash of residential burglaries around here lately and people in the neighborhood must see me come and go in my uniform. I was just about to pay extra for an updated alarm system. You would be saving me money and at the same time, providing this place added security. You carry a gun, don't you?" she asked inquisitively.

Ryker couldn't help smiling at that comment and the fact that this gorgeous woman wanted him to be her roommate.

"That's very generous of you. You've got a deal…on two conditions."

"Only two?''

"Yes. The first one, dinner is on me. The second, you can fire me anytime if I'm a lousy security guard. Just give me a few days notice and I'll be out of your hair, okay?"

"You drive a hard bargain. Italian or sushi?"

"Italian, definitely. No dead fish." He felt ridiculously happy as they got into her car. He was in such a great mood, he didn't even mind the thick, cold fog that was beginning to blanket the city.

CARACAS, VENEZUELA

The flight to Venezuela had taken ten long, boring hours. Viper walked around and stretched his legs before he hailed a taxi. He dreaded getting into a cab after being cooped up on a plane for so long. He made it a point to switch cabs a few times during his trip to the FedEx office in downtown Caracas. After he picked up his package, he drove to his villa, thirty kilometers outside the city.

He opened the windows in the great room. The house smelled musty from being shuttered. He vacationed here during the month of August when he wasn't on a special assignment, otherwise, he used it for an occasional stopover.

By midnight, he had completed final preparations for his trip to Panama and Mexico. When he had finished, he relaxed in the expensive, overstuffed antique chair in front of the cold, dark fireplace and savored a glass of cognac as a candle's pungent fragrance filled the room. It smelled like the perfume *Opium* and reminded him of the dark hair beauty who had eluded him in Paris. Her scent had stayed with him for days.

PANAMA INTERNATIONAL AIRPORT

The command post on the fifth floor of the Panama International Airport Hotel had a perfect view of the airport and more importantly, the parking area where Viper's Jeep might be positioned. Sam McMillan, Costa Rica's CIA's Station Chief and the tactical leader of the operation, looked out of the hotel window. Five teams were deployed in the area. Three were in vehicles, one on foot, and another in a surveillance van. Since arriving two days earlier, McMillan's team had located three Jeep Cherokees they identified as potential targets.

Earlier that day, McMillan had received a change in tactical orders from Langley. Their new objective was to apprehend a suspected assassin, code named *Viper*...a "snatch and grab," as it was commonly referred to in the field...under the pretext of arresting an international counterfeiter.

On any extended surveillance operation, there was always the possibility of compromise, even with the use of electronic tracking devices and satellite coverage. Operating within a neutral government's borders also added an element of difficulty and danger.

"Delta-1 to base."

"Go ahead," McMillan replied.

"I think we might have another target approaching location number three. As soon as he gets closer, I'll get a picture," Delta-1 radioed from inside the surveillance van.

"I got him now," McMillan reported.

The operation was a little easier to cover because the vehicle at location two had left. McMillan glanced at his watch. It was 10:30 p.m. *This could be something,* he said to himself. He tried to get a visual ID on this new target, but it was too dark and he was too far away.

"Alpha-1, this is base," McMillan radioed again.

"Go ahead, base."

"Have your team focus on location number one. The rest of us will try to ID the new target."

"10-4."

"Our guy is definitely headed toward location three," Delta-1 came across slightly broken.

"This is Bravo-1, we just walked by our target. He's late twenties, dark skin, maybe Italian. Build...six feet, muscular, weight...175, carrying a gym bag. Meets the profile of our primary."

McMillan wished he had received more information about the vehicles they were watching.

"Base, this is Charlie-1, do we go on this one?"

"Affirm, let's ID this guy. Charlie-1, you make the grab. Bravo-1, your team has back-up," McMillan ordered.

"Okay, as soon as he makes contact with the Jeep, we'll roll on him," Charlie-1 replied.

"10-4."

McMillan watched through his Nikons as his team leaders started to position for the grab. The Nissan pulled alongside the BMW.

"Charlie-2 and I will make the initial contact. Charlie-3, he is yours if he gets by us. If there's a problem, I'll go high and you go low." Charlie team leader instructed his partner as their vehicle approached the area.

"10-4." Charlie-3 responded.

The adrenaline level in the cars notched up a few levels. Things could go to hell in a hurry.

"Okay, let's get ready," Charlie team leader radioed as he repositioned his vehicle in the same direction as the Jeep Cherokee parked at location three.

"The target is still walking toward the vehicle," Delta-1 crackled across the radio. The Jeep was parked in the tenth row of the north airport parking lot, next to a Mercedes and VW.

"The target is walking straight toward the Jeep at location three. In about thirty seconds, he should make contact," Delta-1 reported.

"Heads up, Charlie team. There is a military police vehicle at the opposite end of the parking lot," McMillan cautioned. "Hold until it clears the area."

"10-4."

Shit. McMillan subconsciously held his breath as he watched the military police vehicle cruise the area, hoping it was a routine patrol.

"Okay, target is at the Jeep and he just opened the back. He's looking around," Delta-1 alerted the group.

Charlie team sat anxiously in position, waiting to get the green light from McMillan. McMillan saw the military police vehicle exit the parking lot and head toward the main terminal.

"He's clear, so go for it," McMillan transmitted.

"Target is still at the back of the Jeep," Delta-1 radioed.

"10-4." The Charlie team leader slowly pressed the accelerator. "Okay, let's roll, nice and easy," he said as they started toward the Jeep.

"He just closed the hatchback and is walking toward the driver's side of the vehicle," Delta-1 radioed.

Charlie-1 wanted to grab him before he entered the Jeep. McMillan could see Charlie unit's vehicles moving in for the grab as he heard an electronic alarm beep loudly from his laptop.

"What now!" He rushed over and read the red captioned, rapidly blinking instant message. It was from Langley and it took a second for it to sink in. He grabbed the radio.

"10-22, 10-22! Abort the mission," McMillan radioed urgently as he looked through his binoculars. Charlie units were within two hundred feet of the target vehicle.

"10-4." All units responded instantly.

"We're on the wrong vehicle. Headquarters advised…target is Jeep Cherokee at location one. I repeat, location one. Reposition all units to location one!" McMillan barked the order.

MONTEREY, CA

Connor and Ryker took separate cars to Monterey, driving in a high-speed formation, moving in and out of traffic like F-18 Hornet fighter jets. Ryker had selected a two-year-old Mitsubishi as his official government vehicle. He loved his OGV. There had been a couple of newer cars to select from, but Ryker chose the faster and higher performance-rated car, even though it had a five-speed manual transmission. Most agents preferred automatic transmissions because simultaneously operating the hand-held radios and gearshift could be difficult during an active surveillance. Ryker hadn't had that experience yet.

Connor observed Ryker's driving skills…aggressive, but not reckless. Ryker maintained a safe distance in the follow car. Not many new agents could keep up.

He sensed that Ryker had the most important basic street instincts…knowing how to keep up with the situation and watching out for someone's back were not easily taught. Ryker had already demonstrated both abilities on land and in the air.

"Not bad driving for a rookie," Connor teased him when they got out of their cars.

"Well, you weren't challenging me today, boss. Why were we going so slow?" he retorted.

"Don't get cocky on me," Connor replied as they headed into the Resident Agent in Charge's office.

"Good morning Jack. How's it going?" Freman greeted them as they walked in.

"Dick, this is Alex Ryker, my new partner," Connor replied. The phone rang before they began their conversation.

"Freman yeah …really? When… what time? Do you know how many people? …I see no, don't do that… okay …thanks for calling." He hung up the phone.

"Our boys are back in town. That was the owner of the warehouse and he said that the same guys we ID'd last time called him, wanting to rent his repair facility for a week starting today."

"That confirms the information we have. The load should arrive anytime now," Connor replied.

"There's an office complex one block from the warehouse that has an unobstructed view of the target location and the marina. One of the Task Force agents assigned to this office got a key for us. His father-in-law is a doctor and has offices on the top two floors. He has given us complete access, day or night. We'll have a fixed surveillance point with minimal chance of compromise."

"Alex and I are going over to the Coast Guard station to see how the operation is progressing from there. Hopefully, they will spot this sub before it gets here. It sure would make things a lot easier if we knew where the sub was before the off-loading occurs."

PANAMA INTERNATIONAL AIRPORT

"Heads up, we might have a possible target walking toward the vehicle. He's coming from the east side of the airport parking lot," the Alpha team leader radioed.

"Smile!" One of the agent in the van snapped a photo from the surveillance camera.

"We got a good shot of him. He's about thirty-five, six-one, black hair, European, carrying a small black nylon case...and he's headed toward Charlie team," he added.

"10-4," Charlie 1 radioed.

"Man, I hope this is our guy. My back is killing me!" The team leader turned to his surveillance team. He checked the time. It was 11:05 p.m.

"Charlie-1, your guys are up again. Bravo is your backup." McMillan tried to get a fix on the new target in the low light conditions with his Nikon. With one trial run under their belts, McMillan repositioned Charlie units to be lead again and placed the Alpha units as perimeter security.

"Charlie-3, you come on the left and we approach from the right. We make contact and you back us up...same as last time," Charlie-1 radioed.

"10-4."

"He's walking straight for the Jeep. Be there in about thirty seconds," Delta-1 replied.

"10-4."

The teams slowly converged and moved into position. This time, it was going down.

U. S. COAST GUARD STATION, MONTEREY

"Mr. Connor, good to see you," Chief Petty Officer Steel greeted Connor and Ryker as they walked into the command center at the Monterey Coast Guard Station.

"Hey Chief, meet my new partner, Alex Ryker."

The men walked through the outdated, stark military-style office space. The scratched and dented steel gray desks and chairs had to have been purchased sometime before the Cold War. Connor always felt as if he were stepping back in time when he was there.

"Got some good news. We spotted the submarine and she should reach port late tonight. Strong currents may have helped her speed. The bad news is, a nasty storm is heading our way, we're in for a wet one," the chief added.

"That's the news we've been waiting for. Let me brief my bosses," Connor replied, and then phoned Freman and Cartwright to let them know.

"Boss, the Coast Guard has located the sub," Connor briefed him quickly.

"Good news, I'll send five agents down to assist in the surveillance of the load. Cade Jenkins will be your point of contact," Cartwright replied.

"Boss, can we leave Jenkins out of this one? Who else do we have?"

"Sorry, we're pretty thin around here and most of the office is on a 24-hour surveillance with group three, waiting around for a hundred kilos of heroin."

"All right but let me know if any of the other agents get freed up. We can use as many as you can spare on this one," he resigned himself to the situation. Jenkins was the last person he wanted on the team. Jenkins was arrogant, stubborn and prone to creating conflict. The newer agents hated working with him because of his condescending attitude. With everything else going on in the case, Connor dreaded the thought of trying to reign in the guy. He sighed and hung up the phone.

"Alex, do you remember how to get back to the Monterey DEA office?" Connor asked.

"Sure."

"Head back there, hook up with Freman and start planning the surveillance. Do yourself a favor and stop and stock up on some food to go, like fruit, energy bars, whatever you like to eat. You never know when you'll get the chance once the load gets in."

"Okay. When will I see you next?"

"Maybe late tonight after the load comes in. I will call you later to let you know what's going on at my end. Cartwright is sending five guys to help out on the surveillance so you'll probably be with them."

"Okay, see you later. Nice to meet you, Chief."

"Likewise."

"Rookie, eh?" the chief asked when Ryker had left.

"Yeah, but a really promising one. Tell me, Chief, what are the chances of the storm getting really bad tonight?" Connor asked staring out the window at the bank of dark clouds overhead.

"This one could be a real blower. The surf is already thundering so bad you can hear it from here," he replied as they stood for a few seconds looking out the window.

"Chief, I think I'll give Mr. Hatfield a call and see what he has to say about the storm."

"Mr. Connor, I know you realize this, but I'm only authorized to tell you about our part of this mission."

"Yeah, I was briefed by Franklin at JTF-5." Connor knew that Chief Steel was not assigned to the Coast Guard, but rather to the classified unit of the Fleet Numerical in Monterey, commonly referred to within the Navy Oceanography Command as the "Ocean Stalkers."

"We were lucky to get a fix on the sub again and we have provided the info to the SEALs so now we are good to go. That sub is very slippery in more ways than one."

PANAMA INTERNATIONAL AIRPORT

The target was about two hundred meters from the vehicle. He suddenly stopped, carefully scanning the parking lot as if trying to detect something or someone. He appeared apprehensive, like an animal sensing a trap.

"Our boy has stopped to sniff the air," Delta-1 radioed in a low tone from the surveillance van.

"Come on, pal, go to the Jeep and let's get this thing over with," McMillan said to himself as he adjusted his Nikons for a better view. Every agent was poised to strike, patiently waiting for the target to make his move.

Another individual was also watching the parking lot from the same hotel. He peered through high-tech binoculars from a hotel room a few floors above McMillan's. His jaw tightened when he saw a small glint of light from inside a van. *"Well, well, what do we have here?"* he thought as he tightened his grip and zoomed in.

"He's moving again. Give him ten seconds and he'll be at the Jeep." The transmission across the radio sounded like an excited whisper.

A man approached the Jeep and reached into his pants pocket for his keys, all the while scanning the area, clearly alert and on guard.

"He's at the Jeep and checking it out. This is definitely our boy," Delta-1 continued.

"10-4, let's roll!" Charlie-1 gave the order.

"We're right behind you."

The teams began to converge. McMillan watched as the Charlie units moved in for the grab. Both vehicles approached from opposite directions toward the rear of the Jeep. As the man placed the keys into the driver's side door, he saw the BMW approaching from his right side. He immediately turned around and saw the Nissan approaching from his left. He momentarily froze, fear written all over his face.

"He's made us," Charlie-1's transmission was curt.

The Nissan screeched to a stop and the agents leaped out of the car. They were joined by the agents from the BMW.

"We got you now, pal," McMillan breathed as he watched the events unfold.

The figure standing alone in the dark room five floors above picked up a small remote from a table as he watched through his binoculars. He slowly pulled the antenna out to full extension and flipped the switch. The red light flicked on and he placed his thumb on the red button. He casually walked to the bathroom and braced himself in the doorway.

"Click."

McMillan saw a bright flash a split second before he felt the shockwave from the blast. The explosion transformed the Jeep into a small inferno of flames and jagged projectiles of metal and glass ripped through everything within a 30 foot radius.

Viper emerged from the bathroom and walked to the window. Amused by the carnage below, he smiled at the column of billowing black smoke. He sat for a moment and enjoyed the cacophony of car alarms punctuated by the crackling sound of the fire. The plaintive wail of sirens in the distance stirred him from his transfixion and he reluctantly stood to leave. His expensive Italian shoes left a soft imprint in the carpet as he walked out of the room.

NAVAL POST GRADUATE SCHOOL, MONTEREY, CA

Watching the four SEALs check their scuba gear reminded Connor of his Marine platoon. They were focused on their mission, but all of them seemed relaxed. The team consisted of Lieutenant Commander (LCDR) Joe Hatfield, Lieutenant Junior Grade (LTJG) Hector Gómez, Chief Petty Officer (CPO) Ron Decker and Petty Officer First Class (PO-1), Payton Simmons. Hatfield and Simmons were assigned to SEAL Team-6 in Norfolk and Gómez and Decker to SEAL Team-5 in Coronado. Simmons and Decker were taking Spanish classes at the Defense Language Institute and Hatfield and Gómez were working on their Master's in Engineering at the Naval Post Graduate School. Hatfield had previously explained to Connor that the orders to utilize the SEALs had been authorized by Chief of Naval Operations himself. As a rule, SEALs did not go on any type of mission unless they were assigned to the same SEAL team. Had this been a combat mission and not a law enforcement support mission, a regular SEAL team would have been assigned. This mission was different. The SEAL teams welcomed the break from their academic training and relished the opportunity to work together on a high profile assignment.

"Sir, are you a swimmer?" Simmons asked as he strapped a Gruber knife to his leg.

"Yeah," Connor replied.

"Military or civilian?"

"Both."

"Any combat dives?" Simmons was curious.

"Five."

"Five?" His tone conveyed his surprise and he added, "Where was the last one, sir?"

"Near Yemen."

Gómez looked up from what he was doing. He was clearly curious. Connor knew that SEALs were always interested in what kind of action other guys had seen. It was one way they decided how much respect to offer up.

"Yemen …I heard about those ops. Those are the ones…"

"Come on, let's get moving. We're running late," Hatfield interrupted.

"Aye-aye, sir," Gómez responded, knowing that Hatfield intentionally changed the subject. Regardless, Gómez made eye contact with Simmons with an approving nod as they continued to pack their gear.

Most SEALs knew about the sensitivity of tracking terrorists in Yemen. Some members of SEAL Team-5 had been trapped during a hot zone extraction. What they didn't know was Connor, had been the lieutenant in charge of the Marines who rescued the team, although one SEAL lost his leg. Connor still remembered that night. He had helped carried the SEAL over a half mile to an alternate extraction point.

He didn't volunteer any more details, but he was glad that they had asked about his experience. He knew that they would respect him now and not question his authority to be involved with their highly secretive, elite club. He had been authorized to go with them as an observer, even though it was a covert mission. He had the military experience and he was the DEA case agent, but he wondered if the CIA had anything to do with him getting the assignment.

They loaded up in Dodge Caravans and headed to the Coast Guard station where the SEALs had staged their Zodiacs. The Navy had an agreement with the Coast Guard which allowed the SEALs to use the southern pier for training exercises. It had long been abandoned by the Coast Guard because of the shallow waters. It was common practice for SEALs on TAD, temporary additional duty, at either the Naval Post Graduate School or the Defense Language School to use the facilities to maintain their proficiency in diving and warfare skills. Many of these exercises took place at night, so the arrival of two vans full of SEALs would attract little attention.

"Here we are," Hatfield said as he parked the van at the entrance to the pier.

"I'll give the Coast Guard a call on a secure line to see if they have a fix on the sub," Connor volunteered.

"There is a secure line in the office if you want to use it. Here's the key," Hatfield replied, tossing the keys to Connor.

Connor entered the office and dialed Chief Steel. "We're in place on our end, Chief. Where's the sub?"

"It's about a mile from our location. The off-load should occur in about two hours. With the weather, my guess is they will move in closer to shore. We got them right off of Lovers Point."

"Thanks, Chief."

"Joe, they got the sub's location. The chief says it's only about a mile out," Connor turned to Hatfield.

"Good."

"How difficult do you think it will be for us to spot it if the weather doesn't let up?"

"Not difficult at all once we put one of these on it." Hatfield handed him a dark, teardrop- shaped object.

So that's the prototype, Connor thought. It appeared to be constructed of a light polymer composite material and was about the size of a softball that had been cut in half and stretched at both ends to make it more aerodynamic.

"It's called the T-82 tracker. We call it a lemon drop. In fact, we took the liberty of visiting the off-load boat, the Windy Sail, yesterday and placed one of these on it. Once the off-load occurs, we'll know exactly where the sub is."

Sneaky bastards, they don't always play by the rules. Once they get a mission, they'll do whatever it takes. Connor admired the forward thinking.

Simmons and Decker walked over to the floating shelter and unlocked the metal door. Several minutes later, twin turbo Mercury motors roared to life as the Zodiac jetted out of the shed and approached the pier. Within minutes, the gear had been loaded.

Connor called Ryker to check in before they deployed.

"What's happening on your end, Alex?"

"Hey Jack. We ID'd the boat..."

You're a day late, Connor thought.

"It's called the Windy Sail and it left a few minutes ago. They definitely have counter-surveillance in the area. They watched it leave the harbor and we are keeping an eye on them. We've been on the go since 5:00 p.m." Ryker reported.

Connor noticed it was 11:15 p.m.

"The Coast Guard has located the sub and it should be here in an hour. The off-load will probably take an hour and then they will be heading back to your location. I'll meet up with you when the Windy Sail returns to the harbor."

197

"Check. Our boys are moving, got to go."

Connor was relieved that Ryker hadn't asked too many questions about what he was doing. He didn't like the fact that he had to conceal this part of the operation with the SEALs from his partner. He returned to the crew outside.

"The Windy Sail left about five minutes ago," Connor relayed, rejoining the SEALs as they tightly squeezed into the Zodiac and headed out of the harbor.

PANAMA INTERNATIONAL AIRPORT

"Base to surveillance," McMillan barked into his hand-held radio. No reply.

"Base to surveillance," he repeated, observing movement in the parking lot.

"Charlie-1 and target are down. Everyone else is okay," Bravo-1 croaked, coughing from the smoke that permeated the air.

"Clear out." McMillan didn't have to give the order, his team of operatives was well trained in emergency extraction situations and damage control. They lifted the agent's lifeless body into the closest vehicle and quickly sped out of the area.

McMillan didn't know what to think. Was this an accident or were they set up? He didn't want to confront the Panamanians officially, he would have to wait and conduct his investigation through back channels. For now, he'd have his hands full with damage control.

MONTEREY BAY, CA

The Zodiac ride out of the port was not as rough as Connor had expected. The cold salt water sprayed Connor's face as the Zodiac hit one wave and glided over the next two. He and the SEALs held on to the outside handles tightly and kept a low profile as the Zodiac jumped across the waves. The storm was still about ten miles offshore and now wasn't expected to directly hit the Monterey Peninsula. The Zodiac was operating without running lights and the chief wore night vision goggles to navigate the craft. Simmons monitored the tracking device and Gómez watched through a pair of night vision binoculars.

"They should be about half a mile to our port side," Simmons spoke over the sound of the motor.

198

"I got em," Gómez replied after a few seconds.

"They should be stationary," Simmons added.

"With the cloud cover and the wind from the storm, we should be able to sneak right up to them," Decker directed his remarks to Connor.

"I can't believe how close they are to the Coast Guard station," Connor replied, trying to be heard over the wind.

"They are avoiding the storm, they're experienced seamen," Gómez commented.

They all nodded in agreement. Connor noticed that their equipment was brand new and much more streamlined than the series he had used when he was on active duty.

"What's that?" Connor asked.

"It's a short-range monitoring device that will guide us to the Windy Sail and back to the Zodiac. Works just like this large monitor, only shorter range."

"We didn't have those in my day."

"These babies are brand-spankin' new! Their range is up to a thousand yards under water," Hatfield bragged.

The SEALs always have the baddest and best new toys, Connor thought. The mission plan called for Hatfield, Gómez and Simmons to make the dive while Decker and Connor stayed behind in the Zodiac. Connor was thankful that it wasn't raining, although his companions would probably disagree. They preferred to insert during foul weather. There were typically fewer obstacles to deal with, notably people. While the SEALs adjusted their dive gear, Connor scanned the area with his night vision binoculars. Hatfield placed a device that looked similar to a watch on his wrist.

"I think I see the Windy Sail," Connor called out to the group.

"Here, let me see," Gómez asked.

Connor passed the binoculars to him and noticed the dark patches of kelp floating on the water's surface.

"That's it," Gómez confirmed as he handed the binoculars back to him.

"Okay, you guys know the drill. Let's go in. Heads up, we're in a kelp bed." Hatfield led the action.

"Aye aye, skipper." Simmons silently slipped overboard, followed by Gómez and Hatfield.

Beneath the dark surface of the waves, the three men swam in a wedge formation toward the two vessels. Their plan was twofold. First, they had to place the lemon drop on the bottom of the sub during the off-load in order to mask any noise they might cause. Second, they wanted to check the tracking device on the Windy Sail.

Hatfield carried the device that he was going to place on the sub in an equipment pocket on his dive gear. Gómez swam close to Hatfield as backup and Simmons provided perimeter security. Each of them was equipped with a special alert device that they could activate if any one of the team needed assistance. The device would transmit a pulse that they could feel from a band worn on their left wrists.

"Agent Connor, there are a couple of M-4s with suppressors in the bag in front of you in if a need arises," Decker said matter-of-factly.

"Thanks, Chief," Connor responded, unfazed. *Nothing like a couple of M-4s to keep you company out on the open sea.* Actually, he would have preferred a couple of .50-caliber machine guns. He tried without success to locate the team in the water. They had probably already submerged.

The three SEALs surfaced approximately one hundred feet from the Windy Sail to get a better fix on it. Hatfield gave a prearranged hand signal and the team submerged. The two vessels were at a dead stop.

When the team was about fifty feet from the vessels, Hatfield signaled to Simmons, indicating he wanted him to take up a perimeter position. Simmons acknowledged, swam to the surface and saw five people on the Windy Sail. Simmons saw a few sparks from an outboard engine and observed a smaller third craft brush against the Windy Sail.

The waves kept splashing his diver's mask as he bobbed up and down, trying to control his silhouette while observing the activity aboard the boat. He saw one of the crew members from the Windy Sail transfer some sort of sealed package to the small craft. Simmons heard voices but could not decipher their conversation. He reached into his swimmer's vest for his starlight night vision camera, but the boat had vanished into the darkness.

He refocused on the sub as the Windy Sail's crew began off-loading. He heard their voices but it was too far away to hear what they were saying. If he had been closer, he could have heard their animated Spanish chatter.

"Amigos, how was your boat ride?" The captain of the Windy Sail spread his arms wide in welcome.

"Bueno, bueno," the sub captain replied with a grin, then added, "Can you throw us your fishing net?"

A young deckhand flung it toward the sub. It hung in the air for a second, but the wind took it and it fell between the two vessels, catching on one of the Windy Sail's props. The deckhand feverishly tried to disengage the net, but it became more tangled with every wave.

"You imbecile! What have you done? You are making it worse. You cannot free it from the propeller while you are standing on the deck! You must go into the water! Go! Untangle it!" The captain roared at the unnerved young man.

"Yes, captain, at once," he replied as he jumped below to change into a wet suit.

Two other deck hands lowered a small inflatable into the water so that they could use it to ferry cocaine from the sub to the Windy Sail. They set up a pulley system so they could pull the raft back and forth between the two vessels, in addition to a crane they operated for the offload. Another deckhand stood guard with a Mac-10 submachine gun.

Hatfield stopped and exchanged signals with Gómez. The vessels were about twenty feet straight ahead.

CHAPTER 12

CIA HEADQUATERS, VA

"Bancroft," she answered sleepily into her cell phone. With one eye open, she squinted at the illuminated dials on the clock by her bedside. It was 2:15 a.m.

"Director, sorry to disturb you. This is the duty officer in the ops center. We have a Code Red situation. We need to go secure." Under normal circumstances, the duty officer would have waited until morning, but he knew the director was interested in all aspects of operation Black Knight.

"Give me one minute and call back," she instructed as she got out of bed and walked downstairs to the study. The phone rang. "Okay, go secure," she continued.

"We've had a situation in Panama City. We're still receiving information, but during the apprehension of Black Knight there was a detonation. One officer and the possible target were killed. I have the situation report and can e-mail it to you now."

"Go ahead"

"Yes ma'am. It's on the way."

"Does Stevens know about this?"

"Yes ma'am. He's on the way and he said he'll brief you when you get in this morning."

"Keep me posted." She hung up the phone and turned on her computer. It read:

FM: PANAMA CITY
TO: DIRECTOR CIA HQS
CC: DEP DIRECTOR FOR OPERATIONS
CC: DEP DIRECTOR FOR INTELLIGENCE
TOP SECRET - AGENCY USE ONLY
REF: HQS MGS #3545
SUBJ: OPS BLACK KNIGHT
AT APPROXIMATELY 2330, COSTA RICA STATION ALONG WITH SUPPORT UNITS FROM PANAMA FRONT OFFICE WERE ON DAY FOUR OF A 24-HOUR SURVEILLANCE OPERATION AT THE PANAMA INTERNATIONAL AIRPORT OF THREE POSSIBLE VEHICLES ASSOCIATED WITH

SUSPECT BLACK KNIGHT. A MESSAGE RECEIVED FROM HQS IDENTIFIED JEEP CHEROKEE VIN #12P21387777H987 AS THE PRIMARY TARGET VEHICLE. A SUSPECT MATCHING THE DESCRIPTION OF BLACK KNIGHT ARRIVED AT THE VEHICLE. APPROXIMATELY FIVE MINUTES LATER, SURVEILLANCE AGENTS ATTEMPTED TO APPREHEND SUSPECT AS HE ENTERED THE VEHICLE. AS THE APPREHENSION TEAM APPROACHED THE SUSPECT, AN INCENDIARY DEVICE DETONATED INSIDE THE TARGET VEHICLE. CAUSE OF DETONATION UNKNOWN AT THIS TIME. SUSPECT AND CASE OFFICER RAFAEL GUZMAN WERE KILLED INSTANTLY. THREE AGENTS RECEIVED MINOR INJURIES, TREATED AT THE SCENE. COLLATERAL DAMAGE IS MINIMAL. NO DIRECT CONTACT WITH LOCAL AUTHORITIES. COS WILL CONDUCT BACK CHANNEL INVESTIGATION. DETAILED REPORT TO FOLLOW IN 24 HOURS.

END

SAM MCMILLAN, CHIEF OF STATION, COSTA RICA

"Another agent killed," Bancroft muttered staring at the carpet. She had full confidence in McMillan but would have to wait until morning to call him and get an update. She went back upstairs to bed and tried to sleep, but her mind wouldn't stop racing. *What have we gotten into?*

MONTEREY BAY, CA

Hatfield pointed at the bow of the Windy Sail. He turned to Gómez, who gave a thumbs up signal. Visibility under water was only about twenty feet.

The young deckhand tugged on his wet suit. It was too small and he felt bound and restrained. He hoped it wouldn't take long as he awkwardly walked to the edge of the boat. He saw the waves lashing against the boat and tried to figure out some way to retrieve the net without going in.

The SEALs had moved within an arm's reach of the sub. They were directly underneath the sub when Hatfield affixed the T-82 tracking device to the sub's hull. He double checked it to make certain that it was properly secured.

Suddenly, something caught Gómez's attention. He spun around to his right. Scanning the area, he moved his eyes left to right and back again. Nothing but darkness. He couldn't shine his underwater flashlight for fear of disclosing their position. Hatfield approached Gómez on his left side, signaling that the device had been installed and pointing in the direction of the Windy Sail.

The deckhand kept staring at the water, dreading jumping into the frigid cold.

"Jump in that fucking water and get that net now!" the captain bellowed, startling the deckhand, making him almost lose his balance.

Gómez saw movement in the water. The surge was so strong, he found it hard to maintain his position. Simmons's eyes broke the surface and he peered through his black scuba mask, eyeing the man on the deck in a wetsuit and scuba gear. *Now's the time to finish this job, guys,* Simmons told himself. He kept his eyes trained on the area where he had seen the movement. At first he thought it was sea life, but as the body broke the surface, he immediately recognized the outline of tanks. Hatfield also saw the intruder but hoped that he wouldn't see them. Simmons submerged and swam toward his teammates.

The shock of the cold water on his face temporarily disoriented the deckhand. He frantically attempted to right himself by grabbing onto the long, streaming kelp. He blew his nose and tried to clear the water from his mask. That's when he made eye contact with the dark figure directly in front of him. He frantically grabbed his knife in disbelief and swung wildly at Gómez. His blade moved in slow motion through the surging water.

Gómez grabbed his wrist and deflected the knife away but doubled over in pain as he struggled. The deckhand was still coming at him, desperately trying to rip his mask off. Gómez doubled over, searing pain ripped through his leg. He couldn't understand it, the knife had missed. As he and the other diver rolled over and over in a violent struggle, Gómez saw it out of the corner of his eye. The white underbelly was unmistakable. If he could have screamed at that moment, one word would have formed on his lips...SHARK!

Hatfield swam toward them at top speed and drew a high-voltage, underwater stun gun from his vest. A military prototype, it had been specially designed to disable sharks, but he couldn't see

204

the shark anymore. All he could see was churning water filled with air bubbles swirling around the two dark forms that were locked in battle. Suddenly, the shark darted directly in front of him. He didn't have time to get a clear shot. He silently shouted Gómez's name.

Jagged teeth ripped into the deckhand's side. Gómez pushed away with all his strength and managed to break free. He swam away as fast as he could. Hatfield headed directly for the shark, leading with the stun gun. He connected with the exposed underbelly. The charge launched the shark upward and it jetted toward the surface, entangling itself in the net as it broke the surface of the water.

"Shark!" the captain yelled, as plastic-wrapped bricks of cocaine bounced out of the inflatable into the water. One of the guards on the Windy Sail saw the thrashing shark's fin in the net.

"Shark!" He shouted and simultaneously fired a wild burst of 9mm rounds from his Mac-10 directly into the ocean.

The captain turned in the direction of the shots and yelled, "Stop, you idiot! Man in the water."

Simmons resurfaced and heard the gunshots. He submerged and swam toward his teammates, hoping they were clear of whatever was going down.

Barely conscious, the deckhand tried to surface. The blinding pain that had ripped through him was starting to dull and his body felt heavy and numb. He let himself float, his eyes half closed, not needing to see where he was going, as long as it was up.

Hatfield saw the bullets leave water string signatures as they zinged past Gómez's head and he pushed his legs through the water as hard as he could, trying to reach him. Gómez winced in pain as he inspected his leg, then gave Hatfield the signal that he was okay.

The great white shark flashed by them and barreled into the limp, dark form floating to the surface. The shark's teeth bit through the black neoprene of the wetsuit into fragile flesh, ripping a jagged hole. A long piece of intestine trailed from the shark's mouth, twisting and twirling in the surge. The diver's eyes were wide open. They glazed over behind his water-filled mask as he slowly floated down.

Hatfield and Gómez started to swim back to Simmons and the Zodiac. Hatfield hit the alert button on his wrist and Simmons felt the pulse instantaneously. He turned on his underwater light, hoping that Hatfield and Gómez would key on the light.

Near the ocean floor, two young sharks mauled the mangled remains in a feeding frenzy. Blood was invisible in the black, frigid water.

Hatfield saw a light ahead and swam toward it. When the three men converged, Simmons saw the dark blood trail frothing from the torn wet suit around Gómez's leg. They placed their arms around his waist and helped him back to the boat. They fought the underwater surge with every movement. Sometimes it didn't feel as though they had made any headway at all.

"Jack, we got trouble," Decker looked at him as he felt the sensor pulse against his wrist. "Do you see anything out there?"

"Negative."

The pain in Gómez's leg was almost unbearable as he struggled to swim. He felt his body getting weak from the loss of blood, but bit down on his mouthpiece and controlled his breathing as he'd been trained to do. Now was not the time to surrender to panic. He knew that.

"Chief, do you think we should try to get closer to them?" Connor asked, his eyes searching the dark swells.

"No, let's wait a few minutes. They'll get as close as they can and then surface. We should see them soon."

Hatfield swam as fast as he could, worried that the sharks might follow the blood trail and attack them again. Their only saving grace was that there were three of them. He hoped the sharks would be less likely to attack a group than they would a single swimmer. He had never been so relieved in his life as when he gave his team the signal to surface. Their heads bobbed on the surface and Hatfield made visual contact with the Zodiac about twenty-five yards away.

"Chief, I see them! There!" Connor pointed. The engines kicked in and Connor caught a taste of briny salt water as a wave broke over the Zodiac's stern.

Hatfield and Simmons stopped swimming when they saw the Zodiac headed toward them. Gómez relaxed and let them support his weight. Hatfield pulled out his stun gun and rotated his body around, facing in the direction of the Windy Sail. The Zodiac came to a complete stop a few feet away from the swimmers.

"Shark bite! Chief, get the med kit!" Hatfield yelled.

Connor swung the M-4 over his neck and helped Decker pull Gómez into the boat. The gapping rip in his leg revealed the slick, dark red of exposed muscle. Water rushed inside the boat as Simmons hoisted himself into the Zodiac.

"Shark!" Connor yelled as a shark jetted by a few feet away. He forcefully jerked Hatfield into the Zodiac.

"Shit!" Hatfield swore…half of his full foot swim fin had been ripped off, exposing his toes.

Decker took control of the Zodiac and headed for the Coast Guard station at full speed. He scanned the water for signs of the predators, but all he could see were whitecaps on the waves.

MONTEREY, CA

"M-5 to M-1."

"Go ahead," Freman answered from the office building that they were using as the surveillance command post.

"They should be finishing the offload shortly," one of the Monterey DEA agents radioed. The last two hours went by quickly as the Windy Sail crew and a few others transferred the cocaine into the warehouse.

"10-4."

"Do you think there will be any movement tonight?" Ryker asked Freman.

"Probably not. Last time they stashed the cocaine in the warehouse for one week. I don't know how they hid it from the day crew, but they did. They could move it anytime, but I think it will be at least a couple of days before they do."

"Why don't you get some sleep, Alex? One of my agents can man the command post." Freman directed more than asked.

"I think I'll hang out here tonight, I'm not tired," Ryker responded enthusiastically. "Plus, I don't want to miss anything."

Freman smiled but didn't say anything. It wouldn't do any good to discourage him. It was Ryker's first operation and neither hell nor high water could have kept him away from the action.

"Hey, anything going on?" one of the Monterey agents asked, entering the command post.

"No."

The agent took Ryker's binoculars and saw the off-loading crew disbanding.

"You know, there were ten crew members when they left. Only nine came back." The agent handed the binoculars back to Ryker.

"What happened to the tenth?" Freman asked.

"Don't know. One is missing." The agent replied.

"M-4 to M-1, they're closing the door. I see two more inside," one of the Monterey agents radioed.

"Copy that. It's your show now. I'm going home to get some sleep," Freman patted the agent on the back on his way out.

"Okay, kid, you've got the helm. I'm going to brief the new shift. If anything happens, hit me on the Nextel, we'll be downstairs in the parking lot, M-2 is my call sign." The agent grinned at the expression on Ryker's face as he turned to leave.

"Yes sir!" Ryker got a cold diet Coke out of his cooler and drank it in a few gulps. He hoped the caffeine would keep him alert.

The first 15 minutes went by fast as Rkyer stared out the window. Suddenly his head jerked to the left. The sound of an approaching slow freight train grew louder as it started to pass in front of the warehouse, as the agents continued their briefing.

Ryker's jaw dropped when he saw the warehouse's huge garage door begin to open. He grabbed his radio, "SF-220 to M-2." No response.

"SF-220 to M-2," he repeated loudly, his tone more urgent.

Ryker watched the brake lights of the thirty-foot U-Haul truck as it backed out of the garage.

"SF-220 to M-2!" Still no response.

"*Shit!*" Ryker looked around the empty warehouse, uncertain what to do now. The parking lot where M-2 was briefing his team was on the other side of the warehouse where he couldn't see them.

M-2 didn't hear Ryker's communications. The radio was in his back pocket and the vibration and noise from the train obliterated the sounds from the radio.

Ryker made a final attempt to raise the agent on the radio as the U-Haul began to drive away. He was shocked to see the truck head the wrong direction down the one-way street, away from the surveillance team. As the train continued to pass, he made his first command decision. He ran down the stairs to his car. When he reached the bottom of the stairs, he tripped and fell. The palms of his hands absorbed the impact of his fall as he slid across the floor. He bounced, got up and ran outside. The truck brake lights were disappearing around a turn.

Ryker jumped into his OGV and felt a brief rush of relief that he had parked on the same side of the railroad tracks as the departing truck. He revved the engine and popped the clutch as the Mitsubishi shot forward. As he turned onto the street to follow the truck, his back end slid out and his tires started spinning, trying to grip the road. He turned the steering wheel to the left to compensate for the slide and brought the car under control, then jammed the accelerator to the floor. The truck was nowhere in sight.

Ryker downshifted into second and made a hard right into two-way traffic. He skidded, barely missing a pickup truck. As soon as he made the turn, he saw the truck's tail lights.

"I got you!" Ryker exhaled in relief. "SF-220 to surveillance team." Still no answer. The truck turned left at the next intersection. Ryker was almost there.

"SF-211 to SF-220," came the reply.

"Connor! Yes!" Ryker said to himself as he keyed his radio, "Jack, the load is on the move. I'm the only one on it, I couldn't raise the surveillance team."

"What's your twenty?"

"Eastbound on Charles Street, headed toward Highway One."

"10-4. I'm two minutes from your location."

M-2 heard his radio squawk after the train finally passed.

"M-2 to SF-220. Status report?" the agent transmitted.

"I tried to raise you! The truck left about four minutes ago. We're on Charles Street headed toward Highway One," Ryker responded.

"Break, where are you now, 220?" Connor interrupted.

"Just entering Highway One, northbound."

"10-4, I see you."

"10-4." Ryker was so relieved, he almost felt faint.

"SF-211 to M-2."

"Go ahead." The agent was running toward his car, embarrassed that he had blown it and that a rookie was saving his ass.

"Your team should be able to intercept us in about fifteen minutes. The target vehicle is only going fifty-five," Connor radioed within eye sight of Ryker's tail lights.

"10-4," the agent replied, out of breath.

Connor switched to a vehicle-to-vehicle frequency that could not be heard by any of the other surveillance team members. "Good work, Alex. What happened?"

Ryker briefly explained.

Connor contemplated the near screw-up and shook his head.

"Jack, I almost lost them. It happened so fast"

Connor interrupted, "You didn't lose 'em and we've got 'em now. The rest of the posse will be here shortly, the rest is easy…don't worry, that U-Haul can't lose that shit hot Mitsubishi of yours, right?"

"Hell no!" Ryker replied indignantly.

LANGLEY, VA

Lynn Bancroft's suburban pulled up to the CIA's front entrance where two armed security guards were waiting to escort her to her office. Because of the possibility of terrorist attacks, the security agents used different routes to and from the director's residence and used different entrances when they arrived at Langley.

"Phil, I don't think I'll be going anywhere today," she told her bodyguard. The director showed no signs of her sleepless night. It was a prerequisite for the job.

Of the many responsibilities of the security division, the most demanding was the director's protection detail. It was like working for the Presidential detail of the U.S. Secret Service. There were many terrorist organizations and individuals who had threatened to assassinate the director of the CIA, but no director in the history of the agency had ever been killed. Her bodyguard was committed to keeping it that way.

"Morning, Emma," Bancroft walked straight to her office.

"Good morning, ma'am. I heard the terrible news about our case officer. There are fresh bagels and coffee if you feel like eating something."

"Thanks. Any updated information?"

"Stevens can brief you in the executive conference room whenever you're ready. We also just received aerial photos of the explosion. They are on your computer screen."

"I don't know what I'd do without you, Emma. Please call Greg and tell him we can start the briefing now. And get the DDO and DDI up here too," she instructed, referring to the Deputy Director of Operations and the Deputy Director of Intelligence.

"They are already in the conference room."

"Morning, ma'am," Stevens greeted her as Bancroft entered the conference room and sat at the head of the table. She motioned for the men to sit down as she looked at the 100 inch plasma monitor on the wall and watched the slow-motion video of burning wreckage in a parking lot.

"I spoke with McMillan about thirty minutes ago. We don't have any leads yet. He expects his investigation will take at least a week." Stevens and the others looked grim as he continued. "There are two big questions. Was it an accident? And is Viper dead, or was this staged to make us believe that Viper is dead? Until we know, we need to assume that Viper is still alive and continues to be a threat."

Bancroft nodded in agreement. The mood in the room was somber. Yet another CIA officer had been killed in the line of duty and they had no idea who was behind it.

Stevens continued, "I'm very concerned about the safety of our source inside the cartel. If this was a setup and Viper or the cartel shot callers think that there's a leak, the first thing they are going to do is to clean house. I'm worried about exposing Striker. I strongly recommend that we contact Bogotá and suggest sanitizing her and having no contact unless there is an emergency. They will kill her...and she'll be tortured for a long time before they let her die."

Bancroft listened intently. He made perfect sense. She remembered the last time he had cautioned her. At that time, he had been a new analyst and he'd told her about another situation that he had insisted couldn't wait. The information he had provided had thwarted an attempted assassination of a former U.S. President on foreign soil.

"I've prepared an emergency action request for Bogotá. Would you mind reading it now so that it can go out ASAP?" Stevens asked.

Bancroft didn't bother reading it, she signed it and pressed the telephone intercom summoning her assistant. "Anything else?" Bancroft asked as she stood up.

"That's it for now."

"Let me know when you develop anything significant."

"Yes, ma'am."

"Emma, please see that this gets sent out now. And, get the FBI and NSA Directors on a conference call."

When the briefing concluded, Bancroft returned to her office and sat at her desk in silence for a few minutes. The familiar aroma of freshly brewed coffee brought her some small relief and she closed her eyes and took a few deep breaths. She picked up a framed picture of her husband. His arm was draped around her shoulders and they were smiling on a beach in Maui...their last vacation together before his death. She couldn't believe how long it had been. She wondered how long it would be until she felt like smiling again as she opened the dead CIA officer's personnel file.

"Ma'am, Stevens would like to have another word with you if you have time."

"Send him in, Emma."

"I just thought about something ...I talked to a NEST technician this morning and he told me that there was a training mission last night off the coast of California," he paused, referring to the Nuclear Emergency Support Team. "They detected a trace of elevated radiation on the Monterey coast. They think it might be another false reading from their new equipment. But, what if it wasn't false? What if it's connected to the cartel and last night's shipment?"

"I'll make a phone call. Thanks, Greg." Bancroft waited until Stevens closed her office door, then dialed a number on her phone.

"Derek, thanks for the heads up last night. Are you still on it?"

"Yeah, as we speak, Lynn. I'll let you know when it reaches its final destination," Derek Schmidt, the NEST Director advised.

"Thanks, Derck." Somehow the coffee didn't smell quite as comforting as she considered how much deceit her position required.

MORGAN HILL, CA

"SF-212 to SF-211."

"Go ahead," Connor responded.

"I need to go to the head, can you get someone to take point?" a surveillance agent radioed.

"I got it, 211," Ryker replied before Connor could respond.

"10-4."

The U-Haul truck had stopped at a run-down, dingy restaurant on the outskirts of town. That gave the DEA surveillance team time to regroup.

Connor felt his Nextel vibrate on his belt.

"Jack, it's Tony," Franklin's deep and formal voice came across the line.

"Yes sir."

"We're getting a strong signal from the electronic tracker and should be able to pinpoint its location when it docks." Franklin was guarded over the unsecured line.

"That's good news. How is Gómez?" Connor asked.

"A few stitches, but he's doing well. Hatfield told me about their outing and said that you were very helpful."

"We were lucky."

"Yeah, you sure were."

"How are things on your end?"

Connor spent a couple of minutes giving him a brief update.

"One more thing, Jack, did your CI mention anything about any other visitors?"

"No sir," Connor lied. He hoped that he could complete his undercover assignment before he was exposed.

"One of the SEALs mentioned that he saw a small craft in the water, but thought it was part of the offload crew. I was just curious, that's all. Gotta run, keep in touch Jack."

Before Connor could put his Nextel on his belt, he felt his iPhone vibrate. He switched phones and saw the words *Secure Incoming* on its screen.

"Jack?" The CIA Director's tone was curt.

"Yes ma'am?"

"Are you guys on the delivery?"

"Yes, we're in Morgan Hill, about an hour from San Francisco."

"Good. Looks like that package your CI mentioned was picked up at sea separately."

"I know, Franklin just told me. One of the SEALs saw the delivery, but he thought it was part of the offload crew."

"What did you tell Franklin?"

"Nothing."

"Good. Hopefully that package will lead us to the terrorist cell. If not, I believe the cartel will. Continue what you're doing, Jack. Focus all your efforts on the cell and the assassin. Anything I get, I'll pass to you immediately. Keep up the good work."

"Yes ma'am," he said as the line went dead.

COSTA RICA INTERNATIONAL AIRPORT

It was a balmy 95 degrees at Costa Rica International Airport. People moved about the open-air terminal, walking hurriedly from place to place. The airport was always crowded on Mondays. Viper stood in the main terminal observing the in-bound flight times. Here, security was very lax by comparison to other airports. He liked that. He knew Roberto would be apprehensive about flying on a commercial flight rather than on his own private jet, but Viper had specified this manner of travel and Roberto had reluctantly acquiesced to his request.

Roberto and his bodyguards took a taxi from the terminal to the Hilton Hotel located on the strip, exactly as he had directed. Within ten minutes, they had checked into their suites. Viper cautiously followed their cab and detected no surveillance. Satisfied that they hadn't been followed, he returned to his hotel. He stepped into the air-conditioned lobby, took the elevator and walked directly to his room.

Roberto picked up the phone on the first ring. "Yes."

"Go back down to the lobby and take a taxi to the Costa Rica Intercontinental Hotel, now," Viper instructed.

Roberto briefly considered arguing. He was tired and hungry and did not want to go anywhere else, but he quickly dismissed the idea. He grudgingly agreed and tried to suppress his annoyance. *If*

Viper requires these measures, he must have a very good reason,
Roberto worried as he came up with the plan to get away from the
hotel undetected.

He told his bodyguards that he would be back in an hour and
that they were not to follow him. They strenuously objected until he
harshly rebuked them. They knew better than to second-guess
Roberto and he knew better than to second-guess Viper.

He arrived at the Intercontinental Hotel in fifteen minutes. It
was high season for tourists and the hotel was booked for a medical
convention. As soon as Roberto entered the lobby, he became
irritated at how crowded it was. He walked toward an empty seat
near the concierge desk and within a minute, the concierge walked
over to him.

"Excuse me, are you Señor Roberto?" she asked.

"Yes."

"I have a message from Señor Victor." She smiled and
handed him a white envelope.

"Thank you."

He opened the envelope and carefully read the note: *Meet me
at the bar near the pool. V*

He stood up and walked to the pool bar. He wondered how
much longer this charade was going to last as he scanned the crowd
for the familiar face. Seeing none, he sat at an empty table. This cat-
and-mouse game was beginning to make him angry.

"Roberto," Viper spoke in a hushed tone from behind
Roberto's chair. "Walk with me," he commanded as he took
Roberto by the arm.

Roberto felt the power in Viper's strong grip. He didn't like
feeling vulnerable or intimidated and he was feeling both. He let
himself be led across the room to a table in a deserted part of the bar
where they sat down.

"You have another mole, Roberto," Viper spit the words in a
harsh whisper.

"We heard about the explosion in Panama. What happened?"
Roberto tried to speak calmly, careful to conceal his mounting
anger.

"I hired someone to pick up the Jeep at the airport. As he
walked toward the Jeep, I saw a team of American agents surround
him in the parking lot. I had rigged the Jeep with the C-4 and used a

remote to detonate the device just before he opened the door. It killed him and one of their agents. For all the Americans know, it was me who died in the explosion. Maybe they think the C-4 accidently detonated, or maybe they think that someone else planned to blow me up when I picked up the Jeep. I don't know if they bought it, but I do think it gives us more time." Viper explained the killings in a tone as casual as a meteorologist reporting sunny weather the day after a hurricane.

"Americans." Roberto replied in distain.

"Yeah, they're not stupid. They know the cartel was behind the hit on Sanchez in Quantico. That embarrassed them. I had no doubt that they would double their efforts to identify me. As you can see, I planned contingencies to counter their lame efforts."

Roberto listened intently and occasionally nodded.

"Someone told them I would be at the airport."

"I...I cannot believe this has happened," Roberto stammered nervously, avoiding direct eye contact.

"There is no need for you to fear. I do not think you betrayed me."

"My friend, I would never betray you. You are like my brother, like blood itself. I will find the traitor among us and the traitor will die!" Roberto replied emphatically as their eyes locked.

"I knew that if anyone ever identified me, it would be because of a communication breach. On my current assignment, we deviated from communication protocol. I set my own trap to see if your communications had been compromised. That's why I requested the C-4 in the note, it was certain to get their attention."

"What do you want us to do now?"

"You have a mole, a highly placed mole who must be exterminated."

"Joaquin is going to explode! We hand-picked everyone around us. I suspect no one yet doubt them all." Roberto's anxiety turned into anger and sweat broke out across his forehead.

"You must find out who it is and eliminate them immediately. The key to the leak is with the list I gave you. Identify every person who saw it and you will have your suspects."

"Very few people knew of the list, even fewer saw it. The possibilities are unacceptable!"

"Do you still want me to carry out the assignment?"

"Yes, but only if you feel certain that your identity has not been compromised. Eliminating that target is Joaquin's highest priority, because he is an immediate threat to our organization," Roberto's tone was emphatic.

"I do not think that I have been compromised. Even with the leak, all the Americans probably suspect is that the hit will occur somewhere in the near future in Central or South America. Best case scenario, they think I'm dead. Worst case, they are still on the alert. But they don't know who the target is, so I think it is safe to proceed as planned."

"What do you propose?"

"We must finalize our plans here and now, in person, so that there is no chance for another breach of our security."

"Agreed."

"Listen carefully, Roberto, I have a few ideas on how to catch your traitor," Viper lowered his voice and leaned across the table.

BOGOTÁ, COLOMBIA

Maria opened the shutters over her bedroom windows and looked beyond the compound toward the village. She saw a green flag hanging from a nearby rooftop, the prearranged emergency signal. She was to leave immediately and meet her contact at the agreed upon location. She left the shutters open, her signal that she had seen the warning. She hurriedly dressed and went out the back, thankful that she didn't run into any other members of the staff.

She got into the staff car and drove to the farmer's market. The market had been a good drop site and rendezvous point because she could always purchase fresh fruit and vegetables without raising suspicion.

When she arrived, a few minutes before 7:00 a.m., the market was opening. All of the merchants were rolling back their canopies and stacking colorful fruits and vegetables into neat rows.

Heist watched her from across the street. He sat on a bench, drinking espresso and reading the morning paper as traffic, mostly taxis, helped shield his surveillance point. He recognized several older women who walked to their favorite vendors and began squeezing the produce to choose the best pieces. He knew their weekly rituals almost as well as he knew Striker's.

Striker stopped and made small purchases at two other stands before she went to Pepe's. Pepe worked for Heist.

"How are the strawberries today?" Striker asked.

"They are fresh, see?" Pepe held the large basket toward her and leaned in closer. "Meet Match at the safe house in ten minutes," he added quietly without moving his lips

"How much?" She paid for the strawberries and pretended to browse at another stand for a few minutes.

She tried not to appear nervous, but she knew something was terribly wrong. She looked down the street, hoping she might see Match, but knew it wasn't likely. She had never seen him on the street. She walked around the block and went through several alleys, making sure that she was not being followed, and then walked toward an apartment that was a block and a half from the café.

She descended the back steps and entered the large underground garage. It was empty except for a few cars and a brown van. She made her way to the parked van and just before she reached it, the driver's side door suddenly opened. She recognized one of Match's associates,

Ricardo Tomales, a new case officer recently assigned to the Embassy. He got out of the van and closed the door behind him as Striker got in on the other side.

"Good morning. It's good to see you," Heist greeted her as usual, but the expression on his face was different.

"What's wrong?" she asked in alarm.

"The cartel may suspect that they have another mole and figure out the connection to the list you got for us. You've got to lay low. You need to retrieve the camera immediately. They could search your room anytime and if they find the camera, they will kill you."

"I understand." Her face was flush and her hands trembled, but she knotted them into fists determined to fight the fear.

"You'll also need to destroy anything else that ties you to me," he cautioned.

"I will go to the meat market after breakfast and drop it off."

"Roberto may set a trap, so be careful. Don't try to get any information, especially from secure areas of the compound, until you hear from us again. If I need to talk to you, I'll signal you. Don't worry, you'll be okay, Maria. We'll get you out if we think they are on to you." Heist rarely used her real name. It sounded foreign to her, as if he was speaking to someone else.

"I have a few ideas on how to keep Roberto occupied. You better get going." He put his hand on her arm and gave a gentle squeeze.

"Thank you for warning me." She touched his hand on her arm and wondered if she would ever see him again.

"You're my best operative and we will keep you safe," he reassured her.

He peeked outside the van window and saw his partner give him the sign that everything was all clear.

"Okay, you'd better get going. Don't worry, Maria, everything will be all right." Heist opened the van door and she was off, moving hurriedly across the cement floor.

In his twenty-year career as a case officer, he'd only lost one, and that had been because a mole within the agency had compromised several highly placed operatives. The Bogotá Cartel was a powerful and intimidating enemy, much like the Soviet Union had been during the Cold War. Each had many highly placed spies. He didn't want to think about what they would do to Maria if they suspected that she was working with the CIA. He hoped he would be able to keep his word to her.

He considered the options after she left. He had come up with an extraction plan a year earlier. He had arranged to have a Special Forces unit assigned to the agency in Bogotá to assist their black operations against the drug cartels during crisis situations. It had caused a shit storm, but in the end, the President had signed a top secret Executive order that allowed the U.S. Special Operation Command to assign a twelve-man unit to the CIA in Bogotá. SOCOM rotated the assignment between the Army's Delta Force detachment and the Navy's SEAL Team Six. Each unit was broken into two teams…A team and B team…six operators each, who stood twelve-hour shifts, seven days a week. They had a rapid deploy time of 30 minutes or less. He thought about Striker and hoped to hell that would be quick enough.

OAKLAND, CA

The surveillance back to the Bay Area was uneventful. Each agent covertly followed the truck to Continental Shipping Lines, located at the Port of Oakland container terminal.

Where to next? Connor wondered as he observed containers from overseas arrive to be transported by truck or train throughout the U.S.

"U.S. Immigration and Customs Enforcement. How may I direct your call?"

"A.J. Steward?"

"Please hold."

"Steward."

"Thank God you're in early, A.J. It's Jack Connor. I need your help."

"What's up?"

"We're following a load that we thought was going to a stash location, but instead they delivered it to Continental Shipping Lines at the Port of Oakland. We're on it now but we need to find out where it's going. Can you help us out?" Connor asked.

"Sure, I'll make a couple of phone calls. We have a crew of inspectors out there and I should be able to find out something pretty quick."

"Thanks, that's great," Connor replied appreciatively.

The surveillance agents sat in their cars, waiting. There was no movement from the truck. Ten minutes later, Connor's Nextel buzzed.

"Jack, according to the manifest, the *goods* will be put into a container in a couple of hours, loaded onto a train across the street, then railed to Miami later tonight. The manifest says it's sugar," Steward reported.

"Sugar and Miami, how original is that?"

"Believe it. Listen, we have an office at the terminal. Do you remember where it is?"

"Is that the office behind the big crane?"

"Yeah. You or one of your guys go over there and ask for the duty inspector. I called him. He'll give you all the details on the delivery and help you out. Do you need me out there?"

"We got enough guys, but come out if you want," Connor replied.

"I'll leave it up to you professionals but call me if we can help out."

"Thanks, A.J."

Connor dialed the number to JTF-5. "Mr. Franklin, please."

"Stand by, sir," the young Marine corporal answered from inside the secure SCIF (Sensitive Compartmented Information Facility) in the op center at JTF-5.

"Franklin," he answered abruptly as he read the classified message traffic on his computer screen.

"Here's a twist for you. We followed the load to Continental Shipping Lines and the cocaine is being railed to Miami."

"Well, well, what are the rats up to?" Franklin paused for a few seconds before continuing, "I got an idea. Can you hold on for a second?"

Franklin dialed an extension within the office and waited for a few moments until another voice answered, "Naval Supply Center." This was a front for the classified NEST office located only a few blocks from the JTF-5 office.

"Hey, it's Franklin, I need a favor?"

"What is it?"

"You guys have any movement scheduled in the next two weeks?"

"Not that I know of."

"Good, would you mind if we used one of the rail cars for a couple of days?"

"Nope. There's an empty one over in building five at the Naval Supply Center. It's ready to go."

"Great! We need it now for a controlled delivery of seven tons of cocaine to Miami. Do you think you could get it moved over to Continental Shipping Lines at the Port of Oakland in the next hour?"

"In the next hour? Are you shitting me?"

"Nope. I know it's short notice, but it's a cartel drug deal and it is top priority."

"All right, I'll get everyone on it," he answered in a determined tone.

"Thanks, I owe you one, big time. I got to go, I got somebody on hold," Franklin reconnected to Connor.

"Jack, can you meet me over at the Naval Supply Center at building five in thirty minutes?"

"No problem, see you then," Connor replied and picked up his Nextel to update the surveillance team.

CHAPTER 13

BOGOTÁ, COLOMBIA

Joaquin stormed into his private study as Roberto poured a half glass of Johnny Walker Black over ice.

"Dios moi! We have another fucking traitor among us." Joaquin roughly drew a commemorative Browning High Power 9mm from under his dinner jacket and pointed it at the window.

"I have had enough betrayal! I will shoot the first five people I see and maybe then people will think twice before betraying me and my family."

"Joaquin, we'll find…"

"I'm tired of talking," he bellowed as he turned toward Roberto, pointing the Browning in his direction and cutting him off in mid-sentence. Joaquin's eyes were bulging and bloodshot, his eyelids swollen from lack of sleep.

"No more!" Joaquin yelled as he pivoted angrily toward the window and fired four rounds, shattering the glass.

"Joaquin! Put the gun down," Roberto shouted over the sound of gunfire.

Joaquin answered with five more rounds.

"I'll kill the traitor!" Joaquin raged furiously.

Roberto rushed toward him in an attempt to take the gun. At that split second, the door to the study slammed open and Joaquin's bodyguards crashed in with their guns drawn.

Joaquin angrily spun away from Roberto and waved the gun wildly toward the door.

"No!" Roberto yelled as he tipped Joaquin's shooting elbow before knocking him to the ground, deflecting the deadly round that undoubtedly would have killed Chico, his most trusted bodyguard. One bullet grazed Chico's right arm, causing him to drop his weapon feeling the burning sensation in his arm. Instinctively, the other bodyguard fired two rounds at what appeared to be Roberto attacking Joaquin. Luckily for Roberto, the force of Chico falling backwards deflected Mateo's shots. They whizzed past his head and embedded in the wall.

"Chico! Mateo! Don't shoot! Don't shoot!" Roberto yelled as he knocked the Browning out of Joaquin's hand, sending it flying across the room into the far corner.

"Joaquin! Please!" Roberto shook his boss by the shoulders, trying to jar him back to his senses. Joaquin struggled to push him away, but Roberto restrained him.

"Joaquin, you are shooting at Chico and Mateo! Please calm down," Roberto lowered his voice and pleaded with him.

"El Jefe, are you all right? Should I kill him?" Mateo waffled, still pointing his weapon at Roberto.

Joaquin looked around the room, seemingly disoriented and confused. They watched as he slumped against Roberto.

"Put down your guns," Joaquin ordered in a weak voice as his rage began to subside.

Roberto released Joaquin. He saw blood on the doorframe, then noticed that Chico was holding his arm. He immediately went to the phone.

"Get the doctor here. Have him come up to the study now, Chico has been shot."

Roberto put down the phone and saw two bullet holes, side by side, lodged in the wall, inches from a portrait of Joaquin's father.

Joaquin stood up and stared at his dead father's face. Angry tears filled his eyes and he began to swear, *"Concha de tu madre! Concha de tu madre!"* It was an oath specific to Colombia. Loosely translated, it meant "motherfucker."

SAN FRANCISCO, CA

The rear tires of Ryker's Mitsubishi screeched briefly as they spun as he shifted. He had ninety minutes to get home, pack for his ten-day trip, and get back to Connor and the surveillance team.

This can't be work, it's too much fun, Ryker thought as he downshifted and approached the Bay Bridge toll plaza.

Connor had briefed him after he returned from his meeting with Franklin. A fortified rail car that was normally used by the government to transport special weapons across the country was going to be used to transport seven tons of cocaine to Miami. Connor and Cartwright had decided that Ryker and Henry Chan, another junior agent, would babysit the cocaine all the way there. Agents from other field divisions would meet them at each stop to help ensure their safety. In Miami, an entire group would follow the cocaine to its destination point and hopefully, to the co-conspirators. To Ryker, it sounded like a plot in a movie.

He planned to keep his eyes and ears open for anything that might relate to the investigation on the West Coast and he was thrilled that Connor had confidence in his ability to be part of this segment of the operation.

Monterey, San Francisco, Miami, and maybe Mexico on a good day, and they pay me to do this. Ryker was ecstatic. He concentrated on driving through the congested traffic. He hoped Tara would be at home, but he was bummed that he wouldn't be able to tell her much about it. It would be cool to see her and at least tell her that he was the lead agent on an operation.

He was home in less than twelve minutes after he took the 9th street exit. He skidded to a stop in the driveway. Tara was in the dining room, going over her own travel itinerary on her laptop when she heard the sound of the tires. Curious, she walked to the front window to see what was going on. She caught a glimpse of Ryker running from his car toward the stairs. Before she could turn around, he was through the front door.

"Hey, Tara! Glad you're home!" he called over his shoulder as he rushed down the hallway to his room.

"Where's the fire?" she asked from the doorway as she watched him grabbing clothes out of his closet and throwing them onto the bed.

"Believe it or not, I'm on a case and I have to leave for Miami in fifty minutes."

"Wow! Sounds exciting. Can you tell me anything about it?"

"Well, it's classified, so if I told you, I would have to kill you." He borrowed the movie line like countless thousands before him.

"You have been watching far too many Bond movies, Special Agent," she scolded as she rolled her eyes.

"There's no such thing as too many Bond movies! Okay, I can tell you that I'll be in Miami for ten days and maybe Mexico after that," Ryker grinned at her, appreciatively inspecting her form-fitting violet blue sweater.

"Sounds mysterious. I leave for Cabo San Lucas in five days. Who knows, maybe we can get together."

"I doubt it...but that would be okay with me!" He replied with more enthusiasm than he intended and she laughed.

"Are you hungry?"

"Now that you mention it, I'm starved, but I'm out of time. I'll get something later. Thanks for asking, though."

"I gotta take care of my roomie, right? I'll make you a lunch to go and you can eat it on the way," she volunteered, heading toward the kitchen.

"Hey, you don't have to do that. I don't want to take advantage of your good will!" he called after her as he continued packing.

He hurried out, threw his single piece of luggage into the G-ride, and rushed back upstairs. He almost ran into her at the front door.

"Hey, I'm a friendly. Don't run me over," Tara laughed as they almost butted heads.

"Thanks Tara, this is great!" He was delighted and surprised when he took the small red and white cooler she offered him. For a moment, they were silent and he felt awkward and tongue-tied. "I'll see you when I get back. Keep the doors locked, okay?"

"Yes sir," she smiled and gave him a sassy salute.

"I'm not ordering you. I just want you to be safe."

"I know. I'll be safe, I promise," she replied playfully as she gave him a quick kiss on the cheek.

He felt a rush of juvenile embarrassment and pleasure and didn't quite know how to respond. She saved him the trouble.

"Oh, I almost forgot," she said, handing him a piece of paper. "This is where I'll be staying in Cabo, just in case you get a chance to say hello."

"Okay. See you in a couple of weeks," he waved as he ran down the stairs to his car.

He looked in the rearview mirror, hoping she was watching as he drove away. He unintentionally revved the tachometer, popping the clutch as he roared down the street. "Shit!" He jammed on the brakes and narrowly missed a Muni bus.

THE PALACE, BOGOTÁ

"Maria, Señor Gusto shot Chico! He shot Chico!" Rosa, one of kitchen staff whispered hysterically as she rushed into the kitchen, wringing her hands.

"Rosa, it was an accident," Maria attempted to calm her down.

"He said he is going to shoot the first five people he sees. *Dios mio!* Please save me," the woman collapsed in tears.

"Maria, Señor Gusto has ordered fruit and wine. Hurry," Angel the butler greeted her as he came into the room. He nervously stared at the woman crying next to her.

Maria prepared a bowl of fresh strawberries, melon, grapes and other fruit she had bought at the farmer's market that morning.

"Don't go, Maria. Don't go! He'll shoot you," Rosa became hysterical again. She ran toward Maria and inadvertently knocked the plate of fruit from her hands. Maria tried to hold onto the dish, but she lost her balance and fell. The camera, bundled in a small towel, fell out of her apron and slid across the tile under the counter.

"I am sorry, Maria, I am sorry," the woman continued to cry as she frantically tried to pick up the wet pieces of fruit.

Maria's heart skipped a beat. She froze for an instant as fear surged through her body in a flood.

"Are you all right, Maria?" Angel asked.

"Yes, yes. Do not worry, I will pick this up. It is no problem," she replied as she pulled herself to her knees.

"Rosa, what you have done. Stop acting loco, you will anger him!" Angel snapped at her.

"What have I done! What have I done!" Rosa continued to cry and rock herself.

"Rosa, stop! You must calm yourself," Maria commanded. The woman stopped sobbing, but tears continued to roll down her face. Angel bent over to help pick up the fruit and silverware. Maria started to move toward the camera when her leg cramped up, forcing her to sit down.

Angel moved toward the bundle and bent down to retrieve it. Maria watched the scene unfold, panic rose in her throat. She tried to speak but could not. The silence that had descended on the kitchen seemed deafening until Rosa's piercing scream ripped through the room.

"We are going to die!" She screamed again as Mateo walked into the kitchen.

"What is happening?" Mateo roared as he surveyed the fruit littering the floor.

Angel turned around, clearly startled by the outburst, and glared at Rosa. Maria slowly stepped between Angel and the partially wrapped bundle.

"Rosa is very upset about Chico's accident, that is all," Angel tried to appease Mateo.

Rosa slumped onto the floor and continued to rock back and forth as she whimpered and cried. Maria managed to gingerly pick up the bundle and slip it into her apron, then continued picking up scattered pieces of fruit. Her hands, wet and sticky, trembled.

"Shut up!" Mateo angrily commanded. "Julio and Jorge will soon join Roberto and El Jefe. Prepare some food!"

"I will bring it immediately. Would you like something to eat?" Maria asked, trying to sound normal.

"No! You must hurry! El Jefe is impatient!" He let the door slam behind him as he abruptly left the room.

"Angel, take Rosa to her room and make her lie down. I will prepare the food and serve it. I must go back to the market this afternoon. If they need anything else while I am gone, please see to it. I will be back in an hour."

Angel nodded deferentially. There was no question that Maria was in charge of the house staff and she was clearly El Jefe's favorite.

Maria quickly prepared a tray of grilled polenta, salsa, avocados and fresh fruit and carried it down the hallway.

"Are you all right?" Maria asked Chico, who was sitting at his post with his arm in a sling.

"Yes, it is nothing."

Maria knocked, then entered the study and put the tray down on the table.

"Maria, my brothers will be here shortly. I do not want to be interrupted during our meeting. Chico and Mateo are aware of this," Joaquin sounded irritated and he did not look up as he spoke.

"Yes, I understand. Should I prepare supper for you and your brothers later tonight?"

"I do not know. Do not prepare anything until I tell you."

228

"Yes, Señor Joaquin," she replied quietly as she left the room. Her heart was still racing. The last time she had seen Joaquin this angry was when he discovered that one of his top lieutenants in Japan had betrayed him and the family. *You must get rid of the camera,* a voice inside her head warned her.

She rushed to her room and took off her apron. She put the small bundle in her bag and headed back to the market.

"Are you all right, Chico?" Jorge asked before he and Julio entered the study.

"It looks worse than it is. It is a flesh wound."

Jorge and Julio had heard what happened almost as quickly as the doctor had and were on their way even before Joaquin called them.

"How bad is it?" Julio asked as they entered the study.

"A traitor!" Joaquin slammed his fist on the desk. Chico and Mateo stared at each other from their post outside the office. This time, they would not rush in at the sound of gunshots.

"We have a serious problem. Viper was almost compromised. He believes that there was a leak…about the list he gave me. The list I showed only to the people in this room a few days ago." Roberto's tone was calm as he paused and took a drink of water. "I am not accusing one of you of being a traitor, but we must determine how the Americans found out about this list. They set a trap for Viper at the airport."

"Americans!" Jorge snorted.

"Fortunately, Viper is very suspicious and cautious. Instead of falling into their trap, he set a trap. He faked his own death and killed one American in the process," Roberto continued.

"We are fortunate he did not kill us for our incompetence!" Joaquin replied in frustration.

"We must determine how we were compromised," Roberto paused, making eye contact with everyone in the room, and then added, "We do not know if the leak came from our end or Viper's. If it was on his end, and he insists it was not, he will be compromised in the near future at little expense to us. Yes, we would lose a valuable asset and resource, but we can live with that. But if the leak is with us, the consequences are unspeakable."

Roberto stood up and walked over to the wall cabinet. He pulled out notepads and pens and gave them to each man in the room.

"I would like for each of us to take 30 minutes to write down anything that comes to mind, anything that could have led to this. Then we will discuss it. I believe that the leak is with us. I know Viper well and he is much too professional to compromise himself. Although anything is possible, my instincts tell me it is on our end," Roberto finished his delivery. He had everyone's attention. For a brief moment, he had complete control over the Gusto family. A rare, uneasy euphoria came over him, but it faded just as quickly as it had come.

FARMERS PLAZA, BOGOTÁ

"I am going to get espresso at the café. Do you want anything?" Manuel Dias asked his brother Fernando.

An impartial observer would have never guessed that the casually dressed, nondescript men were notorious henchman for the Bogotá Cartel. The Dias brothers were well known to the locals and no one challenged them. It was their afternoon off and they were in Bogotá to pass the time.

Maria was anxious to rid herself of the camera. She arrived at the market and walked through the milling crowd, avoiding eye contact with everyone, including her contact, Pepe, who was waiting for her. She was consumed with fear.

Pepe saw her and signaled Heist that she had arrived. Heist, who just seconds before had entered the bookstore next to the café, was out of sight.

Manual Dias took a sip from the hot cup of espresso. He lazily watched the crowd and recognized Maria as she walked quickly through the market. He noticed that she abruptly changed directions when she saw Fernando and she increased her pace.

Fernando! Oh god, I don't want him to see me, Maria almost panicked as she rushed by the vendors. *Manuel must be nearby. I've got to get out of here now.*

When she reached the sidewalk, she abruptly ran across the middle of the intersection. A loud horn sounded from a taxi that had barely missed her. She jumped in fear as she turned toward the sound, then hurried to the other side of the street. The taxi driver yelled out obscenities and waved his fist at her. She clutched her hands across her chest and tried to calm down as she slowed to catch her breath. She looked around nervously, hoping that she hadn't drawn unwanted attention. She didn't see either of the Dias brothers so she continued toward the apartment building.

Manuel got to his feet at the sound of the car horn. Something was wrong with Maria. He called to his brother, but traffic noise drowned out his voice. He put down his cup and walked quickly in the direction he had last seen her. He caught a glimpse of her in the distance, a little over a block away. Within seconds, she would be lost in the crowd. He hurried, roughly pushing people aside.

Heist saw Pepe's signal. He scanned the area, but Striker was nowhere in sight. He left the bookstore and immediately recognized Manuel Dias walking on the street, heading directly toward him. He pulled back for a moment to let him pass by. He was surprised to see him. There had been no intel about the cartel henchman being in town. He followed at a safe distance. He had to find out if Manuel was tracking Maria. It looked like he was headed in the direction of the undercover apartment. Heist took long strides to catch up, constantly scanning faces, searching for Striker.

Shit! he swore out loud. He dialed the apartment's landline. He was relieved when Ricardo Tomales answered.

"We have a problem."

"Go ahead."

"I'm en route from the café. Striker is on the way to make the drop and one of the Dragon's bodyguards is following her. If he makes Striker, we'll have to take him out."

"On my way."

Tomales was a former Navy SEAL with combat experience in Afghanistan. He didn't waste any time. He pulled on a Point Blank ultra-light bullet-proof vest. His Glock 17 fit snugly in a modified Bianchi Black Widow high rise holster. He adjusted the extra magazine on his belt, then pulled the Glock out of its holster and attached a custom silencer.

He pulled on an extra large dark colored t-shirt. The last thing he grabbed before running down the back stairs was his cell phone. He slipped it in the back pocket of his jeans.

Heist dialed the operations center at the Embassy. It was time to activate the Special Forces team.

"Hello." One of two dispatchers manned the secure line.

"This is Match…I got an urgent request."

"Standby," a dispatcher replied.

Heist knew it would only take a few seconds for the voice recognition system to verify his voiceprint. Voice recognition software had been developed years ago by a CIA contractor who worked undercover at AT&T. Its development had been a top secret, government funded operation, but the general public had been led to believe that software developers had engineered it for wealthy executives. The CIA's software was a much higher grade than what was available on the open market and it provided airtight security to field agents, especially in the event hostiles were able to acquire access codes, call signs, or communications equipment that had a direct link to their operations center.

"Go ahead, Match, you're clear."

"I have a Code Yellow priority. I need a team at location A-1 ASAP. Hostile action expected in less than ten minutes. I'm the point of contact."

"Go tell the COS that we have a Code Yellow from Heist," he relayed the urgent message to the other dispatcher. No further authorization was necessary. Match was the assistant chief of station. He and his boss, the COS, were the only two agency personnel in the country with authority to mobilize the crisis team for an operational rescue. The dispatcher rapidly typed in the coded text and transmitted it to all Alpha Team members.

Maria stopped at the street corner and turned completely around to ensure she was not being followed. Manuel stopped, then faced in the opposite direction for a few seconds. Pedestrians walked around him. He could tell that she was trying to see if she was being followed. *But why?*

Heist also stopped and watched Manuel. No mistake about it, Manuel was following Striker. Heist prayed to God the team would arrive in time. The team members' cell phones went off simultaneously. Three of them were driving in their van on the way to Bogotá to get supplies. The other three members of A Team were in the other van on their way to the embassy. While on duty, the team could only split up into groups of three.

"We've got a call-out. It's a priority yellow A-1," Captain Jason Ward announced from the passenger seat of the van.

"We can be there in five minutes if there's no traffic," Sgt. Jackson, the driver, replied.

"Joe, call base and see what's up," Ward directed.

Sgt. Joe McDonald, who was sitting in the back of the van, used the secure phone to call the Embassy.

Tomales ran down the stairs and peeked through the rear door. He didn't see anyone in the garage. His phone vibrated in his back pocket.

"Yeah."

"Ricardo, she's about thirty seconds from you. If he gives us any problem, we take him out," Heist's tone was matter-of-fact.

"I'm at the back door with an eye on the dumpster."

"I called in the team. Hopefully, they'll be here in time to back us up."

"10-4."

"Joe, we're about seven minutes out," Staff Sgt. Mark Dolinski radioed as he and two other team members raced toward the location in a second van.

"Copy," McDonald replied.

"We've got one hostile who's going to compromise Penthouse's top asset at location one. We have two friendlies, Match and his partner. We key off of Match. We have the green light, I repeat, green light," McDonald directed.

Dolinski looked at his teammate in silence. "Green light" was code for the use of deadly force. They were seldom called upon to run a green light in broad daylight.

"We'll be there in two mikes," McDonald replied. The sun beat down on the van as it sped through the streets.

Manuel followed Maria, staying out of sight as she turned the corner and headed for the apartment's underground parking lot. She stopped in front of the entrance for a second, then disappeared into the garage. There was no sign of Match or the van in the garage. She couldn't stop her hands from shaking. She was too afraid to risk going up to the undercover apartment for fear that someone might spot her.

Tomales watched her as she approached the bin, reached under her blouse, pulled out a small package, and placed it in the garbage bin. Manuel entered and ducked behind a truck inside the underground parking lot. He peered around the bumper in time to see her tucking her blouse back into the waistband of her skirt. Maria didn't see Manuel, but Tomales did.

Tomales held his Glock 17 at his side. He did not want to take any action until Striker was clear of the garage. He knew Manuel would not confront her until after he had recovered what she had left in the dumpster.

Striker briskly walked toward the exit. Outside, Heist saw Manuel hiding behind the truck, but decided to wait outside. He did not want to alert Striker. Tomales was inside and he would protect Striker if Manuel confronted her.

Heist watched as Striker darted out of the garage oblivious as she continued in the opposite direction down the street. Once she cleared the area, he unholstered his weapon as he moved toward the garage.

Tomales's Glock was pointed directly at the kill zone between two cars as Manuel approached.

"Shit!" Ricardo swore as he heard the sound of voices in the stairwell. He instinctively reholstered his weapon and started to walk back upstairs so as not to cause any suspicion. A young couple passed him as he reached the first level. He waited until he heard them open the door into the garage, then hurried back down.

"Mark."

"Go ahead."

"We'll be there in about ninety seconds," McDonald advised.

"We're about three mikes behind," Dolinski responded.

Manuel crouched behind a car, weapon drawn, and waited until the couple left the garage. He peered over the hood and didn't see anyone else. He moved behind the bin. The bin was half full and nothing unusual stood out. He climbed up on the ledge near the wall and began to rifle through the top layer.

Heist took cover behind one of the trucks and waited. He could hear the sound of trash being tossed around, but from his hiding place, he couldn't see the stairwell door where he knew Tomales was watching.

Tomales reappeared at the door and assumed his firing position but had no clear shot. He could see Manuel leaning over the bin. He scanned for Heist but didn't see him.

"What's this?" Manuel said under his breath as he retrieved a small bundle from underneath a few pages of crumpled newspaper. He picked it up and a small camera fell out.

De puta! Realization dawned and he ducked behind the dumpster and looked around the garage.

All right, you figured it out. Now come out in the open, Tomales thought, waiting for the right moment, focusing his eye on the front sight of his Glock.

Manuel shifted from behind the dumpster and looked toward the stairwell door. It was slightly ajar. He sensed movement and immediately ducked back behind the steel bin.

Pop, pop! Two rounds from Tomales' silenced Glock hit the wall behind the garbage bin, barely missing Manuel as he dove for cover. He answered with four loud, explosive rounds from his Beretta 92. The shots echoed in the confines of the underground space. The door provided some cover, but it would not stop 9mm rounds.

Heist realized that Manuel had the tactical advantage. He double-tapped twice with his silenced 9mm Sig Sauer 226 at Manuel's position in an effort to draw fire. The rounds pinged into the garbage bin and ricocheted onto the floor.

Manuel, an experienced and disciplined shooter, knew that his second attacker was not an immediate threat to him, based on his own position and the direction of the second volley. He fired four more rounds toward the door, mechanically changed his position, then fired two more in the direction of the second volley.

Tiny bits of safety glass from the truck's windows shattered on the ground around Heist. He ducked and repositioned between two vehicles closer to the stairwell. Manuel caught a glimpse of movement.

Two of the first volley of four rounds had found their mark in Tomales' chest, knocking him violently back against the wall. Pain seared through his chest and he gasped. His ballistic vest had not failed. He regained his balance and fired four rounds through the open door in the shooter's direction.

Manual answered with four more rounds from his Beretta and this time it was flesh that took the impact. One round entered Tomales' forehead and the other ripped through his eye. He spun around as he fell to the ground. Manuel made a break for the street. He ejected his spent magazine and inserted another 15-round magazine into the Beretta. He started running for the exit, firing toward Heist.

Heist took cover while Manuel fired random shots. By the fifth shot, Heist could tell that the rounds were safely off their mark. He popped up, then laid across the hood of an old Mercedes sedan in an attempt to stabilize his shooting platform. He rapidly fired four rounds, each one hitting the wall inches behind the fleeing shooter.

Manuel ran out of the garage and started running down a side street hoping to see his brother.

"Clear!" Heist yelled to his partner and then gave chase.

"There they are!" Ward pointed toward Heist.

"We got contact. Match is pursuing one target. We're engaging now!" Ward radioed the other team as their van entered the street with both Heist and Manuel in sight.

Manuel turned and saw Heist and the van speeding toward him. He fired two more rounds. Heist hugged the building wall as he saw the muzzle flash but continued the chase. The van veered slightly as two rounds struck the grill.

Fernando was outside the café looking for his brother when he heard the unmistakable sound of gunshots in the distance. He ran in their direction.

Heist closed in and Manuel turned to fire, but he never pulled the trigger. Out of nowhere, Heist saw the car. It hit Manuel without slowing down launching him onto the windshield as the car crashed into the corner of a building. The upper half of Manuel's torso lay lifeless across the hood. The other half was pinned between the bumper and the building in a grotesque display.

Heist didn't break stride as he rushed to the crash. The driver saw Heist's gun and sped off down the street. He spotted the Beretta lying in the gutter and the camera on the other side of the street. He ran toward the camera and recovered it.

About fifty feet away, Ward's van came to an abrupt stop.

Heist ran back to the other side of the street and picked up the gun. A man in an apartment above the street stuck his head out of the window, but darted back in when he saw Heist with a gun in his hand.

Heist rushed to the van and ordered, "In the garage, now! Find Tomales. I think he's down. I'll call it in." Heist knew the protocol. The rescue team was on site, he could only hope for the best.

The van made a U-turn and slowly drove back to the garage so as not to draw attention.

"Dolinski."

"Go ahead."

"Meet us in the garage. One target neutralized and a possible friendly down. We need clean up ASAP," Ward instructed.

"10-4. Be on scene in sixty seconds," Dolinski responded.

Heist was about a block away when he looked back to see a few people around the accident. He heard a siren in the distance. He called base and requested that a team close out the safe house in an hour. When he hung up the phone, he felt a sense of dread and feared the worst.

Fernando saw people running down a side street and he followed them. He kept looking around for his brother but did not see him in the crowd.

"Call an ambulance! Call an ambulance!" someone shouted. Fernando pushed his way through.

"Manuel!" he cried out like a wounded animal. "Manuel!"

THE PALACE, BOGOTÁ

The men in the study had put their pens down. No one spoke. Roberto began.

"I discussed the list only two other times. First, with Joaquin…in this study, the day after we initially talked about it. Second, with Jorge…four days later, in the courtyard. While it is possible that one of the staff overheard our conversation, I do not recall seeing anyone near us either time." Each of the brothers gave a similar account of discussing the list only among themselves, when no one else was present.

"I only see one common denominator. Every conversation any of us had about the list was here on the compound. If we have a leak, it is here. Maybe we have bugs," Roberto sighed.

Joaquin lit up a Cuban cigar and blew a mouthful of smoke into the room as he stared at the bullet holes in the wall by the portrait of his father.

FARMERS PLAZA, BOGOTÁ

The team in the second van saw two ambulances at the crash scene about five hundred yards in front of them as they entered the garage.

Ward approached the van as it came to a stop. "Do you have a body bag?"

"Yes," Dolinski replied.

"Ricardo went down, two to the head, never knew what hit him. We need to be out of here in five minutes. Heist has arranged for some of his agents to clean the apartment in an hour."

Dolinski concealed the body bag and walked toward McDonald and another Special Forces operator, who was making sure there was no evidence of Tomales' death. They poured an absorbent bleach solution on the floor where the blood had been. Ward scanned the area to make sure they were not missing anything.

"Dolinski, double-check the brass," Ward instructed, to avoid leaving behind any spent 9mm casings as evidence of the shooting.

THE PALACE, BOGOTÁ

The phone rang in the study and Joaquin answered.

"Yes. Roberto, it is for you."

"What is it?" Roberto asked. "When?...Are you sure?...I'll be there in twenty minutes." Roberto hung up the phone, a stricken look on his face.

"That was Fernando. Manuel was hit and killed by a car one half hour ago. I'm going there to find out what happened."

"It's bad luck!" Joaquin clenched his fist.

Joaquin knew that Roberto had hand-picked the Dias brothers to be his personal henchmen and that Roberto was close to them.

"Do you need any help?" Jorge offered.

"Go to Manuel's house and stay with his wife until Fernando and I get there."

238

CIA HEADQUARTERS

"Director, it's Stevens. He says it's important."

Bancroft stopped writing the draft memo to the President on the terrorism threat at airports and put her pen down on her cherry wood desk.

"Yes, Greg."

"We've got another Code Red."

"Where and how many?"

"Bogotá. One of yours and one of Gusto's bodyguards. They almost took out Striker."

"Who was the case officer?"

"Ricardo Tomales, a relatively new officer." There was an obvious sigh in his voice.

"Can you come and brief me now?"

"Absolutely."

Bancroft called her secretary the instant she hung up. "Emma, please cancel the rest of my appointments this afternoon."

"Yes ma'am."

"Also, get me the personnel file on Ricardo Tomales, please."

Two officers in a few days. More officers are being killed over drugs than terrorism, Bancroft thought. The agency was not accustomed to losing field officers so frequently.

She had the file on her desk in five minutes. Bancroft noticed how thin the folder was as she opened it. The file didn't contain the usual documents such as standard personnel letters of accommodation, letters of discipline, or annual evaluations. The empty file lacked any clues to his personality, his life. It gave her a sick feeling. His life had been cut short and the only evidence of his career was contained in a few pages in a brown, government-issue personnel file.

Her eyes focused in on the left side of the folder. She read the dry summary of information about the slain case officer.

BIOGRAPHICAL SHEET
NAME: TOMALES, RICARDO JAMES DOB: 6-15-88
POB: MCALLEN, TX
SPOUSE: SINGLE
FATHER: TOMALES, JAMES L.

MOTHER: TOMALES, MARIA (GONZALES)
RESIDENCE: MCALLEN, TX
BROTHERS: NONE SISTERS: NONE
EDUCATION: UNIVERSITY OF TEXAS; BS ENGINEERING 05/2010; MS ENGINEERING 05/2011
SPORTS: ALL-AMERICAN UNIVERSITY OF TEXAS WATER POLO TEAM CAPTAIN 2009-2010
PREVIOUS WORK EXPERIENCE: PART TIME BAR BOUNCER/COLLEGE
MILITARY EXPERIENCE: LT. USN 06/2011-12/2017
NAVSPEWARCEN-CORONADO 08/2011-07/2012
NAVSPECWARGRP-1/SEAL TEAM 08/2012-08/2014
NAVSPECWARGRP-2/SEAL TEAM 08/2014-09/2016
DEVGRU 10/2016-12/2017 CLASSIFIED
CAMP PEARY: CASE OFFICER TRAINING 01/2018-12/2018
AGENCY DEPLOYMENTS: 1 ASSIGNMENT
CURRENT ASSIGNMENT: AMEMB BOGOTÁ, COLOMBIA 12-2018- PRESENT

He survived being a SEAL but the CIA managed to get him killed, Bancroft sat back in her chair and closed the file.

CHAPTER 14

SOUTHERN PACIFIC RAILWAYS, NV

Ryker felt the rush of wind on his face as he stuck his head out of the caboose window. He could see the entire length of the thirty-car, Southern Pacific freight train as it snaked through the Sierra Nevada mountain range. The air was fresh and he enjoyed a deep breath before pulling his head back inside.

"It's already been six hours since we left," Ryker turned to the agent with him, Henry Chan.

"Yeah, it seems like we just left Oakland only a few minutes ago," Chan joked as he laughed at Ryker's disheveled hair. "Before you know it, we'll be in Miami."

"Hey, how long before we get to Sparks, Nevada?" Ryker asked the old, lumbering train conductor. Ryker figured the guy had to be at least seventy years old.

Smittie smirked at Ryker for a few seconds and spit a mouthful of Skoal smokeless tobacco into a filthy trash can. "I'd say about another two hours or so." His hands were wrinkled, and his fingertips were stained a dark brown. Dirt showed up in black semi-circles under his nails.

"You reckon you boys are going to get those druggies once you reach Miami?" Smittie grinned, revealing an uneven row of brown teeth, with a couple missing.

"We're planning on it, Smittie," Chan replied in a loud voice so that he could be heard over the noise from the tracks.

"Why don't you boys bring 'em by the yard and let us have a few minutes with 'em? You won't have no more problems with them sum' bitches," he replied with such dogged determination that the agents laughed.

No doubt, it would be a one-way conversation, Ryker thought. Even though Smittie seemed to be as old as the train, he stood 6'4" and weighed at least 240 pounds. He could still hold his own.

"That's not a bad idea, Smittie."

SAN FRANCISCO, CA

"I called Frank Tito, the Country Attaché of Mexico City. He'll have one of his agents, Gill Thomas, meet you at the airport when you arrive," Cartwright told Connor.

"I know Gill, we did some training together in Quantico."

"Good. Here's his number…give him a call before you get there."

"Ok. If Ryker gets back before I return, can he come down here with me? It will be a good experience for him and we could use the help."

"We'll see, it will be good training for both Ryker and Chan to see how other DEA offices work these controlled deliveries. It might be a while before the cocaine shipment reaches its final destination."

"Okay."

"You got everything you need…passport, tickets, money?"

"Yeah, I got it all," Connor replied.

"Hook up with Carlos and debrief him. This is a great opportunity to cripple the cartel. Then, pass the information to Franklin and let the military take care of the sub's base. Do not get involved in that."

"I know, boss. You already warned me about that. I'm just there to observe. I gotta get going. I'm going over to see Franklin, then my wife, and I'm on the plane tonight."

"How is Barrett handling all your travel?"

"Not great, but she's been working on a homicide case so she's busy twenty-four seven."

"Alright, be careful and have a good trip." Cartwright watched him as he left the office and wished he was going too.

CIA HEADQUARTERS

Bancroft stared at Heist's e-mail on her computer screen and rubbed her forehead. She had a splitting headache, but she had to think it through.

He wanted to keep Striker in place, but he needed her approval. His assessment was that the incident in Bogotá happened by chance and that Striker's cover hadn't been blown. They had recovered the camera so there was no physical evidence that could compromise Striker. Heist indicated that Striker wasn't aware she had been followed. It was a calculated risk to keep the op open, but he felt that the advantages outweighed the risks. There was no doubt that the Gustos suspected a traitor in their midst. The question was, did they suspect the traitor was Striker? Bancroft respected his judgment in the field and knew he was in the best position to assess the situation. She saw that the DDO had signed off on it.

"Emma, draft a memo authorizing the continued use of Striker and send it to Bogotá." She hoped she wasn't signing Striker's death warrant.

COAST GUARD ISLAND, ALAMEDA, CA

Connor had never liked closed environments with re-circulated air. The classified operations center at JTF-5 was just that type of place. The room was soundproof and equipped so that it could not be electronically penetrated, but was somewhat outdated in terms of state-of-the-art, high-tech security equipment.

"Jack, we're picking up a good signal," Franklin said as he pointed to the computer tracking the submarine. "At this rate of speed, it should be back in the Baja area in a few days. That should give you plenty of time to complete your debriefing and finalize your game plan."

"Okay. Is Hatfield going to be involved in the operation?"

"I don't know. There's a request to the special warfare command, but that's up to Washington. Hopefully we'll know soon."

"Good luck, Jack." Franklin shook his hand and they started to walk out of the operations center.

Connor focused on the red light above the exit door as he punched in the security code and waited until the light turned green.

"Agent Connor, you've got a call on the STE phone. It's back in this room, on the left."

"Thanks, Chief," Connor replied as he turned around and walked down the hallway.

"Jack Connor."

"It's Lynn Bancroft. Is your phone off?"

Connor reached into his pocket and inspected his iPhone. "Battery is dead, ma'am."

"Jack, that phone cost us ten grand. Try to keep it charged," Bancroft continued, "We have another twist. The targeted cell called someone in Mexico City in the last twenty-four hours; we think it was someone connected to the cartel. We only captured part of the conversation. Apparently, there is going to be an important meeting somewhere in Thailand, but that's all we got. So heads up."

"Yes ma'am...how did you know I was here?"

"Jack I'm the director and you're my project. I know where you are all of the time. Are you en route to Mexico?"

"I will be soon."

"Okay, have a safe trip. Remember that the clock is ticking on this. Keep that damn phone charged! If you need anything, contact me directly."

"I will."

Connor realized that he needed to get home. He dialed his other cell phone as he exited the building and smiled when he heard Barrett's voice. She had that expectant tone, as though she knew it would be him on the other end.

"Hey, babe, did you run yet?"

"No, I'm still in San Francisco, just leaving to go home, want me to wait for you?"

"Yeah, I'm in Alameda and should be home in about forty minutes.

"See you then."

SAN FRANCISCO, CA

"How is everything going?" Steiner looked around as he spoke into the receiver.

"Fine. We're waiting to see if we can go on our trip and if you'll be joining us," the voice on the other end replied.

"I will not be able to make it. I'm still waiting for confirmation of the reservations."

The team leader silently swore as he heard the coded message. The only way he and his men were going to make any money was to knock off the train carrying the load of cocaine.

"Some of the guys have other commitments, so we can't wait too long."

"Listen, I know you want to go on this trip, but the reservations must be confirmed," Steiner emphasized.

"I understand, just remember our time frame."

"I know. I'll get back to you within six hours."

Steiner hung up the pay phone and walked across the street and headed back in the direction of the federal building. He wanted to confirm that there were only two DEA agents on the train and that there hadn't been any last-minute security changes. He needed to get a little more intel from Cartwright before he gave Radcliff the green light to proceed with their plan.

Barrett froze at the sound the blaring horn just as she was going to step into the cross walk, momentarily distracted at the sight of Steiner walking away from the pay phone across the street. *That's weird,* she thought curiously as she continued toward the civic center parking lot.

Steiner had known the team leader, Nick Radcliff, since their fraternity days in college. He trusted Nick like a brother. The two of them once broke into a professor's office and made a copy of their political science final exam. They both aced it.

Nick and Steiner had taken different career paths after college. Steiner decided on a civilian career while Radcliff chose the military, but they stayed in touch. Radcliff elected to go into the Army and volunteered for airborne training. He was selected to serve in a Ranger battalion at Fort Benning, Georgia. He spent ten years in the military with combat time in Iraq and Afghanistan. He volunteered for Delta but had failed the psychological tests. He had become disenchanted with the military and ultimately, wanted to reap higher financial rewards. When he got out of the military, Steiner approached him with a plan to make some money.

Radcliff didn't know about Steiner's association with the Bogotá Cartel. Nobody knew that, and Steiner planned to take that secret to his grave. Because of Steiner's position within the government, he had access to highly classified information which…used in the proper manner…could be extremely financially rewarding.

Steiner's association with the Bogotá Cartel was short-term and potentially volatile. There was always a chance of being compromised, hence his code name…Raven. He didn't particularly care for the stress, but the money was worth it. As he walked away from the payphone, he enjoyed the irony that the cartel was going to wind up paying him twice as much as they thought they were.

REDWOOD SHORES, CA

"You've got a good pace, Barrett," Connor's body told him they were close to a seven-minute mile.

"Well, if this is too fast for you, let me know," Barrett replied in a cocky voice.

He sped up and ran past her, just to prove that he could. She laughed and swatted him on the butt as she tried to keep up.

"Jack, you will be careful when you are down there, won't you?"

"Babe, you know I'm always careful. I'm more worried about you. You're working a homicide case that may have a terrorist connection, not exactly a garden variety felony assignment." He tried to downplay how much concern he actually felt.

"Good point, but I'm not the one going to Mexico where every tenth civilian is either shot at or killed."

Connor listened but didn't reply.

"Jack, what do you think about an AUSA who uses a pay phone about two blocks from his office, when he clearly has his cell phone?"

"Depends, why?"

"I saw Steiner using a pay phone when I was leaving San Francisco," Barrett explained.

"His cell battery could have been dead. Mine went dead today and I got blasted for it. Besides he's a lawyer, who knows what they think," Connor retorted.

"Hey, watch it pal." Barrett was matching his strides but was breathing harder as she spoke.

"He's arrogant and there's something about him I don't like."

"Like I said, he's a lawyer," Connor grinned.

"Okay wise guy, just remember I warned you about him," Barrett snapped as she picked up her pace.

MEXICO CITY, MEXICO

The taxis were lined up in a long row at the Mexico City Benito Juarez International Airport. Viper saw that the lead taxi had its hood up and steam was rising in the air. On days as hot as this one, engines and tempers overheated. As he walked past the line of cabs, he heard two drivers arguing angrily and shouting at each other.

Viper ignored them and walked into the crowded terminal. At the Federal Express counter, five people were already in line.

"We got some real beauties this year, some fresh, young faces," Doug Houser, a Victoria's Secret catalog photographer, addressed the man beside him.

"They're always beautiful," Sean Young, his partner, replied as he rolled his eyes. "You've only got one thing on your mind."

"Yeah? Well, what do you think about when you're taking their pictures and they're wearing thong bikinis…football?" Houser retorted sarcastically.

"I have been doing this for ten years. It's my job."

"Please!"

Viper listened to the conversation but pretended not to pay attention.

"Well, I'll tell you what, there's an Asian model who is one of the most exotic women I have ever seen. I'm glad she is my job."

"Oh! So, you do have a preference! You are so busted!"

"I'm not a dog like you, Doug."

"Well, I'll tell you what, wait until you see the brunette. She might make you bark."

"They're swimsuit models. After a while, they all look the same to me.

"Not this one. She's the real deal. Every man's fantasy. She's tall, has long, straight, dark hair, high cheekbones, full lips…the camera loves her! And get this, she's just now starting her modeling career. She was a flight attendant! Can you believe it?" Houser added.

Viper listened curiously but was careful not to look in their direction.

"Yeah, yeah, how many days are we here?"

"Two days at the University and then we're to go to the Palmilla Hotel in Cabo for a week."

"How long before their plane lands?"

"An hour, they're coming from LA."

"May I help you, gentlemen?" The Federal Express agent waved them to the counter.

"Yeah. We have some camera equipment to pick up. Here's the receipt."

"Please wait one moment," she said as she took the receipt and walked to the back.

"Sir, may I help you?" an employee at the other counter spoke to the next customer in line.

"Yes, thank you," Viper replied as he handed her a slip of paper. She took it and disappeared.

"What's the Sheraton like?" Young asked.

"It's been recently remodeled, probably one of the best hotels in Mexico City."

Viper purposely turned in the opposite direction but listened to every word. When the agent returned with his package, he signed for it and left the area. He repositioned himself near a magazine stand so that he could observe the photographers. They had roused his curiosity and he wanted to see the brunette they had been talking about.

He studied the arrival monitors and saw that United Flight 1530 from Los Angeles was on time, due to arrive in thirty-five minutes. The photographers were sitting outside the security area reading magazines.

He tried to figure the odds that the brunette the photographer had mentioned was the flight attendant who'd slipped out on him in Paris. She was extraordinary, someone a photographer would appreciate. If she was the same woman, he would make sure that she was no longer a threat.

FSB HEADQUARTERS, MOSCOW

"Colonel you know how important it is to apprehend Volkov. I've told you what Defense Minister Ivanovich was going to brief you on before Volkov assassinated him. Volkov is one of the few in the inner circle that knows about operation Red Rising. He could expose our government at the highest level and we could have another collapse of our government, which could set us back decades."

"I understand."

"Then don't fail again. It could have devastating consequences for both of us."

Alexandrov could feel the tension in the director's piercing eyes.

"So, Colonel tell me, what happened? How did you lose two men?" the FSB Director's tone was accusatory.

"Paris was a target of opportunity, a costly mistake, but we were not compromised," Colonel Alexandrov warily rationalized the failed attempt to append the assassin-Viper.

The sound of a fist hitting the desk jarred the floor. "Colonel, we are compromised any time two of our operators are killed on foreign soil while conducting an operation. Do not let it happen again! Do not underestimate your target." the director angrily replied and pointed to the door. It was very obvious the director was not interested in details, only results.

"Yes, Director, it will not happen again," Alexandrov snapped to attention at the harshness of the order, then turned on his heel and quickly retreated into the hallway. What the colonel didn't tell the director was why two of his men acted independent of his knowledge and how close his team came to being compromised when they extracted the two dead operators that night in Paris. That was a mystery he could not solve and highlighted the treacherous danger of his true mission.

MEXICO CITY INTERNATIONAL AIRPORT

Within a few minutes of arrival, the passengers started walking into the terminal. Viper was close enough that he could overhear bits of conversation, in English...most of them were Americans. He watched as a group of three attractive women pulled rolling carry-on bags behind them on their way to baggage claim. He focused on a tall, extremely thin Asian woman in the middle of the group. She was wearing a cream-colored, sleeveless silk blouse with a tan, linen mini-skirt. Her jet-black hair draped down her back. She was striking, more exotically feline-looking than beautiful.

Another group of women followed...all blondes. He craned his neck to look around them. He saw her in the distance. She was walking alone, wearing a pair of designer jeans, a snug white top, and a navy blue Ralph Lauren baseball cap. She had on a pair of Rudy Project sunglasses which accented her high cheekbones and glossed lips.

He knew it was the flight attendant, Tara, before she got close enough for him to recognize her. Even though her face was partially covered by the cap and sunglasses, her distinctive natural beauty set her apart from the other beautiful women around her. He watched her as she walked, taking purposeful strides with long legs that covered ground quickly. Her shoulders were squared, and her chin was tilted up, very slightly, giving her a regal bearing.

He saw one of the photographers point in her direction. *We will meet again my beauty, we will meet again,* Viper bit his lower lip as he watched her walk away.

Two terminals away, Connor stood in line at customs. When it came to clearing Customs into Mexico City, there were no special privileges with the host government for Connor or any other DEA agent not assigned to the Embassy. The political climate was too corrupt and dangerous for DEA agents to reveal their true identities in Mexico.

The airport was a little more modern than he had expected. It had all the flare of an international setting with duty-free stores, Gucci and Chanel, lining the terminal. Brightly colored ads filled the storefronts, beckoning weary travelers with promises of luxury items for less.

"Jack!" Gill Thomas called out to him and waved.

"Gill, how are you doing?"

"Great! How's Barrett and life in San Francisco?"

"Barrett is doing great, and as for the city…well, it's not as crowded as this place."

"How long has it been?" Thomas asked.

"Too long."

"Time flies! Did you check any luggage?"

"Nope, just brought a carry-on."

"Fantastic, baggage claim is a zoo. Let's get the hell out of here."

They walked out of the airport into the unusually clear, cool afternoon. A couple of cab drivers rushed toward them to offer their services.

Thomas waved them off, avoiding eye contact, as he pointed in the direction of the parking area. A line of fifteen to twenty green and white cabs lined the lanes outside the baggage claim area, clogging already heavy traffic. The smell of exhaust and diesel was overpowering.

"Jack, don't get in a cab. It increases your chances of getting robbed about 100 percent.

Only use the yellow and white ones, if you have to. They are the safest here in the city. Hopefully, you won't have to. I made a reservation for you…at my place. It's a deluxe, three-bedroom apartment, with two full bathrooms. There are some perks that go with being assigned to the State Department and having diplomatic status."

They made it to the apartment in less than thirty minutes and parked in the underground garage. They caught up on small talk on the way over and discussed the case.

"Security is tight at this apartment building, or should I say, as tight as anything can be around here. You never know who's on the take here. We just assume they all are."

Connor was impressed with the living space inside the apartment. The place was at least twenty-five hundred square feet. A comparable place in San Francisco would go for at least six grand a month. *This is some perk,* Connor thought.

"Your room is at the end of the hall on the left," Thomas pointed.

"Gill, are you still single?"

"Hell yeah! There are some knock-out, gorgeous women in this town who just love Americans and dream of becoming an American wife and U.S. citizen. If we have time, I'll introduce you to my newest acquaintance. I met her couple of weeks ago at the Ambassador's birthday party."

"Does she know you are a confirmed bachelor?"

"Of course not, and don't blow my cover. Besides, we work our butts off down here and it would be hard to have a normal family life in this environment. Don't get me wrong, there are married couples down here, but I'll be damned if I know how they manage. Half of them wind up divorced anyway."

He listened distractedly as he checked out the furnishings. *For a single guy, Gill has good taste,* Connor thought as he examined an obviously expensive, classic Mexican antiquity on the sofa table.

"Jack, are you listening to me?"

"Yeah. Where did you get this piece? I didn't know you were a collector. Is this the real deal?" Connor asked curiously.

"Absolutely," he replied, clearly pleased that Connor had noticed.

"Where did you find it?

"It's a long story. I'll tell you over dinner, I don't know about you, but I am starved!"

"Okay, let's go," Connor replied as he carefully placed the intricately carved piece back on the table.

"Did you bring a gun?"

"Of course not, I know the rules."

"Just checking, Jacky boy. Anyway we've got different rules down here, ever since Eduardo's murder and Dominic's torture." Thomas's expression hardened as he walked down the hall to his bedroom.

"And what's that?" Connor called out after him. There was a pause.

"Shoot first and ask questions later," Thomas replied as he walked back into the living room.

Every DEA agent knew the history behind the brutal murder of Eduardo Marquez and the torture of Dominic Hilarus. Dominic's fate would have been the same as Eduardo's, if not for the valiant efforts of a few DEA agents who had rescued him from a Mexican jail.

"Here, take these."

"A Glock? You got any Sigs?" Connor asked as he examined the Glock 19 and spare fifteen-round magazine.

"The issue weapons down here are all Glock 19s and 17s not like the states where they issue .40 cals. We don't use .40 cals down here since all Mexican military and police use 9mm and .45 cal. We don't want to stick out."

"I still carry a 9mm. I don't like the kick in the .40 cals."

"Then you won't miss a beat. Hey, if for some reason we get into a shooting, the official story is that this is my back-up weapon that I only loaned it to you so that you could defend yourself. We absolutely cannot risk being taken hostage. So use it if you have to, and answer questions later. Washington knows the deal down here. Believe me, OPR will not come down on you for staying alive." He tried to sound convincing, not at all sure that the Office of Personnel Responsibility really would have their backs, but better to be terminated than...*terminated.*

Connor held the Glock 19 in his hand, then tucked it inside his waistband. The Glocks were lighter than SIGs and it fit snugly

252

inside the waistband, even without a holster. Connor preferred the Sig 228 because he was a bit more accurate with it, but he was also proficient with the compact Glock 19.

"You still a firearms instructor?"

"Yeah."

"Good, then you just certified yourself," Thomas announced in an official tone of voice, then grinned.

"Where are we going?" Connor asked.

"It's Mexico's version of an Italian trattoria. Great food and I know the manager."

"Is it safe to drink the water?" Connor asked.

"Only if it is in a bottle and the label is in English," he replied emphatically. "Oh, one more thing before I forget," Thomas turned around and faced Connor just as he was going to open the front door. "Do you still get up at the crack of dawn to run?"

"You have a good memory, Gill."

"You're an exercise fanatic, how could anyone forget that? Anyway, don't run in the city. The air is five times worse than L.A. We have a mini-gym with a couple of treadmills here in the building and I am quite sure you will not have to wait to use the machines in the morning. There's a better gym at the Embassy that the Marines use if you want to work out there."

"What, you aren't going to join me?" Connor asked in mock surprise.

"Not at the ungodly hour you get up. No sir."

Horns sounded, and tires screeched in the heavy evening traffic in Mexico City. Everybody drove like maniacs. It took them twenty minutes to get to the restaurant and another ten minutes to park.

Thomas's OGV was a compact, four-door BMW 325i. He parked on a side street next to an alley. When Connor got out of the car, he surveyed the area. He adjusted the Glock 19 and was glad that he had a weapon.

"How does the night life in Mexico City compare to San Francisco?" Thomas asked.

"It appears a lot more crowded than the city, but so far I'm impressed. Mexico City is more *Americanized* than I realized," Connor replied as he observed the yellow arches of McDonald's on the corner.

Thomas led him into a small restaurant decorated with a bright red and blue sign, *La Cantina.* Inside, it was tastefully decorated and most of the customers looked like well-dressed professionals. An upbeat salsa tune played in the background. Thomas walked up to the maitre d' and spoke briefly to him in Spanish. In a few minutes, the manager appeared.

"Jack, this is Caesar, the manager of this magnificent establishment. I call him Caesar the Great."

"Glad to meet you," Connor said, extending his hand.

"The pleasure is mine. Gill is one of my best customers. I reserve a very special place for him. Enjoy your dinner."

"Thank you, Caesar," Gill smiled warmly and patted him on the back.

"Busy place," Connor remarked as they walked through the restaurant. He could smell the smoky aroma of the mesquite wood fire lingering in the air.

As they approached their table, Gill caught a glimpse of a large man, sitting in a corner booth with two young, beautiful women, one on each side.

"Jack, you see the ugly fat guy in the booth with the two babes?"

Connor raised his eyes from the menu and glanced in the direction of the booth. "Yeah, why?"

"That's Javier Mora, better known as El Capitán. He's one of the most corrupt cops in Mexico...provides protection for Francisco Felix, the head of the transportation cell in Mexico and West Coast cocaine distribution into the United States for the Bogotá Cartel."

"Really?" Connor listened carefully, his interest peaked.

"I wonder what he's doing in Mexico City. He's a police captain in Cabo San Lucas, so he's a long way from home. The guy is trouble. He'll kill anybody for the right amount of money."

"Have you gentlemen decided what you'd like to order?" the waitress asked in perfect English.

"Two chicken enchiladas with Spanish rice. Jack, trust me on this, it's the best in the city."

Connor nodded, he wasn't that hungry. He shifted his eyes from Thomas and noticed that El Capitán was staring at their table. The men made direct eye contact with each other and El Capitán gave him a challenging stare.

"Jack, hey Jack," Thomas interrupted, concerned.

Connor broke eye contact, because El Capitán suddenly turned and looked toward the door. Connor turned to see what he was looking at.

A man was walking toward the booth, pointing a gun directly at his face, but it was El Capitán who fired, as he grabbed one of the women and used her to shield himself. A blast from under the table wounded the intruder, but he still managed to get a shot off before he hit the floor. It missed its intended target but struck the frightened woman in the chest.

Thomas and Connor instinctively ducked for cover and Connor pulled his weapon.

"Connor, no!" Thomas hissed.

Connor hesitated. His eyes were fixed on the booth. El Capitán pushed the woman off himself and swore irritably as he wiped her blood from his arm. He stood up, pointed his gun at the floor and fired two rounds into the gunman's torso.

"Jack, put it away. This is not our fight."

Connor reluctantly placed the Glock back in his waistband, but stayed on the floor, not taking his eyes off the scene. People were screaming, and the faint smell of gunpowder mixed with the smoky odor of grilled meat.

"Get that bastard out of here," El Capitán ordered the two bodyguards who were standing over the intruder's body.

"Help her! Help her!" The woman beside him screamed as she reached out for her friend.

"Shut up!" El Capitán barked as he backhanded her across the face.

Connor made another move to draw his weapon, but Thomas grabbed his arm.

"Welcome to Mexico, Jack. Let's get out of here before this gets any more out of hand and the police storm the place. We can't take him and his bodyguards, because we don't know how many more he's got in here."

"Alright," Connor grudgingly agreed, his jaw clenched, as he quickly got to his feet.

"Follow me!" Thomas led the way toward the rear of the restaurant. Most of the patrons were running out.

"We'll come back another night," Thomas called out to Caesar as they reached the back door.

"Dios mio!" Caesar held his head in his hands as he watched the crowd flooding out of the restaurant and heard women screaming.

El Capitán holstered his .45 pistol and spit on the corpse. He searched around the room and stared at the table where he had seen the two Americans. They were gone.

"Cowards!" he yelled, and then laughed out loud as he picked up the shot glass and drained it in a single swallow. He slammed it on the table, sending silverware flying onto the floor.

CHAPTER 15

FLAGSTAFF, ARIZONA

The sound of the high-pitched engines and rotor blades did not break Nick Radcliff's concentration as he sat next to the pilot in the lead helicopter. The team was conducting their second full-scale, night-assault practice-run under Radcliff's stopwatch. There were thirteen men on the assault team, including the pilots. All of them were experienced military combat veterans, just like him, except for one who only had law enforcement experience. *This time they will get paid what they deserve, not paltry government paychecks.*

Looking through his night vision goggles, Radcliff saw the operator from the second chopper begin fast-roping down to the top of the moving semi-trailer that they were using to simulate a moving freight train. Fast-roping is the quickest method of insertion and affords the assault team the element of surprise. Radcliff, like all Special Forces personnel, was acutely aware of the danger of this preferred technique, especially on a moving platform. This time, the risk was worth 150 million dollars instead of *God and Country,* which made the challenge much more appealing.

The assault called for five operators inserting themselves onto the moving train during the cover of night. Two operators would be responsible for commandeering the engine, while three operators neutralized the DEA agents and the others at the back of the train in the caboose. Timing was essential because there were only two locations along the route where the off-load could occur. At one of the two locations, the remaining team of operators would be waiting in two vans to transfer the cocaine.

Radcliff wanted to be part of the insertion team, but his overall responsibility as the commander of the mission dictated that he be seated in the co-pilot seat of the lead chopper. Radcliff monitored his watch and wondered if they would get the green light to go through with the actual assault. The first possible assault location was five hours away and the second was just under ten.

"Eagle-1 to Eagle-2. You're clear for your run," the lead pilot radioed the second chopper pilot.

"10-4," came the response as he veered to the left and began zeroing in on the fast moving semi.

Radcliff was watching three operators sprawled out on the top of the semi when he felt his cell phone vibrate. He reached down and pressed the button that lit up the screen and saw the numbers 111.

"Yes!" he said out loud as he clenched his fists and punched the air. The pilot, focusing on the run, didn't notice. The second chopper turned sharply to the right. The last operators had inserted onto the trailer.

"This is Tower, we've got the order to go. Let's wrap this up and do it for real."

The pilot next to Radcliff turned to him and signaled.

Each of the team members was equipped with bone microphone headsets that connected to Motorola shortwave radios, providing reliable communications throughout the tactical operation. The equipment had belonged to the First Ranger battalion in Fort Stewart, Georgia. *The idiots at Fort Stewart probably don't realize they're missing the equipment yet,* Radcliff laughed to himself.

SOUTHERN PACIFIC RAILWAYS, ARIZONA

Ryker shifted around as he tried to get comfortable. It was his second night aboard the train and he had not quite adjusted to his makeshift bunk. The noise in the caboose was deafening. He thought it was a miracle that Smittie could hear at all. Ryker couldn't believe that Chan was dead asleep. *The guy must be on drugs to sleep through this crap,* Ryker thought as he got up and sat in a seat next to the window. He stared out at the outline of dark freight cars in front of the caboose. He reflected on the meeting earlier in the day with the DEA agents from the Las Vegas office. The stop had been short and uneventful. No one would ever guess they were escorting 150 million dollars' worth of cocaine. Security was low key, they didn't want to raise suspicion.

"This is Eagle-1, we have contact. Dead ahead, about two hundred yards," the lead pilot radioed.

"10-4." Eagle-2, the second pilot responded.

Right on time, Radcliff thought as the radio traffic echoed in his headset.

The two helicopters were flying at low altitude in an attack formation approaching the train from a perpendicular angle. Both choppers banked sharply to the left. The attack plan called for an approach from the rear to avoid detection by the engineers in the front of the train. They were intercepting the train right at the beginning of the target zone, a hundred-mile stretch of an operational oil drilling field.

Ryker was relaxed even though he still couldn't sleep. The noise from the train was irritating, but he was learning to block it out. Something in the sky caught his attention. He focused on the horizon and caught a glimpse of a silhouette of a helicopter above the mountain ridge. He leaned closer to the glass and strained his eyes to get a permanent fix on what he thought he saw, but it was gone…nothing but the outline of the mountain range in the distance. *It couldn't have been a chopper, they don't fly without lights.*

"This is Eagle-1. We are in final approach," the lead pilot radioed.

The assault team, dressed in black fatigues, conducted their final checks before the insertion. Pirate-3 was in the cargo bay of the lead chopper and was holding the two-inch thick rope as they prepared to fast-rope. He concentrated on the task at hand as he signaled his team. The raid teams in both choppers were oblivious to the roar of the helicopters' turbine engines.

Radcliff held on as the lead chopper finished a high banking turn and entered the final approach, approximately five hundred yards directly behind the train.

"This is Tower. Drop is in thirty seconds. Give me a radio check, over," Radcliff addressed the team.

"Eagle-1 ready."

The rest of the team counted off.

"We are good to go!" Radcliff ordered as he started the stopwatch feature on his Indiglo G-Shock watch. They had thirty minutes to take control of the train, plus a ten-minute grace period before the train reached the drop site.

"Steady," the lead chopper radioed over the intercom as he began the attack run and rapidly descended toward the train, now one hundred yards directly in front of him.

The pilot concentrated on the eleventh car from the caboose. There was minimal light as he looked through the night vision goggles and counted the freight cars.

"Got it," the pilot announced as he slowed down and matched speed with the train, directly above the targeted freight car.

Pirate-3 felt the vibration inside the helicopter as it aligned itself with the eleventh car.

"Go!" The lead pilot ordered the crew.

Pirate-3 dropped the rope out of the chopper's side door. Pirates-4, 5 and 6 nodded to each other, then made their rapid descent. Radcliff saw the silhouettes of the first three operators glide down the rope onto the top of the freight car. He held on as the lead chopper banked right, allowing the second helicopter to make its approach.

"We're going in," the second pilot announced as the helicopter dropped altitude and zeroed in on the train.

Ryker continued to stare out the window. He still couldn't shake the sense that something wasn't quite right. He strained his eyes searching into the darkness but saw nothing out of the ordinary. The sky was overcast, and he could barely make out the oil rigs in the distance. He stood and walked toward the exit door of the caboose.

"Pirate-4 to Pirate-7. We are secure. Come on down." The loud sound of rushing wind echoed over the radio net.

"10-4."

Within a few seconds, the second chopper was in position.

"Go!" Eagle-2, the second pilot called over the intercom.

Pirate-7 signaled Pirate-8 and they jumped out of the chopper on the ropes. Pirate-9 remained in the chopper, providing security, carefully watching the team as they fast roped out. The wind jostled them as they glided down the ropes to join the other operators already on the train. The second chopper banked to the right and maintained a holding pattern.

Radcliff concentrated on the luminous dials of his stopwatch. They were five minutes ahead of schedule. He felt a sense of satisfaction as he watched them execute the plan exactly as he had trained them.

He felt his cell vibrate. His eyes widened in disbelief as he read the screen: "444"…the code signal to abort.

"Fuck!" he yelled, but it was drowned out by the noise of the engines.

"This is Tower. Abort! I repeat, abort!" He turned to the pilot, "Let's pick 'em up!"

"Copy." The pilot jerked hard right and started his approach toward the rear of the train.

"Heads up! Signal your copy," Radcliff radioed the teams.

Within seconds, all members of the raid team acknowledged.

"Eagle-2, recover your team first, then provide cover," Radcliff spoke into the chopper's intercom.

"10-4," he responded. He had been focusing his attention on the caboose before the abort order had been given.

"What the fuck is going on?" Pirate-4 called out to the two operators next to him. They didn't reply but watched the chopper as its outline got closer to them in the darkness.

Pirate-9 held the recovery ladder in his hands and leaned out. The chopper maintained air speed with the train as it traveled directly above the raid team below. He saw the five sprawling figures on top of the train as he dropped the ladder. The recovery altitude was slightly lower than the insertion. It only took about one minute for the first two members to return to the second helicopter. "We're clear," the pilot radioed as he banked to the right.

Pirate-3 prepared to drop the recovery ladder as the lead helicopter approached the remaining members of the assault team.

"Tower, this is Pirate-9. We have movement at the caboose."

Radcliff immediately twisted around to look over his shoulder, but he couldn't see the caboose from his position.

"Looks like the rear door of the caboose just opened."

"10-4," Radcliff replied. There was no need to give any orders or to jam the radio with unnecessary traffic. His team was well trained and had planned for such contingencies. *I hope this is not the fucking reason why we are aborting,* he angrily considered the possibilities.

"Where're you going, Alex?" Smittie asked, brown spit dripping down the side of his mouth.

"Can't sleep. I just want to get some fresh air," Ryker's concerned expression gave away his uneasiness.

"Nobody's gonna steal your treasure."

"Yeah, I know," he replied defensively, embarrassed that the old man had read his concern so easily.

"Put those gloves on. That ladder is cold and slippery, son. If you fall, you're gonna be flatter than an Aunt Jemima pancake!" Smittie grinned as he stuffed a wad of tobacco in his mouth.

"I'll be careful," Ryker replied grudgingly as he put on the gloves and went out the door. The noise was louder than he had expected. The rhythmic pounding of the wheels on the tracks made it barely tolerable. He pulled himself onto the ladder and held his position for few seconds.

"We've got movement outside the caboose. Male target on the ladder," Eagle-9 reported. He had already grabbed his H&K sniper rifle, slung the shoulder strap under his right arm, and started to zero in on the target with his night scope.

It's got to be one of those DEA pricks, Radcliff speculated as he watched the last operator make his way up the ladder.

Pirate-9 had the target in the cross hair of his scope as the target started to climb up the metal ladder on the rear of the train. The vibration of the chopper bounced the scope away from his shooting eye, but he still maintained visual contact with the aid of the aerial sniper support platform. If the target reached the top before the last helicopter cleared the area, he would fire two rapid rounds. If the rounds didn't kill him, the fall from the train would.

Ryker was halfway up the ladder when his foot slipped, and he almost fell. He grabbed tightly onto the ladder as he regained his balance. He bent his elbow and hooked it around the ladder, pulling himself close to the side of the train, his heart pounding, grateful he hadn't fallen to his death.

"What a moron!" Pirate-9 sneered as he watched the figure through his scope. "Come on, make it to the top so I can shoot your ass."

"All right, we're clear. Let's go," Pirate-3 radioed as he pulled the last operator into the helicopter.

Both pilots turned their birds hard right and accelerated, departing the area at full speed.

"You lucky bastard!" Pirate-9 shouted as he lowered his H&K rifle to his chest. He leaned out of the chopper and the wind plastered his hair against his scalp. With each passing second, the train became smaller and smaller, to a point where he could no longer distinguish which freight car had been the target.

Ryker pulled himself on top of the car and a blast of rushing wind hit his face. He searched in both directions but saw nothing on top of the train. He squinted and he could swear he saw the outline of two helicopters on the horizon, but only for a second. He turned and faced in that direction but the image was gone. He wasn't sure he'd seen anything at all.

"Son! What are you doin' up there? Come on down before you fall on your ass," Smittie bellowed above the noise.

The wind was so strong that Ryker didn't hear him. He kept staring at the horizon, but still didn't see anything. He carefully negotiated down the metal ladder and returned to the caboose.

"What the hell you doin'?" Smittie asked, irritated, as he spit a thick brown stream into a can.

"I couldn't sleep. I thought I heard something, so I decided to get some fresh air and check it out. That's all."

"Back here in the caboose, we hear all kind of noises. You'll get used to it."

Getting used to it was the last thing Ryker wanted to do. He crawled into his bunk, determined to get some sleep, but he couldn't stop thinking about helicopters.

BOGOTÁ, COLOMBIA

Joaquin and Roberto's near-naked bodies dripped sweat as they laid beside the pool. Perched on a plateau, a little higher than the villa, the artistically designed, Olympic-sized swimming pool surrounded by Greek columns was center stage in the Gusto compound.

"Simple things are treasures to me now," Joaquin said as he bit into a piece of crisp, chilled melon.

"I agree. I would like to ask you a favor," Roberto replied.

"What is it?"

"My mind is consumed by the fact of our betrayal."

"As it should be, our lives are at risk," Joaquin replied as he picked up a towel and sponged sweat from his chest.

"The only people I trust are you and your brothers. The other members of the council...I do not fully trust them, but I do not think that they would betray us because we share a common economic interest."

"Yes?"

"I am concerned about the household staff. That is the only possible area of weakness that I can think of. I had everywhere swept for bugs, but found nothing," Roberto explained with trepidation in his voice.

"What is your plan?"

"I want to search Maria's room and place her under surveillance."

Joaquin sat up in his lounge chair and stared at Roberto for a few seconds without speaking a word. "She's a trusted member of our family."

"The other night, when I showed you the list from Viper, I left it in the study. When I returned an hour later to get it, Maria was in the study…"

"What was she doing?" Joaquin interrupted, frowning. "Did she do something to cause suspicion?"

"No." Roberto knew Joaquin had feelings for Maria and was overly protective of her.

"She was cleaning the room? It is her job to clean the room!" Joaquin protested.

"I will be very careful. She will not know that I am watching her."

"I will not insult her. She is loyal to the family."

"She may be, but we must consider every possibility. She will not learn of this, I give you my word."

"She must never know of it, ever. I am certain that you will find nothing."

Roberto was relieved that Joaquin had not been angry. He didn't necessarily suspect the woman, but she had seemed startled when he had come into the room.

"Roberto, what have you learned about Manuel's death?" Joaquin changed the subject.

"It is still a mystery. We have found no other witnesses. There are rumors that he was being chased by a gringo, possibly an American, before the car struck him. Also, we know he had fired his weapon."

At that point, Roberto's watch alarm beeped. "I must get back to work."

"I will go in as well. The sun has grown too warm."

The men dived into the pool and swam to the other side. They used thick white towels to dry off as they walked back to the main villa.

"What is going on in Mexico City?" Joaquin asked as they walked through the manicured garden surrounding the pool.

"I haven't heard from our friend, so I am confident that everything is going exactly as planned."

MOBILE, ALABAMA

The phone rang in the caboose and Smittie answered. "Yeah, okay," he replied then hung up.

"We'll be here for at least thirty minutes," Smittie updated Ryker.

Ryker looked out the window and saw lines of freight trains on parallel tracks.

"Let's go check our package," Ryker was eager to get fresh air.

"Man, I'm happy for any excuse to stretch my legs," Chan replied as he stifled a yawn.

Ryker jumped from the last step onto the gravel beside the tracks. A mechanical, oily smell permeated the air and warm air rushed out from under the train around their legs.

They watched another freight train pull into the station five tracks away and felt the ground vibrate. The chief engineer waved at the two agents as they approached the eleventh freight car; the one ferrying the coveted cargo.

"I had my first good sleep last night," Chan stretched his arms.

"I don't know how anybody can sleep on this damn thing."

As they walked up to the side of the freight car, Ryker noticed that his feet sank deeper into the gravel, making it increasing difficulty to walk.

"Here it is. Nobody has stolen it yet," Chan wryly observed.

Ryker wasn't so sure. He wanted to inspect the car with a magnifying glass. If a chopper had been flying around the train in the middle of the night, through a deserted oil field, it was for one reason only.

Ryker double checked the security lock on the freight car's door, noting that it appeared intact. There were no telltale signs of tampering, such as scratches. He inspected the door closely and saw no signs of attempted forced entry. His cell began ringing. He checked and saw a ten-digit number that he did not recognize.

"You mind taking this call? I want to check something out," he tossed Chan the phone.

Ryker walked between the connecting freight cars and climbed up the ladder, hoisting himself on top of the rail car. He planted his feet solidly on the roof, maintaining his balance. It was not a flat surface; it peaked in the middle at a slight angle. He carefully traversed the length of the car, inspecting every inch.

"Hey you up there!" A rail yard worker shouted at him from two tracks away.

"He's with me, it's okay," Smittie yelled back.

Ryker couldn't see Smittie, but saw the worker acknowledge him with a wave. He turned around and started to walk back toward the other end. He continued to scan the top of the car, but he didn't know what, if anything, he was looking for.

Out of the corner of his eye, he saw something dark on the edge of the roof, near the middle of the freight car. He gingerly approached the object, trying to keep his balance. He knelt down and inspected it. It was a piece of cloth, caught in a rough edge on the side of the car. He tugged at it to loosen it from the metal, but it was difficult to break free. He patiently worked it back and forth until he pulled it loose. He examined the cloth and a chilling thought crossed his mind. The texture of the material was consistent with black, cotton, rip-stop material…the type used by SWAT teams and military personnel. It was the same material his SWAT style BDU pants were made of, the pants that had been issued to him at the DEA Academy.

"Alex, what are you doing?" Smittie called from directly behind him.

Ryker jumped, startled by the unexpected voice. "Just checking the rooftop," he replied as he clenched the cloth in his hand.

"Son, ain't nothing happening to that train car. The only way to get in is through that locked door."

"Just being cautious. I don't want anything to happen on my watch, that's all," Ryker replied somewhat sheepishly.

"We'd better get down from here. We're going to be on the move in about ten minutes."

"Alex, hey Alex!" Chan yelled from down below.

"Yeah, we're coming down," Ryker replied as he followed Smittie toward the ladder. Ryker looked at the *Big Ben Davis* patch on the back rear pocket of the conductor's pants and noticed that railway employee uniforms were not made of rip-stop cotton.

"That was the local DEA office. They had a shooting last night. Nobody got hurt except for the crooks. Anyway, they are tied up with the crime scene. They were going to send two agents out, but I told them we'd be gone before they got here."

"Sounds good to me. We'll be out of here in ten minutes anyway," Ryker replied as they all walked back to the caboose.

The possibilities raced through his head. *What am I going to do now? Only a few DEA agents and a small number of railroad types know what we're carrying. Shit, if there is some kind of leak, who can I trust? How the hell can I get in touch with Connor? Maybe I should call Cartwright and tell him? Tell him what, you idiot...that you thought you saw a helicopter flying at night and that you found a tiny piece of what looks like BDU material on the roof top? Sir, I saw helicopters flying at night in the middle of an operational oil field. I think they may have been trying to rip off a moving freight train. What do you think, sir?* Ryker imagined how far-fetched it sounded. He tried to shrug it off as rookie jitters, but he couldn't stop obsessing about it. He sighed as he climbed back on board. He'd keep it to himself...for now.

MEXICO CITY, MEXICO

The black marble countertop and matching floors contrasted dramatically with the gold fixtures and white porcelain sinks in the lavishly appointed hotel lobby bathroom. Viper rinsed his hands with cold water and lightly patted his face as he starred in the mirror. He was pleased with his altered appearance. His new mustache, longer hair, and wire rim glasses gave him an almost scholarly appeal.

His eyes darted to the bathroom door as it opened. Two individuals were engaged in conversation and didn't notice him at the sink.

He recognized the two photographers he had followed from the airport; the ones who had led him to Tara. He slowly wiped his hands then returned to the hotel lobby. He knew that she would be close by. He could sense it. He scanned the lobby and chose a corner section occupied by three older women. Tracking two targets at the same time intrigued Viper.

His favorite aspect of his profession was stalking his prey. The final act of killing was anticlimactic for him as an assassin. He focused on his primary target, Diego Cuevas, as he positioned himself on a sofa next to two American tourists. The manicured and stylishly dressed women looked like rich doctors' wives on holiday. He ignored their admiring glances in his direction as he continued to watch Cuevas and set his stopwatch.

SAN FRANCISCO, CA

It was an unusually high 80 degrees in the shade when Raven pulled up to the gate of his recently renovated, ten-story condominium complex in San Francisco's South of Market district. His condo's climate control was set at 60 degrees. As soon as he opened his front door, he closed his eyes and enjoyed the cool air. The door closed behind him with a thud. The next thing he felt was a blow that knocked him forward. His face was pinned against the wall by a huge hand, roughly twisted around his neck.

"Hey asshole. How you doin' today?" Radcliff hissed viciously. "Fucker, you jeopardized my men during a mission. What was so goddamned important that we had to abort? You don't tell me to pull out when I'm screwing a beautiful woman and you don't tell me to pull out after I've inserted with my team! Do you know how much money it costs to operate this kind of operation!" Radcliff let up slightly on the death grip he had on Raven's neck.

"They had additional security that we didn't know about," Raven coughed as he grabbed the hands that were crushing his neck.

"I hope you don't mean that limp-ass DEA agent in the caboose. If you called it off because of him, I'll snap your neck off."

"Listen to me, you idiot! DEA got their hands on a special rail car with a built-in titanium chamber. One that the government uses to transport special weapons across country. You special ops boys do know what they are, don't you, Nickolas? They are impregnable!" Raven sputtered as he struggled to break free. "DEA put a new prototype motion sensor pinhole camera on the door. That would have gone off as soon as you'd attempted to open it and I do mean attempted to open it! Now let me go you crazy motherfucker!" he spat.

"Go on." Radcliff roughly let him go.

Raven rubbed his neck and angrily shot back, "Listen you crazy son- of- a- bitch. I have just as much to lose as you do. Or have you forgotten that?"

"I haven't forgotten a damn thing. And frankly, your intel sucks! You should have known about that shit way in advance. That's your problem, not mine."

"Yeah, well it ain't a perfect world, Nikolas. Just so happens that the night of the mission, I was out drinking with a DEA tech. After a few pops, he tells me the whole scenario, including the fact it was being monitored from the ops center at DEA Headquarters. There would have been no way for your team to open the titanium chamber, and when you tried it, the whole fucking world would have seen you on camera. Can you hear me now, asshole? So, big time Ranger...my intel was real-time and actionable, so get the fuck out of my face!" Raven shouted and shoved Radcliff back with both hands and tried to control his rage.

"Shit! We just lost 150 million bucks!" Radcliff hit his fist against the palm of his own hand in frustration.

"Maybe not," Raven glared at him sullenly as he rubbed his neck, then reached for a bottle of Scotch.

MEXICO CITY, MEXICO

His eyes focused on the elevator doors as they opened. Diego Cuevas followed his two bodyguards into the lobby. Viper preferred to stalk his victims as long as possible. At 6'4", Cuevas was easy to stalk. He towered over most of the country's citizens and weighed in at 280 pounds. Viper analyzed the way Cuevas walked and dressed. He monitored his facial expressions and mannerisms. It was clear that Cuevas was arrogant and enamored with his own power, but at a hundred yards, under a night scope, he was just another fat, helpless rabbit. He watched the men as they walked through the lobby and approached the hotel's main entrance. The doorman, anticipating their departure, opened the door and dropped his head in submission as they walked out.

Viper paused for a second. The elevator doorbell rang and a flood of beautiful women and several photographers strutted into the crowded lobby. All eyes focused on the women. Even the receptionists stopped to stare as they passed the check-in counter.

He first recognized the exotic Asian model engaged in an animated conversation with Tara. He was close enough to hear them speak.

"Hoshi, we are going to have a blast shopping today!" Tara spoke excitedly.

"No doubt! We need some retail therapy after all this work," she answered as she swept her hair away from her face and they continued outside to the awaiting charter bus.

Business before pleasure, Viper reminded himself as he turned his attention from the women and focused on Cuevas. He stood up and walked toward the side exit.

"Hoshi, I forgot my bracelet! I want to match it with a new pair of earrings. Tell the driver to wait for a few minutes while I run back to the room."

"Hold on, I'll go with you."

"Hurry up, we don't have all day," the driver raised his voice impatiently. They flashed him a smile and his frown melted away.

They quickly walked back into the hotel and Tara caught a side view of a man walking across the lobby and a sick feeling struck her as she strained to get a better look.

"What's wrong?" Hoshi asked as she noticed Tara's stricken facial expression.

"I saw a guy who looked like someone I met in France. A really scary guy."

"Where is he?" she asked in alarm.

"He just left through the side entrance. His face was different but he had the same walk...posture...there was something so familiar about him."

"Do you want to call security?"

"It probably wasn't him, just someone similar that's all. Come on...we'd better hurry up or the bus will leave without us."

God I hope that wasn't Devinuer, Tara worried fearfully. She never wanted to see him again. She still didn't know what had really happened that night. He had seriously injured or killed two men who had attacked them, but why didn't he call the police? What was he hiding? Tara looked around before she stepped into the elevator. She wished that Alex Ryker was with her.

"Tara, are you sure that you're all right?" Hoshi asked.

"I'll be fine, let's go." The elevator doors closed slowly behind them.

AMERICAN EMBASSY, MEXICO CITY

"Hey boss, let me introduce you to Jack Connor from San Francisco," Gill Thomas said as he walked into the office.

"Glad to meet you, Jack. Bill Cartwright told me you were coming down on your case," replied Frank Tito, the Country Attaché of DEA's Mexico City office. A twenty-year DEA veteran, Tito had held many positions during his distinguished career.

"Well, I haven't started working on my case yet. Let's just say our night out on the town was cut a little short last night," Connor added.

"What?"

"It was El Capitán, again!"

Thomas gave Tito a blow-by-blow account of the shooting. Tito hardly seemed surprised.

"It's a real hornet's nest down here. As long as none of our agents get hurt, I don't care what these thugs do among themselves. Jack, I need a favor," he shifted gears.

"What's that, sir?"

"There's a certification conference going on down here for the next two days and I need all the agents I can get to assist. I know you need Gill to go to the coast with you and interview your informant, but would you mind delaying your trip for two days until the conference is over?"

"Sure, not a problem."

"Thanks. Stick with Gill and he'll tell you what you need to know. I heard rumors that the AG might come down with the NSA for this and everybody in the Embassy will be working on it. After this is all over, you can have whoever you need on your investigation."

"Gill, could you do me a favor?"

"Sure, boss."

"Go over to the Mexican governor's house later this afternoon and take our flag and the AG's flag and place them with the others? Also, see if there is anything else we need to add to the conference room for the meeting."

271

"No problem. I'm going to show Jack around and then we'll all go over there and hang the bird." Thomas cracked a smile as they left the CA's office with the light blue and white DEA flag. Agents called the seal on the flag the *Flying Goose* because of the corny insignia.

Connor felt a little disappointed at first. He had wanted to meet with Carlos right away, but then he realized the next two days might give him a taste of what it's like to work in a foreign post.

"Your boss seems like a good guy."

"He is. It's a whole different world down here. We can't trust anyone outside DEA and sometimes street justice is the only way to take care of business. Frank will be glad when this conference is over. There are a lot of headaches with a certification conference like this one. The U.S. delegation has a dozen or more VIPs from Washington, including the National Security Advisor and now maybe the AG."

"How many agents are assigned to the Embassy?"

"Well, we have fifteen agents and the bureau has two agents. The third floor is all Agency. God knows how many they have here. They're good guys, we cover each other down here. Just don't believe anything they tell you and you'll be okay."

"Yeah?" Connor didn't take any offense at the stereotyping. After all, CIA agents lied for a living. He knew that first hand.

WASHINGTON, D.C.

The phone rang a fifth time before the Attorney General hung up. *Why does he have a private line if he never answers it?* Henderson thought as he looked up the regular number in his phone contact list. This time, someone answered on the first ring.

"Jordan, Hank. Looks like we are going to be drinking margaritas together."

"Oh yeah?"

"On the flight down, we can go over some issues about the conference."

"Sure, sounds like a great idea. I'll see you at Andrews in the morning." Zif hung up, then answered the phone when it rang again.

"Hi, Lynn. What's up?" He recognized the CIA Director's voice.

"Still no fix on Viper. The best guess we have is that the cartel has some rival they want removed. Be careful down there, I'm sorry we don't have better intel."

"I will, Lynn. Thanks for calling."

The phone line went dead. Bancroft sat back in her chair lost in thought. She flinched at the sound of thunder and lightning crackling in the distance. The weather report had predicted scattered showers, but it looked like it was turning into a thunderstorm.

MIAMI, FLORIDA

The train slowed as they pulled into the Miami Civic Center train station. Ryker was glad the trip was over, but still felt apprehensive. He had little more than a hunch about the choppers and didn't want to make a fool of himself, but if someone was trying to rip off the cocaine, it was his responsibility to inform a supervisor. He decided to contact Connor.

"Hey, Alex. I think I see one of our guys over at the terminal."

A tremendous weight lifted from his chest as he saw a familiar face. "You're right, Henry. That's Ron Williams, the case agent from Washington."

"You know him?"

"Yeah, we were on surveillance together in DC."

"What do you mean? I thought your first assignment was in San Francisco after Quantico."

"Right, but I met him through Connor at one of our training surveillances at the academy." Ryker carefully clarified his response.

"Those training exercises were never realistic, you know?"

"Right," he replied, thinking back to the night when he and Connor arrested two suspects in the middle of the surveillance. That was realistic enough.

"I wonder if the crooks have anybody in the yard watching the shipment," Chan replied.

"Undoubtedly. Let's make contact with Williams inside the terminal."

There was no question in Ryker's mind now. He trusted Williams and would tell him everything and let Williams make the call as to what to do about his suspicions.

"Smittie, thanks for the ride. When I get back to San Francisco, let's go out and get a beer. I'm sure you have a lot of good stories to tell," Ryker called out.

"That goes for me too," Chan chimed in.

"You're buying. You college boys, take care of yourselves." Smittie waved them off.

They jumped down off the caboose and negotiated ten railroad tracks in the freight yard before they reached the train station.

"For a junior boot, you've found yourself in the thick of things, haven't you, Alex?" Williams greeted them with a wry smile.

"Yes sir, I have. We're just a couple of hard-charging rookies. Ron, this is Henry Chan. He's also assigned to San Francisco."

"Henry, glad to meet you." Williams' handshake was solid.

"Let's go upstairs to your observation point and I will brief you two on the operation."

They went to an office on the second floor at the south end of the building, overlooking the train with the freight car containing the shipment of cocaine.

Williams picked up the radio. "DC-111 to Miami-111."

"Go ahead," the Miami team leader responded.

"We're in position."

"10-4."

"This is the plan, guys. There are ten Miami agents watching the train right now. It will take about four hours to unload the freight car. Yesterday, we learned from the freight company that the entire shipment is going to DC. The load could leave as early as tonight. The Miami team will follow the load halfway to DC, where agents from my group will meet them and escort the load the rest of the way. Henry and Alex are going with us."

"Anything is an improvement over riding on that train," Chan replied emphatically.

"Miami-111 to DC-111."

"Go ahead."

"Could you send one of your guys over to location two? They're moving some video equipment to get a better vantage point and they need some help for thirty minutes or so."

"10-4," Williams responded.

"I'll go. I want to stretch my legs and I'm good with tech equipment," Chan volunteered.

"All right, go downstairs and one of the agents will take you to the building."

Ryker was a little uneasy at first but after a few minutes of small talk, he got up his nerve and told Williams his concerns and showed him the piece of material that he had found on the roof of the train.

Williams carefully inspected it.

"It's rip stop all right, but I'm not sure what to make of it. I'm glad you told me."

"I have to admit, I was afraid you'd think my imagination got the best of me."

"Have you told anybody else?"

"Hell no! I didn't want anybody to think I was some overzealous rookie."

"I'm glad you haven't told anyone, but not because of what they may think of you. If what you suspect is true, we have a serious leak on the inside, a leak with high-level connections. Only serious players would attempt an air assault on a moving train in the dead of night."

"I know! It doesn't seem logical…too Hollywood, you know? I didn't think anybody would believe me." Ryker's relief was evident in his tone.

"Well, for now, I'll call Washington and talk to someone I trust. This could get complicated very quickly," Williams replied as he kept a closer eye on the train.

CHAPTER 16

GOVERNOR'S MANSION, MEXICO CITY

The governor's mansion was resplendent. DEA agents called it the Grand Palace, even though it was somewhat less ornate and imposing than the Presidential mansion located just outside of Mexico City in a surreal country setting.

"Twenty million dollars! That is double what we are paying now, your Excellency. The attorney general is cracking down on us and some of our important federales have been arrested," Diego Cuevas spoke in a tone of disgusted amazement. *What is this puppet governor thinking? I will have him killed if he tries to steal from me,* Cuevas thought.

Agitated, Cuevas became less formal with the governor. "Since the attorney general took office, he has tried to crush the cartels. He raided four warehouses last month and knocked a hole in one of the distribution networks. He has higher political ambitions. He is trying to impress the Americans. He will use the certification conference in a few days," he paused, then added, "How do you plan to stop that swine López?"

"Leave Attorney General López to me," a new voice replied, entering the living room where the men were gathered.

Cuevas immediately recognized the powerful voice. "Vice Presidente."

"Señor Cuevas, we all have our vices, including our attorney general. I have recently obtained a bit of intelligence on the good Señor López that I think will change his political attitude on a few issues."

Cuevas had heard rumors about the Vice President but had no direct knowledge of him working with any Colombian or Mexican cartel. *Perhaps 20 million wasn't such a bad deal after all,* he pondered his new secret investment.

"Tell me, Vice Presidente," Cuevas's eyes narrowed into thin slits as he waited for a reply.

SAN FRANCISCO DEA FIELD OFFICE

"Good morning. Is Bill in?" Steiner greeted the receptionist through the bulletproof glass window of the San Francisco DEA Field Office.

"Yes he is, you can go back." Steiner heard the familiar click as the main door unlocked, when the receptionist hit the hidden release button allowing access to the secure DEA office space.

"Bill, did you get the arrest warrant on the heroin fugitive?" Steiner asked as he walked into Cartwright's office.

"Yeah, it came in this morning. It's in my in-basket. Molly, please make me a copy," Cartwright instructed his secretary as she peeked her head through the door frame.

"That's ok, Molly, I'll do it, I have nothing to do right now," Steiner volunteered.

Cartwright nodded his approval. She had more than enough to do, so one less menial task was fine with her.

"What's the latest on the Bogotá connection?" Steiner changed the subject.

"The load is en route to Miami and we think that the final destination is DC."

"Interesting." Steiner started thinking about the possibility of another shot at the cocaine somewhere between Miami and DC.

"Sir, the SAC would like to see you," his secretary interrupted.

"Got a few minutes?" We can grab an early lunch after I see what the SAC wants."

"Sure, I'll make that copy."

Steiner walked over to the desk and went through the in-basket. He found the arrest warrant from the Eastern District of California, then continued to shuffle through the documents. About half way down the stack, he noticed the bold lettering: "Operational Plan/Operation Bright Star."

Bingo! Steiner recognized the codename for the Bogotá Cartel investigation. His eyes raced across the stapled documents. *This is it!*

"Find the arrest warrant yet?" Molly asked as she walked by the office on her way to the crypto room.

Steiner's heart jumped as his body stiffened at the sound of her voice.

"Took me a minute. The pages stuck together in the stack."
He flashed her a calculated smile.

"They'll make you an agent yet," she smiled back.

Steiner knew he only had a few minutes. He slipped out of
the office and headed for the copy room, praying that no one else
was using the copier. It took him less than 30 seconds to copy the op
plan and the arrest warrant. He folded his copy of the documents,
slid them into his jacket pocket, then went back into the office.

Yes! He gloated as his mind went into overdrive. He could
make this work.

"Molly, will you please tell Bill that I got a call from the
office and I had to get back. Tell him we'll go out to lunch next
week."

"Sure."

As soon as Steiner exited the building, he dialed the number.
It was almost lunch time and the street was starting to fill with
government workers in business attire, getting a jump on the noon
lunch hour.

"Hello," a familiar voice came from the other line.

"Are you doing anything right now?"

"Why, what's up?" Nick Radcliff replied.

"I think we might have another chance on our project. Pick
me up at the corner of Van Ness and Golden Gate in 30 minutes. I'll
show you what I've got," Steiner directed.

"This better be good!"

"It is, believe me, it is."

"Mr. Cartwright, Ron Williams from the DC office is on line
two."

"Thanks Molly."

"Hi Ron. How's it been going?"

"Fine, so far. My ASAC wanted me to call you and give you
an update. Your two agents arrived here in Miami with no problems.
We are in the process of offloading the cocaine now. No sight of the
suspects yet. We think that since the load is going to DC, we won't
see any of them until we arrive in the Washington area. We already
approached the trucking company and they have no problems with
one of our guys driving the rig up there."

"Good, your office faxed me a copy of your op plan this
morning," Cartwright responded.

"We found a Dade county narc officer who has a commercial license and moonlights as a trucker on the side. He's been assigned to us for the delivery."

"Seems like you got everything under control."

"Hope so. There's one more thing," Williams paused.

"What's that?"

"One of your agents, Alex Ryker, had some interesting information. He was a little nervous bringing this up as a new agent, but I think his observations may have some merit." For the next ten minutes, Williams briefed Cartwright on Ryker's suspicions about the helicopter.

"I've got a good feeling about Ryker. I met him in DC during training and he seems to have good instincts. If we did almost get raided, we have a serious leak," Williams concluded.

There was a pause on the phone line for a few seconds. "You're right Ron. Have you told anyone else about this?"

"Only my ASAC. I thought I would call you next since this info came from your agent," Williams replied.

"I appreciate that Ron. Okay, I'll inform my SAC. I don't think you have to worry about the transport to DC…there are too many agents involved. The train was a different matter because there were only two agents covering it. If Ryker is correct, serious professionals are involved. They'd have to be highly trained and well-funded. Your SAC may assign a few more agents to the detail for extra security. Tell Ryker he did a good job," he added.

"Will do sir, have a good day." Williams was glad he had taken Ryker's observations seriously.

Cartwright went through his in-basket looking for the ops plan for the escort to DC. He found it and briefly looked it over. He noticed that the last page was duplicated. He ripped the duplicate page off and threw it in his shred box, then took the ops plan and walked straight to the SAC's office.

"George, you got a minute? We might have a problem."

Steiner walked a couple of blocks away from the federal building and ducked into an alley where there were no street surveillance cameras. He heard the sharp blast of a horn from the corner and recognized Radcliff in the driver's seat.

"You made pretty good time." He got into the passenger seat of the van and handed the op plan to Radcliff.

"What's this?"

"This, my friend, is DEA's operational plan for their escort of the cocaine from Miami to DC, where they believe it's going to be picked up by local dealers. This is what DEA calls a controlled delivery," Steiner added smugly.

Radcliff scanned the document for a minute. "Where is the last page?"

"It should all be there...I copied the entire plan myself," he replied in surprise.

"Looks like you are missing the logistic page with the hospital numbers and other bullshit, contact numbers, but all the important stuff is here. Tell you what...I need to review this with my team to determine whether this is possible. I'll get back to you tonight."

Radcliff examined the document in silence for a few minutes. Steiner could tell he was calculating the options. That was a good sign.

"Okay. I'll call you tonight." Radcliff looked in his rear-view mirror and watched Steiner as he quickly walked away.

GOVERNOR'S MANSION, MEXICO CITY

Viper pressed the eyepiece of the scope against his dominant right eye and scanned the second-story balcony of the governor's mansion. He was in a full trial run, dressed in a ghillie suit, situated in a shooting position approximately one hundred yards from the mansion. By comparison, this assignment was far less challenging than his last one. But, he was compulsive and meticulous, taking nothing for granted.

The balcony, almost the size of a full basketball court, afforded a panoramic view of the countryside. Viper could see movement through the wide glass doors of the balcony entrance but could not get a positive identification of the people inside. It was enough for target acquisition and a kill if necessary. He would calculate the shot for deflection and distance.

That's it, Viper thought as the unsuspecting practice target stood in the room, engaged in conversation with another person. He raised his crosshairs upwards so that the shot would be dead center.

The entrance doors to the balcony opened and both men passed through the lens of his scope. He lowered his scope a notch to get a better visual as they walked outside onto the balcony.

"Man, this is living! This balcony has more square footage than my condo back in San Francisco," Connor exclaimed as he and Thomas walked across the balcony.

"You know, Jack, you and Barrett should think about going overseas. Truth be told, there are a lot of nicer duty stations than this, but this isn't exactly slumming it."

"No, it isn't," Connor replied as they approached the elegant hand-carved wooden railing that enclosed the balcony.

Viper's targets stopped at the edge of the balcony overlooking the valley. *Americans,* Viper's lips moved slightly as he focused on them. *Security force or agents, definitely enforcement or military personnel,* he surmised as he took in their lean muscular forms. One of them answered a cell phone.

"Jack that was the embassy. Franklin is trying to contact you. You can use the STE phone when we get back," Thomas relayed the message.

Viper watched as they turned around and walked back into the mansion and zeroed in on the back of one of the men's head. For the next three seconds, he focused, exhaled, and slowly squeezed the three-pound trigger until he heard the dry click of the firing pin.

SAN FRANCISCO, CA

The cold, blustery wind whipped up white caps on the dark water below, but it was not a distraction for the two warmly dressed men who stood among the throng of tourists at the lookout point on the San Francisco side of the Golden Gate Bridge. Some wearing shorts and summer shirts hurried back to their tour buses, eager to get out of the frigid air. They were often unprepared for the dramatic drop in San Francisco's temperatures when the damp fog rolled in. The city skyline sparkled in the distance and dramatic beams of soft white light backlit the towering suspension bridge. It provided a proper backdrop for this clandestine meeting.

"If we agree to this, there will be no turning back like last time. There will definitely be multiple body counts on this mission. Can you handle that?" Radcliff asked as the two men walked away from the lights.

"Excuse me, *General,* but just because I was not in the military doesn't mean I don't know what the consequences are," Raven snapped irritably.

"This can be done, especially in the Carolinas. That's where we all trained and it's a whole different animal than the fucking left coast. That operational plan you got is only a day old and there is time to pull it off."

"Then let's stop wasting time and get on with it," Raven replied defiantly.

"Good." He pressed a programmed number and spoke into his cell phone. "Pick me up in five minutes." He hung up without waiting for a response. "All right, we're on the clock now. We will fly out tonight. This will happen in approximately forty-eight hours. If you get any real-time tactical intel about the convoy, contact me immediately on this cell phone only. Once the hit is made, no contact between us for five days."

"No problem," Raven agreed as he typed the number into his phone's contact list under *Golden Gate.*

"If things get fucked up, we'll have no contact with you at all. It's better if you keep clean so your cover's not blown. You will be more useful that way."

"Right. Don't screw it up," Raven added.

Radcliff gave him a death stare and walked away. Within a few seconds, a black van pulled up and he got in. It disappeared into a red sea of taillights.

"Any contact from Bobby?" Radcliff asked one of his team members.

"Yeah boss, about twenty minutes ago. He just arrived in Miami and did a drive-by at the train station. He spotted three of the five DEA vehicles listed on the op plan. He's in an ideal location and will be able to observe everything when the semi leaves the train yard," Eric Hickson reported.

"Any cartel surveillance?"

"None spotted."

"Doesn't surprise me, they're better trained than the feds." Radcliff doubted the cartel had any surveillance, but if they did, they'd be harder to spot. He despised government agents.

Radcliff had met Hickson during Airborne training at Fort Benning, Georgia. After initial training, Hickson had been assigned to the 82nd Airborne Division, Headquarters Company. He was a transportation specialist and his entire military career had been marred by disciplinary actions. He was forced out after a general court martial, suspected of being involved in an auto theft ring. Radcliff had tracked Hickson down after his discharge and asked him to join his team. Besides being a tough soldier, Hickson was one hell of a mechanic and an expert driver, skills that would be soon tested.

The van headed southbound toward San Francisco International airport. Radcliff mentally rehearsed on the way. He hoped that he hadn't missed anything in his planning. His timetable was drastically short, but he had been able to adapt since his team had already prepared for the earlier assault. He hadn't told Raven that he had already deployed his men to the East Coast. He liked being one step ahead. After Raven gave him the ops plan, he assembled his team and discussed all the logistical and tactical elements of the assault. Two hours later, the team members had their assignments and the mission was a go. Radcliff closed his eyes. It felt great to be operational again.

AMERICAN EMBASSY, MEXICO CITY

"Jack, the STE is in the CA's office," Thomas spoke as they entered DEA office space.

"JTF-5, this is a secure line," a recently assigned Marine lance corporal answered the phone.

"This is Agent Connor from the DEA office in Mexico City. Is Mr. Franklin there?"

"Hold on, sir, I'll check." The sound echoed over the secure line.

You would think with all the modern technology, they would get these damn phones to sound right, Connor thought.

"Jack, how do you like Mexico City?" Franklin came on the line.

"Not bad, at least so far. I was at the governor's mansion helping the office prepare for the certification conference when you texted a couple of hours ago. Sorry I couldn't get to a secure line before now."

"No problem. I just want to give you an update on the sub. They ran into some rough seas and it put them back about a day, so they should arrive in two to three days. I hope they got seasick. I've coordinated with the Navy. Those guys are going to be in for a surprise."

"Good, I'll need the time. I'm helping out DEA with the conference," Connor replied.

"Do you know the National Security Advisor?"

"I met him briefly at Quantico."

"Well, he's a friend of mine and he's a friend to DEA. If you see him, tell him I said hello."

"Will do."

"Gotta go. Talk to you soon."

"When do the AG and NSA arrive?" Connor turned and spoke to Thomas.

"Later tonight. A security detail's going to pick them up at the airport and escort them to the ambassador's residence. Tomorrow the conference will start and the reception will follow at the governor's mansion in the late afternoon. Another two days and this will be over."

"Let's go get a bite to eat. We should be back at the Embassy an hour before the VIP's arrival. We won't be needed for the detail, but I told the boss we'd be in the office in case they need us. Any particular place you want to go to eat tonight?"

"I can think of one place I don't want to go," Connor grimaced.

"What's wrong, Jack? You don't like the live-fire dinner exercises we have down here?" Thomas feigned surprise.

"I prefer to do my dining and tactical training in separate locations, if you don't mind."

"Hey, we could go to another place where wearing our Kevlar is optional, but preferred."

"Oh… that's just what I should tell Barrett the next time we discuss an overseas assignment. *Oh dear, you need to add a ballistic vest to your overseas wardrobe,*" Connor used an appeasing tone of voice for effect.

They laughed as they headed outside. It was getting dark.

FOUR SEASONS HOTEL, MEXICO CITY

Viper woke from a sound nap in his hotel suite, rested from his reconnaissance patrol. The next few nights were going to be spent in the field, so he wanted to get as much sleep as possible before the mission. He got out of bed and took a long shower. He mentally went over his list to double-check that he had all his equipment and supplies lined up for the next few days. He never used written notes once a mission was in progress. Doing so would constitute a security breach that could compromise him or his mission. In two hours, he had memorized the checklist and every step of his battle plan. Working as a GRU agent early in his career had ingrained in him the need to be as efficient and self-contained as possible to the point of perfection. The planning was over. The mission was now underway.

CIVIC CENTER TRAIN STATION, MIAMI

"I talked to my ASAC and your GS and told them about your suspicions and concerns." Ryker tried to conceal his anxiety as Williams continued. "They're both on board. In fact your GS told me to tell you it was a good call to let us know."

Thank God, Ryker thought in relief.

"He agreed with me that you might have stumbled onto something. Not to mention raised concerns about a major breach of security. As of right now, our plan remains the same. We continue this controlled delivery and see how far it takes us up the food chain. We have to be more alert and provide enough manpower to deal with any threat that comes our way."

"Miami-113 to DC-111."

"Go ahead," Williams replied.

"Hey, Ron, looks like we'll be moving in five minutes. They're are doing a check on the rig and we'll be ready to move shortly," the Miami unit related.

"10-4. I'm located outside the yard. I'll be in the trail car with Ryker."

Three blocks away and six stories up in a corner hotel room, Radcliff's scout, Bobby Fields, watched Williams and a younger man shake hands through his binoculars. He had reconned the area, located the container, and identified most of the DEA surveillance team with the op plan Radcliff had provided. He double-checked the op plan. So far, everything was correct. He watched patiently as the younger man spoke with Williams.

Fields watched the semi leave the yard followed by the convoy of DEA surveillance vehicles as he reported to Radcliff. "The boys are headed back to town. All the cars accounted for."

"Excellent. We've all made it down to the vacation house and the guys are out practicing now," Radcliff replied cryptically, just in case anyone with high-tech listening devices was monitoring cell phone transmissions in the area.

"I should be seeing you soon. If anything changes, I'll give you a call."

"I'll do the same."

GOVERNOR'S MANSION, MEXICO CITY

Viper was accustomed to predawn insertions. He carefully placed a camouflaged net cover over the SUV and collected his equipment. He changed into camouflaged clothing and retrieved his night vision goggles. He cinched up his backpack and adjusted the goggles. Once they were tightly fastened, he turned them on and within a few seconds, the familiar green glow lit up the countryside. He adjusted the light and cued the timer on his stopwatch. The trek to the firing point would take at least sixty minutes. The insertion began.

INTERSTATE 95, NORTH CAROLINA

"Yeah," Radcliff answered his phone.

"We're about sixty minutes from your location," Fields reported. "It just started raining down here. What about where you are?"

"Rainy here too, we just landed. We should be rolling in 30 minutes."

Bobby Fields was the point man for Radcliff's team. He was a rare breed of Ranger, a pathfinder. He had been one of the Rangers' finest snipers until he shot the wrong target in Afghanistan. That, including punching a top-ranking officer, ultimately led to his downfall. Radcliff had heard about the incident and recruited Fields about two months after his discharge. Fields' hatred toward the government had intensified. He was ecstatic about joining Radcliff's team of mercenaries.

Radcliff knew the rain would be a tactical advantage. He dialed another number.

"Trace, Bobby says they're sixty minutes out."

Trace Griswall was another former Ranger grunt and frustrated gung-ho type who had never seen action. Radcliff had no problem recruiting him.

"Roger," Griswall responded

Radcliff made another call.

"A.D., I just talked to Bobby. They're about sixty minutes out. How is it on your end?" Radcliff asked Drum, another member of his team.

"They're all accounted for. The weather could not be any better. It's really pouring down right now. We're about ninety minutes from your location."

"Good."

"We'll contact you every fifteen minutes to give you an update," A.D. replied.

Radcliff was extremely pleased with the versatility of his team. He diverted a two-man team to DC, a couple of ex-Rangers Andrew Drum, was a weapons specialist whose nickname, A.D, short for "accidental discharge", had stuck with him into civilian life and Pat "Patcher" Doolittle, a Special Forces medic. Radcliff, a stickler for detail, wanted them to establish a loose surveillance at the DEA Washington Field Office, verifying any changes in the op plan before rejoining their team.

The DEA team left right on time in the vehicles listed on the op plan. Radcliff hated to admit that he was impressed with DEA. They were detailed, organized, and thorough. But he wasn't worried. His team was just as good…and they had the element of surprise.

"DC-111 to DC-112…DC-111 to DC-112, over. They must not be in range yet. I'll have to check in on my cell," Williams explained to Ryker as he made the call.

"Hey, Jerome. Where are you guys?"

"We're about sixty minutes from the truck stop. The rain is falling pretty hard right now, so we slowed down a bit. We've got to make one more pit stop for gas before we hook up with you guys. How's everything on your end?" asked Special Agent Jerome Samuel, the team leader of the DC crew.

"So far, so good," Williams responded. "Anything on your end?"

"No. So far it's been smooth," Samuel replied. He thought the whole situation had been blown out of proportion by a rookie agent who had watched the movie Bad Boys one too many times.

Samuel, an eight year DEA veteran, was born and raised in Harlem. He spent his first seven years undercover in the Bronx, targeting a Jamaican organization distributing cocaine in Harlem and in the Bronx. He had recently transferred to the Washington Field Office after things got nasty in one of his investigations and he had received death threats.

"Good. I tried to get you on the radio, but the repeater must not be working down here. The car-to-car should work once you get near the truck stop."

"Okay." Samuel hung up.

I can't believe Ron seriously thinks some unknown force is going to attempt to take us on. What the hell has he been smoking lately? Samuel continued to grouse to himself as he glanced at his Eagle bag containing his Colt M-4 assault rifle in the passenger seat of his g-car approaching the freeway exit.

Well, well, what have we here, Max said under his breath as he looked out the van's rear window. *The cavalry has arrived too gas up.* He glanced over to his right and saw A.D. parking his vehicle near his location.

He strained to see through the rain pouring down on the window. He recognized all six of the DEA vehicles as they got off the freeway. He watched as four of them turned into the Shell Mini Mart and the other two pulled into the BP station across the street.

"Nick, they're gassing up," A.D. phoned in.

"Good, come on down and set up," Radcliff replied.

"Roger that."

Samuel caught a glimpse of the van leaving the gas station out of the corner of his eye noticing that a white male was driving the vehicle. He recognized the van from a hundred miles ago, as it approached the south I-95 exit.

"Hey, Jerome, want anything inside?"

"No, thanks."

Because of the job, Samuel was always suspicious of vans. Criminals and law-enforcement types used them in their respective operations. He looked back in the direction of the van, but it was gone. He made a mental note that the driver intentionally avoided eye contact with him as he pulled out of the gas station.

Before you know it, you are going to be as paranoid as that rookie agent, he scolded himself.

"Are you ready back there?" Matt asked his cousin Max.

"Yeah. Just take me to the target zone and slow down."

Max Finder was the explosive expert on Radcliff's team and the only member who had served under Radcliff's military command during his entire enlistment. Finder had barely avoided a court martial and received a less than honorable discharge from the Army for being too aggressive as a bomb tech. His mistake resulted in a premature detonation that had caused his best friend in the squad to lose his arm. Radcliff liked Finder because he was a risk taker and was always trying to improve his skill level.

Matt Finder was the only team member who had not been in the military. He was a former Miami police officer whose career had been cut short. He had resigned to avoid an internal investigation regarding his extracurricular activities. Internal Affairs suspected he was on the take but could never prove it. He filled out the complement of rogue warriors on Radcliff's team.

Max rolled down the rear window. *What a perfect location. The Carolinas are so accommodating,* he thought in smug anticipation. The thick tree line came within fifty feet of both sides of the intersection.

"Max, we're coming up to the location. Standby." Matt looked in his rearview mirror and did not see any headlights behind him as he started to slow down.

"Okay…now!" Matt directed.

Max opened the right-side panel door, pointed the remote device straight at the tree line, and pushed a blinking red button. A puff of white smoke went up when it ignited the fuse.

Matt drove very slowly, still keeping an eye out for traffic behind them. Max repositioned to the rear door window and pointed the second device toward the other side of the freeway.

"Here comes the bang!" Max announced as both fuses raced in single file toward the tree line.

The first explosion rocked the right side of the interstate. They saw the flash of the explosion before they heard the sound. Max veered to the median on the left and saw the fuse's final sizzle up to the tree line, followed by a blinding flash. The second charge exploded and rows of trees on both sides of the freeway came crashing down on the two southbound lanes of I-95.

"We have some lights behind us. Yeah, baby!" Matt exclaimed as he watched traffic in his side mirror. "Damn, that was perfect!"

Max had wrapped the detonation cord around a large tree on each side of the interstate and had positioned the blasting caps and detonation cord so that the force of the explosions would cause the trees to fall directly into the southbound traffic lanes.

As a precautionary measure, he rigged two more trees on each side of the highway in the event that the trees did not fully block the two southbound lanes. His calculations were right on the mark and all four trees sprawled in broken disarray, completely obstructing all southbound lanes of travel.

"Matt, I think we got a couple of semis headed our way," Max said as he saw the small liner lights on top of the cabs through his binoculars. "Pull over! I gotta see this," he added, as excited as a child on Christmas morning.

"Hey Kenworth, you got your ears on, son?" The driver of the brand new Kenworth cab radioed a fellow trucker as he changed into the left lane and started to pass the slower semi on the right.

Before the other trucker could reply, he jolted in horror and disbelief. Because of the heavy rain, he didn't have time to apply his brakes and crashed into the trees in front of him.

What happened next was a chain reaction that the most skilled professional driver could not have avoided. In the right lane, the cab of the semi lurched forward and over the trees as its trailer disengaged and slammed into the cab and trailer in the left lane. The driver of the second cab tried to control his rig during the impact, but the trailer jack-knifed, crushing the cab between the trees and his trailer. The rear wheels of the first cab caught the last tree, causing it to violently cartwheel onto its right side, throwing the driver into the roof and knocking him unconscious as his trailer rolled over onto its side.

"Fuck! Did you see that?" Max's tone was gleeful.

"Oh yeah cuz!" Matt responded as he dialed the preset number.

"It's done."

"How long?" Radcliff asked.

"Hours…if not days," Matt smirked.

"Excellent."

"We'll be there in ten." Max concentrated on the road. Rain and sleet were pelting the windshield like gravel.

CHAPTER 17

MEXICO CITY INTERNATIONAL AIRPORT

The exhaust fumes from the dark blue Chevy Suburban rose into the warm humid air as the engine idled in a special parking area adjacent to the terminal at the Mexico City International Airport. An American security detail was waiting for the arrival of the U.S. delegation headed by the U.S. Attorney General and the National Security Advisor.

The security detail consisted of a squad of Marines, dressed in civilian clothes, from the Marine Security detachment and the State Department's Regional Security Officer (RSO) all assigned to the U.S. Embassy. In addition to the Embassy detail, an escort of Mexican federal police also waited in the staging area in four military vehicles. The U.S. Air Force C-40B was on time and on final approach.

The RSO and the Marine captain looked toward the black Motorola radio shaped like a lunch box that allowed them to overhear the communications between the aircraft and the tower. The National Security Agency had recently retrofitted and modified the standard lunch box radio to allow direct communication to the presidential VIP fleet of Air Force jetliners.

"Let's go!" the Marine captain directed and all vehicles in the security detail began to move in the direction of the aircraft. Within a few minutes, they had surrounded the plane as it came to a complete stop.

Only the RSO and captain maintained a visual on the forward hatch. The rest of the Marines maintained a 360-degree visual outward from the aircraft.

The captain surveyed his squad to ensure they were all in position. He didn't care about the Federal police. He neither trusted nor was he concerned about how they were deployed. He knew if things went to shit, it was going to be his Marines that would protect U.S. personnel...or die trying. Each Marine was equipped with an M-4 assault rifle and a Beretta 9mm pistol, and each vehicle had two LAW rockets.

Within five minutes, the delegation had been loaded into the Suburbans. The convoy drove through the streets of Mexico City to the Ambassador's residence under the watchful eye of the CIA operatives who were stationed throughout the route. Their job was to monitor the route for trouble. Only on special occasions would the agency support operational security for visiting dignitaries. In this situation, there were two significant cabinet-level VIPs, one of whom was the President's best friend.

The phone in the DEA duty room rang twice before Thomas answered.

"All is well. The AG and National Security Advisor just arrived at the Ambassador's house safe and sound. We can secure here and go back to my place. It's going to be hectic the next two days."

"Sounds good to me," Connor replied as he turned off the office lights. The two DEA agents headed out of the office toward the Embassy compound.

GOVERNOR'S MANSION, MEXICO CITY

The morning sun had crept above the tree line and Viper could feel the warmth. It was not as hot and humid as it usually was this time of year in Mexico. He felt little discomfort in his ghillie suit. He was used to it. Enduring the natural elements required as much skill and talent as pulling the trigger.

He held his high-powered binoculars and analyzed the movement in the target area. In less than twenty-four hours, the mission would be complete. He slowly crawled to his shooting position. The likelihood of anyone being within a one hundred yard radius was practically nil, but he took every precaution, as if he was situated in the middle of an enemy camp. Every piece of his equipment had been blacked out to avoid any possible reflection.

He inched into his shooting position. It took him more than twenty minutes to crawl ten feet. A sniper's deadliest skill was the art of stealth and he was a master.

He raised his Remington sniper rifle and scanned the targets on the balcony through a different scope, a Trijicon ACOG or Advanced Combat Optical Gunsight. The ACOG scope was perfect because it was designed with tritium-illuminated reticule patterns to provide maximum hit potential in all lighting conditions and was easier to conceal during international travel. If the hit went down after dark, backlighting from inside would not be a problem.

He zeroed in on two officials standing at the edge. Ideally, this was the desired position...to take the victim at the edge of the balcony so that the body would fall to the ground below. The technical shot would require target assistance. He preferred this angle of attack. It ensured confusion and allowed him a few more minutes for his escape.

He concentrated on his breathing as he focused his crosshairs on an individual who was standing in the target location. As he started to exhale, his finger slowly began to squeeze the trigger.

Click. The firing pin snapped forward. Viper could see the target standing very still.

"This is your lucky day my friend," he said out loud as he completed his final practice run.

I-95, NORTH CAROLINA

Radcliff watched the truck stop entrance as Matt and Max arrived on the scene. There was no need for unnecessary communication. His team knew their assignments. The truck stop was packed due to the rain; a blessing in disguise for Radcliff. Everybody wanted to get out of the rain and get some hot coffee and food. He felt his own stomach growl.

Radcliff picked up his cell phone on the second ring. "Yeah."

"We're on station," Bobby reported.

"Good. We're all in place. Our friends should be arriving soon."

Razor Byrd and Bennie Beaufort, both ex-Airborne troopers, were the lookouts to ensure that there were no surprises from the interstate. They were equipped with military-issued Remington 7.62mm M40A1 sniper rifles with a Redfield, twelve-power scope and M-4s with attached M203 grenade launchers to make their presence known if required.

"Miami-111 to DC-111, over."

"Go ahead."

"Ron, we're approaching the exit now. Any word from the DC crew?"

"Not for the past twenty minutes or so. I'll call them to get an update."

"10-4."

"Yeah," Radcliff answered his cell.

"The Miami crew just took the exit and should arrive within minutes," Razor reported.

"Good." Radcliff reached for his Motorola radio. "Okay. We're operational. Let's give it ten minutes to see how they set up."

All four of Radcliff's teams relayed ready. He had designated five shooters, two lookouts and two snipers. The key to the attack was the element of surprise, coupled with the bonus of inclement weather.

As Samuel and the rest of the DC agents pulled out of the gas station, he noticed a North Carolina trooper zipping southbound with his lights on. *Somebody is gonna get a ticket.* They merged back onto the interstate and headed toward their rendezvous with the Miami agents. The flicker of a blue strobe light in his rearview mirror caught his attention in the darkness though the rain. *Another trooper with light bars flashing. Maybe it was more than a speeding motorist,* he speculated.

"Heads up, guys, we probably got a wreck up the road," Samuel radioed his team.

About five minutes down the interstate, the agents saw a stream of brake lights lining up in a long red row.

"Oh no, we might be here for a while," the lead agent radioed. All traffic had come to a stop, but the agents couldn't see any police or emergency vehicles because of the bend in the interstate.

"Hey Ron, we're only three exits from you, but there's some kind of wreck ahead of us and right now the interstate is a parking lot. We could be delayed thirty to sixty minutes, and the rain is not doing us any favors," Samuel reported.

"Don't worry about it. We just got to the truck stop and I know the guys are hungry, so we'll eat here. See you when you get here."

"Okay. Hopefully, it won't be too long," Samuel sighed and stared out the watery windshield at the blur of red taillights stalled in front of him.

Radcliff watched as the agents got out of their vehicles and walked into the restaurant. He noticed that four agents had remained in their vehicles, maintaining surveillance on the semi. They had to park behind the restaurant due to the traffic congestion in the parking lot.

Well, we're soon going to find out just how good these DEA boys are, Radcliff anxiously anticipated.

"Unit fifteen to dispatch," the state trooper radioed as he got back in his cruiser.

"Go ahead."

"How long until the ambulance arrives?"

"Probably another ten to fifteen minutes."

"We've got a real mess out here. That DOA...well, he's not DOA. In fact, he's trying to crawl out of the cab of his semi. It beats anything I've ever seen. I don't think he's in all that bad a condition. Like I said earlier, the other driver is ok as well."

"What?"

"You heard me. Has the Hazmat team responded?"

"10-4, about five minutes ago. They said it will take about sixty minutes at the earliest before they reach you."

"The good news is that we stopped the oil leak from spreading on the interstate, but we'll still have to shut it down for at least four to five hours. You better start having the substation up north re-route traffic on the southbound lanes at the crossroads."

"10-4," the dispatcher responded.

Radcliff turned down the volume on his police scanner and picked up his cell phone. He had tried unsuccessfully to secure a DEA radio because their frequency was secure and could not be scanned. "Matt, get this," he paused.

"What?"

"One of those semis was an oil tanker and the freeway will be shut down for at least four hours. It is fucked up, big time. The DEA boys bringing up the rear will be stuck in that shit for hours!"

"Lucky fucking break, huh?"

"Go inside the restaurant and see what they're up to. Probably going to eat, but I want to double check before we start," Radcliff directed.

"Okay, I'll call you back in five minutes."

"Listen up, Matt's going inside to check on the feds before we start, so everybody stand by." Radcliff watched the parking lot.

GOVERNOR'S MANSION, MEXICO CITY

Viper looked through the scope. He saw that there was finally activity on the balcony and in the adjoining room. The conference must have taken longer than anticipated. According to his intelligence, the reception should have commenced in the early afternoon. He had planned for a daylight hit, but he actually preferred a night hit. It was always safer to pack out under cover of darkness.

The reception had just started. In less than twenty minutes, complete darkness would fall. He had been motionless in his shooting position for the past six hours but did not yet feel fatigued. In fact, with night fast approaching, he felt a new surge of energy sweep through his body.

"Jack, have you met the National Security Advisor, Jordan Zif?" Frank Tito, the Country Attaché pointed his glass of wine in the direction of a group of prominent businessmen.

"Yes sir, at Quantico, during a conference." Connor felt somewhat underdressed in a dark blue suit for this semi-formal occasion. He had borrowed it from one of the local DEA agents and the jacket was a bit tight.

"Jordan," Tito called out.

Zif graciously bowed out of his group and made his way toward them.

"Frank, this was a very good conference. I'm impressed," Zif looked at Connor and recognition dawned.

"What brings you to Mexico City…is it Jack or John?"

"Jack, sir," Connor answered, rather surprised.

"I attended a briefing you gave at Quantico last year about the Bogotá Cartel."

"Sir, I'm impressed you remember that."

"That's a big case Jack, it impacts our national security. Are you assigned to Mexico City?"

Before he could answer the question, Connor noticed Thomas over Zif's shoulder in the corner, discretely mimicking him and rolling his eyes as if Connor was brown nosing the NSA.

"I'm working the case; that's why I'm here, sir," he replied as he tried to suppress a smile.

"I sincerely hope you nail the bastards," Zif lowered his voice.

"That's the plan, sir," Connor replied as he shot Thomas a dirty look and then grinned.

CIA HEADQUARTERS

"Oh shit!" Stevens suddenly realized the time. His mother was coming over for dinner tonight and he would be dead meat if he left his wife alone with her. The days were running short and he still had no assessment from Panama whether Viper was dead or alive. He had increased his daily review of all intercepts and their code 1 informants. He was almost through the pile of intercepts when he noticed the words: TOMORROW, WATCH THE NEWS. Stevens paused and started over, rereading from the beginning:

JORGE: "ANY NEWS YET?"

ROBERTO: "TOMORROW, WATCH THE NEWS."

Fuck the prick is still alive, Stevens muttered. He immediately glanced at the top of the e-mail to verify the date and time.

"Last night, what the hell?" he said aloud.

Stevens dialed the op center. "This is Stevens, is the director on property?"

"Yes sir, she's in the science wing."

"I need to talk to her now!" He waited impatiently for about thirty seconds.

"What's up?" Lynn Bancroft's tone was concerned.

"The hit is today, it's the conference."

"Are you sure?"

"Nothing is a hundred percent, but I'm looking at an intercept where Jorge asks Roberto if there's any news yet and he replies *Watch the NEWS.*"

"That's it?" The director sounded skeptical.

"Ma'am, that's why you pay me the big bucks. I advise you to call the COS immediately and put the AG and NSA under tight security, right now."

Bancroft heard the alarm and urgency in Stevens' voice. She glanced at the clock; it was 6:35 p.m. in Mexico City.

"Okay, I'll make the call. Greg…?" Bancroft jerked the phone back to her ear before hanging up. "What time was the intercept?"

"Last night. There was a screw-up. I should have received the info with the morning traffic but somehow, it came in with the evening batch. I'll correct that problem."

"Damn it!" Bancroft hung up, then redialed. "This is the director. Get me the chief of station, Mexico City, ASAP. It's an emergency. I'll be back in my office in five minutes."

"Yes ma'am," the duty officer replied, his back stiffening at the director's tone. He immediately searched the computerized list of station chiefs' phone numbers around the world and found Mexico City.

Stevens dreaded the next phone call. "Hi honey. Do you really love me?"

"Greg, not tonight," his wife's tone was hostile. She knew what was coming.

"I'm so sorry. Something serious has come up and I have no idea when I'll be home."

"Please! It's always something serious. I am so sick of this…" This wasn't the first time he'd heard a dial tone abruptly end a conversation.

"Ma'am," the duty office's voice belted over the intercom, "I just talked to the duty officer at the Embassy. The conference took longer than they anticipated. The station chief is currently at the reception with the ambassador. The National Security Advisor and the Attorney General are at the reception at the governor's mansion. The in-country's duty officer and I have notified the station chief. He should be calling you in the next five to ten minutes."

"Thanks." Bancroft's lips set in a thin line. She hoped the call wasn't going to arrive too late.

GOVERNOR'S MANSION, MEXICO CITY

Viper adjusted the ACOG scope for the backlighting on the balcony. He had not yet ID'd his prey among the guests. Instead, he had selected a target zone and focused on the individuals in that area. The majority of the guests who walked onto the balcony walked into the target zone.

He felt his adrenaline level rise as he anticipated Señor Cuevas's arrival. The crowd began to increase rapidly. He knew he would soon be stalking his prey.

Connor was standing at the bar when he noticed a familiar military uniform. A tall, distinguished man in full dress uniform at the other end of the bar gave Connor a brief smile as he waited to be served.

"Admiral, Jack Connor, DEA San Francisco," Connor introduced himself.

"Hal Jarcowski. You wouldn't be Mike Connor's son, would you?" The admiral's handshake was firm.

"Yes sir."

"You look just like your old man. I'm glad to meet you, Jack," he smiled warmly.

The men took their drinks and walked toward a less crowded area in the room.

"I served under your dad in the Gulf as CO of the Black Knights F-14 Fighter Squadron. He was one hell of an aviator. I remember when he told me you wanted to be a Marine. That's not something he wanted to admit to his staff, considering your family's Navy heritage. He told me you got an early promotion to captain."

"It was a field promotion, sir, but thanks for your kind words. What brings you to Mexico City, Admiral?"

"We're part of a joint natural disaster exercise with Central America. Mainly a support role, but it's a good drill for our medical staff and other non-combatant units in the task force. How about you, what are you doing down here?"

"I'm working on a case," Connor said, noticing Thomas at the other end of the room, trying to get his attention. "Admiral, it was a pleasure meeting you. If you will please excuse me, I've got to get back to work." Connor excused himself.

"The pleasure is all mine. If there's anything the Navy can do for you while you're down here, let me know. You can reach me through the Embassy. They know where to find me."

"Thank you, sir." Connor walked toward Thomas.

"Not bad, Jack, you really know how to work the circuit…the National Security Advisor, Admiral Jarcowski. The Ambassador is over there talking to Mexico's Attorney General.

You ought to hit them up next, get all the VIPs out of the way."
Thomas enjoyed ribbing him.

"Give me a break, Gill. Is that all you wanted, to bust my chops?"

"No. You see that guy walking toward the hallway?"

"Yeah." Connor saw the individual walking rapidly toward the stairs to the first level.

"He's the agency's station chief here in Mexico City." Thomas was referring to the top CIA official assigned to the American embassy.

They watched him as another man met him at the top of the stairs. They couldn't hear the conversation.

"Sir?" The assistant was immediately on full alert as the CIA station chief greeted him in a hushed tone.

"I got two messages; one from our office and one from the CIA Director. I need to get to the car and use the secure phone to call Langley."

"Yes, sir. Follow me."

Connor and Thomas watched curiously as the two men quickly left the room.

"I haven't seen too many spooks this evening. They're usually out in droves trying to develop new sources. There's an interesting chap over there," Thomas pointed.

"The big guy wearing the white dinner jacket?"

"Yeah, that's Diego Cuevas, one of the wealthiest businessmen in Mexico."

"What the hell is he doing here?" Connor replied in surprise.

"Believe it or not, he's the one responsible for this conference."

"What?"

"Politicians and money…that's what they call diplomacy down here. Rumor has it that he used to be one of the agency's top informants."

"Really?"

"Mexico is its own little world. We ain't in Kansas anymore."

Viper caught a glimpse of his target through the well-lighted reception area and began tracking Cuevas from window frame to window frame. Cuevas stood in the door of the balcony entrance for a few seconds. He had him dead to rights, but mentally and physically he knew this was not the right moment. The scope's magnification allowed him to focus on Cuevas's face. He anticipated every move.

He watched a guest brush by Cuevas as he reentered the building and began his death march toward the target zone. His large torso and shoulders loomed above everyone else as he made his way through the crowd. His toothy smile was broad and relaxed. Viper slowly exhaled.

"This is Robert Fernandez."

"Hold on, sir. The DCI is expecting your call," the duty operator replied.

The secure line went silent for a few seconds as Fernandez peeked out the side window from the back seat of his Mercedes sedan.

"Robert, this is Lynn Bancroft."

"What's up?" Neither wasted any time.

"Greg Stevens, one of my top intel analysts, is convinced that the assassin is not dead and that he is going to hit either Cuevas, the Governor, or López…most likely at your location. We have an intercept from the Bogotá Cartel that suggests this will happen tonight," Bancroft hurriedly explained.

"We have heard rumors that there might be conflict between Cuevas and the cartel. My guess is it's him. We have taken some extra security precautions in the event that the assassin is still alive. I've deployed a Marine Force Recon squad in the field in case there is trouble tonight. A few of my guys are watching the perimeter around the residence. We may not be able to stop the bastard, but it might be our best shot to nail him or grab him."

"Be real careful on this one," Bancroft cautioned.

"Director, the only way we are going to get this bastard is to nail him in his own game. I'd better get back…Anything else?" Fernandez knew that in order to flush out the assassin, he needed a decoy and he had no problem using Cuevas.

"No, just take care of business on this one." The secure line went dead.

"Advise all personnel in the field that Mother Goose believes that the action is going down tonight. Tell everybody heads up!"

Fernandez advised his bodyguard as he made his way back to the reception.

CHAPTER 18

NORTH CAROLINA

Samuel had no tolerance for traffic. Growing up in the Bronx, he hated traffic almost as much as he hated the drug dealers he had arrested. He felt antsy and paranoid. The convenient traffic jam, the van driver who purposefully avoided eye contact, and the new agent's conspiracy theory all weighed on his mind.

"DC-112 to DC-114," Samuel radioed.

"Go ahead."

"Take your 4x4 onto the median, get to the front of this mess, and see what's going on? Find out how long they expect us to be parked out here."

"10-4. I'm on my way," the DC agent radioed, as the low growl of his Tahoe's V-8 engine started up and he slowly made his way on the muddy median. He reached under his seat, placed his portable blue light on the dash, and plugged it into the adapter. The strobe light began whirling, causing surprised motorists to turn and stare as the Tahoe moved down the median.

As soon as he approached the curve in the interstate, he could see the patrol vehicles alongside the freeway and the two crushed semis.

"DC-114 to DC-112."

"Go ahead."

"Two semis crashed. The interstate is completely blocked. I'm approaching the scene now."

"10-4," Samuel transmitted.

"Hey, are you part of the Hazmat team?" the state trooper asked as soon as he got out of the Blazer and walked toward the accident. The lights from all of the emergency vehicles illuminated the carnage in flashes of red, white and blue.

"No, I'm with DEA, out of DC," the agent replied.

"DEA?" the trooper asked, confused.

"Yeah, eight of us are caught up in this mess. We're part of a moving surveillance team."

"Well, you won't be going anywhere soon. The freeway will be closed for four or five hours, at least. A hazmat team is on the way for clean-up. Hope you're not in a hurry," he replied as another trooper joined them.

"How the hell did those trees get on the interstate?" the agent asked.

The troopers exchanged a pointed look and the first one spoke, "He's with DEA. A bunch of them got stuck in traffic. They're on a case."

"So, what do we have now, drug dealers using explosives?" the second trooper asked.

"What do you mean?"

"I think someone intentionally caused this wreck. I worked explosive ordinance disposal when I was in the Navy and it looks like somebody used explosives to blow these trees onto the interstate. If it wasn't raining and pitch dark out here, we'd be able to collect enough evidence to prove my point."

"That's bizarre. Why would someone want to blow up trees?" the agent asked.

"I don't know, you tell me. You're a fed, you guys have all the answers," the trooper replied sarcastically.

"It's not related to us." *Or is it?* He felt a flash of concern.

Sirens wailed from the south, growing closer. The rain kept falling.

"Anything we can do?" the agent added.

"We got it covered. No reason for you feds to get wet," the trooper replied dismissively.

The agent ran back to his car. "DC-114 to DC-112."

"Go ahead."

"There's one hell of a wreck up here. A couple of motorists are banged up pretty good. Two semis collided. It's a mess, man! One was an oil rig and now they got oil all over the place on the southbound lanes. They're waiting for the Hazmat team, minimum four or five-hour delay."

"You've got to be shitting me!" Samuel sighed irritably.

"That's only the half of it. One of the troopers thinks the wreck was planned."

"What do you mean?" Samuel listened intently as he took in the traffic jam around him.

"One of the troopers worked EOD in the Navy and he thinks somebody used explosives to blow the trees down, to intentionally block the interstate."

"Can our cars make it to the location?" Concern gave way to fear as Samuel contemplated the consequences.

"No, only the 4x4s. Cars will not make it in the mud in this weather."

"Listen, go the restaurant as fast as you can, this has to be a rip! Go! Go!"

Samuel speed dialed William's number and cursed under his breath as he waited for the connection to go through.

The rain continued its steady downpour outside the restaurant. Visibility was less than fifty feet.

Radcliff could barely see Matt running from the restaurant back to his van. He looked at his tactical radio, anticipating Matt's voice.

"Three to base."

"Go ahead," Radcliff replied.

"They're just ordering food. We are good to go."

"Good. Let's do it. Razor, get ready to watch our backs," Radcliff ordered as he activated his stopwatch.

"All right." Razor responded. He and Bernie were hidden on the opposite side of the freeway at the highest portion of the slope in the tree line, watching both directions of I-95.

Six of the ten DEA agents were in the restaurant. The other four maintained their surveillance positions outside near the semi.

The doors to the back of the white Bobcat, which had parked in the lot only a few minutes earlier opened as A.D. and Grizswall, team one, stepped out into the rain-drenched parking lot. They were dressed in blue jeans, plaid shirts and rain ponchos, hoping to blend in with the truckers.

"Team one is out toward the vehicle to the south with two Ds," Matt radioed as he and Max got out of their vehicle. The D was code for DEA agents. Within seconds, the tactical radio net was active again.

"Team two is out toward the north side of the vehicle with another two Ds," Hickson said into the bone mic attached to his head.

Radio traffic was kept to a minimum and transmission would not be acknowledged unless assistance was required...Radcliff's orders.

"Damn," Samuel swore as he slid over to the passenger side of his car to reposition his phone in hopes of catching a signal. On the third try, the call connected and finally started ringing.

Two of Radcliff's teams approached their respective target vehicles without detection. The two DEA agents closest to the semi sat in a Ford Taurus, watching the semi through the rain, blissfully unaware that death was on its way.

"Ron, it's a rip! Watch out!" Samuel yelled into the phone. Before Samuel could utter another word, Williams turned on his headlights, illuminating the semi and the Taurus.

"It's a rip!" Williams blurted to Ryker as they saw the two figures approaching the Taurus with their weapons drawn.

Williams keyed his mic, warning the other agents, as he and Ryker simultaneously looked out the back window. Williams stepped on the brakes. There was just enough backlight to illuminate two more dark shadows approaching the rear of their vehicle.

Ryker, out of sheer fear of not wanting to be trapped inside the car, flung open the door and leaped out of the car sideways and rolled straight onto the ground. Startled, one of the attackers sidestepped and fell backwards, firing two rounds into the passenger seat where Ryker had just been. Ryker capped off two rounds point-blank into his chest. The shooter flew backwards from the force of the shots and slammed into the ground.

Williams didn't hesitate. He fired two rounds through the rear passenger window at the shadow that hugged the rear quarter panel of his vehicle. The sound of the gunfire was muffled by the pelting rain. A second shooter simultaneously fired two rounds directly into the vehicle, in Williams' direction. Williams' first round missed but the second round exploded in the shooter's throat as he stumbled to the wet ground gasping for air.

Williams felt a slight stinging sensation in his left arm and he looked down to see that one round had grazed his shoulder. He jumped out of the car and took cover. He could see that both shooters were down.

"Razor, you two get back here! We got a problem and we need backup, now!" Radcliff ordered.

Samuel flinched. He had grown up with gangbangers and drive-by shootings and immediately recognized the sound of gunfire, even though it was muffled by the rain.

"Ron!" Samuel yelled into the phone, but there was no answer.

"All agents, listen up! Miami team is being hit. 113, 115, and 118, park your cars to the side and join up with me in my 4x4. Get your raid gear and move it! The rest of you guys, get in the other 4x4. We've got to get to the truck stop, now!" Samuel shouted.

He grabbed his op plan and checked the last page for the agent contact numbers. He focused on Miami-113's cell number and texted: Williams' call sign, 111, plus 911.

"116, call 911! Multiple shots were fired at the restaurant! Get an ambulance on the move," Samuel ordered.

"10-4."

Within thirty seconds, all the agents were in the two 4x4s racing along the shoulder of the interstate. Samuel prayed that they would not get stuck in the mud with this much weight in the vehicle.

"Hickson, the semi…now!" Radcliff yelled as both Hickson and Patcher ran straight toward the 18-wheeler in a hail of gunfire.

A.D. and Griswall had fired four rounds through the windshield of the Taurus, wounding one agent in the leg as the other agent returned fire through the broken glass.

"Ron, you all right?" Ryker shouted.

"Yeah!"

Ryker ran toward the semi, exchanging gunfire with one of the shooters crouched behind it.

It took Hickson seconds to hotwire the big rig while Patcher returned fire. The diesel engine roared to life.

"Let's get the fuck out of here!" Hickson yelled as he shoved it into gear.

Patcher ran alongside the semi for cover as he sprinted back to his car.

Radcliff saw the semi pull out of the lot and looked at his stopwatch: 2:05. *Go go go!* He yelled to himself.

Inside the restaurant, Miami-113 jerked toward the window at the unexpected sound at the same time felt his cell phone vibrate. He slammed his coffee down on the table as he read the text. His eyes opened wide as he recognized Williams' call sign and the 911 emergency code. "Guys!" he yelled.

DC-114 jammed the brakes of the 4x4 as the semi appeared out of nowhere in front of him. The 4x4 crashed into the rear of the semi, blew out the right rear tires and the huge rims folded under the truck. The force of the driver's airbag exploding knocked the DEA agent unconscious.

"Shit!" Radcliff swore, slamming his fist on his steering wheel as he witnessed the crash. He jumped out of his car.

"911 guys. It's Ron!" The agent jumped up from the table and drew his Glock 21 from his shoulder holster. The entire team immediately drew their weapons and rushed toward the exit. The waitress froze when she saw their guns, then dropped the tray of food. A glass shattered on the tile floor, spraying dark, bubbling soda.

"DEA! Police! Everyone down! Stay inside!" one of the agents yelled.

Radcliff and A.D. saw the movement.

"Activity inside the restaurant! They're coming out!" A.D. keyed his bone mic and concentrated on the front entrance, his M-4 trained on the door through the rear window of his van. There was a direct field of fire between the van and the door leading into the truck stop.

A.D. and Griswall repositioned themselves in the back of their van and fired a volley of .223 rounds from their M-4s at the first agent approaching the entrance door. The first few rounds missed one of the agents as he breached through the glass door of the restaurant, but he hit the second agent in the shoulder and sent him backwards into the agent behind him. Miami-113 dove to the ground next to a parked car and tried to focus on the direction the shots came from. Ryker and Williams ducked down, oblivious to the wet and muddy ground as .223 rounds whizzed past them.

A.D. and Griswall fired a second volley into the restaurant and at the other agents outside. Two of the agents returned fire toward the muzzle flash coming from the rear window of the van parked in the parking lot. Their rounds were not true to their target and a third volley of M-4 fire erupted, pinning down the agents inside the restaurant.

"Okay pigs, deal with this!" A.D. hissed as he pulled the pin on a flash bang concussion grenade and tossed it into the darkness directly at the front entrance.

He pulled a second pin and tossed another flash bang in Ryker and Williams direction.

Focusing on the gunfire in front of them, the agents never saw the flash bangs. Miami-113 heard a loud explosion, then passed out from the noise concussion.

Radcliff ran to the back of the semi and struggled as he picked up multiple heavy heat-sealed bundles of cocaine that had fallen to the ground after the crash. He yelled at A.D. to do the same. He didn't fire at the downed agent who was unconscious and pinned inside the 4x4 as he ran back to his vehicle.

"Razor, take out their vehicles," he ordered the two team members, who had just arrived.

They jumped out of their vehicle, shouldered their weapons and fired controlled bursts into the agents' tires.

Radcliff's mission was deteriorating rapidly, and he needed a diversion. He reluctantly reached behind his front seat and pulled out a grenade and threw it at the semi. The explosion was deafening, and the big rig was quickly engulfed in flames.

"Let's get out of here!" he ordered as his tires spun out on the wet payment. The rest of his crew pulled out of the parking lot in a frenzy of squealing tires. Their vehicles swerved wildly and skidded on the slick roadway as the rain pelted down. Their tail lights disappeared in seconds. Not a single DEA agent was in sight.

GOVERNOR'S MANSION, MEXICO CITY

The CIA chief of station quickly walked back to the reception area with a heightened sense of awareness as he scanned the crowd. He immediately made visual contact with the governor, Attorney General and Cuevas before approaching a group of embassy personnel in the rear of the bar area.

"Frank, I need your help tonight." Fernandez looked at Tito.

"What do you want my guys to do, bug the ambassador's office?"

"No, that's already done," he said with a conspiratorial grin.

Tito smiled, thinking that Robert should have been a DEA agent, instead of CIA…what a waste of talent. "What can we do for you?" Tito replied.

"How many agents do you have here tonight?"

"We've got ten, including Jack." Fernandez briefly glanced at both Connor and Thomas.

"I just got off the phone with the DCI. Langley seems to think that there will be some trouble tonight. Intel is that some Mexican government official or prominent Mexican citizen might be hit tonight."

The DEA agents immediately scanned the room while they leaned in and hung on every word.

"There's no intelligence that any Americans are at risk. The top three likely candidates here are Mexico's AG, the governor, and Cuevas."

"So what do you want us to do?" Tito asked.

"I want to minimize the exposure of our VIPs from association with these targets. We first need to get our guys off the balcony and away from the windows without attracting too much attention."

Thomas and Connor looked around the room and saw the American AG, NSA, and the ambassador standing out on the balcony with many other guests. Cuevas was within ten feet of them with his entourage.

"I do not want to cause any panic in here or start rumors that the CIA thinks there's going to be an assassination tonight at the mansion. Brief your agents and have them be alert for anything suspicious. Frank, maybe you and I can keep the AG and NSA busy for a while and draw them away from the potential targets."

"Don't worry about the ambassador. My guys have him covered," Fernandez assured him as he walked away.

Fernandez had always been a field agent. When there was a hint of trouble, he liked to have as much manpower available as possible. Even though his office was large, by agency standards, DEA was larger and welcomed their help.

"Gill, go brief our guys and give them a heads-up," Tito instructed Thomas.

"I'm on it."

"Jack, let's go out to the balcony," Tito turned to Connor.

Connor started milling among the guests, assessing each one as a potential shooter.

"And I thought our office was busy," Connor whispered to Tito as they approached the balcony.

"You ready to transfer down here?"

"Too early to tell."

"It's different down here, Jack. Like the incident in the restaurant the other night. We play by their rules or we lose. We help each other out down here...CIA, FBI, military. It's us against them. Tell you one thing, Fernandez is a pro, a seasoned field agent and if he thinks there's trouble, count on it."

Connor felt the blast of warm air as soon as they walked out onto the crowded balcony and surveyed the area. "Jack, go check the reception area and the head. I want to make sure we get all the agents on this ASAP."

"Okay, I'll be back in a few minutes."

Viper had briefly focused on the two men when they walked onto the balcony. He recognized one of them from his earlier recon of the mansion. The tip of his barrel shifted back toward Cuevas who was still outside the target zone. He sensed the time was drawing near and refocused his crosshairs on Cuevas's head.

Staff Sergeant Baker knew he would only get one chance at the assassin and that was the very second when he fired his weapon. The flash from the muzzle of his weapon would be the weak link, revealing the shooting position. Baker had a squad of six Force Recon Marines, stealthily deployed in pairs, within a fifty-yard radius of the mansion.

It was a waiting game now and it had been so for the past two days since he deployed his Marines. Based on the foliage, tree cover, and position of the mansion, he had concluded that if there was a hit, it would most likely come from the balcony side of the residence. The only slight advantage he and his team had was that Viper would not expect Marines to be stalking him. Baker knew that the assassin was a pro and would take extreme precautions to observe for surveillance and avoid detection.

Come on, show yourself, you snake, Baker said to himself as he laid by his partner on the ground and looked through his night vision binoculars. He knew that the slightest noise or movement could compromise their respective positions. Each team of Marines acted independently, with complete radio silence. This was a Special Op assignment direct from SOCOM and the use of deadly force had been authorized, if and when the assassin was located. Baker had positioned himself and his teammate in the direction of the line of fire that he knew the assassin would choose.

Come on, come on, show yourself, you red bastard, Baker kept telling himself. He was convinced that assassin had been a Spetsnaz operator and was determined not only to even the score, but to one-up it. He planned to show him the true meaning of the Marine Force Recon motto: *Swift, Silent, Deadly…*with emphasis on deadly.

Realistically, he knew that he and his team would only get one shot at the assassin. Baker did not concern himself with the assassin's target. He knew that the target, in all probability, was a dead man, no matter what. He did not delude himself into thinking he could actually stop him from making his kill. The assassin had demonstrated that he was a master sniper in Quantico. The completion of his mission was a foregone conclusion, no matter the time or place. Their only hope was to eliminate the future threat.

Viper watched as Cuevas walked back in from the balcony. It was too early for him to be leaving the party. Viper surmised that Cuevas was either getting a refill at the bar or taking a piss. He saw the activity on the balcony and refocused his crosshairs. Some of the guests were pointing out into the wooded area. He shifted his weight very slowly in that direction. There was a small herd of deer at the border of tree line.

The deer froze, motionless in his crosshairs. They sensed something. He systematically scanned the wooded area around them. A large buck suddenly leapt away from the rest of the pack and arched its body in long, fluid moves deeper into the tree line. The rest of the herd followed and disappeared into the shadows in seconds. Viper maintained his concentration, looking through his scope. He stopped when he saw movement in the left side. He panned to his left a few inches. For the next thirty seconds, he did not draw a breath. Another slight movement in the scope.

Blyad! Viper silently swore, using the Russian word for fuck, when he spotted two individuals in camouflage fatigues. They were well hidden. He saw a spotter with binoculars and a sniper with a rifle. He guessed they would be Marines. The question was, how many were there? He mentally marked their location with a landmark and refocused his sights on the mansion. Cuevas was still inside standing next to the bar.

Viper's new concern was how many were stalking him. He knew the Americans would definitely be after him since he drew

313

blood on the last two missions. He gave it some thought. The Americans probably guessed at potential targets and sent teams to each target's location, hoping to snare him. One thing he was sure of, the Americans did not know his present location. He knew, as did his enemy, that there was only one vulnerable moment in his mission. Now that he was aware that a team was on him, the score was even. He speculated that they had between six and twelve men. As the seconds ticked away, he calculated there would be only six. They knew he would be more likely to spot one in a group of twelve.

He felt a surge of confidence. He hoped they were Recon Marines and was all too familiar with their reputation. He planned to test just how good they were. After his Charlie Barracks hit, he knew they would be motivated by wounded pride. It had been his experience that snipers were more likely to screw up when they had something to prove. They would be anxious and overeager. He put his eye to his scope and felt in control. *That's right, Cuevas, have another drink. It will be your last.*

Connor finished searching the men's room and walked down the hall toward the reception area. As he walked past a pair of swinging doors, he looked through one of the porthole windows and saw Thomas talking to a waiter near the back of the kitchen. What caught Connor's eye was that Thomas was trying to give the waiter an envelope, but he refused to take it. The envelope tore before the waiter finally accepted it.

"Hey Gill, everything all right in here?" Connor called as he stuck his head through the doors.

"Yeah, hold up. I'll be right there." Thomas patted the waiter on the shoulder and walked out of the kitchen. "He introduced me to his sister. She is a ten plus. I tried to give him some tickets to next month's bullfights, but he wouldn't take them. Have you ever seen a bullfight? Man! Talk about an experience."

"Sounds like the sister must have been an experience too."

"You could say that," Gill grinned.

"Has everyone been briefed?" Connor asked.

"All but one agent. Some of the guys thought he might be in the kitchen when I ran into the waiter. I thought you were with Frank?"

"I was, but he wanted me to go back inside to check the head and reception area for any other agents. The AG and NSA are out there in intense discussion. Frank was trying to usher them back inside when I left," he replied as they entered the main room.

"I'm going downstairs. I think one of your agents might be near the entrance."

"Okay. I'm going back to hook up with Frank." Connor headed back to the balcony.

Viper relied on his instinct. If a six-man team of Marines was deployed, they would be in three sectors in front of him, based on the fact that the east side of the building was the best angle of attack. He had made the team on his far left flank but was primarily concerned with the location of the team on his right flank because that was his escape route.

Another one, Viper saw something at the base of the tree line about 50 yards in front of him and to the right. He froze for thirty seconds on that position. It was another spotter and a sniper. *Very clever,* he thought, certain that he could still complete the mission now that he had located the second team.

He knew that there would be at least one more team between the two positions he had located. He refocused on the mansion and saw Cuevas walk onto the balcony and he adjusted his plan of attack as the now-familiar figure reentered the target zone.

Connor tracked Cuevas as he walked onto the balcony. He looked around and saw the NSA talking to Tito. At the opposite end of the balcony, the American and Mexican AGs were engaged in conversation.

He scanned the crowd, trying to determine if anybody or anything appeared suspicious. This is impossible, he thought in frustration. He stared out toward the hillside, acutely aware of the sniper threat. *How the hell would you stop that, short of evacuating the place and causing an international incident? How does Secret Service do this?* He looked at his watch. In less than an hour, the reception would be over. It seemed like an eternity away.

I-95, NORTH CAROLINA

"It's up ahead," Samuel said as the Blazer carrying the five agents sped toward the truck stop.

"God, no!" Samuel saw the emergency lights of an ambulance and the burning semi. The rain seemed to have no effect on the flames. It looked like a full-scale disaster zone. He got out of the Blazer before it fully stopped and ran toward an agent standing near a Ford truck at the restaurant entrance.

"Ron!" Samuel yelled after recognizing Williams, with a dressing around his upper arm, standing next to Ryker. "What happened?"

"It was a rip," Williams said, enraged. "Your call saved our lives. Five agents were wounded, but nothing too serious. We got two of them. One of your team crashed into the back of the semi, then they blew it up. What a nightmare! The bastards tossed a flash bang at us! My friggin' ears are still ringing, and my head feels like it's cracked open!"

Samuel saw the rest of his agents gathered under the awning at the front of the restaurant talking to the Miami agents. He noticed light glinting off the shattered glass on the ground near the entrance and saw a couple of bullet holes in the restaurant's door frame.

"Did you get a plate or description of any of the vehicles?" Samuel asked.

"No it was dark and raining. I think they were in vans. It happened so fast. They had at least four or five guys. It was well executed. They shot out all the tires on our OGV's so we couldn't go after them. They may have blown up the semi, but at least they didn't get it," Williams sighed holding his head.

"Yeah, well, that's only the half of it," Samuel replied.

"What do you mean?"

"Somebody blew up a couple of trees lining the interstate and caused one hell of a wreck. Now it's clear it was all part of a plan to slow us down, so they could hit you guys." Samuel's face was grim.

"Shit."

"Have you notified Washington or Miami yet?" Samuel asked

"Yeah. We've got a serious problem, Ryker's information was right on, which means they've definitely got somebody on the inside," Williams lowered his voice.

"Yeah, I know." Samuel shook his head not knowing what to think *...dead suspects, wounded agents, a traitor, automatic gun fire, grenades...what the fuck?*

GOVERNOR'S MANSION, MEXICO CITY

Viper took a slow, shallow breath. He calculated that he could get off two, possibly three, shots before they could zero in on his location. It would be challenging going up against the Americans, but the odds were at least even, now that he was aware of the threat.

Baker painstakingly covered every inch of the terrain assigned to him and his partner in the remote chance he could spot the assassin in a full ghillie suit, buried in the undergrowth, practically impossible to detect at night.

He estimated that the party would last at least a couple more hours. He was in no hurry to go anywhere. He was grateful that he and his men had been given the chance to hunt down the assassin who had embarrassed the Charlie Barracks Marines. Payback was a bitch and he planned to get some.

There you are again, Viper thought as he studied one of the men on the balcony. For a few seconds Viper studied his purposeful stride and erect posture sensing he would be a formidable opponent. He inched his scope back toward the target.

Connor purposely avoided eye contact with Cuevas who was in an animated conversation with both Attorney Generals. *It's time to get our AG back inside,* Connor decided, as he made his way toward them.

Viper concentrated on the target's head. He did not notice the man approaching the group. He slowly exhaled as he started to gently squeeze the trigger of his silenced weapon.

"Mr. Attorney General, how do you like our hospitality?" Cuevas asked in a booming voice.

"Señor Cuevas, everything so far has been excellent!" Henderson diplomatically replied.

"Let me tell you a secret?" Cuevas leaned toward him.

"Sir?" Connor interrupted, and Henderson turned.

Cuevas's movement coincided with Viper's final trigger pull. He knew immediately that his first shot would not be a direct hit and instinctively fired a second. The first round only grazed

317

Cuevas's ear, but ripped a jagged, gaping hole in Henderson's neck. Connor lunged toward Henderson. The second round, a fraction of a second later, slammed into Cuevas's back, directly between the shoulder blades. The force and velocity of the high-powered sniper rounds violently propelled Henderson and Cuevas over the balcony railing and they plummeted to the ground below. The force of Cuevas's body weight split the wooden railing, causing AG López to lose his balance and fall through the railing, but he managed to grab one of the broken posts. He looked terrified as his body dangled off the side. Connor dove for him and managed to grasp his hand.

"Left at ten o'clock. About 70 yards, three clicks up, two rounds," Baker whispered urgently to the Marine corporal lying next to him.

"I saw it too," he replied as he adjusted his shooting position and pointed his rifle toward the area where they had seen the muzzle flashes.

Baker broke radio silence and spoke into his bone mic, "Charlie-2, you got him?"

"Working on it."

Viper automatically zeroed in on his next objective. He jerked, and his heart skipped a beat at the sight of an eight-legged insect magnified through his scope. He felt the chill of goose bumps on his arms. Despite all his training, he had a phobia of tarantulas. He realized this wasn't one, flicked it off the barrel and regained his concentration.

Baker strained his eyes, observing some movement, but before he could transmit, he saw two more flashes.

"Shit! Charlie-2, come in…" Baker searched through his scope for a sign.

No answer.

Baker felt sick. One of his team had been hit. The two remaining teams fired toward the area where they had seen the muzzle flash.

Viper expected the retaliation. The hum of rounds zipping through the air above him did not alter his course of action. He was going to evade and evacuate the area as planned. He began to low-crawl through the brush.

Sgt. Jones rolled from his shooting position as soon as he saw the first flash. He knew that a second round was earmarked for him. When he felt the warm blood drip from his hair, he knew it was a superficial wound. He hardly felt it; his attention was fixed on Smith.

"Ray, Ray?" Jones whispered as he wiped the blood out of his eyes so that he could see his friend. He knew there wouldn't be an answer.

"Charlie-2 to Charlie-1 over," Jones paused for a few seconds. "Charlie-2 to Charlie-1, over." He reached down and touched the portable radio, still on his duty belt. He ran his hands up the mic wire to his head and realized that his headset was broken. *Shit, no comm!*

"Charlie-1to Charlie-3."

"Go."

"I think Charlie-2 is hit. Let's start moving to his position. The target's extracting, so be alert," Baker radioed. He saw the frantic movement around the mansion, but that wasn't his concern.

Viper was now at least fifty yards away from his shooting position. He knew that his ambush on the Marines would stall them, if not totally negate their pursuit. After every five minutes of movement, he would stop for thirty seconds to see if anyone was following him. He panned the area through his night vision goggles and started to move again. He studied his watch and estimated that he would be at his vehicle in ten minutes.

Sirens began to fill the air as Connor kneeled over the body of United States Attorney General Hank Henderson. He tried to analyze what he had witnessed in the last five minutes. He remembered Cuevas leaning forward as if to whisper something to the AG. *Was the AG's death a mistake or was he the target?* He pondered as he stared off into the darkness.

Connor heard voices behind him and turned around. The Mexican Attorney General was surrounded by Mexican federales.

"That's him, over there," one of the them pointed at Connor.

"Señor, what is your name?" López called out.

"Jack Connor, DEA."

"Señor Connor, you saved my life. I am grateful." López embraced Connor, taking him by surprise.

I didn't save him, Connor felt morosely, looking at Henderson's covered body.

"Señor Connor, I will do everything in my power to find the one who did this." López' face was sweating and flushed, his voice strained.

So will I. So, will I. The words echoed in Connor's mind.

CHAPTER 19

CIA HEADQUARTERS

The duty operator connected the urgent call to the DCI's direct line. "Lynn, it's Robert. Bad news," Fernandez spoke over the phone static.

"Viper?" Bancroft held her breath.

"Yeah. He got Cuevas and Hank about fifteen minutes ago."

"Oh my God! Hank? How?"

"Hank and López were on the balcony talking to Cuevas. From what we can piece together, it seems that Cuevas leaned toward Hank just as the shot was fired. The first round glazed Cuevas but struck Hank in the neck."

Bancroft squeezed her eyes shut as Hernandez continued. "A second shot hit Cuevas in the back. They never had a chance."

"My God! What about the Marines?"

"I don't know. We haven't heard from them yet."

Bancroft paused, "What else do we know?"

"Jack Connor, one of the DEA agents witnessed the shooting. According to him, there were two shots fired. The force of the second shot knocked Henderson and Cuevas off the balcony. López fell through the railing but was pulled to safety by the DEA agent. We don't think Hank was the intended target. All my agents are out there. We're trying to piece it together."

"Do the best you can. Call me back in two hours with an update. I'm going to inform President Cromwell. Is Jordan Zif there?"

"Yes, ma'am. It will take a few minutes to track him down. Hold on."

Bancroft concentrated while waiting, thinking of the violent deaths that had recently occurred in association with the Bogotá Cartel.

"Lynn?"

"Jordan, what's your plan?" Bancroft was straight to the point

"I'm going to see if we can leave tonight."

"Good, I'll pick you up at Andrews, then we'll brief the President with the FBI."

Bancroft's next call rang directly into the personal living quarters at the White House. "Allison, this is Lynn Bancroft. Sorry to bother you."

"Hi Lynn, how are you?" the President's wife greeted her warmly.

"Frankly, I've had better nights."

"I take it this is business."

"Yes, unfortunately."

"Hold on, he's coming. Listen, Lynn, on the twentieth of this month, I have to give a speech on women in government at the Commonwealth Club. Would you mind joining me?"

"I'll check my schedule and let you know tomorrow."

"Thanks. I really appreciate it. Here's Russell. Hope you can make it. See you soon."

"What's up, Lynn?" the President asked in his deep, low voice.

"Mr. President. I have some bad news."

"It's about Hank Henderson..." she paused. She knew their friendship went back to their college days at Harvard. "He was killed about twenty minutes ago," her tone was solemn.

"What! How did it happen? Where?"

"Hank was at the governor's mansion in Mexico City. We believe a Bogotá Cartel sniper shot and killed Diego Cuevas, a wealthy Mexican businessman and our Attorney General."

"I sent Hank down there to attend that conference at the last minute..." the President's voice trailed off.

Lynn knew how he felt. "Mr. President, Hank was aware of the risks before he signed on. Based on our preliminary information, Cuevas was the intended target, not Hank. Embassy personnel who witnessed the assassination reported that Cuevas leaned toward Hank and that the first round hit Hank in the throat."

The President listened intently without responding.

"A second shot, fired instantly, hit Cuevas."

"My God!"

"I also spoke with Jordan Zif and Robert Fernandez. They witnessed the assassination and an investigation is in progress. When I get off the phone with you, I'll notify the FBI. We're sending a joint crisis team to Mexico City."

"Has the wire service or news picked up any of this yet?"

"No sir, I don't think so, but it won't be long until they do."

"Allison and I will go over to Hank's house and tell Maggie."

"I know Hank would appreciate that, sir. Jordan is leaving tonight with Hank's body and will be back in Washington early this morning. We'll brief you first thing."

"The earlier the better."

"I'm really sorry, Mr. President. I know how close you were to Hank."

"I can't believe this has happened. I cannot believe it."

"None of us can, Mr. President."

THE PALACE, BOGOTÁ

"Señor Joaquin? Julio called and told me to tell you to turn on the television." Maria stood in the doorway as Joaquin picked up the remote and scrolled to cable news.

"Maria, is Roberto still on the grounds?" Joaquin asked.

"I think so."

"Find him and tell him I want to see him."

"Sí, señor."

Reporting live from the governor's mansion in Mexico City. Just a few feet away from me   lie the bodies of United States Attorney General Henry Henderson and prominent Mexican businessman Diego Cuevas. Preliminary reports indicate that the two were killed by a sniper.

Joaquin's eyes were fixed on the screen when Roberto entered the room.

"Roberto, we have two for the price of one," he exclaimed excitedly as he lit his cigar.

A panel of talking heads began speculating about the international implications of the assassination of a U.S. official on foreign soil.

Joaquin turned to Roberto with a smug, satisfied smile as he tilted his head up and blew smoke rings. "What do you think about that, amigo?"

"If we continue killing Americans, we will enrage them. They will remove their gloves of diplomacy and bloody us. The American Attorney General was their President's close friend. The

323

President will be relentless in is his pursuit. Viper is not invincible. He must not lead them to us."

"What do you suggest?"

"We should retire Viper for a while. We know the CIA suspects him. The FBI and CIA will now be vengeful and unpredictable. I will contact Raven to see what information he has."

"Should we increase our security?"

"No, not yet. We should do nothing. If we increase our security, the Americans may think we fear retribution. If we are blameless, we have nothing to fear," Roberto reasoned.

"Ok...What have you learned about Manuel's murder?"

"Nothing. We have not found a single witness. That is very strange and disturbs me greatly."

"Do you think the Americans were involved?"

"We have no evidence that they were involved. What is the motive?"

"What about Maria?" Joaquin asked quietly as he looked outside the doorway to be sure they were alone.

"I have been watching her closely but have seen nothing suspicious. Perhaps I was mistaken."

"I told you she is not a traitor!" Joaquin replied defiantly as photos of the governor's mansion beamed live across the screen.

The phone rang. "Hello...yes Jorge, he is here...are you certain?"

"What is it?" Joaquin asked in concern.

"There is a problem. He will be here in a half hour."

GOVERNOR'S MANSION, MEXICO CITY

SSgt. Baker's squad had stealthily regrouped. They patrolled the area in a standard wedge formation for any signs of the shooter. Baker feared their efforts were futile, but the Marines continued the mission relentlessly. He hoped that they would find evidence any evidence that would lead them to the sniper. He was haunted by the fact that their efforts at Quantico had produced nothing, despite searching the area for a week. He was not accustomed to losing men. He hated the feeling of loss but welcomed the feeling of rage. It motivated him like nothing else could.

He tried hard to be objective about what had happened at Quantico. Viper had methodically killed a protected witness on his own home base and killed four Marines. Baker prided himself on being the best, yet he had been bested twice, probably by the same adversary.

Baker saw the Marine on point give a hand signal, indicating a break in the terrain. The Marines converged in the brush on the edge of the fire road. They knew that crossing it could be a trap and were acutely aware of just how deadly the enemy they were tracking was. They silently and quickly crossed the road in the dark, on high alert for an ambush.

Baker was the last to cross and the team waited for a few minutes before they moved on. On the far left flank Jones gave a hand signal indicating that he had alerted to something. Baker slowly moved to Jones's position while the other Marines provided 360-degree perimeter security. Jones pointed to the ground.

It was quite clear that a vehicle had been hidden in the area. There were fresh tire tracks and broken brush. Whoever it was had only humped in a few miles. Getting back to this site from the governor's mansion would have been quick and easy. One thing was certain, the bastard was gone...long gone.

Baker motioned for Jones to survey the site without disturbing any evidence. The two men started to slowly inch their way forward when a horrified expression flashed across Baker's face and he gave the immediate signal to freeze. Jones stopped in his tracks and focused on the ground.

Baker pointed two fingers at his eyes, then the ground. A thin, dark trip wire lay partially concealed mere inches in front of their boots. They recognized it immediately...the device's military configuration was disturbingly familiar. Baker slowly crouched to his knees and followed the wire for about ten feet until he spotted the M67 fragmentation grenade partially hidden under wild brush.

"Shit! The bastard hotwired his escape."

For the next five minutes, they secured the grenade while the rest of the team cautiously searched for more traps but found none. It was their first victory, but it stank of defeat. Baker decided to call it a night. They needed to preserve and protect what little evidence might be lying there in the darkness. They would have a better chance of collecting it during the day. God knows, they needed every shred of evidence possible if they had any chance of following the cold trail. Baker assigned two Marines to guard the site. He and the rest of the team headed back out. They had to take one of their own home.

MEXICO CITY INTERNATIONAL AIRPORT

Ryker breathed in the smog choked air as he walked outside the airport at 5:30 a.m. He had been lucky to get a red-eye flight from Raleigh, North Carolina, to Mexico City, given the surreal circumstances of the past 12 hours. Connor pulled up in front of him.

"I just saw it on the TV in the terminal," were the first words out of Ryker's mouth. "What happened?"

As he navigated out of the airport, Connor gave a detailed account of the assassination while Ryker listened in wide-eyed disbelief and horror.

"Christ! What do we do now?" he asked.

"Nothing, it's a CIA and FBI gig now. Our agents will probably be involved, but I think that since you're here, we'll be cut loose and we can debrief my informant, Carlos. We need to be at the Embassy at 8:00 a.m.

Ryker began his story, starting with the train ride.

THE PALACE, BOGOTÁ

"That is all I know at this time," Jorge finished telling Joaquin and Roberto about the news coverage of the attempted cocaine heist in North Carolina.

"Do you think it was one of our loads? We need to check on the status of our inbound deliveries," Joaquin worried out loud.

"It seems that DEA has a traitor within their ranks. What do you think, Jorge? Roberto?" Joaquin's eyes narrowed into thin slits as his anger stewed in his stomach.

"If it was our load, the problem must be in the distribution cell. The question is, where? West Coast, East Coast or, perhaps Mexico," Jorge spoke first.

"Roberto, what do you think?"

"I agree. It has to be with the distribution network."

"We must find the traitor and make an example of him, an example that no one will forget. We will meet again in two days. Contact our people in Mexico and the U.S. Tell them that we offer a reward, a big reward. Money loosens tongues."

326

AMERICAN EMBASSY, MEXICO CITY

Connor and Ryker had just sat down for breakfast at the Embassy Suite's buffet when Connor's cell phone rang.

"Jack?" He heard his wife's familiar voice and her concern. "Are you okay? I heard about the assassination on the news and when I couldn't reach you last night I got worried."

"I'm fine, but it was busy last night." Connor wasn't surprised that she had tracked him down. He should have called her. He knew that she would be worried.

"Can't really go into detail, but everything is okay." Connor didn't know if anyone was monitoring the phone and he knew that Barrett would understand.

"Did you hear about the DEA agents in North Carolina?" she asked worriedly.

"Yeah, Ryker is with me now and he was there, but he's okay."

"Oh my God! Jack, I'm glad you guys are safe. Be careful and don't get yourself shot down there. Watch out for Ryker, too, or I'll kick your ass. I love you."

Connor smiled, loving her sense of humor. "I love you too, Barrett. Don't worry, okay? The drama down here is all over. I'll call you tomorrow." He knew that was only half true, but he wanted to reassure her. "Hey how's your case going? Any leads yet?"

"It's funny you should ask. I found something very strange, but I don't know what to make of it. It's too complicated to discuss over the phone, but I would like your input when you get back."

"Sure. Hon, will you do me a favor? Go upstairs and look in my cabinet in the storage area and find the file of old newspaper clippings. There is an article on the assassination of Venezuela's President years ago and another article on Romanian defectors and Russian Special Forces snipers. I need the date of those articles and the name of the newspaper. I also wrote down a file number on the paper on one of those articles. I need that number too. There may be a connection to one of the cases we're working.

"You want me to find it right now?"

"No, I have to go. But as soon as you find it, text me. Thanks, Barrett. I love you."

"I love you, too." Barrett hung up the phone and sat back down at her desk.

The Attorney General of the United State...killed. DEA agents...wounded. The President of Venezuela...assassinated. Russian snipers...and defectors. Is the drama over or is it just getting started?

Barrett focused on her file and three photographs paper clipped together with a handwritten note attached. One was the seal of the U.S. Attorney's office, the second, a picture of her murder victim, and the third, a blurred photograph of a moving Redwood City police car. The note read:

"You're looking in the wrong place for the person who murdered Simi Shiriff. This telephone number will lead you to the answers you seek. Followers of Allah."

WASHINGTON, DC

The Air Force jet landed with a jolt on the runway at Andrews Air Force Base. Jordan Zif had awakened a few minutes before landing. Despite the circumstances of the last twenty-four hours, he had managed to get some sleep on the flight.

As soon as Zif stepped out into the cool air, he saw the DCI's black armored Suburban waiting for him. The rear passenger door opened, and Bancroft stepped out to greet him as he walked down the stairs onto the tarmac.

"You all right?" Bancroft asked.

"I was never in any danger."

"I asked Bill to join us in your office, so we could have a short meeting before the three of us brief the President."

"Anything new since I left?"

"We had a Marine Force Recon team surrounding the Governor's mansion. Viper made them and killed one of them seconds after the assassination. Like I said, he's the best I've seen."

"Believe me, after that stunt at Charlie Barracks, we are not underestimating him. But, containing him is another thing altogether," Bancroft sighed in frustration.

"How's the President taking it?"

"Not too well."

Their car, with its blue lights flashing, sped along in the HOV lane toward the White House. The lights had been custom-built into the grill of the car and were not visible unless activated. Zif gazed through the dark, tinted windows unaware of the commuters staring at the SUV as it breezed through the morning commute. Within twenty minutes, they were in the Old Executive Building.

"Morning, Sir. Are you okay?"

"Fine, Lucy, thank you," Zif replied as he and Bancroft passed the secretary's desk.

"The FBI Director is waiting for you in your office and the President's running a bit late. The White House requested that your meeting be pushed to 8:45," she called after him.

"Thanks."

"Any new developments, Bill?" Zif asked as he and Bancroft entered the office.

"Not really. Our team is on site along with Lynn's guys. The Marines located the area where they believe Viper stashed his getaway vehicle. Hopefully, we'll find some evidence. He rigged the area with explosives to cover his tracks, but the Marines found them and secured the area."

"At this point, nothing about Viper surprises me and he is surely not dead. It is definitely time to brief the President..." Before he could finish the next sentence, his intercom sounded.

"Yes, Lucy?"

"The Commandant of the Marine Corps is on line two."

"Morning General. Lunch sounds fine. See you then." Zif hung up the phone. "Seems everybody wants Viper's ass this morning."

"You're right. We need to tell the President about Viper, but we also have to make sure we keep a lid on this," Bancroft replied.

"Bill, any other ideas?" Zif asked.

"No, we just tell him what we've got and what we're doing to resolve the problem."

"Okay. Let's do it." The three stood up and headed for the Oval Office.

REDWOOD SHORES, CA

Barrett had dozed off after her third glass of wine and woke up just past midnight feeling woozy. She remembered that Jack had asked her to find old newspaper articles. She got up from the sofa and stretched before she walked upstairs to the storage area in the loft of their condo.

"It's not friggin' here," she mumbled, frustrated, sick and tired of combing through the file folders packed in the drawers. *Slow down Barrett,* she told herself, realizing that she had one too many glasses of wine. She started over and concentrated on the files.

She breathed a sigh of relief when she located a manila folder that was stuck to the inside of a similar folder. She pried the folder open and one of the newspaper articles fell out.

"Suspected sniper shot and killed President of Venezuela from two hundred yards." She read the article with interest, wondering what connection it had to Jack's investigation. She started reading another article but decided to finish it downstairs.

"Ahhh!" she yelled out as she tripped on one of the steps and grabbed the hand rail to keep from falling down the flight of stairs.

"Shit!" The file flew out of her hands and scattered all over the hardwood floor below. As she collected the newspaper articles she noticed a small white laminated card partially sticking out of a concealed pocket on the inside of the folder. At first, she thought it was a credit card. She fished it out of its hiding place and read the bold writing on the back.

RETURN POSTAGE GUARANTEED
IF FOUND RETURN TO:
P.O. BOX 365441
WASHINGTON, D.C. 20016-0006

She turned the card over and stared in stunned disbelief.

AMERICAN EMBASSY, MEXICO CITY

A flood of international press vans and satellite dishes were camped in front of the Embassy gates. Connor could definitely feel the change in intensity at the Embassy. Everyone seemed focused and determined. It reminded him of his battalion headquarters during his tour in Iraq.

Ryker could not stop thinking about the assault at the truck stop and how close he had come to death. Connor had been preoccupied all morning thinking about the mission ahead and the events of the past twenty-four hours. He did not initially pick up on the fact that his new partner was acting a little distant. Connor's silence did little to relieve Ryker's anxiety.

"I think I'll be able to issue you a Glock 19 from the Embassy," Connor finally spoke after gaining access to the Embassy grounds.

"Yeah, okay," Ryker's tone was cool and detached.

Connor could tell Ryker was preoccupied but didn't say anything until they were inside.

"Alex, listen. I don't want to sound cold or jaded, but this is like a combat situation. I know that was your first shoot-out. I know it's scary. But, you did what you were trained to do. That's why we put you through all that weapons and tactics training. We're in a foreign country, one that's practically hostile toward our enforcement efforts. We have to focus on completing our mission here, because, believe me, this place is extremely dangerous. Just remember that you have received the best training the government has to offer, and you will do fine." Connor hoped that he was not overdramatizing the point, but he wanted Ryker to stay sharp.

"Thanks, Jack. You're right, it was scary…the shit happened so fast, but it was weird…it was like the whole thing was happening in slow motion."

"That's all your senses and energy focusing on the threat, Alex. Sometimes it slows down the action of violence. It's normal. Remember what they taught you in the academy about tunnel vision. That's what we've trained you for. You took the right course of action. You'll shake it off."

"Yeah, I guess you're right," Ryker agreed and felt somewhat relieved. "Let's get inside and find out what's going on. What did you say earlier about the Glock?"

"I think I'll be able to get a Glock issued to you while you're down here," Connor replied.

"Uh yeah, a gun would be nice."

The tone in his voice made Connor laugh. Guns always seem to cheer up the new guys.

"Jack, would you mind if I grabbed a sandwich to take with us. I'm still a little hungry."

"No problem. Come up to the third floor when you're finished."

"Thanks. See you in a few minutes." Ryker darted into the café and made a beeline for the coffee.

He wants a gun and he's hungry, he's back on line. Connor felt a little better.

"Baker?" Connor asked in surprise as he recognized the muscular, tall figure in Marine camouflage fatigues standing in line at the elevators.

"Sir, how you doin'?"

Connor immediately smelled the all-too-familiar stench of a Marine who had been in the field one too many days.

"Man, have you been out in the bush?" Connor slapped him on the back.

Baker nodded and walked away from the elevator with Connor in tow.

"Were you at the governor's mansion last night when the assassination went down?" Baker asked.

"Yeah."

"Well so was I, with a team of my men. We tried to set a trap."

"Really?"

"Remember Sgt. Smith?"

"The Marine I met at Charlie Barracks?"

"Yeah, after the shooter tagged the two civilians, he opened fired on us. Ray was hit."

"What!"

"Shot in the head. This sniper is the most deadly, accurate shooter I have ever been up against. Now, two of my Marines are dead and two others. We tried to track him after he opened up on us, but he slipped out. We found where he parked his getaway vehicle and a team of FBI and CIA agents are up there right now working on forensics. I'm here to brief the CIA Station Chief. Apparently, he's friends with the commandant. He's the one who requested our presence. What about you, what are you doing here?" Baker asked curiously.

"It's the same case I've been working on in the States against the cartel. This shooter definitely gets around. First, the cartel witness in Quantico, now the Attorney General and a wealthy Mexican businessman with cartel connections."

"The word is that the AG's death was a mistake and the target was the local," Baker continued to speak in a hushed tone.

"Yeah, that's what they are saying at this point. So, where to now?"

"I don't know. I'd like to send for a few more Marines and hunt this asshole down," Baker said through gritted teeth. "What about you?" he added.

"My partner and I will be heading for Cabo to continue our investigation today or tomorrow."

"After my debriefing, I'm going back out in the field with my Marines."

"Be careful. The last two times we've met have been because of this shooter. Let's make sure that the next time we see each other, we're talking about his funeral, not one of ours."

Connor walked into the elevator and checked his cell phone. He frowned as he read the text from Barrett. It was unusually formal and abrupt.

"Mr. Connor, Mr. Tito is having an all-hands meeting now and has requested your presence," the DEA receptionist greeted him.

Connor placed the iPhone back in his pocket and joined the group already assembled in the DEA Country Attaché's office.

REDWOOD SHORES, CA

Barrett tightly gripped her shoestrings and forcefully tied a double knot on her running shoe as she stared at the official seal, the eagle's head, and the familiar face on the identification card.

CENTRAL INTELLIGENCE AGENCY
JACK C. CONNOR
CASE OFFICER
OFFICE DIRECTORATE OF OPERATIONS

He fucking lied to me. He worked for the CIA or maybe he still works for them, Barrett seethed as she ran down the steps from the condo.

Assad momentarily glanced at his GPS screen. He was only a few blocks away from the advertised apartment rental. Hakeem had directed him to secure another safe house for some additional

333

Jihad -7 freedom fighters who were essential for the completion of their mission.

Assad caught a glimpse of the blonde runner out of the corner of his eye as she ran into the crosswalk. He slammed on his brakes and laid on the horn.

"Watch out, asshole!" Barrett yelled as she abruptly stopped and thumped the driver's-side door.

"Fuck you bitch!" Assad screamed as he flung open his door and angrily attempted to exit the van.

Barrett…already emotionally enraged, spontaneously responded with a lighting quick right jab to his face. He jerked back in astonishment.

A horn blew as screeching tires brought a second vehicle to a full stop behind the van.

Assad slammed his door, gunned the engine and roared off in a cloud of exhaust.

"Are you okay?" the driver asked from the safety of his car.

"Yeah, but that guy nearly ran me down when he blew through the stop sign! Did you get his plates?" Barrett demanded. He shook his head side to side…. meaning no. She ran after the van as it burned rubber down the street and flipped him off as he veered around the corner.

Assad swore in his native tongue as he glared into the rear-view mirror, outraged that a woman had the audacity to strike him. "I will kill you! I will kill you! I will kill you!" he chanted, pounding on his steering wheel as he sped out of the neighborhood.

THE WHITE HOUSE

"Come on in," the President greeted the three most powerful people in his administration.

"Good morning, Mr. President," Bancroft answered as she entered the Oval Office. Huntington and Zif greeted him as well. The President stood up and walked around his desk to the chairs in front of it. The group waited for him to sit down first.

"You know how close I was to Hank. I want this straight. Cut the crap and give me the hard facts. I will not make this personal. A cabinet member of this administration has been murdered and I plan to get to the bottom of it as quickly and as judiciously as possible." His face was stone-like, his tone direct and decisive.

"Mr. President, you know a sniper shot and killed a government witness being protected, under Marine guard, in the witness protection program," Zif began the briefing.

"Yes, at Quantico. The victim was a high-level Bogotá Cartel accountant operating in the Far East, wasn't he?"

"Yes sir, he was. We believe that the person who killed the government witness is the same person who murdered Hank. We think that he is responsible for several other high-level cartel-related hits in the past few years."

The President listened intently as the National Security Advisor outlined the facts.

"Based on our intel to date, we think this assassin is working for the Bogotá Cartel. All the hits have been drug-related."

"One of our top sources within the Bogotá Cartel intercepted a note that was written by the assassin. We established surveillance on him at the airport. He rigged an explosion in the parking lot, which we think was an attempt to fake his own death when we tried to grab him. One of our agents was killed in the explosion," Bancroft replied.

"Have we identified the assassin?"

"We only know him by his code name, Viper," Zif answered. "Bill and Lynn have crisis teams on this. They are trying to ID the guy, but so far, we have no clue who he is. We know that he is one of the deadliest assassins we've encountered. It was Hank's and my decision not to brief you until we were able to identify him. We found out at the last minute that his next target was the conference and we immediately made efforts to protect our personnel."

"Why didn't you tell me earlier…is it because you thought he might assassinate me?" The President frowned.

"Mr. President, you know how it is in Washington. We didn't want to spark any rumors. Moreover, we didn't want to publicly acknowledge Viper's existence. We thought it was the best way to stop him and we still do," Zif explained.

The President stood up abruptly, walked back around his desk and stared out into the Rose Garden.

Shit, he's pissed, Huntington thought as an uncomfortable silence filled the room.

"Hank gave his life for this job. In my heart, I know he agreed with your assessment, that's why he didn't tell me. He always protected me, no matter what the cost!" The President's voice cracked.

The uncomfortable silence seemed to last an eternity.

"So, where do we go from here?" The President turned around and faced them. The FBI Director was the first to respond.

"Sir, Lynn and I sent a joint crisis team to Mexico City last night and they are on scene as we speak."

The President sat down at his desk and they briefed him on every detail of the investigation. At the conclusion, they agreed that the subject of Viper would not leave the Oval Office...not even the chief of staff would be brought in at this point...and Zif would brief the President once a week, or whenever there was a break in the case.

"Where's Hank now?"

"He's en route to Bethesda." Zif answered.

"Could I have a word alone with you, Jordon?" the President asked.

Bancroft and Huntington glanced at them on their way out.

"Do you think Hank suffered?"

"No, Mr. President. I was there. He never knew what hit him." Zif saw the President's eyes begin to water.

The two men were silent for a few seconds, both trying to keep their composure. Zif's throat tightened as he witnessed a man grieve over the loss of a close friend. He knew the feeling and he hated it.

CHAPTER 20

CABO SAN LUCAS

Viper opened the door to his two-room luxury suite. He put his bags in the closet and walked onto the patio, overlooking the Sea of Cortez. The warm breeze engulfed him as he stepped outside. He was pleased with the success of his mission but was irritated that he had underestimated the Americans. He was positive that he had killed one of them and was confident that he had escaped undetected.

He thought about the deer. He pictured them, frozen, then fleeing, signaling the danger to him, allowing him to strike first. Nature was oddly reassuring.

He had killed Cuevas, the U.S. Attorney General, and probably two Marines. It wasn't as clean as he had wanted. The Americans had gotten in the way. That small detail did not detract from his sense of satisfaction and accomplishment. He had proven that he could outwit America's finest…not once, but twice. He smiled as he took in the sun reflecting off of the whitecaps. His next mission was partly business, partly pleasure. He relished the thought.

Viper stared at the adjacent Palmilla Resort and focused on the one person, outside of the cartel, who could compromise him. The likelihood of him ever meeting or seeing the flight attendant again was remote, but she was a loose end and that was unacceptable. She had narrowly escaped in London. That was not going to happen this time.

He decided to take a shower and have an early lunch on the patio. He wanted to be refreshed. It was warm and breezy, inviting weather for a hunt.

MEXICO CITY INTERNATIONAL AIRPORT

"Attention, attention! We will now begin boarding Flight 227 to Cabo San Lucas. Please have your boarding pass ready for the gate agent."

Connor and Ryker got in line with the other passengers. Families with small children were pre-boarding at a snail's pace.

"I can't believe we are finally on our way to Cabo," Ryker said as he and Connor waited in the stagnant line. I figured that we were a lock to stay behind and help out with the investigation at the Embassy."

"The Attorney General's death is definitely a top priority as far as our government is concerned, but there are other priorities and right now ours is the Bogotá Cartel and the hit in North Carolina," Connor replied, wondering how or if this mess was related. Bancroft had made it clear to Connor that time was running out and he needed to develop some leads between the cartel and the terrorist cell in the San Francisco Bay area.

Within thirty minutes, they had lifted off and were en route on the ninety-minute plane ride to Cabo. Tito had given Connor the name of a CIA contact, they would meet once they arrived. Connor wondered if it was anyone he knew but dismissed the notion as improbable. Like DEA, the CIA had also been monitoring the activities of Felix Francisco's transportation organization and would provide logistical support to Connor. Because of the Mexico City assassination, Tito couldn't spare any of his agents. Under the circumstances, Connor completely understood, and relished the idea of working outside the umbrella of DEA. Ryker was fluent in Spanish and he was well versed in the cryptic, coded language of drug transactions. His interactions were heavily peppered with Spanish profanities, a skill that others admired and coveted.

Ryker thought about Tara as the flight attendants prepared for lift-off. He tried to remember the name of her hotel. *Was it the Palmilla Resort?* That would be too good to be true, staying at the same hotel. The thought of seeing her excited him, but he wasn't exactly optimistic with the work schedules that faced them both. Still, no harm in trying, he pondered with a smile.

Ryker looked out the aircraft window, wondering if the pace would slow down. Maybe these last few weeks on the job were routine for a DEA agent. On one hand, it was exciting and challenging. On the other hand, people got killed. A pocket of turbulence jarred him from his thoughts and he double checked his seat-belt to be sure he was locked in.

CIA HEADQUARTERS

"Lynn, our new prototype needs a few adjustments, which we are working on. We believe the package is somewhere in the Hollister area, south of San Jose, about forty minutes from the target location. I doubt it will be long before the prototype is back online. We know that the package is stationary. We don't know the exact location, but we know the general area," the NEST Director reported.

"That's reassuring," Bancroft replied skeptically.

"Don't worry, we'll be back online soon. My guess is that the package is in a staging area for some reason. Anything on your end?"

"No, not in the past twenty-four hours. One of my officers is in Mexico and hopefully he will develop something," Bancroft replied.

"Okay. I will call you when I have any updated information."

"Please do." She felt pulled in a dozen directions as she considered all the moving parts of the multiple investigations. They needed a solid lead…soon.

PACIFICA, CA

From his bedroom window, Radcliff watched the Pacific fog roll in. He was unpacking his suitcase when he heard the knock at his front door. He picked up his Beretta 92, placed it in the small of his back and proceeded to the door. He looked through the peephole and recognized the familiar face on the other side. Raven's hair was blowing around his face. Cold, gusty wind was normal year-round in the coastal town of Pacifica just south of San Francisco.

"I'm surprised you're not at work." He opened the door and waved him inside.

"I went to a two-day conference and they finished up early, so they let us go," Raven replied as he walked into the room. "Is everything okay on your end?" Raven asked hesitantly.

"Of course it is, we know the risks. Why do you ask?" Radcliff snapped back.

"Oh, I don't know, five wounded DEA agents, two of your men dead, explosions, cocaine blown up, live 24/7 news coverage!" Raven threw his hands up in the air in frustration.

"Listen, I warned you that it could get ugly. My men are good. We just caught an unlucky break, that's all. Hey, at the end of the day we're still getting paid. We got about a ton of coke, so there's two less to split the money with. It's still a good payday, even with the extra headaches. Case closed."

"I know the deal. I just want to know what happened, that's all," he snapped.

Raven had been so stressed that he hadn't slept the previous night, but he had finally managed to get his nerves under control, for the moment. He knew DEA's reputation for tracking down people who killed or wounded agents. The idea of Cartwright finding out that he was the mole put the fear of God in him. He knew exactly what Cartwright was capable of doing, and it was not necessarily within the confines of the criminal justice system.

"Everything is fine. The rest of my men are all back and we are taking separate vacations, lying low. The cocaine is in a safe place. They probably don't realize that we got some of the shipment. Also, there's the matter of the murder of the AG. That will take some of the heat off us. Hey, at the end of the day, ten plus million of coke is still worth the effort." *This asshole has no clue what he's dealing with or what DEA is about,* Raven thought as he tried to suppress his nervous irritation.

"The only thing you have to do is warn me. If by some miracle they develop any leads that could compromise us, we'll keep a low profile before we start phase two of this operation. Any questions?" Radcliff sounded like a principal talking to a schoolboy.

"No. I'm still in the loop and I will let you know when I hear something." Raven sounded like he was trying to reassure himself.

"We should minimize our contact with each other for a while. Keep your nose to the ground and only contact me if it's important. Otherwise, don't contact me at all for a month."

"Alright. Hopefully, in six months' time, you and I will have a few extra pennies in our pockets."

"That's the plan." *What a friggin' wimp,* Radcliff scowled as he closed the door behind him.

SAN FRANCISCO, CA

Raven noticed the blinking light on his old-school answering machine.

"Hi, my name is Steven Higgins and I'm a good friend of your brother. I am trying to contact him, but his number has been changed. I'm in town and would like to see him. I'll call you back around eight tonight, or if I miss you, I'll call you back in the morning. Thank you." Beep, beep, the recording sounded, ending the message.

What the hell does the cartel want now? He looked at his watch and noticed that his hands were shaking. He picked up his keys and headed out to meet his Bogotá handler.

PALMILLA RESORT, CABO SAN LUCAS

The taxi pulled up to the entrance of the Palmilla Resort. Ryker did not want to appear awed, but he couldn't believe that as a new agent he was at a luxury resort in Cabo San Lucas on a work assignment.

His eyes followed the long, tan legs of a stunning woman wearing tight shorts, as she glided through the lobby toward a bar that opened up to the sandy beach. *This is too good to be true.*

Connor saw Ryker's face and watched him as he stared at the woman.

"Beats serving subpoenas and analyzing phone logs, huh?"

"You got that right!" Ryker cracked a smile. "You know, I think this is the resort where Tara is staying."

"With any luck, you may have enough time to give her a phone call."

"Hey, boss. Don't ruin it for me," he sighed dramatically.

"All right. Maybe you can have breakfast with her on the day we leave."

What I wouldn't give if it were breakfast in bed, he fantasized, but refrained from saying.

"Sir, we have a slight problem."

"What's that?" Connor responded to the reservations manager.

"We only have double suites. All of the singles are gone. Your reservation indicates that you booked two rooms, but under the circumstances, will you accept a double suite until single rooms become available?"

"Not a problem, that'll be fine."

"This is a much more expensive suite, but there is no extra charge. Sorry for the inconvenience."

"Thank you," Connor signed the reservation card and picked up the key-cards.

"Alex, let's put our stuff in the room and then I'll make that call to our contact here."

"You lead the way and I'll follow."

Soaring white Corinthian columns lined the walkway. The dress code seemed to be designer swimsuits and strappy Prada sandals. The suite was far more elegant than they expected. The two bedrooms were master suites, equipped with sunken tubs that could more appropriately be described as mini-spas. The rooms were connected by a large living room with oversized white sofas and a lavishly appointed kitchen accented with colorful tiles and a Subzero refrigerator. Each room had a commanding view of the ocean. The rock formation known as *The Arch* rose majestically out of the water in the distance.

"I wouldn't mind staying an extra few days down here when we finish," Ryker's tone made Connor smile.

"I bet you would, but somehow I think our boss would have our asses when we got back," Connor replied as he picked up the phone on the coffee table in the living room.

Ryker walked onto the balcony and took in the clear, blue sky and frothy waves hitting the sand below. The fairly calm waters were deceiving. Dangerous riptides plagued the area and swimming was forbidden at some of the beaches, but not this one. He hoped he would have time for a swim. The water looked inviting and sweat was starting to bead up on his forehead from the midday heat.

"Hey Alex," Connor called from the living room. "We're on. We're going to meet our contact in an hour. Why don't you go to the lobby and rent a car?"

"Can we get a Porsche?"

"Yeah, if you're paying."

"Seriously? We're undercover, right? We need a fast car."

"Alex, this is a debriefing, not a buy-bust. The last thing we want to do is attract attention, right? So, find us a Ford or VW, okay?"

"Damn, I had my hopes up," Ryker replied in mock seriousness as he headed for the door.

"Rookies," Connor replied in an exasperated tone and rolled his eyes.

FISHING HARBOR, CABO SAN LUCAS

"Any contact yet?" Francisco asked as Carlos entered the harbor office.

"They just made radio contact with the sub. It should be here later tonight."

"Excellent! I want to load her up again and send her out as soon as possible. We need to locate another route into the States. It is too risky to take the same one. I'm thinking we could set up a route in the Gulf of Mexico and establish an operation somewhere on the coast of Mississippi. Have you ever been to Mississippi, Carlos?"

"Only once. I traveled through there on my way to New Orleans."

"I may need you to take a trip to the Gulf Coast and check possible locations."

"I have some contacts in New Orleans."

"Good. Did you find out anything more about the assassination?"

"Very little. My contacts think that Cuevas was the target, not the U.S Attorney General."

"Cuevas was arrogant and greedy," Francisco's tone was bitter as he stood up from his desk and walked toward the window overlooking the harbor and the fishing vessels docked at the pier. "He told me he was a man of vision. He once said that his power would one day rival the Colombians. Well, he pissed off someone because they short-circuited his grandiose plans."

"Do you have any idea who could have killed him?" Carlos asked.

"No, but his brother Sal is very angry. He has made it well known that he plans to avenge his brother's death. The killers will think they are in hell when Sal finds them."

"Carlos, I don't care what it costs. Pay whoever you need to but find out who killed Cuevas. I need to know." Francisco was adamant.

The phone rang loudly, interrupting their conversation.

"Yes, okay...about an hour. Okay." Francisco hung up. The other load just came in. It's in town. Let's go back to the hotel and get something to eat and then we can go inspect our package after dinner. Go get the car." Francisco ordered.

Carlos departed, feeling a little edgy. *Where is Connor? Why hasn't he made contact yet?* His mind raced as he tried to figure out what to do next.

BAHAMAS TRAVEL, CABO SAN LUCAS

Connor and Ryker drove for fifteen minutes before they came to a street lined with rundown warehouses. It took them an additional ten minutes before they located the address and entrance to the CIA undercover business front. Considering that it was situated near a resort area, nowhere near one of the larger Mexican cities, the area seemed quite busy. The majority of the businesses either related to commercial fishing or the travel industry.

They entered a business with a small sign posted above the entrance...*Caribbean and Bahamas Travel Incorporated.*

"May I help you, señor?" the receptionist greeted them. The walls of the small office were covered with scenic posters of beaches, palm trees, and travel destinations in the Bahamas.

"Good afternoon. Is Mr. Winston in?" Connor replied in Spanish.

"Yes, he is. May I ask who is calling, please?"

"Mr. Connor and Mr. Ryker, from Mexico City."

The receptionist picked up the telephone and briefly spoke into it.

"He'll see you now, please, this way," she said as she opened the door, allowing them access into the next office.

"Welcome to Los Cabos, Señors Connor and Ryker." The tall American invited them in.

"Alex Ryker." Ryker extended his hand and noticed that Winston avoided eye contact with him and focused on Connor. Ryker turned around only to see his partner's mouth wide open in surprise.

"Herman?" Connor said in an astonished tone.

"Actually, I'm presently Mr. Gerald Winston."

"Herman, damn, I had no idea!"

"I wanted to see your expression and to be honest, I didn't know your names until a day ago," Winston laughed.

"Herman, I mean Gerald and I..." Connor paused, "served together in Iraq a few years back when I was in the Marines and he was in the Navy. In fact, he saved my butt, or I should say my

344

career, when he stopped me and my Marines from hitting the wrong target."

"You know, I almost forgot about that."

"We were a couple of boots back then, weren't we?" Connor smiled.

"We were." A phone rang in another adjoining room and Winston excused himself.

"We lucked out on this partner," Connor told Ryker.

Winston returned, "Jack, it's Franklin. He wants to talk to you."

Connor went into the next room. It was a little larger than a walk-in closet, filled with various portable crypto and communications gear. Connor picked up the STE secure telephone.

"Sir."

"Well, Jack, I see you finally made it to Cabo. You've had an interesting couple of days. Have you made contact with your CI yet?"

"No, not yet. We just got in. I wanted to check in with Gerald first. I plan to try to contact him tonight."

"Good. The tracking device on the sub worked beautifully. We now know the exact route. Gerald will brief you. Contact Carlos as soon as you can. We should get great intel," Franklin instructed. "The SEAL team is in position, waiting to move in once the sub is back. Jack, remember, there are only three other people in DEA who know about the SEALs...the administrator, your SAC and your GS. We need to keep it that way, understand?"

"Yes sir." Connor recognized the change in Franklin's voice.

"Gerald has been briefed into the entire program, so if you need anything in the field, go through him. He's your contact. Any questions?"

"What about my partner, sir?"

"Keep that minimal and use your own discretion as operation needs dictate. If you need to contact me, use this phone or go through Gerald. Good luck, Jack."

"Thanks, sir."

"And Jack? I read the after-action e-mail on the assassination. That was some fast thinking on your part. Good job."

"Thank you, sir."

Connor noticed the open briefcase on Winston's desk when he returned to the office.

"Have one of these yet?" Winston asked as he picked up Glock's smallest subcompact 9mm capable of interchanging magazines with larger glocks and firing up to 31 rounds.

"The twenty-six? Yeah, it's an accurate little gun."

"Well, I tell you what, sign these property cards and they're yours while you're in Cabo. One thing, though. Before you touch them, remember I get them back. I know about you DEA guys. I just got these in and they are hard to come by down here. Deal?" Winston grinned.

"That is an offer we can't refuse. Of course you'll get these beauties back," Connor grinned in return, glad to be armed again after they had to return the DEA Glock's when they left the embassy.

"These are yours. Here, take four magazines, four boxes of ammo and a couple of the inside the waist holsters."

Connor noticed that two of the magazines were Glock 19s, each carrying fifteen rounds, and the remainder were the smaller Glock 26 ten-round mags, equipped with finger extenders which gave it a 12-round capacity, all very concealable.

"As you know, these boys play for keeps down here. It's a totally different game." Winston locked eyes with Connor.

"Yeah, I know," Connor replied as he and Ryker started loading the magazines.

"We don't have many reinforcements down here, especially after the assassination a few days ago. What you see is what you get, but I'll try to cover you as much as I can," Winston spoke with concern.

"We're going to track down Carlos tonight and call you later."

"Sounds good to me. Here's my cell number. Give me a call when you find him."

PALMILLA RESORT, CABO SAN LUCAS

"That's great, Tara. Sexy, sexy, sexy! Okay, now tilt your head back to your right. Good, now look up at the sky. Great, that's a wrap."

346

The photographer fired staccato commands at the tall model. She responded instantly and naturally, as though she had been born a supermodel.

Tara looked down at her feet, submerged in the crystal-clear, warm ocean water. It felt soothing. She closed her eyes thinking she would no longer be standing on her tired feet after those long international flights. *I must be in heaven now.*

"Tara? Tara! You can stop daydreaming. You were great! I think you're going to make it big in this business."

"Thanks, Doug, I'm going to love this," she smiled, clearly pleased by his praise.

"I want you to come out two hours earlier tomorrow morning, so that I can take some additional pictures of you with the sun rising in the background. I know you models hate early-morning shoots, but the light will be perfect."

"No problem. I like mornings," she replied enthusiastically.

"Okay, see you bright and early then."

As she walked past him, he lightly swatted her on her butt. A shiver of anger shot through her and she paused for a second, then decided to say nothing. It was an occupational hazard that she hated. A frown creased her forehead as she crossed the warm sand.

About thirty yards away, sitting on the beach in one of a row of private cabanas, Viper watched her through a pair of Nikon mini binoculars as she walked away. *You didn't like the photographer grabbing your ass? What a waste of talent. You would have been a tremendous asset in one the specialized units of the FSB,* he speculated as he tracked her across the sand. As she drew closer to the cabanas, he marveled once again at her natural beauty. People impolitely stopped to stare at her, but she pretended not to notice. *She is probably used to it.* She turned and glanced at several cabanas including Viper's as she walked by.

I wonder how many VIP perverts hang out in these cabanas, she thought as she pulled her white mesh cover-up closer to her body. She caught a glimpse of a man with his face buried in a book and heard the sound of ice hitting the side of a glass. She suddenly realized how thirsty she was.

Viper waited until she was out of sight and took a sip of his Scotch. *I have to finish her soon.*

347

HIGHWAY 1, CABO SAN LUCAS

The drive back always seems shorter, Connor thought as he and Ryker sped along the two-lane road back to their hotel.

"Do you think you will be able to hook up with Carlos tonight?" Ryker asked.

"Hope so."

Connor didn't notice the patrol car until it pulled out onto the highway with its red lights flashing.

"Shit," he swore and immediately took his foot off the accelerator. "I've got enough cash, so this shouldn't take long." Connor adjusted the rearview mirror, so he could see the car behind him and pulled over to the side of the road. There were two uniformed officers inside the patrol vehicle. He watched the driver get out and slowly approach.

"Alex, you handle the questions. Your Spanish is a hell of a lot better than mine."

"Passports and rental agreement?" The officer's expression was serious and his tone was demanding.

"Is there a problem?" Ryker asked in fluent Spanish, trying not to sound disrespectful.

"Speeding," he replied coldly.

Connor reached in the glove box and retrieved the rental contract. He noticed Ryker's Glock 26 in partial view under the passenger seat and his heart rate shot up as he handed the contract and his passport to the cop. Earlier, Ryker had taken his Glock out of the holster to avoid the discomfort of wearing it in the car and had tucked it under the seat.

"Momento." The officer abruptly turned and walked back to the patrol car.

"Alex, I hope to hell he didn't see your gun under the seat!"

"Shit! I'm sorry…"

"Don't touch it now. They'll see you bend over. Try to shove it under the seat with your foot."

Ryker gave it a nudge with his heel. He felt sweat running down his back as his heart pounded in his chest.

Connor watched the officers in the rearview mirror. Both of them got out of the patrol car and approached. Connor stared in disbelief as he recognized the second officer, who was resting his hand on his .45 cal as he approached the driver's side.

"Heads up, Alex. This could go to shit real fast. The one on your right…I saw him kill a man in cold blood in a restaurant in Mexico City two days ago. He didn't even stop eating. He's a pig, one of the most corrupt, murderous cops in Mexico." Connor spoke rapidly but sat calmly as he watched them approach.

"We have a problem, señor," the first officer began. Connor kept his eye on the rearview mirror, watching El Capitán. "We need to go to the station to see the judge on this speeding ticket…or you could pay the fine of two hundred dollars today and be on your way." He flashed a threatening grin and exposed his uneven, brown teeth; a single gold cap was the only evidence of dental care.

Connor watched in the rearview mirror as El Capitán approached the passenger side and stood at the window.

"Are they paying?" El Capitán asked in English.

At that moment, El Capitán's radio squawked. He reached down on his duty belt, pulled off the radio, and spoke into it rapidly.

"Let's go now!" El Capitán blurted. He rattled off the rest of the sentence so rapidly that even Ryker had difficulty understanding.

The younger officer threw the passport and rental agreement through the open window and into Connor's lap. "Another day, amigo." He abruptly turned around and ran back to his car.

"What the hell was that all about?" Ryker exclaimed as he watched them jump back into their car.

"Hey, you're the expert Spanish speaker."

"Something about a shooting. I didn't catch all of it." They watched as the patrol car sped away with its flashing red lights. Within seconds, the sounds of a siren rang out.

CHAPTER 21

PALMILLA RESORT, CABO SAN LUCAS

"How many girls do you think we can finish tonight?" The lead photographer downed he rest of his Corona Longneck.

"Let's take eight of them, split 'em up, and shoot four each. It'll probably take us two hours and then we can call it a night."

"How's that flight attendant coming along?"

"You mean Tara?"

"Yeah."

"Just fine. In fact, tomorrow morning I'm going to shoot a sunrise special with her." Houser gave a leering grin.

"Is she coming out tonight?"

"No, I gave her the night off."

"She'll get plenty of work tomorrow."

Viper eavesdropped as the photographers discussed the models. He was positioned with his back to them, sitting at an adjacent table at the pool. His disguise was rudimentary, but he blended in with the crowd of tequila drinking tourists.

"Houser, do I detect that you have a little bit of a hard-on for the flight attendant, or is that my imagination?"

"Get real!"

"You know the rules. Don't get personal with the models. It doesn't matter how long you've been around in the business. You get blacklisted and you're done," Young warned.

"You mean I should cancel the thong shoot tonight in suite B-210?" Houser smirked and raised his right eyebrow in a crooked scowl.

"It's your job on the line."

Viper couldn't believe his ears. Was the guy joking, or was the suite number B-210 correct? There was only one way to find out. He buried his head in his newspaper pretending to read as the photographers continued their conversation. He wasn't interested in hearing their lecherous small talk. They were pathetic.

Viper stood up and stretched. His face was partially shaded by a smart, sand colored, wide-brimmed hat and Guess sunglasses. He sported a heavy mustache on his tanned face. He picked up a white embossed terrycloth hotel towel to wipe the sweat from his forehead and walked toward the bar outside the lobby entrance. He felt confident that he could pass Tara without a chance of her recognizing him. He decided to return to his room for a massage at the spa.

Tara approached the lobby, clutching the inexpensive but treasured watch her father had given her for high school graduation. He had died shortly after that and it was the one thing that reminded her of him. She couldn't believe that she had left it on the beach after the photo shoot. Thankfully, she had put it behind some rocks and no one had seen it there. She was determined to lock it in a safety deposit box for the rest of her stay in Cabo.

As she walked up to the front desk, she caught another glimpse of him. Something about him seemed familiar but slightly menacing. She held her breath. She couldn't get a good look at his face, but the way he walked, the way he held himself, was familiar…or was her imagination playing tricks on her again? She ducked into the gift shop and fixed her eyes on him as he walked out of the hotel.

Could it be Jacques Devinuer? It can't be, she thought nervously as she strained to get a good look at his face. The hat and sunglasses were in the way. Her eyes followed him through the exit, then he was gone.

"May I help you, señorita?" the gift shop attendant asked.

Tara jumped, clearly startled.

"No thank you, I'm just waiting for a friend," she answered self-consciously as she met the inquisitive stare of the young woman. She continued scanning the lobby, but he had vanished. *God! I hope I'm wrong. It can't be him,* she mentally assured herself.

The car rolled up to the hotel's main entrance. "Here you go," Connor said as he handed the keys to the hotel doorman and got out of the rental car. "We'll probably need the car later tonight," he added.

Viper heard him and stopped and turned. His eyes narrowed as he recognized the man. *Coincidence or fate?* He clearly recalled watching that profile in his crosshairs at the Governor's mansion. *Those two are working,* he concluded as he casually walked toward the parking lot. He began to rethink his plan.

"Jack, I'm going to get some gum. Do you want anything from the gift store?" Ryker asked as they walked into the hotel lobby.

"No thanks, I'll check the front desk to see if we got any messages."

Ryker turned the corner and his eyes lit up with delight when he saw her. He tried to make eye contact, but as he drew closer, she didn't acknowledge him at all. In fact, she seemed distracted. He frowned.

"Tara?"

"Alex!" She was clearly surprised. She threw her arms around him and held on for a few moments.

"Whoa! For a minute, I didn't think you were happy to see me."

"What are you talking about? I'm thrilled to see you!" She smiled brightly and tried to conceal her uneasiness. She had no intention of mentioning her irrational fears. She didn't want him to think she was crazy.

"Are you working now?" She tried to sound cheerful.

"Yeah, my partner Connor is at the front desk," Ryker motioned. "We're trying to meet someone, but we don't know where he is right now. I might have some free time later. What's your schedule like?"

"I have the rest of the day off. I start early in the morning and am booked all day tomorrow."

"What's your room number?" Ryker asked.

"B-210," Tara responded without hesitation.

"Mine's C-225. As soon as I find out what's going on, I'll call you, and hopefully we'll be able to get together later today."

"That would be great!"

Her brilliant smile made him feel weak. He tried to focus.

"Tara, remember don't tell anyone what we do." Ryker lowered his voice.

"Obviously Mr. Bond. I get what your job is about," Tara whispered with a slight grin.

Ryker noticed the expression on her face change and he turned around to see Connor approaching them.

"Hi, good to see you again."

"Thank you, it's good to see you too."

"Alex was wondering if we would run into you down here," Connor smiled.

"It's nice to see friendly faces." Tara gave his hand a firm shake as she smiled warmly.

"Any messages?" Alex directed his attention to Connor.

"Yeah, we got a message from our friend. Hopefully, we'll be able to see him tonight."

"Great," he replied in a less-than-enthusiastic tone that was not lost on Connor.

"Tara, it was a pleasure to see you. When we get back to San Francisco, I'd like to introduce you to my wife Barrett and have you and Alex over for dinner."

"I'd like that, thanks."

"Alex, I'm going to the room to make a few phone calls. I'll see you two later." Connor left them standing outside the gift shop.

"I'll go find out what the real deal is and call you in fifteen minutes. Hopefully, we can spend some time together either this afternoon or later this evening."

"Okay," she said in a conspiratorial tone.

Ryker took a few steps back and realized what she was wearing.

"What is it?" she asked self-consciously.

"Damn, I just realized how amazing you look!" Ryker exclaimed as his eyes traveled down the white mesh cover-up that revealed the bright turquoise bikini beneath. Her skin was golden, and the contrast was striking. But what blew him away was her flat, firm abs. He wondered how many sit-ups it took to achieve that figure; he guessed at least five hundred a day.

"Well, thank you, Agent Ryker. Now, get going so you can give me that call."

"Fifteen minutes," he answered as he reluctantly tore his gaze away. He couldn't help looking back over his shoulder as they went in opposite directions. Her body was to die for.

DEA HEADQUARTERS

"Okay, what do we have?" Joseph O'Leary the DEA Administrator addressed the three senior DEA managers seated in the executive conference room on the sixteenth floor of DEA headquarters in Arlington, Virginia, and one on the teleconference screen from San Francisco.

"We have very little sir," replied Lucas Crenshaw, SAC of the Washington Field Office, noting the administrator's demanding tone. "This was carefully planned and expertly executed, like a military operation."

"Lucas, I've heard that already. What else do we have?" O'Leary fired back.

Before Crenshaw could continue, Gino Domingo, the SAC from Miami spoke up.

"Sir, we really don't have that much. We know the two dead suspects in North Carolina were cousins and we know that one was an ex-Army Ranger and the other an ex-Miami police officer suspected of being on the take. We did search warrants at both residences and unless Lucas has anything to add, we've got nothing to tie them to anyone of significance. We're waiting on the phone logs. Hopefully that will tell us something."

"What about the stolen van? Any leads on that?"

"No sir. We were on that as soon as it was located. The van was stolen from a used car lot in Savannah, Georgia a couple of days ago, but no leads on that end. The plates had been changed, so it took a little longer to trace it," Domingo added.

"What about the new recruit who initially suspected the plot?" O'Leary continued.

"Yeah, Alex Ryker. He's pretty good under fire. I talked to him yesterday. I don't think he knows anything else that will help us develop any additional leads in this case. I let him join Jack Connor in Mexico to help on the Bogotá Cartel investigation," George Melconi, SAC of San Francisco reported from the telephone conference screen.

"Have we confirmed if they got any of the cocaine?" The administrator continued his cross-examination.

"Sir, it's hard to tell. Forensics says that the semi was too burned to confirm whether the entire load was destroyed. All the agents in Washington and up and down the East Coast have been alerted to be on the look-out for the one-handed monkey symbol on the kilos. A priority e-mail has also been distributed to the field worldwide. If any of this stuff shows up on the street, we'll work the case in reverse if we have to. We'll track down leads from street dealers and work our way up from there. We're still logging calls from the various state and local law enforcement agencies and pursuing leads they are generating," Crenshaw reported.

"Okay," O'Leary replied, seeming somewhat reassured. "Now, the sixty-four million dollar question: where did the leak come from? Who is the fucking mole?" O'Leary's tone could have cut glass. The room was silent as a tomb.

"I think the leak is either in Miami or Washington," Gino Domingo, the Miami SAC spoke quietly. "My OPR staff is working with OPR at headquarters. They are conducting a full-scale investigation right now."

"I agree with Gino," Crenshaw added. "The leak had to come from one of our two offices. It's like they had a copy of our op plan. They knew the route, made the semi, and got away without being followed."

"Michael, anything you want to add?" O'Leary motioned toward his brother.

"No, like Gino said, we're working on it. There is a rat, and we will flush him, or her, out."

Michael O'Leary was the DEA chief inspector of the Office of Professional Responsibility…the second-most feared person in DEA. The fact that he and the administrator were brothers unnerved a lot of agents.

"All right, here's how I want to play this. Lucas, Gino, conduct your own investigations and coordinate your results through Michael here at headquarters. George, got anything to add from San Francisco?" O'Leary asked.

"Nope."

"I know that every agent in this room is highly motivated to find out who did this. Do whatever it takes but do it strictly by the book. When we catch these bastards, we need to make sure it sticks in the courtroom," the administrator said pointedly as he locked eyes with his brother. "One definite weak link is the op plan. Find out everyone who had access to it and then start a process of elimination. Hopefully, that will lead us to the traitor." The administrator paused as he looked around the table. "Okay, if there is nothing further, let's get to it."

PALMILLA RESORT

Viper carefully folded a pair of dark pants and placed them into the gym bag along with the white uniform shirt with the palm tree insignia of the Palmilla Resort embroidered on the pocket. Most of the support staff at the various resorts in Cabo had similar uniforms. Obtaining one from housekeeping had been simple.

Viper reached for a larger piece of his luggage and opened a secret compartment built into its hard frame. He took out a Beretta 950 BS Jetfire .25-caliber semi-automatic pistol fitted with a custom silencer and loaded .25 magnum hollow-point rounds. He slid the weapon into a suede holster and secured it inside his waistband on his right side. He imagined two silent, swift shots to the head. *She'll never know what hit her.*

He took out his make-up and hairpiece and walked into the bathroom.

DULLES AIRPORT, VA

Stevens got off the plane from Mexico and entered the terminal. Most CIA agents prefer Dulles over Reagan National Airport. It is less congested and closer to Langley. He recognized one of the staff assigned to the Office of Security from the director's detail.

"Phil, you didn't have to pick me up."

"No problem, Greg. I had some work to do down here and the director wanted to see you as soon as you arrived," Goodman explained as they walked toward baggage claim. "How was the trip?"

"It was a tough one. We've got very little evidence at this point," Stevens answered in a clipped tone.

Phil Goodman knew better than to pry into Stevens' business and he had no desire to. Stevens worked for the Director of Intelligence, a completely different directorate than the Office of Security. He was not cleared for the information generated from Stevens' department and that didn't bother him one bit. He had more than enough bullshit to keep him busy.

The evening air felt cool and breezy, a welcome relief from the stifling humidity in Mexico. Stevens didn't talk during most of the trip back to headquarters. He was mentally preparing for his briefing with the DCI.

"Thanks for the ride, Phil. I really appreciate it." He got out of the car.

"No problem. See you upstairs," Goodman replied. He phoned the director's office to let them know Stevens was on the way up.

"Welcome back. She's expecting you," the secretary greeted him as he walked in.

"Thanks, Emma."

"Greg," Bancroft waved him in.

"Thanks, ma'am."

"Well, what do we have?" Bancroft got right to the point.

"The Marines found the staging area where he parked his getaway vehicle. The FBI lifted a tire print. They think it was probably a SUV. They also located the area where he fired his weapon. As you know, the Marines got off a shot at him. They found bits of his ghillie suit and a piece of a plastic canteen. They think they may have nicked the canteen with a bullet. A few more inches and the story could have had a happy ending."

"That's more detail than I expected." Bancroft was pleased. Viper wasn't invincible and the next time he might not be so lucky.

"We've learned that he prefers using sport utility vehicles. This is the second time he's used one. It's not much, but it's a start. The Bureau, Marines, and our techs will be there for two more days and we hope that they'll find out a lot more. One thing is certain," he paused, "he knows we're on to him. I wonder what went through his mind when the Marines opened up on him."

"I hope he was scared shitless. I don't care how we stop this guy. I just want it done. The President is livid." Bancroft's voice was tense.

"Yeah, I bet he is. I'm gonna go home and get a good night's sleep. Tomorrow is a new day." Stevens rubbed his eyes. They felt swollen and dry.

PALMILLA RESORT

Ryker felt elated after he saw Tara and could barely contain his excitement.

"What's the deal?" he asked as soon as he closed the door to the suite.

357

"Carlos left us a message saying that he will contact us between eleven and midnight." Connor had changed into gym shorts and was lacing up his running shoes.

"Great!"

"I'll make a deal with you. I need to send out an e-mail, but I want to go for a short run first. You stay in the room and watch our weapons and rest of our gear. When I get back, I'll write the e-mail and chill in the room until Carlos calls. Then, you can go have dinner with your lovely roommate or do whatever you single guys do."

"Sure, that's fine with me." Ryker tried to act nonchalant, even though he was so jacked up he wanted to do cartwheels across the room.

"I'll be back in forty minutes."

Ryker was thrilled, it was only 7:00 p.m. Four hours, what a deal! He whistled the theme song to Cops for the next five minutes. After Connor left, he dialed Tara's suite.

"Tara, want to meet me for dinner in about an hour? I'm free until eleven."

"Sounds great, except for one thing."

"What?"

"They just dropped off thirty dresses for an evening-wear shoot tomorrow. I've got to try them all on and pick out six. Why don't you come by and help me select the dresses and we'll order room service?"

"My own private fashion show? Seriously, who could resist that!"

"That's right, your own personal show, Alex," she laughed.

"I'll be there at a quarter 'til."

"Good. See you then."

"Yes! Yes! Yes!" Ryker pumped his fist in the air as he rushed to the shower.

Viper studied the map of the resort in his suite. The location of the target suite was ideal. It was at the end of the building, which made his escape route easy. His main concern was the point of entry. One method of access was through the front door. He could use a ruse or obtain a room keycard. He mentally weighed the possibilities of obtaining a keycard. *Plausible,* he thought, *considering the number of support staff on duty.*

The other method was through one of three balconies attached to the suite. It was a two-bedroom suite and that meant that the models were probably sharing. A double hit would add a different dimension to the subsequent police investigation. It would complicate matters for them and help confuse the issue of motive and intended target. He looked out at the ocean and silently welcomed nightfall as he poured a single glass of wine from the $350 bottle. He decided to enjoy the moment before determining his point of entry.

Ryker had just finished dressing when he heard the front door open.

"Hey, you're back early," Ryker called, keenly aware of the time.

"Had a good run," Connor called out as he walked in the kitchen and took a cold bottle of water out of the refrigerator.

"Jack, you can reach me at Tara's suite. She can't leave, so I left the number by the phone in the living room."

"She's a prisoner in her own suite?"

"She has to work tonight! They sent her a bunch of evening dresses and she has to pick some of them for a session tomorrow. I'm going to help her over room service," Ryker replied with a sheepish, yet satisfied grin.

"I see." Connor gave him a don't-do-anything-I-wouldn't-do grin.

"If you hear from Carlos early, call me and I'll come right back."

"I'm sure you hope that happens, right?"

"Come on, Jack, don't bust my chops. This is Victoria's Secret, for God's sake!" Ryker replied as he hurriedly put his wallet in his pants pocket. Connor chuckled as the door closed behind him.

FISHING HARBOR, CABO SAN LUCAS

Carlos stood on the pier and watched the top of the sub as it followed the fishing trawler back to the dock area and into the enclosed warehouse.

"Carlos," one of Francisco's drivers yelled out.

"Yes, what is it?"

"Señor Francisco wants to see you. He's in his office."

"Okay. I'll be there in a few minutes."

It was a calm, clear night in the harbor and the stern of the trawler knifed through the smooth glassy surface.

"The sub is back in the shed," Carlos greeted Francisco starring in astonishment at a man standing in the corner. He recognized Jorge Gusto.

"Señor Gusto," Carlos bowed his head. He was surprised by Gusto's presence, but not surprised that his two bodyguards were watching Carlos' every move. It was a rare occasion for one of the Gusto brothers to visit an operational site. Carlos had no idea what was going on.

"Carlos, I am glad to meet you again. I heard from Francisco you continue to do great work."

"Thank you, señor," Carlos replied in a highly deferential tone.

"Carlos, we have a small change of plans. The Gusto family wants us to transport another package for them," Francisco said.

"What do you want me to do?" Carlos responded, focusing on the package on Francisco's desk. It appeared similar to the last package that was sent to Monterey.

"Just let me know when the sub is ready to leave."

"Yes, señor. It's an honor to meet you again, Señor Gusto." Carlos bowed out of the office curious as to what was in the package.

PALMILLA RESORT

Ryker knocked one time. The door swung open and his eyes lit up at the sight of Tara wearing a floor-length black silk column dress with a plunging neckline and a slit running up the entire length of her right thigh.

"This is dress number one." She stepped aside and let Ryker walk inside.

"That dress has extreme potential." He looked at her appraisingly and tried to sound professional.

"Well, there are twenty-nine more to go, so grab that pen and paper and write down your top six favorites." She handed him a thin pad of paper and twirled around.

"Hey, you didn't tell me this was going to involve paperwork!" he exclaimed in mock horror.

"I think you can handle it," she teased.

He sat on the sofa and watched as she used the center of the room as a makeshift runway. He was in awe as she modeled a dozen dresses in rapid succession, taking only seconds to change from one to the other. She looked stunning in each one. He seriously could not believe this was happening to him.

There was a knock at the door. Tara was in the back room changing, so he opened it and greeted the two waiters. They pushed in a cart and uncovered one of the most impressive room-service meals he had ever seen. Jumbo prawns, broiled lobster tail, and cracked crab were elaborately displayed on silver platters.

"Is that dinner?" Tara called from the bedroom.

"Well, it's a feast, if that's what you mean by dinner."

"Great, I'm starved!"

The waiters set up fine china and crystal on the dining table and opened a bottle of Dom Perignon and left the chilled bottle in a sterling silver ice bucket. Ryker was relieved when they didn't ask him to sign anything, so he handed one of them a ten dollar tip. He figured that a tip on a spread like this had to be fifty bucks, but he was short on cash. The waiter accepted it graciously. *They must think I'm the cheapest bastard ever.* He was relieved when they left the room before Tara came back.

When she reemerged, she was wearing a pair of white capri pants with a blue halter top. Ryker forgot the tip and stared at her. She was drop-dead gorgeous.

"A toast, then." She took the bottle of champagne out of the bucket and reached for a glass.

"Sorry, I'm working. I'll have to pass."

"Well, I'm not going to drink without you. Bubbly makes me tired the next day, anyway, and I'd rather spend the calories on prawns and lobster. Can you tell me anything about your case?" She gracefully sat beside him and began filling a salad plate with appetizers.

"Only that it's the same case I've been working on."

"You can't tell me anything?" Her tone was wistful as she handed him the plate.

"Not really, sorry, it's just how the job goes," he replied apologetically.

"I get it. Top secret and all that. Hey, I watch TV." She grinned at him and winked.

"Yeah, well, so do I and we can stay plenty busy talking about your glamorous Victoria's Secret gig. That is way more interesting."

"I have to admit, I never got room service like this when I was working as a flight attendant. Too bad they opened the bottle of Dom, we could have saved it for later, when you are off duty," she replied quietly, her voice full of innuendo.

The next hour passed like minutes as they shared the decadent spread and Tara regaled him with funny stories about the unruly or flat-out crazy passengers on some of her flights. Ryker couldn't help thinking that she was intelligent, fun, sexy, beautiful, witty and wonderfully single. He felt like a man who had won the lottery. He was acutely disappointed when he glanced at his watch and realized it was past 9:30 p.m.

"We better resume the fashion show, or I won't have time to give you my final vote."

She jumped from her chair and headed into the bedroom, "I'll be right back."

"Housekeeping!" A call came from the hallway after a brief knock at the door.

"Alex, would you mind getting it?"

Ryker opened the door at the same time his cell phone buzzed. A new waiter pushed an empty cart into the room.

"Alex, sorry to interrupt your party, but our friend just called and there's a slight change of plans. Get back here at 11." Connor was careful not to use Carlos' name over the phone.

"I'll see you then," Ryker replied as he watched the waiter.

Viper made little noise as he cleared the table, trying to listen to the man's phone conversation. He decided not to make a move for the .25 caliber pistol that was neatly tucked into the front of his uniform pants.

What the hell? Viper calculated, as he recognized the face. He quickly tried to piece together the possible connection between the three. *First, the other one at the Governor's mansion, and now here in Cabo. This man...a friend of the other? A coworker? What is their connection to this woman?*

Viper avoided eye contact as he went about the task of cleaning up with professional efficiency.

"I'll be out in a few minutes."

Viper turned slightly at the sound of Tara's voice. *There are too many loose ends here, the timing is not right.* He pushed the cart out the door and let it close behind him. The plush carpets in the hallway muted the sound of the shifting china and crystal as he pushed the cart into a small storage room at the end of the hallway and walked down the stairs.

"Who was that?" Tara asked in a sultry voice, pushing her hair up in a sexy tangled pile on top of her head.

"Just housekeeping, cleaning up after dinner...now *that* I like!"

"It's the last one," Tara grinned as she walked into the room wearing a short, figure-hugging red dress with platinum high heel sandals that made her ankles seem as delicate as the stems on champagne flutes.

"That one definitely makes the top of the list," Ryker whistled appreciatively as she twirled around in front of him.

"Add it to your list and I'll be right back." She hurried back into the bedroom.

"You know, choosing just six is more difficult than I realized it was going to be," he called behind her as she disappeared through the door. He reviewed his list of favorites and grinned. The common theme was tight, low cut, and sexy.

"Alex, what time is it?" she called from the other room.

"Ten."

"You've got to go at eleven?"

"Yeah."

"Well, I'm only going to show you one more. I wish you didn't have to go so soon."

Ryker was thinking the same thing as she came into the room.

"If you had to pick one as your favorite, which would it be?" she asked in a soft, serious tone.

Ryker could not believe his eyes as she slowly walked toward him, sleek and tawny. He stared at her intently and hoped his eyes were not deceiving him. She was wearing a short, turquoise blue sheer camisole...not an evening dress like the others, this one was lingerie.

"Any ideas on which one is your favorite?" Her voice was soft, and there was no mistaking the sexy undertone as she brushed the straps from her shoulders and it floated to the plush carpet. Her smooth bare skin shimmered in the low light. Her lace thong was a thin line of barely-there blue and her legs looked long and lean in stiletto sandals.

"I really love those shoes. Prada?" Ryker grinned mischievously. She stood in front of him, waiting for him to make the first move. He loved the tentative look in her eyes.

"Yeah. Maybe I can get you a pair."

"I wear a size thirteen," he warned, not yet moving toward her.

"I'll just ask for an extra large," she emphasized, looking pointedly at his crotch.

"You do that," he whispered as he took her in his arms.

Tara could not believe how quickly she had reached a state of sexual euphoria. She was embarrassed that she had clung to him with such desperation, urging him on, coaxing him inside her, holding him inside for the long, slow moments leading up to the blinding finish. She lay against his chest now, trying to slow her breathing, trying to figure out what the hell she had just gotten into. All she knew is that she felt safe and did not Ryker to leave.

They both closed their eyes for a while, almost dozing. Ryker came to and quickly checked his watch. It was 10:55 p.m.

"Tara, I hate like hell to go, but I'm late." His face was pained as he rolled out of the bed and hurriedly began pulling on his pants.

She gave him a lazy smile as she leaned on her elbow and watched him dress. *Dear God, he has a hard body!*

"I don't know if I will be able to see you again while we're down here, but you can be sure that I will try like hell..."

Before he could finish his sentence, she jumped to her knees on the bed and put her arms around his neck.

"Hey, I'm clear on the concept," she grinned.

"Shit, I hate to go! I'll try to call you sometime tomorrow." He kissed her tenderly.

"Make it in the late afternoon. I've got that beach shoot tomorrow. If I'm not here, you can leave a message with my roommate, Hoshi."

"Your roommate? Where is she now?" He looked around nervously.

"A few of the models had to fly back to Mexico City to re-shoot a location. They won't be back until tomorrow afternoon."

"I'll talk to you tomorrow. You really are incredible. What a night!" He gave her one long, last passionate kiss before he hurried out of the suite.

"Yeah, what a night." She felt like she was dreaming as she locked the dead-bolt behind him.

Viper caught a glimpse of an individual running from the building. Other than that, there was no movement. It was 10:58. Most of the rooms still had their lights on, and he could see the bluish reflection of television screens behind some of the partially drawn curtains.

He continued surveillance. He felt annoyed more than anything. This was the second time she had evaded him and there wasn't going to be a third.

This might take a little more preparation, he grudgingly admitted to himself as he started back to his room.

CHAPTER 22

USS SEAWOLF, SEA OF CORTEZ

"No word yet. I wonder when JTF-5 is going to contact us," Lieutenant Junior Grade Hector Gómez said as he returned to the small table and sat down across from Lieutenant Commander Joe Hatfield in his compact stateroom. The USS Seawolf, SSN-21, had been recently retrofitted and it was one of the most advanced nuclear-class attack submarines in the world.

"What are the guys up to?" Hatfield asked.

"Well, Simmons challenged Decker to a push-up contest and they were up to one hundred and twenty-five when I left."

"Your move," Hatfield smiled.

Gómez picked up his knight and placed it in front of Hatfield's queen.

"This might be a long night," Hatfield observed.

"Well, at least we picked the right game for it," Gómez replied as he inadvertently touched his leg, noting that the ten stitches caused by the shark bite had dissolved, with only a minor scar remaining.

PALMILLA RESORT, CABO SAN LUCAS

Connor had just finished loading his spare magazine when Ryker rushed into the room.

"Just in time. How was dinner?"

"Great. One of the best meals I've ever had!"

It was sure the best date I've ever had, he thought, but didn't say. Partners didn't need to know everything.

Connor had too much class to pry, but he couldn't help noticing Ryker's flushed face and wrinkled pants. Ryker avoided eye contact and hurried into his room.

"We're meeting Carlos at the Presidente Resort in twenty minutes. Winston's en route."

"No problem." Ryker tried to keep his tone nonchalant, but he was damn glad that Connor had not interrupted him any earlier. He was still reeling from the faint, sweet smell of her on his skin.

They met Winston in the side parking lot of the Presidente Resort. They agreed that they would not introduce Winston to Carlos. Instead, he would provide counter-surveillance during the meeting to be sure that Carlos had not been followed. Winston had significant counter-surveillance experience as a CIA operative and Connor was grateful that he could count on an extra set of eyes.

"My friend…over here," Carlos called as Connor and Ryker entered the moderately crowded lounge area in the resort's main bar.

"Amigo, it's been a long time since our last meeting," Connor greeted him warmly, genuinely pleased to see his most productive and loyal informant.

"Carlos, this is my new partner, Alex Ryker."

"Señor Ryker, it is a pleasure to meet you." The men shook hands.

Carlos looked around the room and said quietly, "I don't have much time. Here's a keycard to a safe room. I'll meet you there in five minutes."

"Nice to see you again, goodbye," Carlos spoke in a louder voice as he shook Connor's hand and pressed the keycard into it.

Ryker was intrigued by his first encounter with one of DEA's most valued CIs. "That was interesting."

"Don't be impressed just yet. Wait 'til after the debriefing." They moved quickly into the crowd.

"Where do you think he went?" one of Jorge's bodyguards asked the other as they walked into the bar and scanned the crowd.

"I do not see him. We lost him. He could be anywhere by now," the other bodyguard replied, irritated.

"We will search the bar by the pool. If he is not there, we must return to Jorge."

Connor made sure there was no one else around when he knocked at the door once and used his keycard to enter. Carlos locked the door behind them and directed them to the coffee table where he had carefully arranged photos of the harbor, warehouses, and office area with their respective locations written on the back.

Carlos spent the first ten minutes describing the exact location of the harbor and the details of the loading planned for later that night. Connor was somewhat concerned about Jorge's unplanned visit.

"Do you think they suspect anything?" Connor asked.

"I don't think so. I have been very careful," he replied.

Connor told him about the ambush on the East Coast but kept the details to a minimum. Carlos hung on every word.

"There's no doubt the cartel knows that there's a high level leak in their organization. You can bet they will try to flush it out. Carlos, at some point we are going to have to pull you and your family out and put you into witness protection. We've talked about that…"

"Not before the Gustos are behind bars," Carlos fiercely interrupted.

Ryker excused himself to the bathroom.

"What about that information about the other package that was on the sub?" Connor asked quietly while Ryker was out of the room.

"I have no other information, but Jorge brought another identical package for us to deliver."

"What!"

"Yes, Francisco was told to keep it with him at all times up until the sub leaves."

"Any idea what's inside?"

"No, only that it is extremely important."

"What's important?" Ryker asked as he came back into the room.

"Looks like the cartel might be transferring some money. Carlos, we should probably meet tonight after the off-load. Any suggestions?" Connor wanted to deflect any more conversation about the package.

"I rent a small apartment in a village three kilometers from the harbor. Here's my key. No one is living there now, and I only use it once or twice a week. It is safe there; no one else knows I use it. Let's meet there at 2:00 a.m., after the sub has been loaded."

"Good," Connor replied, impressed with Carlos' resourcefulness.

Carlos scribbled directions to the apartment on a scrap of paper.

"I must get back to the dock. I will see you in a few hours." Carlos stood to leave.

"Be careful, Carlos." The two men shook hands and looked at each other for a long moment. They both knew what was at stake.

Ryker watched from the sidelines. It felt sort of like watching a movie. He couldn't wait to see what happened next.

MILL VALLEY, CA

"Hi dear, it's good to see you. Bill's in the study working. Come on in," Carol Cartwright welcomed her son-in-law with a hug. She was grateful that he continued to visit them despite the fact that their beloved daughter had been dead for four years.

"I was on my way to the mall and I wanted to know if you needed anything?" Steiner replied with a synthetic smile, his calculated deceit cleverly masked by a facade of shared loss.

"You're so sweet to offer." She speculated that her son-in-law often made excuses and drove across the Golden Gate Bridge just to visit them. "Thank you. But I haven't felt like shopping in a long time. There is nothing I really want," she replied as she fought back unshed tears. Seeing him made her acutely aware that she would never go shopping with her daughter again.

"Carol, who's at the door?" Cartwright called from the study.

"He's got radar ears and the curiosity of nine cats," she said as she brushed a tear away and tried to smile. "It's…" Her reply was interrupted by the sound of a smoke alarm coming from the kitchen.

"Oh no! I'm cooking chicken. I'll be right back." She hurried toward the sound of the loud buzzing.

"What the hell is going on, Carol? Hey, guy! How are you doing?" Cartwright's concern switched to pleased surprise as he came into the living room and saw their visitor.

"Jason was on his way to the mall and stopped by to see if we needed anything," Carol called out as she passed her husband in the doorway.

"You know, I need some lead pencil refills for a Mont Blanc. Would you mind?"

"No, not at all."

"Come on back to the study. I'll give you the box they came in. I'm the only old-school guy who still uses pencil lead."

Steiner wasn't surprised when he saw the case file and papers on Cartwright's desk.

Cartwright was consistently methodical and organized, paying attention to the smallest details. He walked over to his desk, opened the top drawer and retrieved a small, now empty tube that had held .5 mm lead pencil refills. He handed it to his son-in-law.

"I would greatly appreciate it if you'd get a few. We don't have them at the office.

"No problem. I need some supplies. Working on the North Carolina case?"

"Yeah," Cartwright nodded.

Steiner tried to unobtrusively scan the desktop for anything that seemed important, but nothing stood out among the memos, notes, and photos.

"Anything yet?"

"Nothing. Not one damn thing. I know the agents on the East Coast are trying their best to develop leads. This is going to be a tough one to crack. We need a break but I think we will get one, sooner or later."

Steiner focused on the walls, covered with plaques and awards for outstanding service. He felt a chill at the grim determination in Cartwright's voice.

"Yeah, something will turn up sooner or later."

"I hope it's sooner. I want to get my hands on those bastards!"

"Well, if I can be any help, let me know," Steiner replied, hoping he sounded convincing.

"Believe me, we've got plenty of people working on this one."

"I'll get going. I'll drop off your refills later."

Steiner felt extremely uncomfortable. All he wanted to do was get out of there.

"Don't you want to stay for dinner? I think we're having burned chicken." Cartwright smiled and patted him on the back as he walked him to the front door.

"No thanks, I've got a lot of errands to run."

He walked to his car with a mental image of the awards hanging on the wall in Cartwright's study. His palms were sweaty when he put the key in the ignition.

CABO SAN LUCAS

After the meeting with Carlos, Connor sent Ryker on an errand to the newsstand to give him time to meet with Winston. Connor and Winston walked down the sidewalk on the far end of the Presidente Resort while Connor summarized the earlier meeting with Carlos and told him about the additional package.

"Hey, what's up with this DEA routine? Are you still one of us?" Winston asked curiously. This was the first time that the two men had been alone. He had known better than to break Connor's cover in front of the younger agent.

"Yeah, but that's classified. Thanks for not giving it up. That would have given me a whole a lot of explaining to do." Connor wondered what the odds were of running into his bunk mate at The Farm, the unofficial name of Camp Peary, the CIA's training academy in Williamsburg, Virginia.

Winston knew his tradecraft. As a working case officer in the field overseas, rule number one was to never give up another case officer's true identity to anyone not authorized to know unless, you knew unequivocally that they too were Agency personnel.

"Does Franklin know that I work for the Agency?"

"Certainly not, not unless you told him. Come on, I know the rules. He's an outsider."

"Yeah, I know you do," Connor cracked a smile.

Winston also knew not to ask Connor about his assignment or why the hell he was posing as a DEA agent. If Langley wanted him to know, they would have told him.

"What do you think about a low crawl tonight? It's not every day that one of the Gusto boys leaves the nest. I would love to get some current photos of Jorge. I've got a new low-light camera back at the office that is perfect for long-range night close-ups. Afterwards we can go over to the apartment and hook up with Carlos," Winston added.

"Sounds good to me. I'll go get Ryker and we'll follow you to your office. Afterwards we'll debrief Carlos."

"Alright, you guys go first, and I'll follow you. Here, take this. It's the latest field radio," Winston said, handing Connor the newest compact Motorola radio with a micro earpiece.

"Damn, this is small. Looks like a smart phone. No antenna either," Connor exclaimed, impressed by the sleek, high-tech equipment.

"We have all the new gadgets. This one is classified, and it's a lot better than a Nextel, so keep it to yourself."

"Is there anything you have that's not classified, Gerald?"

"My underwear."

Connor burst out laughing.

FISHING HARBOR, CABO SAN LUCAS

"Anything?" Jorge asked the senior bodyguard who walked into Francisco's office.

"No, señor. We followed him back to Cabo but lost him on the strip. We did not see anything unusual. He probably went to dinner."

"How did you lose him?"

"A truck broke down in front of us on the strip and we were trapped in the traffic. He was in front of the truck."

"Has he returned?" Jorge asked.

"No, but he should be here soon. We will begin loading within the next hour," the bodyguard replied nervously.

"You two provide extra security for the loading. I will be fine up here."

"Yes, señor!" the bodyguards replied in unison and left the office. Francisco passed the two men as he walked into the room and confronted Jorge.

"Anything?"

"No."

"I told you that he was clean! Carlos is loyal. My trust in him is not misplaced." Francisco's tone was a mixture of relief and triumph.

Jorge said nothing. He hoped Francisco was right.

USS SEAWOLF, SEA OF CORTEZ

The executive officer knocked sharply on the door to the operation officer's quarters.

"Come in."

LCDR Joe Hatfield and LTJG Hector Gómez stared intently at the chessboard in front of them without looking up.

"Joe, we just got an op order from SOCOM. The skipper has ordered the boat to the drop zone. We should be there in thirty minutes. It'll be your show then. You're good to go?"

"Affirm," Hatfield replied, not looking up from his chess board.

"It's time you earned your pay, Hector. Ready?"

Hector moved his rook directly in front of Hatfield's king again.

372

"Checkmate!" Gómez smiled triumphantly.

"What!"

"Let's go. Game over, you lose, sir," Gómez's grin was diabolic.

"You lucky son of a bitch!"

Hatfield was pleased that Gómez had won the game. It was Gómez's first mission and he wanted him to start it off feeling confident. But, he was pissed off that he hadn't seen that move coming.

FISHING HARBOR

"This is an ideal spot," Connor whispered to Winston as the three of them sprawled on high ground, eyeing the harbor area through high-power binoculars. They were positioned on a rocky ridge that provided an excellent view of the harbor, warehouse and the personnel working around the area. Connor looked back to ensure Ryker, who was about 20 feet behind them, was providing adequate rear security.

"There's Carlos, waiting on the pier near the warehouse." Connor pointed.

"Jorge's coming out of the warehouse with Francisco." Winston zoomed in.

Connor refocused on the individual coming out of the building, barely able to hear the quiet whirring sound of the camera freeze-framing the figures in the distance.

USS SEAWOLF

"See you in a few," Hatfield called as he secured the hatch of the submarine after the last SEAL was in the chamber.

The ocean waters were deep enough that the captain of the USS Seawolf had been able to position the sub less than a mile from the target.

The team cleared the sub's external hatch and made their way up to the DDS, the dry deck shelter that housed two new high-speed, open-cockpit, two-man SDVs, the prized swimmer delivery vehicles. Within fifteen minutes, Gómez and the other three SEALS were zipping through the water toward their target.

FISHING HARBOR

What the hell? Ryker was alarmed as he counted ten to twelve figures crouching on the ridge to their left, carefully descending down toward the wharf area. All of them were heavily armed. He tossed a small pebble and hit Connor on the shoulder, then pointed to the ridge. Connor refocused his binoculars.

"What the fuck!" Connor whispered as he watched the unidentified force divide into two groups and slowly creep up on Francisco's men and the warehouse.

"This is not good," Winston said in a low tone.

"Are they federales or locals?" Connor asked.

"I doubt that crew is law enforcement, they're too well armed."

Ryker got Connor's attention and pointed directly behind them at the top of the ridge. Two armed men were kneeling at the top of the ridgeline just above them.

The SDVs sliced through the dark water like sleek sharks, delivering the SEALs to the target exactly on schedule. This was considered an in-and-out mission, one with no direct action with the target. SOCOM had allowed the SEALs who'd installed the tracker in Monterey, Hatfield, Gómez, Chief Decker and PO-1 Simmons, to follow up with the mission, with the addition of PO-1 Sid Santiago, a demolitions expert from SEAL Team-5. The plan was for Decker and Simmons to provide cover while Gómez and Santiago swam to the sub and installed the underwater mine. Gómez signaled Santiago as he was first to gain a visual of the sub's hull.

Ryker gave the alert again as he, Connor and Winston froze in position as they watched the two figures about 40 yards above them on the ridge line. Connor tucked the H&K MP-5 9mm submachine gun close to his body. He automatically calculated the distance and angle of attack.

Ryker didn't move as he laid on his side behind the cover of two sizeable boulders. He pointed his weapon in their direction as he watched the two men on the ridge. The men had not spotted them and seemed intent on watching the action down below. Given their circumstances, Connor felt confident that he and Ryker could dispatch the threat.

Connor directed his attention back toward the sub base, relying on Ryker to secure the rear. Winston focused the camera and zoomed in on the scene below. The dark figures were getting closer to the warehouse.

Multiple intruders snaked toward two of the guards standing on a path about twenty-five meters north of Francisco's office. Within seconds, three of the attackers leaped. There were no gunshots, only the silent motions of a brutal knife attack. When they moved away from the bodies, they were joined by two more men as they cautiously approached the office. Three moved toward the front door, while the other two scurried around the back, out of view.

Winston maintained his aim with his MP-5 submachine gun in the direction of another six armed figures that surreptitiously surrounded the warehouse near where the sub was docked.

Francisco jumped when the phone on his desk rang loudly, breaking his concentration.

"Yes?" He hung up the phone and announced, "They will finish loading the sub in twenty minutes," Francisco informed Jorge and his two bodyguards.

The unmistakable thunder of a Remington 870 shotgun echoed loudly as Carlos fired at one attacker, then another, dropping both of them at the back of the office.

Where is the shooter? Connor wondered, not expecting weapons fire from the invading group because they had not yet reached the warehouse. He speculated that the invading force had been detected.

"It's Carlos!" Connor whispered to Winston, as he recognized the familiar profile rack another round and boldly advance toward the attackers' position near the side of the office.

The first two blasts from Carlos' folding stock riot shotgun were direct hits; two bodies down. He had seen the guards approach and knew he had to make it to the front of the building to Francisco.

Within a split second of Carlos' shots, three attackers reached the front door and kicked it in. Francisco was behind his desk and reached for his .45 automatic when he heard the gunshots. The front door crashed open and two attackers, each holding a pair of Uzi's, opened up with a wild hail of 9mm rounds at Francisco.

"Ricardo's spirit sends you to hell!" one screamed.

The volley of 9mm rounds entered Francisco's chest, propelling his body into the wall. His eyes were frozen in a mask of terror and surprise and his mouth formed the word *no* as he slumped onto the floor, leaving a bloody trail on the wall.

Carlos turned the corner and fired his shotgun at the attacker positioned at the front door. He felt the recoil slam into his shoulder as the deafening blast created a surreal sensation of slow motion. For a horrifying moment he imagined he saw a flash from the attacker's pistol and a round speeding straight at his head.

The bodyguard closest to Jorge shielded him, then forced him to the ground. The bodyguard at the opposite end of the office fired a volley from his 9mm Beretta at the attacker closest to him to draw his fire. Both attackers swung their machine guns toward the new target and let out another burst of rounds, hitting the bodyguard and knocking him off his feet. He would never have the satisfaction of knowing that his volley was a direct hit on one of the attackers.

Carlos flattened himself against the exterior wall for a moment when he heard the gunfire inside, then rushed through the front door and saw one man standing, the profile of an Uzi silhouetted in his hands, taking aim at two bodies on the floor.

Jorge's bodyguard had raised his arm to fire his weapon at the exact moment Carlos fired his last round. The point-blank force knocked the assailant into the desk, sending the lamp, phone, and everything else crashing over the side. The light bulb shattered into tiny pieces, sending sparkling white flecks into the growing pool of dark blood that was forming around the shooter's head.

"Francisco, Francisco?" Carlos called frantically as he stood in the doorway. The pungent odor of gunpowder burned his nose and his eyes watered. He could only make out the dark shadows of bodies sprawled across the floor.

"Carlos, don't shoot!" Jorge called desperately.

Carlos lowered his shotgun and took a few halting steps toward them.

"Jorge, are you shot?"

"No," he cried as he struggled to his feet. Francisco and one of Jorge's bodyguards lay lifeless on the floor in a huge crescent of their own blood.

"Jorge! We must go! There are others," Carlos ordered as he reloaded the shotgun.

The bodyguard picked up one of the Uzis and snapped in a new magazine he grabbed off the belt of the dead man in front of him.

The SEALs were only a few feet away from the sub. Gómez adjusted his facemask and cleared the water as he had been trained to do. Santiago set the timer on the mine and pressed hard as he attached it to the sub. He tugged against it, testing the strength of the attachment.

The side door of the warehouse flew open and the second assault team stormed through it, spraying 9mm and 7.62 rounds from their submachine guns and AK-47 assault rifles at every moving target. Two of Francisco's loadmasters went down first. They toppled onto the load of cocaine piled in neat stacks on the dock.

Two of Francisco's guards who had taken cover fired back, sending the intruders diving behind a dry-docked fishing boat. More attackers burst through the front entrance, outflanking the guards. A deadly volley scored a direct hit and one of the guards went down with a bullet to the head. He knocked the other guard off balance, opening an opportunity for the shooters to get behind the boat. They fired their weapons and lobbed an American-made M-67 hand grenade.

It landed in a metallic thud on the floor, spinning in tight circles like a pinwheel. The guard paused for a split second as he recognized the object skittering toward him. He fired wildly at the last place he saw muzzle blasts, then turned, ran, and dived behind a forklift. The grenade came to a lazy stop, just touching the neat stacks of cocaine piled up in kilo-sized bricks on the dock in front of the sub. The explosion launched the bricks into the air like missiles, sending a powdery snowfall over the water. Hard fragments fell on the sub and into the water, kicking up splashes across the surface like hail from a summer storm.

The SEALs felt a slight turbulence and saw the sub tilt to one side. They stopped moving, floating motionless as they watched the water around them. Plastic-wrapped blocks sank past them, then bobbed back toward the surface. Santiago and Gómez signaled each other that it was time to get the hell out of there. Santiago double checked to be sure that the mine was operational, then raced towards Gómez's fins as they swam back toward the SDVs.

The eardrum-rupturing sound of the explosion left everyone inside dazed for a few seconds, then the gunfire suddenly ceased. The guard behind the forklift felt something moist on his knees and looked down fearfully for signs of his own blood. He sighed in relief when he saw that the fluid was clear, but then he smelled the pungent diesel fumes. His relief turned to panic when he jerked around and saw the steady spray streaming from the bullet holes in the fuel drums. At that moment, gunfire erupted again.

The main hatch of the sub flew open and a guard inside opened fire with a Beretta submachine gun directly at the attackers crouching behind the dry-docked boat. The guard behind the forklift used the diversion to fire at the second group of attackers near the front entrance as they trained their weapons on the gunfire coming from the sub.

A loud shotgun blast muted the machine-gun fire as two of Francisco's men emerged from the far side of the warehouse, firing wildly at the attackers. Rounds from the shotgun blast caught one of the attackers in the shoulder, spinning him off his feet, while the other two dove for cover and returned fire. An all-out gun battle ensued, and ricochets became as deadly as bullets in the crossfire.

Carlos, Jorge, and one of the bodyguards rushed from the office toward the dock, scanning the area for more attackers. They dropped to the ground at the sound of automatic gunfire and crawled toward the warehouse, flinching every time a stray round pierced the warehouse's thin exterior walls.

"Grenade!"

The guard behind the forklift was the first to see the metallic ball hurtling through the air toward the sub.

"Grenade!" He yelled again as it hit the ground and bounced toward the guard who had rushed to defend the firing position at the sub.

The guard lunged to catch it on the second bounce. As he closed his fingers around it, two 9mm rounds pierced his skull, knocking him off the dock and into the water. His lifeless fingers relaxed in death and let go of the shotgun and the grenade.

Gómez checked the rear as they retreated. He saw the silhouette of a shotgun, butt-down, spiraling down through the water. He paused momentarily and spotted the body above in a slow descent. It was a clear night and rays from the noon light filtered through the clear water.

Simultaneously he saw the smaller object spiral through the water leaving a trail of bubbles. A brilliant flash of blinding light was the last thing he saw. Seconds later, the mine on the sub prematurely detonated, sending seawater raining into the warehouse.

Connor watched as the explosion ignited the fuel storage tanks in the warehouse, ripping out the backside of the building, while flames shot out through all the windows. Within seconds, the entire building was engulfed.

"It's definitely time to get out of here," Winston snapped.

Connor made eye contact with Ryker with only one thought in mind. Ryker responded by giving a hand signal indicating that the threat from above was gone.

Connor turned back to Winston. "I've got to go down there."

"What!" Winston frowned in disbelief.

"Yeah." Connor signaled Ryker to join them. "Gerald, I have to find out what was in the package from Jorge. It's part of my assignment and the reason I'm undercover. It's one of the DCI's top priorities."

"Ok." Winston knew not to question a DCI priority. "You two can cover me. I just need a quick look in that office."

"What's up?" Ryker was breathing hard from his rapid descent.

"Alex, listen there's not much time. I need to go down there and check out the office."

"You're kidding right; it's a fucking hornet's nest down there...they're still shooting!"

"But not at me. You two can provide cover closer by those rocks. It's a good firing position and you'll have better eyes on. We got comm, alert me if there is any danger. It's worth the risk." Connor's commands were not subject to debate. "Here take this," Connor passed the machine gun to Ryker, "Give me all your magazines."

Ryker handed Connor three magazines including one from inside his Glock 9mm pistol.

"I have plenty of firepower. Let's go!" Connor jammed the magazines in his back pockets as they descended toward the rocks.

The SDV shielded Decker from the blast and the shockwave from the underwater explosion. Unfortunately, the rest of the team wasn't as lucky. Decker, momentarily stunned, scanned the clear waters for Simmons and saw him pinned him against a large rock formation on the bottom.

Decker headed towards him, but Simmons waved him off and pointed to the area where Gómez and Santiago had been. Decker redirected his engines and darted off. Within seconds, he saw Gómez's body floating, his tanks dangling from a hose that was bubbling air into the water.

Nearby, Santiago moved weakly. Santiago saw Decker and motioned for help. Decker recognized that the problem was with the oxygen supply and reached for a back-up breathing unit on the SDV as he approached. When he handed it over, Santiago grasped the device and hungrily inhaled the fresh oxygen. Decker left him momentarily to secure Gómez's body to the SDV.

Santiago took controlled breaths of oxygen and struggled to get his bearings. He swam toward Simmons. Simmons had almost freed himself from between the rock and SDV. Decker nudged the SDV forward and Simmons managed to break away. The three men stared at Gómez for a long moment, then fired up the SDVs and headed out.

Carlos covered his head as the explosion showered pieces of metal and wood from the building onto the ground. He clenched his jaw from the pain in his ears and winced at the loud ringing inside his head. He checked on Jorge and the bodyguard. They looked stunned, but alive.

"Carlos!"

Carlos struggled to his knees and surveyed the flaming building.

"Everyone inside is dead. We must get Jorge out of here! Now!" the bodyguard commanded.

"Señor Jorge, are you okay?" Carlos asked, noting that the other man was covered with dirt and bits of broken glass.

"I think so," Jorge groaned as he slowly pulled himself to his feet.

"Carlos, Carlos!" One of Francisco's men yelled as he ran from behind the building, his face black with smoke and his clothes singed and torn. "They were Ricardo's men! I recognized one of them when they attacked us inside," he called frantically.

"Round up everyone. Search the area for the rest of them. I'm going to take care of Señor Jorge. Get the wounded to our doctor and clean up this place! I will return later." Carlos ordered.

Connor side-stepped around two dead bodies with gaping chest wounds at the rear office entrance. He pointed his gun towards the door as he cautiously opened it, then burst into the room, moving his pistol in a horizontal motion ready to engage any threats. His first sight was Francisco's body sprawled behind a desk. He looked to the other side of the room and saw three more bullet ridden bodies. The odor of gunpowder still permeated the air.

"I'm cleared in here. I'll be out in one minute," Connor transmitted.

"Copy," Winston whispered into his radio.

Connor holstered his weapon and started inspecting material on and around the desk. He grabbed a pen from the floor and used it to sift through the various items, to avoid contact with the splattered blood.

He froze for a split-second, at the same time Winston's voice gave him the warning in his earpiece. The barrel of a shotgun breached the frame of the rear door. Connor, with his back to the door, only had one option. He turned and grabbed the barrel, launching the individual into the room. Connor drew his weapon with lightning speed.

"Jack it's me…Carlos!" He blurted as he raised his hands. Connor recognized him as his Glock zeroed in on Carlos' face.

"You've got to get out of here now! Jorge is coming back to the office and…"

"Carlos where is the package the cartel gave you?" Connor cut him off.

"That's what I'm trying to tell you, they're coming to get it."

"Where is it?" Connor said impatiently almost yelling.

"It was over there on the desk before the shooting started."

Connor followed the debris trail and focused on the corner where the desk chair was upside down.

"Is this it?" Connor held a plastic container the size of a cigar box that was riddled with bullet fragments. Before Carlos could respond, Connor saw the electronic circuit board the size of a credit card nestled inside the box lined with Styrofoam.

"Jack! You've got two hostiles coming your way, be there in about two minutes. Get out now!" Winston's transmission was broken.

"10-4."

"Jack, you have to give that to me that or they will think something is suspicious. They know it's here." Carlos warned.

Connor grabbed his iPhone from his back pocket, placed the device on the desk, and took several photos of it. He picked it up and struggled to snap it into two pieces. He put one of the halves onto the floor and crushed it under his heel, then carefully placed both pieces back into the container.

"Jack, what are you doing?" Carlos frantically asked.

"Tell them it was damaged in the attack. They cannot have it."

"Jack you've got less than one minute, get out of there now," Winston transmitted.

"Leaving."

Connor tossed the container and device to Carlos. "Did Francisco keep any records in his office?"

"There's a safe built into the desk on the right side, he keeps some records there."

"Try to delay them!" Connor hustled behind the desk and opened the drawer where he spotted the small safe. He reached down and touched the dial and turned it slowly. To his surprise, he turned the lever and the safe opened. Whoever had opened it last hadn't securely locked it. He looked inside, took out a 9mm pistol, a Rolex watch, and one ledger, then closed it and made sure it locked.

"I'm clear." Connor keyed his radio, tucking the ledger in his waistband as he hurried toward the ridge.

Carlos met Jorge and his bodyguard about 30 feet from the door. He saw blood dripping from the bodyguard's right leg as they stopped.

"Did you get the package?" Jorge asked as he recognized the distinctive shaped box.

"Yes, but it was damaged in the shootout. Let's get out of here."

Connor was the first to reach the top of the ridge. Winston told Connor that three assailants had run up to the ridge only five minutes earlier. Connor's senses were heightened as he approached. He cautiously watched the dirt road. Satisfied that there were no surprises, he waved for Ryker and Winston to join him. He scanned the road for an additional thirty seconds with the scope to detect concealed threats. Seeing none, he signaled, and they hurried quietly across the road to where their Trooper was hidden behind brush and trees.

Winston opened the front door, reached under the front seat and pulled out a pair of night vision goggles. The vehicle had been previously equipped with a cut-off switch, preventing the interior door-activated light from illuminating their position and making them a target.

"Jack, there's another pair of goggles behind Alex's seat," Winston said, slightly winded from the exertion.

Ryker reached in the back, opened a small gym bag, and tossed Connor the goggles.

Within seconds, they were backing down the road toward the highway. Connor had the passenger window open and an MP-5 in his hands, as he focused intently on the road and surrounding underbrush.

Ryker saw the glow of the fire and thick black smoke. He wished they had a few more agents with them as he brushed dirt and leaves off his shirt.

"The highway is just up ahead," Winston said with a hint of relief in his voice.

Connor didn't breathe any easier. The night was far from over.

As Carlos and Jorge reached Jorge's Mercedes, Carlos turned around at the sound of automatic weapons fire coming from the ridge.

"Carlos," the bodyguard called to him, "You drive." He threw the keys over the top of the car and Carlos caught them in midair.

"Where are we going?" Carlos asked as he slid into the driver's seat.

"The Palmilla Hotel in Cabo." Jorge's face was tight and drawn, a mask disguising the rage that boiled beneath the veneer.

USS SEAWOLF

"Captain, we've got trouble," the senior petty officer announced as he adjusted his headset.

Hatfield turned toward the captain. They had suspected something was wrong ever since the sonar crew had detected the premature explosion.

"What is it?" the captain asked.

"We received a distress signal from the SEALs. They're en route back."

"Skipper, I'll go below and suit up as an assist on the recovery." Hatfield didn't wait for a response.

Within five minutes, he had suited up and was out of the special hatch used for special ops missions. He hoisted himself through the narrow hatch into the cold water and saw the SDVs and the SEALs. A sick feeling overcame him as he recognized Gómez's body tied down to one of the SDVs.

Hatfield rapidly swam toward them, inspecting each man for any visible sign of injury. He saw slight damage on two of the SDVs, but the men appeared to have functional tanks. Santiago was protecting his right arm and his suit was ripped on the side. Because Simmons appeared somewhat dazed, Hatfield helped him re-enter the tight confines of the Dry Dock Shelter first. The SEALs loaded the SDVs inside, secured the hatch, and evacuated the seawater.

"Hang on bud," Decker encouraged as Santiago shut his eyes, clenched his teeth and fought the pain.

The rest of them carried Gómez's body into the sub.

"What happened?" Hatfield asked.

"I don't know. Simmons and I had the perimeter. Gómez and Santiago had attached the mine and were on the way back when it prematurely detonated. It had a lot more kick than we expected. Maybe Santiago has a better explanation," Decker replied in frustration.

Hatfield completed the distasteful task of placing Gómez's cold, blanched corpse into a body bag and securing it in the ammunition storage compartment.

"Are you guys okay?" Hatfield asked, his face full of concern.

Simmons and Santiago nodded affirmatively, starring at their dead teammate's body as the reality of the situation began to sink in.

"I've got to go to the comm room. I'll be back in ten minutes," Hatfield added. *Shit! We are not supposed to lose a man on a piss ant mission like this one,* Hatfield swore.

CHAPTER 23

CARIBBEAN AND BAHAMAS TRAVEL INC, CABO SAN LUCAS

"What's happened?" Louisa asked in alarm as Winston, Connor, and Ryker walked into the CIA undercover office looking dirty and disheveled.

"We stepped right into the middle of a cartel shoot-out," Winston replied as Connor placed the gym bag containing the weapons and gear on Winston's desk.

"Louisa, I need to use the STE phone. Would you mind stowing the gear?" Winston asked as he went into the back room and closed the door behind him.

"Sure."

"It's loaded," Connor warned as Louisa reached into the bag for the MP-5.

"I treat all weapons as if they are loaded. Don't worry, I know what I'm doing," she replied confidently as she expertly unloaded the weapon.

"Sorry." Connor smiled apologetically. He remembered that during his CIA agent training all field secretaries were trained in weapons and special ops equipment.

She is my kind of secretary. 2:00 a.m. and still working, Ryker thought in admiration.

Ryker heard footsteps outside, but before he could react, the office door crashed open and a hulking man in a dirty uniform stood in the doorframe, pointing a .45 automatic at Ryker's head. Two uniformed thugs stood behind him, their weapons drawn and aimed into the room.

Connor did a double take. It was El Capitán.

Louisa made the deadly mistake of pulling the MP-5 the rest of the way out of the bag. El Capitán fired one round that hit her squarely in the middle of her torso and killed her instantly. Her small frame crashed into the door behind her desk.

"Do not move!" El Capitán shouted in Spanish as he pointed his weapon at Connor's face.

Winston, where are you? Alarms were going off in Connor's head as he watched the ugly, snarling fat man standing in the doorway with his finger on the trigger of his .45.

Ryker's eyes darted between them, as he waited for his partner to make the first move. In the other room, Winston dropped the STE phone and drew his Glock. He walked softly to the two-way mirror that was concealed in a picture frame in the outer office. The hair on the back of his neck bristled when he recognized El Capitán.

"What were you doing at the harbor this evening?" El Capitán barked, then paused, "I have seen you before…Search this place!" El Capitán ordered one his men.

Connor started to slowly exhale, anticipating Winston's attack. A gunshot blast rang from the doorway, diverting everyone's attention for a split second. In that moment, Connor and Ryker simultaneously drew their Glocks and double-tapped their respective targets in the heads.

El Capitán and one of the uniforms crashed into the wall. Connor continued firing point blank into the huge man's chest until the lumbering body collapsed onto the floor.

"Carlos?" Connor called in stunned surprise as he turned his weapon on a figure in the doorway holding a shotgun in his hand.

"Yes," Carlos replied as he walked into the office, looking over his shoulder cautiously.

"Where did you come from?" Connor asked, but before he could respond, Winston pushed open the door that Louisa's body was leaning against.

"Louisa, Louisa?" Winston cried out loud as he dropped to his knees and gathered her into his arms. Grief etched deep lines into his face.

"Alex, you and Carlos check outside. Here, take this." Connor picked up the MP-5 and tossed it.

Ryker caught the weapon and vanished into the darkness. Connor changed his magazine as he looked at Winston rocking Louisa back and forth, whispering her name over and over. He knew it had to be rough to lose a trusted secretary, but he was taken aback at Winston's unchecked expression of grief.

"Gerald, man, I'm so sorry!"

"Jack, she was my wife. We were a husband-and-wife team." He began to cry and his tears dropped onto her pale face.

"My God, I'm so sorry!" Connor gripped the man's shoulder in stunned disbelief. "We've got to clear this area…now, Gerald."

Winston stopped crying and stood up. His wife's blood streaked his clothes.

"We'll need fifteen minutes. I'll call Langley and they'll send a reaction team. We need to go through the emergency procedures!"

"We don't have fifteen minutes! We have got to go now before the whole damn Mexican police force descends on this place."

"We can't let some of this stuff fall into the federales' hands. You know the drill." Winston spoke calmly and deliberately.

"Are you alright?"

Winston took a deep breath, "Yeah…I don't have a choice," he replied.

"All clear outside," Ryker interrupted, trying to control his anxiety, knowing that the local police could arrive at any minute.

"Alex, keep a lookout with Carlos. We've got fifteen minutes of clean up, then we're out of here."

"Fifteen minutes?" Ryker asked in surprise, thinking that they needed to get the hell out now.

"Yes. Did they come in one car?" Connor stared at him without offering an explanation.

"Yeah."

"Get the keys and relocate it down the block with Carlos, now!"

He turned to Winston. "Let's see if we can clear in seven minutes." Connor holstered his weapon and started evacuation procedures.

Connor was impressed as he watched Winston go through and methodically select only the most sensitive material from the office. They were done in six minutes flat. The final order of business was the most difficult. They gently relocated Louisa's body into the equipment room along with other dead bodies.

"Let's go." Winston swallowed hard as he visually inspected the room one last time. They headed outside. Connor was not surprised to see that Ryker and Carlos had returned.

"Carlos, do you have any idea who attacked you guys?" Connor asked.

"It was Francisco's cousin Ricardo's men. Francisco killed Ricardo last week. They were avenging his death. I'll explain later."

"What about Jorge?" Connor asked.

"Where are they now?" Winston interjected.

"They are back at the Palmilla Resort," Carlos replied nervously.

"What?" Connor replied in alarm.

"Yes, Jorge knows the general manager. That's where they are staying until sunrise and then they'll go back to Bogotá. I told them that I had to go and check on my men, but they want me back soon."

"What room are you in?" Connor asked.

"Room 580, a suite by myself. It faces the beach."

"All right, we'll go back to the hotel and will contact you shortly."

Connor and Winston walked together toward their cars on the other side of the building.

"Where's your safe house?" Connor asked as he saw Winston frown and saw the controlled emotion mixed with fatigue.

"It's the Palmilla Resort, but I'll be safe," Winston replied and shook his head as if he couldn't believe it himself.

"Are you serious?" Connor asked incredulously.

"Dead serious."

"Looks like we'll be one big happy family tonight."

Connor bit his lip, wishing he could take that one back.

PALMILLA RESORT

Tara checked the clock for at least the hundredth time. It was 3:30 a.m. and she couldn't sleep. *Where is he?* She tried to suppress the anxiety building in the pit of her stomach. She had left Ryker an urgent message asking him to call her no matter what time he got in. She had decided to tell him about London...the whole story. Ever since she had seen the man in the lobby, she had felt unsettled and afraid. She wanted to tell Alex everything. She anguished over what he would think of her for getting involved with Devinure and for agreeing to cover it up. She stared at the phone, willing it to ring.

Connor and Ryker were wide awake during the drive back to the resort. They had enough adrenaline in their bloodstreams to keep them up for at least another twenty-four hours. Connor noticed that

389

Ryker was quiet. They had talked about the shootings briefly, but Ryker seemed distracted again as they made their way back to the hotel room.

Ryker couldn't believe that he had been in two shootings within a few days. *It was different this time.* Having a gun pointed at his head was unnerving, but he had reacted instantly. *Maybe I was more confident this time,* he pondered, as Connor interrupted his thoughts.

"Alex, you did just fine back there."

"You were right about the training," Ryker admitted.

Connor knew that Ryker was starting to adjust to the realities of the dangerous elements of the job. There would be plenty of time to talk later, but for now Connor felt confident that Ryker was adapting.

"Well, I'm glad you guys finally decided to show up," Winston greeted them as Connor opened the door to their suite.

Connor dropped his hand away from his holster and stared at Winston who sat calmly on the couch. Connor was impressed that Winston was still functioning given the circumstances.

"My contact here gave me a master key to all the rooms at the resort."

"Gerald, sneaking into my room is a good way to get your ass shot!" Connor shook his head.

Ryker noticed the flashing light on the room phone. He listened to the message and sensed that something was wrong. Tara's voice sounded troubled and she had insisted that he call, regardless of the time.

"Jack, listen to this message," Ryker handed the phone to Connor.

"Looks like you've got your first domestic crisis. Just make sure it's not related to us. We're down for at least the next four to five hours and I doubt if either one of us will get any sleep anyway," Connor reassured Ryker. He wanted to spend some time alone with Winston and it was obvious that Tara was troubled about something.

"Thanks," Ryker replied as he dialed Tara's room. "Hey, what's up?" Ryker asked. "I'll be there in five minutes." He hung up. "Something's up, but she wouldn't say what. She sounded a little worked up."

Ryker went to the bathroom to clean up.

"Okay, about ten minutes. What room?" Connor put the down the receiver. "Carlos says he wants us to meet him now in his room. He can't leave. He said that Jorge and his bodyguard are in a suite in another building drinking beer and it's safe to meet," Connor advised as Ryker entered the living room.

"Let's get down there to find out what's up. Hey, what are you doing?" Connor continued as Ryker picked up the phone.

"Telling Tara I'll be delayed for a while."

"No. I'm serious, go see what this is about. Gerald and I can do this. It won't take long; we don't a need crowd meeting Carlos. You'll be in the next building. If I need you, I'll reach you on this." Connor tossed him a field radio.

"10-4," Ryker was out the door before Connor finished the sentence.

"I think your partner is in love." Winston smiled.

"I definitely think there's a spark there. Listen, Carlos told me he's holding another package." Connor's tone turned serious.

"What!"

"Yeah, we need to check it out and be real careful. That's why he can't leave his room."

The Sea of Cortez lapped soft waves against the beach as the moon played a game of hide-and-seek behind the clouds. Viper had strategically hidden in a row of thick foliage that was a natural barrier between the resort and the beach. He had painstakingly staked out Tara's room for the past few hours. He was confident that she was alone. Her only visitor had left hours ago.

Viper knew the risk factors in this operation were higher than his other hits. He had taken more time to plan and recon those. He had impressive skills and a huge ego that had been insulted to the point he was obsessed with killing her. No target had ever eluded his crosshairs. He looked at his watch and started a last-minute equipment check. He gave a quick tug to the nylon rope he had slung over his shoulder and tightened the slack. He drew the Beretta .25 caliber automatic pistol fitted with a silencer from his hip holster and ensured that the magazine was properly seated. He scanned the building one more time and was pleased that all the lights were off except for the emergency exit. He silently slipped into the darkness.

Ryker was halfway to Tara's room when he realized that he had left his Glock in his suite.

391

"Shit!" he swore softly as he stopped and turned around. He wasn't going anywhere without his weapon, especially tonight.

"I forgot to tell you about this!" Carlos pointed to a locked briefcase as Connor and Winston entered his suite.

"What?"

"Jorge told me to keep the package temporarily, not to let it out of my sight and not go anywhere with it till morning."

Connor stared at the briefcase and considered his options. Winston interrupted his thoughts.

"Someone is scaling the end of the building! Looks like he's trying to break into one of the end suites. Carlos, do you have binoculars?" Winston demanded, looking out of the balcony door.

Connor rushed to turn off the lights. Winston opened the sliding glass door and crouched on the balcony while Carlos darted to the bedroom to get the binoculars.

"What the hell is going on? That's Ryker's girlfriend's suite. Give him a heads up on the radio," Connor snapped.

"Shit, I left it in the room," Gerald replied in frustration.

"Gerald, give me the master key. I'm going over there to check it out. You go upstairs now, get the radio and warn Ryker! Carlos, you stay here…and don't let anything happen to the package!" Connor ordered as they both rushed out of the room.

Viper scaled the three-story building in less than ninety seconds. He silently hoisted himself up onto the balcony. As soon as he was firmly on his feet, he drew his weapon. The cool ocean breeze gently moved the sheer drapes through an opening in the sliding glass patio door. He lay face down on the balcony and slowly scanned the room. The light in the bathroom was on and the door was partially open, casting a pale shaft of light into the deserted bedroom. He slowly slid the door open, just wide enough for him to snake-crawl into the room. He stood up and concealed his tall frame behind a large wardrobe.

Tara roused from her nap on the sofa when she heard a quiet tap on the front door. She ran to open it.

"Alex, I'm so glad to see you," she whispered as she put her arms around his neck and pulled him into the room. The door slowly closed behind him as he held her in his arms.

"Hey, what's wrong?" She felt frail and small in his arms. He loved the way she pressed her body against him. Her breasts were firm under the soft cotton t-shirt.

"Alex, I need to tell you about something that happened in London. It has been driving me crazy." She pulled away slightly so that she could look up into his face. She was very worried about his reaction.

"What is it?" he asked soothingly.

"About ten days ago, I met this man on my last flight to London. I had a layover there, so I agreed to have dinner with him the following evening. He seemed nice enough," she paused as they sat down on the sofa. He nodded for her to continue.

"After dinner, we were walking back to his hotel when we were attacked by two guys who tried to rob us. They looked like freaky skinheads," her voice cracked as her eyes brimmed with tears. "They had knives and one of them cut him. It all happened so fast…they were fighting, and the next thing I knew, they were lying on the sidewalk and there was blood, lots of blood. He said he had a friend at the police department, but I never saw anything in the paper or on the internet."

She paused and swallowed a few times, trying to regain her composure. He squeezed her shoulder and let her continue.

"I was so scared, Alex. I didn't know what to do. He took control and insisted we leave the scene. He told me that he would call a detective friend who would handle it discreetly. He said they were alive, but they looked dead to me. He kept telling me we had to get out of there." She started to repeat herself, visibly shaking. "I…I don't know why I listened to him." She looked at Alex with pleading eyes.

"What happened after that?" Ryker asked, his forehead creased in a slight frown. He didn't know what to make of the story so far.

"He took me back to his hotel room and said he could take care of the cut on his arm. He told me to go downstairs and get some first aid supplies and take some money from his wallet to pay for everything. When I did, I found a different driver license. His picture was on it, but it had a different name. At first, I thought he was some kind of agent, like you are, but then the more I thought about how skilled he was at attacking those guys, the more scared I

393

got. I didn't know what to do…I just didn't know what to do, so I ran out of the hotel. The reason I am telling you all this now is because I think I saw him in the lobby yesterday. I'm sure it was him, and I don't know what to do. I should have gone to the police, Alex…I don't know what I was thinking…"

Ryker interrupted her breathless account as he saw her getting increasingly agitated and tearful.

"Tara, calm down. It's going to be okay. Let's turn on the lights and talk about it. First of all, what is this guy's name?"

"Which one? He had a few. Let me go to the bathroom before I launch into the whole story. I'm sorry I'm rambling. I'll be right back." She fought to control her emotions. His comforting presence was a relief and for the first time since London, she felt the weight of it all lifting off her shoulders. He would help her figure it out.

Viper heard their voices as he inched closer to the hallway. He was intrigued by the fact they were talking in the dark. There were two voices, one female, and one male. He clenched his jaw as he heard vibrations of light footsteps on the carpet as Tara walked down the hallway toward the bathroom. She froze when she saw the gun and recognized the figure in the dark shadows. She desperately wanted to scream, but she could not make a sound.

He motioned with his weapon, directing her toward the bed, but she stood like a statue, rooted to the floor. Her chest felt as though it was about to explode from holding her breath. Her eyes were wide open, her pupils alternately constricted and dilated in unrestrained, primal fear. He knew immediately that her body had locked up. In fact, he had expected it. Women always froze like wild animals caught in the glare of bright lights. He put his finger across his lips, signaling silence, as he gripped her arm and guided her toward the bed. His touch jolted her from her paralysis and she felt a scream rising in her throat along with the bile. She didn't even feel the cold metal circle settle against her temple.

Winston ran as fast as he could up the stairwell and sprinted down the hall to his suite.

"Hey Alex! Heads up! You might have an intruder!" Winston's voice crackled over the radio.

Viper, annoyed rather than startled at the crack of the radio sound, jerked the trigger of his silenced .25 caliber Beretta.

Click was all that was heard. Viper experienced his first misfire as the primer on the center-fire cartridge malfunctioned. He became momentarily enraged at the American manufacturer for costing him precious seconds…seconds that could turn him into a target.

Ryker, alerted by the radio traffic, turned toward the hallway. In that second, Tara's voice came to life. "Alex!" she screamed.

Ryker jumped, then drew his Glock and rushed down the hallway. The backlighting from the bathroom shed some light into the hallway through the open bedroom door.

Viper racked the slide back, cleared the defective round, and racked a fresh one into the chamber.

Tara leaped toward Viper, just as he started to sight in on Ryker. The force pushed him into the hallway, off-balance.

Ryker abruptly stopped, surprised by the emergence of the figure dressed in black, then he focused on the weapon in the figure's hand. Startled, he jerked off a round. The 9mm bullet grazed Viper in the left shoulder.

Viper fired back. Ryker saw the flash, instantaneously feeling a stinging pain to the side of his head. He spun around and side-stepped backwards as his Glock flew out of his hand.

Infuriated, Viper turned to Tara. She had retreated into the bedroom and was now gripping a heavy lead crystal vase in her hands like a baseball bat.

"Alex!" Connor called out in alarm from the doorway as he entered the room just in time to see his partner fall backwards onto the floor. Ryker's Glock hit the floor with a thud.

Viper heard the new threat. Enraged and wanting to eliminate Tara, he fired his weapon…CLICK…again! Tara threw the vase as hard as she could and partly hit him on the side of the head. Survival overcame fear as she ducked back into the bathroom. Viper pissed more than disabled, automatically racked another round into the chamber and fired two shots at her shadow. He instinctively spun around, seeking cover behind the bedroom wall.

Connor, his gun drawn, heard the muffled sound of the silenced weapon and crouched against the wall. He stared down at Ryker as he caught a glimpse of a moving shadow. For a split second, he felt his heart stop until Ryker gave him the thumbs up and reached for his Glock. Connor advanced warily into the hallway, leading with his gun.

Viper flattened himself against the wall. He had heard the second male voice after shots were fired. *Another threat,* his instincts told him. He waited, taking short and shallow breaths. Uncharacteristically, his palms began to sweat. He hated the clammy feeling of his skin against gunmetal. He gritted his teeth, his jaw locked. He inched toward the door.

Connor saw the telltale flicker of movement in the shadows across the floor. He didn't know where the girl was, but he had to assume the worst from the eerie silence. He waited a split second, then the shadow moved again. This time, he zipped the wall with a volley of 9mm rounds. The blasts broke the silence. The first two rounds penetrated the sidewall but ricocheted to the floor. The two rounds that followed pierced the wall, millimeters away from Viper. Viper dropped to the floor, not returning fire. Anger struck him when he realized that his magazine was missing. Unbeknownst to Viper, his magazine release button had been jarred, causing the magazine to fall on the carpet. He instinctively replaced it with a spare from the magazine pouch on his belt. He knew that his .25 caliber rounds could not penetrate the wall.

"Jack, how many?" Winston yelled, coming through the front door with his weapon drawn. He winced briefly at Ryker, on the floor and holding his head with one hand and his weapon in the other.

Viper swore in Russian, realizing that he was out-manned and out-gunned. He made a dash for the balcony.

Connor heard the movement and fired another volley into the wall, narrowly missing Viper as he scrambled onto the balcony and began rappelling down to the ground below.

"Gerald, the balcony," Connor directed as he gestured toward the living room.

Winston was on the balcony in an instant. He dropped into a crouched position and then quickly peeked over the railing.

Viper anticipated that tactical move and fired two rounds at Winston's silhouette positioned next to a huge flower pot. One round lodged in the railing and the other tore through Winston's jacket sleeve, singeing the hair on his arm.

Connor heard the muffled sound of silenced gunfire and ran into the bedroom. The sheer drapes were swaying back and forth in the breeze and the light from the bathroom cast a soft glow onto the slender female, obviously in pain, holding her shoulder.

"I got her. Get that fucker!" Ryker blurted, oblivious to his own wound.

Connor didn't respond as he ran back down the hallway and out of the room, heading directly for the exit stairs.

Winston stood up and fired four rounds in the direction of the shots as he saw the shadow on the ground taking aim at him again.

"Hey, what is happening here?" A security guard yelled, running in the direction of the squatted figure, not realizing the death zone he had just entered.

Viper fired two rounds point blank into the guard's chest, then whipped around and fired two more rounds, barely missing Winston. Viper, keenly aware that his time had lapsed, stood up and bolted for the corner of the building.

Winston fired the remaining rounds in his Glock, trying to lead his target as Viper approached the building.

Viper jolted backwards onto the ground…not from the shots fired from Winston's semi-automatic pistol, but from the force of a blind-side collision with Connor as the two crashed face-to-face at the corner of the building. In that fraction of a second, Connor's arms flexed close to his body like a linebacker bracing for impact, while the unsuspecting Viper was focused only on the bullets that chased him.

Viper recovered remarkably, attempting to grab his weapon as Connor raised his own weapon at Viper's head.

"Policia! Policia!" Two local police officers yelled in Spanish, drawing down on the two figures that now stood only a few yards in front of them.

"Policia…DEE AH…DEE AH!" Connor yelled back in Spanish, ever mindful of being shot by friendly fire. The officers keenly aware that *DEE AH* in Spanish translated as DEA, observed the familiar gold-and-blue DEA badge around Connor's neck targeted their weapons at Viper.

Viper, infuriated but not suicidal, froze in pain and stared at his captors.

"Arrest this man. He just shot a DEA agent and an American tourist!" Connor commanded in Spanish. He was obeyed. Connor issued a few other instructions and then ran back upstairs.

Startled, Winston pointed his Glock at the man standing tentatively in the doorway.

"Don't shoot! I'm a doctor. Can I help?"

"Come in." Winston lowered his weapon as the man walked toward the bedroom. "We're Americans, federal agents. We have two Americans with gunshots."

"I'm Dean Roseberg, a surgeon from San Francisco. Please get me some clean towels," the doctor replied as he looked past Ryker to Tara.

"It's okay, an American doctor is here now and you're going to be fine," Ryker said in a comforting voice to Tara, who was still lying on the bedroom floor.

"Winston!"

"Back here, Jack," Winston called.

Connor cringed as the doctor worked to control Tara's bleeding. He was relieved to hear the pounding of footsteps as several medical personnel entered the room with supplies.

"I'm an American doctor and these are my patients. We need to get her to a hospital now," Dr. Roseberg greeted the ambulance crew as they rushed into the room, jerking up the extending folding legs on the stretcher. He gave a series of quick medical orders that sent the medics into a frenzy of activity. Connor was impressed with the efficiency of the medical crew as Tara was moved onto the stretcher. In the same breath, the doctor turned to the agents, "She should be fine once we get her to a hospital. Your partner is fine. He just needs a sterile dressing, but he should take a trip to the hospital as well to check for any eye damage. He's very lucky. You guys okay with that?"

"Great, doctor," Winston replied, thankful that an American surgeon was on hand.

"Go with her, Alex." Connor motioned to Ryker. Connor had initially thought of contacting Admiral Jarcowski to request an emergency medevac but decided against it. He felt comfortable with the doctor.

Connor briefed Winston on the situation with the assailant.

398

"Gerald, we need to get back to Carlos and secure that package. I'm going downstairs to check on the police for a few minutes and find out who that guy was…something is not right here."

"Was that gunshots?" Carlos exclaimed after letting Winston into his room.

"Yeah. Everybody's okay. Listen, do you still have the package?"

"Yes, it's in the closet."

As soon as they reached the bedroom, there was a knock at the door. Both men froze and stared at each other as they heard the second soft knock.

"That should be Connor," Winston whispered.

Carlos walked up and looked through the peephole.

"Carlos, open the door!" Carlos jumped at the change in the pitch of the voice.

The knocking got louder as Winston immediately reached for his gun.

Through the peephole, Carlos recognized three of Jorge's bodyguards.

"Go! Hide! I'll see what they want, it's okay," Carlos whispered.

"Here, take this. Keep it on you at all times and don't spend this," Winston commanded as he flipped Carlos a quarter and darted back to the bedroom. Carlos waited for a few seconds, and then opened the door.

"Carlos, Jorge needs to see you, it's important. You need to come with us right now. Where is the package?" The biggest bodyguard indicated as he grabbed Carlos' arm as the men entered the room.

Winston strained to hear them as he walked into the living room after he heard the door close. He tried to formulate a course of action but there was no time. He heard multiple voices.

He silently darted back into the hallway, drawing his weapon, and then slipped into the closet, almost stumbling over the suitcase.

"I will check the bedroom and bathroom." He heard one intruder say.

"Search everything," a male voice replied, as the two men walked into the bedroom.

Winston drew his weapon as his heart pounded like a jackhammer. He waited inside the cramped closet, ready to fire…until he suddenly remembered that his Glock was out of ammunition. He started calculating the distance and angle of an attack as the voices grew nearer. He would cold-cock whoever opened the closet door and then hope for the best. He could hear drawers opening and closing.

"Check the closet and bathroom," a deep voice commanded.

Winston stared directly at the sliding closet doors inches in front of his face, anticipating that they would be jerked open at any second. He felt the footsteps as though they were touching his feet. The doors vibrated slightly as one side began to slide open.

"I found it!" Before Winston could react, there was a blur of a huge hand and the suitcase disappeared from the closet.

The door stopped moving. Winston froze, trying to anticipate what was going to happen next. He focused on the slight opening, his body tense, waiting to strike at the first sign of movement.

Once the big guard saw the package in the suitcase, he slammed his fist into Carlos' stomach. "Carlos, you fool! Señor Joaquin will chop off your head and send it to your mother! Let's go, the plane is leaving. You traitor!" he sneered.

Winston cautiously peered down the hallway and saw the backs of the men departing with Carlos. He waited a few seconds and then returned to the living room. The eerie silence was interrupted as the phone rang. Winston grabbed it on the first ring.

"Something's up, there are no signs of the police," Connor said.

"Three guys just grabbed Carlos! They know he is working for us and they took the package. Meet me in the lobby!"

"Shit!" Connor swore to himself.

As soon as Winston reached the lobby, Connor asked, "What happened?"

"Somehow Jorge found out that Carlos was working with us. They took the package and Carlos and said they were leaving on the plane. There were three of them. My gun was fucking empty! They grabbed him so fast I just couldn't do anything. We've got to try to get him back!"

"Yeah. We would not be here if it weren't for him.

"We've got to get to the airport, now!" Winston blurted, as they ran to his car.

As soon as Winston closed the driver's side door, he dialed a number on his cell phone.

"Miguel, it's Gerald. That plane you've been watching…is it still here?"

"Yes, but not for long. It's about to lift off."

"Is there any way you can stop it?"

"No way, too many people around it."

"Did you see who boarded it?"

"Yes, the main guy, at least three others and one who looks like their hostage. They just arrived."

"Okay, get our bird ready. We're going to follow them. We'll be there in less than five minutes," Winston instructed as his tires screeched out of the parking lot.

The two police officers abruptly escorted Viper to the unmarked police van parked in the back of the hotel. One of the officers opened up the van as another officer jerked Viper into the van and secured him to a bench along the side panel.

"Ivan, you are a traitor to Mother Russia. You'll die a slow death, only after every drop of your blood is out of your body," Colonel Alexandrov vehemently threatened Viper. The van engine started as the members of the Russian FSB Alpha Counterterrorist Group, masquerading as police officers, left the area.

Carlos tried to free his hands. They were handcuffed behind his back, as he sat in a cramped window seat in the small aircraft. He knew that he did not have long to live. If only he could free himself, he would try to take them all down, even if it meant his own life.

"Stop moving!" The bodyguard slapped Carlos across the face.

At this point, he had no choice. He dropped his head in submission.

CHAPTER 24

CABO SAN LUCAS AIRPORT

Winston's car skidded around the corner and came to an abrupt stop at the hangar. The CIA Gulf Stream was on the tarmac, doors open, ready for takeoff. Connor still couldn't believe Winston's revelation that he had managed to slip Carlos a miniature GPS tracking device. He jumped out of the car and inhaled the jet fuel fumes. Daylight was less than an hour away.

Within minutes, Connor looked out the window as it smoothly lifted off the short runway. Seconds later, the small municipal airport was buried beneath the clouds.

"My guess is that they'll fly to one of their airfields near Bogotá. Flying time is about four hours and fifteen minutes. They've probably got about a ten-minute lead on us, but we may be able to make up the time, depending on their airspeed," Winston said as he unbuckled his seat belt. "Come on, let me show you the comm gear on this bird."

Connor followed him to the back of the plane where the communications center consumed the entire rear end of the aircraft. *There is more comm gear on this plane than on an AWAC,* Connor thought in amazement.

"As long as the tracking device works, we'll be able to plot their course and pinpoint where they're going to land," Winston explained as he flipped a couple of switches on the console.

"Without this device," Connor said, "Carlos would have little chance of survival. That was good heads-up thinking on your part."

"Well, there is still no excuse for having an empty gun…hey, explain the deal again with you and DEA now that we're alone."

"I am undercover into DEA, tracking a terrorist cell in the Bay Area. I don't want to sound corny, but it's *CC* and it's a category four level."

"Complicated and classified? I haven't heard that for a long time." Winston chuckled for the first time in two days, remembering the phrases that came up when they were trainees at the Farm. He understood the significance of the category four classification which meant CIA Director-level only. He didn't need to ask Connor any other questions.

"I believe the package was being transported to that cell. God only knows what was in the suitcase." Connor dreaded thinking about the possibilities.

The phone at the end of the console rang before Connor could continue.

"Go ahead. It's secure, and it's probably Langley."

"Jack Connor."

"I was hoping it would be you, Jack. We analyzed those pictures you sent. I take it there was no way to recover the device."

"That's right ma'am."

"It was part of a detonation platform and I suspect that the other package contains the remaining firing elements. One item was damaged, but I'm told it can be fixed," Bancroft explained.

For the next few minutes, Connor gave the director a brief description of what had occurred in the past twenty-four hours.

"Jack, do what you can to get that suitcase and Carlos back. There's a detonation device in that package, so we need to get it at all costs. Winston is fully briefed on our capabilities in Bogotá and he's a good field operative, so you guys come up with the rescue and ops plan. Good luck Jack. Let me speak to Winston, please."

"Gerald, this is Lynn Bancroft. I'm so very sorry to hear about your wife."

"Thank you, ma'am." Winston took some solace in her heartfelt words.

"You know our capabilities in Bogotá. Contact the Embassy and coordinate the rescue. I have a lot of faith in your abilities and I trust your judgment Gerald. Let's get our CI back...and that package. Good luck."

"Thank you, ma'am." Winston had to admit that the director's pep talk was inspiring. He smiled at Connor. "We'll need a little luck on this one," Winston said as he dialed the number to the American Embassy in Bogotá.

"This is Cabo-1, I need to speak to the COS or assistant COS. We have a priority A-one HRT situation." Winston used the abbreviation for the phrase *Hostage Rescue Time-Sensitive*.

"Understand, Cabo-1. I need voice verification. Standby," the operator replied as he hit the intercom button to Hugh Heist's office.

"Sir, this is dispatch. We have a priority HRT call from Cabo-1. I'm in the process of voice verification."

"On the way," Heist replied as he rushed to the operations room.

"Cabo-1, go ahead with voice authentication."

"This is Cabo-1 five four nine four nine zero zero one four. I have a priority A-1 HRT request."

"Stand by, Cabo-1. The assistant COS is on his way down. He should be here any second."

"Heist?" Winston asked.

"Yeah. Gerald, what's the situation?" Heist's baritone voice came over the line so clearly, it almost sounded as if he was in the plane.

"Hugh, we have a problem. We're headed your way and should be there in about four hours." Winston briefed him and described the kind of assistance they would need. He also described the shootout with the assailant, requested they contact the COS in Mexico and follow up with the locals on the suspect in custody.

"Okay, I get the picture. I'll get back to you in ten minutes."

Winston flipped the GPS switch on the console. In a few seconds it lit up and a dot showed up on the screen. An intermittent beep started to transmit.

"Bingo! There's Carlos. As long as he has the device I gave him, we should be able to track him, no matter where he goes. Here, take this." Winston handed Connor a small remote unit.

"We have two field units which have 95 percent of the functions of the main console." Winston pointed to the device he gave to Connor.

"If you want to know where he is in the air, for instance, you press this button. If you want to locate him on the ground, press this button and you'll have him within three meters." Winston demonstrated.

"What does the tracking device look like?"

"It's a coin, a quarter to be exact."

CIA HEADQUARTERS

"Derek, I just got a call from my agent in the field in Mexico. I can't believe this, but we may have another possible device inbound to the cell. I told the ground units it was a detonation unit. We are tracking it right now to Bogotá. Do you think you can get the new project online for an intercept? We have about two hours," Bancroft told the NEST Director.

"I'll do my best," he said, already working on some calculations in his mind.

"What about the other package? Are we back online on that?" Bancroft paused, hoping for the right response.

"Yeah, we just got back online. I think we'll have movement soon."

"Keep me posted."

"Will do."

AMERICAN EMBASSY, BOGOTÁ

"What's up?" Captain Jason Ward snapped as he entered the operations center.

"Jason, you're going to need Goldstein's team to back you on this one. Do you know where he is?" Heist asked.

"Yes sir. They are on a training mission with five Marine Recon snipers who are TAD with us."

Heist briefed him as they reviewed maps and satellite data.

"My guess is that they're probably going to land at the new airstrip they built in this area about seven months ago. It's near a new processing plant that we suspect went operational this year," Ward added as he walked over to the field radio set up in the corner of the room.

"Base to Bravo-1, Base to Bravo-1" Ward spoke into the portable field mic that allowed secure communication to the teams during training exercises.

"Go ahead, base."

"Bravo-1. What's your location?" Ward asked scanning the map hanging on the wall.

"We're in grid D-four, at the southwest corner."

"Good," Ward replied as he put his finger at the location on the map.

"Bravo-1 will meet you at latitude 4° 35' N and longitude 74° 4' W. That is about one click due south from your present position in thirty mikes. Copy?"

"Copy that," Bravo-1 responded.

"We've got a hot HRT. I'll brief you when we link up. Out."

"10-4. Guys, our training mission just turned live," Goldstein informed his team.

BOGOTÁ CARTEL JET

"Carlos, you're good, especially in the last couple of hours. I would have loved to have met your control agent. It's a shame you will never be able to introduce us," Jorge said as he stood in the aisle and stared at Carlos with utter contempt and loathing.

"I do not know what you are talking about! You have made a terrible mistake, someone is giving you wrong information!" Carlos responded forcefully, knowing he was wasting his breath.

"Do not speak to me! Do you think the Americans are the only ones that can check out phone records? I know you are working for the DEA!" Jorge shouted as he slapped him across the face. "I should have trusted my instincts when I met you, I knew you were a liar!"

Jorge's bodyguard stood up from his seat, but Jorge motioned for him to sit down and the bodyguard reluctantly obeyed.

"My brother will have the last word with you, you *hijo de puta*!" Jorge spit the words, son-of-a-bitch, as he stalked off.

Carlos stared straight ahead as the plane pitched in the turbulence. He choked back the bile that was building in his throat and distracted himself by imagining his hands around Jorge's neck.

CIA AIRCRAFT

"Go ahead."

"This is Captain Jason Ward from the Embassy. May I speak to Gerald Winston?"

"He's in the head, captain. This is Jack Connor, DEA. I'm working with Winston on this operation."

"Got something to write on?"

"Go ahead."

"Copy this. Latitude 4° 35' N and longitude 74° 4' W. There's an old airstrip and you should be able to put down there. We think the target will land at a new airstrip they recently built about thirty mikes from your L-Z. We have been tracking Carlos too. When you land, position the aircraft at the south end of the strip. We'll meet you in the southeast corner, about twenty meters into the bush and will brief you there. When you're about thirty minutes out, notify us at freq one-seven-five-point-three foxtrot."

"10-4. I copy one-seven-five-point-three foxtrot."

"See you on the ground."

"What happens if they don't land at that airstrip?" Connor asked.

"Let's hope that's not the case. You should have a good read on their landing intention when you're thirty mikes out."

"Roger that. Winston is standing by; do you want to talk to him?"

"Negative, we've got to go."

"Copy."

Connor watched Winston as he began pulling gear out of a locker. They had their work cut out for them and Connor hoped like hell that it wouldn't be in vain.

Winston returned to the console, noticing the flashing red light that indicated an incoming message. He read the message in disgust.

"Jack, read this." The tone in Winston's voice was obvious disappointment as he walked back to the locker.

"Shit." It took only a matter of seconds for Connor to digest the contents of the classified e-mail. The message explained that their suspect had escaped and killed the two police officers. They had no further information, ID, or whereabouts on the suspect.

Connor had no idea how close he had come to stopping the reign of terror of the world's most notorious and deadly assassin.

THE PALACE, BOGOTÁ

"Joaquin, when do you want to go to the plant?" Roberto asked as they walked through the stables. Joaquin stopped and admired one of his favorite thoroughbreds, standing gracefully in her stall. Her coat shined from the grooming brush.

"I almost wish I could trade these horses for a den of lions. I would feed them the bones of the bastards who betray us," Joaquin growled. "How long until Jorge returns?"

"Less than an hour," Roberto replied uneasily. He could see that Joaquin's mood was growing blacker by the minute.

"We'll leave now." Joaquin stroked the horse's long neck and salivated about how much pleasure he would take in slitting Carlos' throat.

SPECIAL FORCES SNIPER TEAM, BOGOTÁ

Army First Lieutenant Elton Goldstein would not admit it, but he was impressed with the Marine Force Recon unit. During the limited exposure he'd had with them, he had found them to be tough and reliable, extremely efficient, yet deadly. They would be a welcome addition to this mission. The men stopped for a minute to check the coordinates.

"Lieutenant, we are right on course, it's just over the next ridge. We should be there in twenty minutes," Staff Sergeant Peters reported.

"Let's move out. I want to get there before Alpha team."

CIA AIRCRAFT

"Jack, we've made good air speed. The pilot said that if we keep going at this speed, we should land thirty minutes ahead of Jorge."

"Great!" Connor replied enthusiastically. He felt wide awake, despite the fact that he had very little sleep during the past twenty-four hours.

OLD BOGOTÁ CARTEL AIRSTRIP

The air was humid and still, as dawn cast rays of light across the airstrip. The silence was interrupted by the occasional sound of wildlife in the tree line where Bravo team was concealed. Staff Sergeant Baker was the first one to turn his head in the direction of the faint sound of engines from the road leading to the airstrip. Within seconds, the entire team heard the approaching convoy.

The Alpha team arrived in two vehicles, five minutes apart. After both vehicles were hidden in bushes along the tree line, Ward and his team met Goldstein and his crew at the designated site.

"Hey Elton, when did you guys get here?" Ward asked.

"About ten minutes ago. Everything is quiet so far. I've got three men on perimeter security."

"Good. How are the Marines doing?"

"Great so far."

For the next five minutes, Ward discussed his ideas with Goldstein and the two agreed on a primary and secondary rescue plan. Goldstein then deployed his team.

CIA AIRCRAFT

"How's it look?" Connor asked.

"We're still tracking them," Winston replied as he kept his eyes on the red dot on the console.

"How much longer 'til we make contact with the ground units?"

"Another fifteen minutes should do it."

AMERICAN EMBASSY, BOGOTÁ

"Sir, I just got a call from Langley. A satellite will be passing over in approximately ten to fifteen minutes. Hopefully, we'll get some good tactical info for the op," the base operator reported.

"I hope so. They will need all the help they can get," Heist replied.

Please don't let this be the cluster fuck of the year, Heist prayed as he stared at dated surveillance photos of the airstrip.

BLACK MOUNTAIN RANGE, BOGOTÁ

"El Jefe is here," one of the plant processors told the foreman as he inspected the shipment headed to Miami later that night. The facility was one of two secret staging plants that the cartel operated as their transshipping points for the cocaine they distributed throughout the world. The Gusto family paid dearly for the protection of the highly sophisticated equipment, enlisting the highest level of officials in the Colombian government. The plants were officially designated as cattle ranches. In fact, acres of land surrounding each plant were littered with cattle to create the appearance of a ranch.

Visits by the Gusto family were random, but not uncommon. Security was extreme, but slightly more discreet than security at Joaquin's hacienda. The foreman inspecting the shipment satisfied himself that everything was in order. Then he left the warehouse to meet his "Supremo Jefe".

CIA AIRCRAFT

"Cabo-1 to Alpha-1, over," Winston paused.

"Go ahead, Cabo-1." Ward responded.

"We are about ten minutes out. We're still tracking our primary. They are on course to land at the site previously identified."

"10-4. We'll see you shortly."

"Hey, Jack, pick out what you want to carry," Winston directed as he opened a wall locker and side compartment.

"Are all of your planes equipped like this one?" Connor exclaimed as he viewed a small arsenal and an incredible collection of tactical equipment. He picked up a load-bearing vest and web belt, both made by Eagle Industries, and identical to the equipment he used in San Francisco. He noticed a pair of 226 Sig Sauer 9mms and two Black OPS 1911, Para Ordinance .45-caliber pistols. Connor picked his weapon of choice, the Sig, considered one of the finest 9mms built, in lieu of the more powerful .45 weapon.

Now we're talkin..., he thought grabbing the 226. He examined the long guns in the locker and selected a shortened M-4 with an M-203 grenade launcher.

"Where're the LAW rockets?" Connor asked facetiously.

"In a locker in the back. You want one?" Winston replied seriously.

"God almighty! I can't believe all the toys you guys get to play with in the field. Let me guess, they're working on installing Sparrows and Sidewinders on this aircraft?"

"That's classified, level four," Winston replied seriously, then grinned.

Connor shook his head, smiling as he selected ammo for his weapons.

SPECIAL FORCES RESCUE TEAM, BOGOTÁ

"McDonald, contact Bravo units and make sure they copy that," Ward directed.

If that satellite comes through, we'll have a good run at this, Ward thought as he contemplated the sheer number of things that could go wrong.

"10-4," Sgt. Ricardo Salinas radioed as he placed his short-range PRC 112 hand-held back into his tactical vest.

"Lieutenant, Alpha team just confirmed their contact with Cabo-1. They're due to touch down in ten minutes. We're still tracking the target and we're good to go with our primary mission. They estimate the target will land in twenty minutes." Salinas gave the details in a subdued tone. The scanning capabilities of the radio net allowed each team to monitor more than one frequency so that the teams could keep up with all aspects of the operation at the same time.

Goldstein gave Salinas a thumbs-up as they pressed on toward their destination and his team negotiated through the densely wooded terrain.

Within a matter of minutes the Gulf Stream landed. All three climbed down the narrow aircraft steps and headed to the rendezvous point. Alpha team spotted them first. Alpha team members emerged from their camouflaged positions as Connor, Winston, and Miguel walked into the center of the Special Forces team circle. Connor was caught off guard.

"You must be Jack Connor."

"Yes."

"Jason Ward, Delta Detachment, Alpha platoon and you must be Gerald Winston."

"That's right. This is Miguel Perez, our pilot."

Before anyone else spoke, another figure appeared from behind a tree seven feet away.

"Staff Sergeant Baker reporting for duty, sir!" He spoke crisply, directing his attention too Connor.

"Oh my God, this mission is doomed," Connor joked, then added, "How the hell did you get here, Marine?"

"Sir, after the assassination at Quantico, my men and I got invited to do some cross-training with our Army counterparts down here and now we're operational again."

"Are you still tracking the target?" Ward asked.

Winston pulled his portable receiver from his tactical vest, "Yes. Their plane should land in five to ten minutes at the new airstrip. It is about two ridges from our present location. We think they're going to transport the hostage to their processing plant, located about thirty kilometers from the airstrip.

"Yeah, we agree. Our plan is to hit them while they're transporting the hostage to the plant, at a junction about fifteen minutes from our present location," Ward explained.

Connor saw the rest of the team providing perimeter security while Ward conducted the briefing. It was clear that everyone on Ward's team knew their assignments.

"I have broken the team into three elements. The first element will be the rescue group comprised of my men and you, Jack. The second element will be the support fire group from the sniper team that has been already deployed and should be on station by now. The third element will be the Marines who will provide security for the plane and airstrip with Gerald and Miguel."

"Mr. Winston, you've got comm, so set your PRC to channel four. Connor, one of my men will give you a headset and tactical radio for the rescue. We all have comm so we'll be able to communicate with one another. After we secure the hostage and package, we'll return to the strip. You can take off, we'll return to base, and we'll be done," Ward added.

"What's my role?" Connor asked.

"You'll be with me. I'll brief you on the way down to the target location. If something goes wrong, or if somebody gets hit during the rescue, we'll medevac them to a carrier group that is conducting an exercise off the coast. They will have some choppers up in the area if we need them. If for some unforeseen reason this gets fucked up, we're on our own. There's no backup, we'll have to adapt to the situation. I suggest the two of you get in the plane with the Marines and get the hell out of here if that happens," Ward directed. His command presence was apparent.

"We're not going anywhere, Captain. We're here to support you," Baker adamantly replied.

"I appreciate that, staff sergeant, but I don't know what you could do for us in the event shit happens."

"We all have GPS. You can radio your coordinates and we'll find you." Baker's Marines were not taking the easy way out.

"Hopefully, it won't come to that."

"Let's move out," Ward ordered.

412

Baker dispatched his Marines into two teams, providing cover while he and Connor walked over to the modified Isuzu Trooper hidden in the tree line near Ward and his team.

"Just like the old days," Baker said quietly.

"Different continent, different enemies, same fight," Connor wryly observed.

"Take care of our Army buddies." Baker smiled. Marines believe that they are superior to all other military personnel.

"Make sure nothing happens to that jet. That's our ticket back home."

"Don't worry about it, just get our boy back." Baker gave him a thumbs-up sign and they headed out.

NEW CARTEL AIRSTRIP, BOGOTÁ

A blast of hot air hit Jorge's face as he walked down the steps and off the plane. Three armor plated Suburbans were parked in a straight line beside the aircraft, flanked by security guards waiting to take them to the processing plant.

"Señor Jorge, welcome home," the driver greeted him as he opened the rear door.

"Is my brother at the plant?"

"Yes, he is waiting for you and the prisoner."

One of the bodyguards roughly grabbed Carlos by the arm, pushing him as they descended the narrow steps. Carlos winced in pain as two sullen-looking thugs grabbed both of his arms and forced him into the back seat of the Suburban parked at the end of the line.

The caravan drove off the airstrip and onto a narrow dirt road leading to the processing plant. Dust swirled in a powdery brown wake as they drove away.

OPERATION ROOM, U.S. EMBASSY, BOGOTÁ

"Hugh, come down. The photos are coming in now," the duty officer radioed from the operations room. The agency's operations room within the Embassy was not the same caliber as the one at Langley, but it was adequate to support real-time covert field operations in-country.

By the time Heist reached the ops room, the dispatcher was already on the radio providing intelligence to the SF team. Heist

413

studied the satellite photo frames and could see that a male was handcuffed and being escorted into the last vehicle in the line. It was gray. The first two were dark blue. *Thank God for color imagery,* Heist told himself as he realized their luck. He left the ops room to advise the station chief of the latest developments.

SPECIAL FORCES RESCUE TEAM, BOGOTÁ

"He is in the last Suburban, the only grey one We don't know which vehicle the package is in." Ward turned to them after he heard the radio transmission from the Embassy.

"Let's hope they don't switch vehicles," Connor replied cautiously.

"Yeah, that would be unfortunate. We'll reach the intercept point in five minutes. It will take them at least fifteen minutes to reach us. We'll take on Carlos' vehicle after we neutralize the others. The snipers will neutralize anyone who gets out of the vehicles during the initial assault. Jack, it will be your job to clear the inside of the grey Suburban since you know Carlos. Hopefully the package will be in the same vehicle."

Connor nodded.

"I will provide cover for you after you get him out. We'll make it back to your vehicles, retreat to the plane, and you're outta here," Ward continued.

"That will work," Connor replied, but thought, *God, I sure hope it does.*

NEW CARTEL AIRSTRIP

"I thought we no longer used the old airstrip," Jorge's pilot said as he walked into the small camouflaged office at the end of the runway.

"We don't, why?" the airstrip manager asked curiously.

"When I flew near the strip, I saw the tail of a plane parked at the south end of the runway."

"It is not one of ours," the manager replied as he picked up the phone and dialed the security office at the plant.

"Hello?"

"Where's Juan?"

"He's with Señor Roberto and El Jefe in the plant. Why?"

"Antonio, there may be a plane at the other airstrip. The pilot thinks he saw one at the south end of the runway. I want to let Juan know."

"We will investigate," he replied as he hung up the phone. Antonio, the newly appointed assistant security chief, did not want to interrupt Juan's meeting with Jorge. He wanted to show some initiative, so he rounded up four security guards and decided to inspect the airstrip himself. He knew a short-cut down a fire road that would cut their time in half.

SPECIAL FORCES RESCUE TEAM

Hiding the vehicles in the trees was a simple task for Ward and his team, who were now in position waiting for Carlos and his captors. Connor felt his adrenaline level rising as he and Ward silently waited. He checked the GPS and saw that Carlos' signal was still active. He was getting closer.

"Alpha-2 to Bravo-2"

"Go ahead."

"We're all set down here. How's it look up there?" Jackson spoke softly into his bone mic.

"We're zeroed in and ready," Salinas responded as he looked through his scope.

MARINE SECURITY TEAM, OLD AIRSTRIP

"Charlie-2 to Charlie-1"

"Go ahead," Baker answered.

"We've got company. Looks like two vehicles are headed this way. ETA two minutes," Jones reported as he scanned the winding road below through his binoculars.

"Okay, listen up. Ruiz and Rocky, come back to my location, ASAP!" Baker ordered the two Marines who were providing security at the opposite end of the runway near the Gulf Stream.

"10-4," Sgt. Ruiz replied as they ran toward Baker's position.

"Charlie-1 to Alpha-1."

"Go ahead."

"We've got hostiles. ETA ninety seconds," Baker radioed.

"10-4," Ward replied. He knew that the Marines would have to deal with the threat, if in fact it was a threat.

"Jones, engage any hostiles using any phones, radios, or any other type of communication equipment, you and Fluentes take out the lead vehicle. Rocky, you and Ruiz concentrate your fire on the second vehicle. Assault both vehicles from the right flank. I'll be your backup. Jones, you two provide cover. Stay put unless we need help." Baker gave the rapid fire orders.

"Copy. Copy." Both teams of Marines replied. The first pair had a bit of high ground and could effectively provide cover if the situation required.

Turning to Winston and the pilot, Baker added, "You two concentrate on the aircraft. If they just come up for a peek and do not use comm, do not engage unless they get within thirty feet of the aircraft or try to board it."

They nodded affirmatively.

"I see a total of five in two vehicles. They should arrive in thirty seconds," Jones radioed.

Baker and his team could hear the sound of the approaching vehicles. Jones's eyes were glued to his binoculars, scanning both vehicles for weapons and any signs of comm.

"I got weapons inside the vehicles," Jones radioed as the vehicles reached the strip.

"Look! That's a brand new Gulf Stream. I don't think we've got one of those yet. What are the tail numbers?" A cartel security guard asked as he pulled out his cell phone and began to dial the plant.

Jones aimed his M-203 and pulled the trigger. The guard's call was interrupted by a 40 mm, high-explosive projectile grenade. It pierced the back window of the Range Rover and detonated in an eardrum shattering blast.

The initial force of the explosion caused the back end of the lead Range Rover to spin loose, but not before Fluentes fired his M-203 into its side. It exploded into flames and skidded to a halt. The team could not see the cremation taking place in the flaming wreckage. The other two Marines fired their M-203s at the second vehicle with equal accuracy and the threat was eliminated.

Baker's men cautiously observed the infernos as huge flames spit black smoke into the dawn sky.

"Charlie-1 to Alpha-1."

"Go ahead."

"Two vehicles and five targets neutralized," Baker transmitted.

"10-4," Ward replied.

"Heads up, they know we're here," Ward radioed his team.

"All right, everybody except Jones on the strip. Let's clear that debris. We've got to clear the runway," Baker yelled to his team and waved them forward.

Ward and Connor made eye contact without saying a word. They knew that it was a matter of time before cartel reinforcements arrived. The only question was when and how many.

CARTEL PROCESSING PLANT, BLACK MOUNTAINS, BOGOTÁ

"Where's Antonio?" Juan asked the security guard who answered the phone.

"He took some of the men up to the old airfield to check on a report that a plane landed there."

"What? Why wasn't I informed of this?"

"Antonio said he did not want to interrupt your meeting with Señor Jorge."

"Get him on the phone immediately! Call me back with a report." Juan could barely contain his rage. Antonio should not have made such a decision without his approval. He would deal with him harshly when he returned.

"What is wrong, Juan?" Roberto asked.

"I am not sure. Someone may have spotted a plane at the old airstrip. Some of my men went there to check."

Roberto did not like the sound of this news. He knew that Jorge was on his way to the plant, escorting the traitor. Before Roberto could speak, the phone rang.

"Yes. Did you contact him?" Juan replied impatiently, then paused and listened. "Get fifteen men there now. I am on my way." Juan hung up the phone.

"What's wrong?" Roberto demanded.

"I do not know. They tried to contact Antonio, but he is not answering his phone. I am going to the airstrip to see what is going on," Juan replied.

"We need to contact Jorge. If there is any trouble, we need to be with him," Roberto replied in grim determination and left to find Joaquin.

"I'm going with Juan and some of the men to meet up with Jorge. There may be a plane at the old airstrip…and it is not one of ours."

"Where's Jorge?" Joaquin asked, a note of alarm in his voice.

"He's on his way to the plant."

"Wait for me," Joaquin ordered as he left the room.

"Joaquin," Roberto objected.

"He is my brother, Roberto, I must go."

"Yes, Jefe." Roberto knew that Joaquin sensed, as he did, that something was not right.

"Let's go," Roberto said as he dialed a number on his cell phone. "Jorge, where are you?"

"About thirty minutes from the plant."

"You must be careful. There may be some intruders in the area. There is a plane that does not belong to us at the old airstrip and we are out of contact with the men who went to investigate. We are on our way and should meet you at the fork in about twenty minutes."

"Pull over," Jorge directed the driver after he hung up the phone. Jorge signaled the other two drivers to join him.

"Roberto called and he thinks there may be trouble ahead. He's on the way to meet us, so be alert. If we run into any trouble, kill the traitor."

"Sí señor," the bodyguard snapped back.

"Let's move," Jorge commanded as he ran back to the blue Suburban.

SPECIAL FORCES RESCUE TEAM

"What's wrong?" Ward was alarmed.

"Either they stopped or the device has been compromised," Connor replied.

"Shit!" Ward swore when he saw that the red dot had stopped moving on the GPS.

"Jackson?" Ward spoke into his mic.

418

"Wait," Connor interrupted. "They're moving toward us again."

"Heads up. They should be here shortly," Ward radioed the team.

SPECIAL FORCES SNIPER TEAM

Two of Goldstein's sniper teams were in position on the ridge providing crisscross fields of fire at the target intersection for Ward's rescue team. Sgt. Hoffacer glued his strong eye to his telescope and aimed in on the intersection. His spotter skillfully scanned the roadway with his optics. Sgt. Salinas and his spotter scanned the target zone through binoculars. The air was stiflingly hot and humid. Everyone was on high alert.

"Our party has arrived," one of the sniper spotters radioed. The two sniper teams, hidden high on the ridge, had the best long-range view of the intersection where the rescue attempt would occur. Goldstein's sniper teams provided security from the north while he and Peters provided security from the east.

CARTEL REINFORCEMENTS

The gravel kicked up along the side of the road as Roberto's five-vehicle procession raced toward an intercept course. Juan led in the first vehicle, followed by Roberto in the second with Joaquin. The guards, armed with machine guns and LAW rockets, were in the three vehicles bringing up the rear.

SPECIAL FORCES RESCUE TEAM

Ward's team split into three two-man units, each assigned a target vehicle. The trickiest part of the rescue was to disable the third vehicle without injuring Carlos. That was the responsibility of Ward, Dolinski and Connor. Jackson and McDonald were assigned the second vehicle and Gallo and Mendez would take on the lead vehicle.

Connor rested his trigger finger along the side of his M-4 assault weapon as he rolled his shoulders, trying to keep his body loose. He hoped they still had the element of surprise.

The driver of the lead vehicle cautiously approached the intersection, anticipating...along with everyone else...that it was a possible ambush site. Everyone inside held weapons, ready to use them at the first sign of a trap.

Both sniper teams had their crosshairs zeroed in on the windshields as their respective target vehicles approached the intersection. Connor and Ward heard the hum of the engines as the big Suburbans neared the target zone.

The lead vehicle approached at a high rate of speed, then power-braked through the intersection. The driver almost lost control of the rear-end as it spun wide to the left, but he regained control and headed west on the narrow road. Dirt and gravel threw up clouds of dust.

"They know something's up. Hit them now!" Ward radioed. Mendez and Gallo tracked the first vehicle with their weapons as it slid into the westbound lane. Ward's men fired their M-203s immediately after the vehicle completed the turn.

The lead vehicle was tossed into the air as if it had driven onto a trampoline. The blast erupted into a fireball as the vehicle fell heavily to the ground in a shower of glass and debris. The direct hits between the front wheels detonated in the engine compartment. The occupants never felt the heat or burning metal sear into their bodies, because the merciful force of the blast killed them instantly.

"Hold on!" the driver of the second Suburban screamed as he braked at the sight of the carnage in front of him. He turned the wheels sharply and his tires plowed through the gravel, jarring his hands from the vice-like grip he had on the steering wheel. He maneuvered the Suburban around the burning pile of twisted metal in the intersection and sped forward, distancing his vehicle from the target zone as quickly as he could.

Seconds later, Jackson and McDonald fired their M-203's simultaneously at their targets, now swerving sharply in response. One round ricocheted off the metal trim on the second vehicle's rear window. The second round glazed the front windshield, cracking it before detonating on the side of the road. The driver slammed his foot on the accelerator and drove blindly through the thick, acrid smoke. Within seconds, he was out of range.

Dolinski fired one M-203 round at the base of the third Suburban's front wheel and it detonated, disintegrating the front tires and half of the engine block. It shattered the bulletproof windshield, causing the vehicle to come to a violent stop as the naked front disc brake ground into the dirt.

The driver of the third vehicle yelled as he felt the shrapnel from the floorboard pierce his left leg. Coughing from the singeing stench of smoke, he grabbed his thigh. Enraged by the pain, he drew his 9mm pistol from his shoulder holster and spun around, taking aim at Carlos.

SPECIAL FORCES SNIPER TEAM

One of the snipers tracked the action as he marked the vehicle in his crosshairs throughout the assault. He fired one high-powered round and hit the driver's neck as the driver aimed his weapon directly at Carlos' head. Blood spurted into the back seat and sprayed the bodyguard's face behind him, temporarily blinding him. The bodyguard screamed in horrified disgust as he wildly raked his hands over his face, trying to wipe away the warm, sticky fluid.

SPECIAL FORCES RESCUE TEAM

Connor and Ward reached the right rear passenger door within seconds of the blast, while Dolinski zeroed in on the driver's side of the vehicle, being careful to position himself far enough away to avoid crossfire from Ward and Connor's position.

Carlos, momentarily stunned by the blast, reached over with his elbow and hit the unlock button on the right rear passenger door. He swung his legs up and violently kicked the bloodied guard next to him, pinning him to the left passenger door.

Connor jerked the passenger door open. "Carlos," he yelled as he fired a short burst from his M-4 point blank at the guard, who never managed to raise his weapon. The guard's body violently jerked against the door frame and his weapon clattered to the floorboard.

"Carlos! Let's go," Connor shouted. He quickly released Carlos' seat belt while Ward provided cover.

"You okay?" Ward yelled.

"Get these cuffs off me!" Carlos pleaded as he rolled off the high bench seat onto the ground, his ears ringing in pain.

Connor reached for his handcuff key, while Ward trained his weapon on the perimeter. Connor hurriedly keyed the cuffs and they fell away. He helped Carlos to his feet.

"Where's the package?" Connor asked, quickly inspecting inside the charred SUV.

"It's in Jorge's vehicle." Carlos' voice was hoarse, and he was having a hard time hearing anything. His head was pounding after close range gunshot fire.

"Shit!" Connor slammed the vehicle with the butt of his weapon out of frustration.

"Alpha-1 to Alpha team, we have our primary. Secure and evacuate," Ward ordered.

"Alpha-3 is clear, target neutralized."

"Alpha-2 clear, but target fled the area untouched."

"Bravo-1, this is Alpha-1. Stay and provide rear security. Give us a heads-up if you see any more intruders," Ward continued.

"Check."

SPECIAL FORCES SNIPER TEAM

"Lovazzo, Aznack! You two get closer in with those M-203s. We'll need your fire support if we get any more visitors," Goldstein ordered the spotters, reluctant to separate them from the snipers.

"10-4."

They gathered their gear and started their descent down the ridge toward the wreckage strewn across the road.

CARTEL CARAVAN

"Who attacked us?" Jorge shouted as he turned around to see that the third vehicle was no longer behind him.

"Bastards," he screamed as he pounded his fist on the dashboard, startling the driver and causing him to momentarily yank the steering wheel, sending the big vehicle swerving into the other lane. Jorge angrily dialed his brother on the cell phone and wiped sweat off his forehead.

SPECIAL FORCES RESCUE TEAM

Ward, Connor, and Carlos rushed to the concealed Trooper. They ripped the camouflaging brush away from the doors and climbed in.

"I owe you my life," Carlos' voice cracked as he hugged Connor.

"We're not out of here yet, my friend," Connor cautioned. The engine sputtered, then revved into high gear as they shot onto the road. The rear wheels sent a spray of dirt and rocks behind them.

CARTEL REINFORCEMENTS

"Joaquin, we were ambushed! They got Carlos!" Jorge shouted into the phone.

"Where are you?"

"We are almost at the falls." Jorge eyed the roadside for identifiable landmarks.

"We will meet you on the road, in less than five minutes. We will find them!" Joaquin shouted furiously as he saw ribbons of black smoke in the distance.

Roberto tried to calmly analyze the facts as he heard Joaquin angrily recount the assault over the phone. It was difficult to concentrate with a mixture of fear and anger overtaking him. He would be blamed for this breach of security. Finding out who was responsible was not enough. He would have to personally deliver their corpses…and even then, that might not be enough.

MARINE SECURITY TEAM

"Alpha-1 to Charlie-1," Connor radioed.

"Go ahead," Baker responded.

"We got our primary and neutralized two of the three targets. Be on the lookout for a blue Suburban. Occupants are heavily armed. We will arrive at your location in fifteen minutes."

"10-4." Baker turned to his team, "Marines! Listen up.

CHAPTER 25

CIA HEADQUARTERS

"Hi, Lynn. I'm running late for a meeting, but you know that package in Colombia we were talking about earlier? We need to leave it at its current location. It shouldn't come here. So, if your ground crew comes in contact with it, all I need is one minute and fifty yards of clear space and it will not be of interest anymore," Derek Schmidt, NEST Director reported as he paced back and forth behind his desk.

"Okay, Derek, I'll let you know if we come in contact with it. Thanks for the update," Bancroft replied. *Oh my god*, the director thought. *What did he find out?* The only thing that raced through her mind was the fact that Derek had just given her a coded message.

SPECIAL FORCES SNIPER TEAM

"Lieutenant, we've got company," Sgt Salinas reported as he looked through his sniper scope, counting six Suburbans, including the one that got away. Six more armored Suburbans coming our way. The lead has a turret with a .50 caliber mounted on top. ETA is sixty seconds," he continued.

"Lovazzo and Aznack, you guys in position yet?" Goldstein asked.

"A-firm," Aznack replied, as he crouched next to a tree and pointed his M-203 at the approaching convoy.

"I'll be there in three," Lovazzo responded.

"Try to take out as many as possible with the M-203s," Goldstein directed. "When they get to the intersection, blast them! Salinas! Radio Alpha units, tell them they have ten minutes max if we don't stop them," Goldstein ordered as the roar of the caravan's engines drew closer.

"Lovazzo! You in place yet?" Goldstein asked as he calculated the angle of attack.

"Damn!" Lovazzo heard the crackle of the leaves and branches as he tripped over an exposed tree root, which sent him airborne, causing him to drop his weapon as he fell.

CARTEL REINFORCEMENTS

The lead driver brought the Suburban to a complete stop just before the intersection. They cautiously took in the spectacle of the disabled and debilitated Suburbans enveloped in smoke.

Jorge looked around nervously, contemplating the possibility of a second attack.

"There is movement up ahead to the left," Juan pointed from where he sat in the front passenger seat of the lead vehicle, to an area of slight motion in the foliage.

SPECIAL FORCES SNIPER TEAM

Goldstein and Peters crawled to a position where they had decent cover and took up a firing point.

"Heads up, they stopped about fifty yards out." Goldstein adjusted his bone mic using his binoculars. "Light them up...light them up!"

CARTEL REINFORCEMENTS

"Drive!" Roberto yelled to his driver, and all of the vehicles accelerated toward the intersection.

The roof of the armed vehicle opened and a security guard sprang up in front of the turret, grasped the handle of the .50-caliber machine gun, and fired at Lovazzo's position.

SPECIAL FORCES SNIPER TEAM

As Lovazzo fell, he automatically rolled onto his side, close to the nearest tree, as he heard the .50-cal rounds whistle past his left shoulder. He saw potholes appear around him, spraying his face with dirt.

Goldstein and Peters dropped their heads and flattened their bodies close to the ground as the .50-cal rounds ripped through the foliage, tearing off branches and ricocheting off trees. The guard shifted position and began laying down fire in the direction of the intersection.

"I guess they don't want any surprises this time," Peters quipped as he and Goldstein lay very still, waiting for the shooting to stop.

"Yeah, well neither do I," Goldstein whispered.

"Lieutenant, you guys okay?" Salinas radioed as he readjusted his firing position and zeroed in on the hostile firing the .50 cal.

"They're just clearing the area. They don't have a fix on us," Goldstein replied.

"10-4." Salinas started to squeeze his trigger, but Hoffacer fired first and the guard slumped through the opening in the roof and the piercing sound of the .50 cal gunfire abruptly ceased.

The sounds of 40mm rounds from an M-203 rang out, hitting simultaneously on each side of the Special Forces sniper's location. They had been focusing on the vehicles and were caught off guard by the explosions.

"Shit!" Salinas hissed under his breath as he and Hoffacer repositioned their rifles in the direction of the new threat.

CARTEL REINFORCEMENTS

Roberto, anticipating a second strike, had prepared his own counterattack by deploying four security guards from the rear Suburban, armed with M-203s and plenty of 40mm grenade rounds. He counted on the .50-cal suppression fire as a diversion for the snipers who were laying in wait. He knew he had signed the death warrant of the .50-cal gunner and he fully anticipated that he would lose the four M-203 shooters as well.

SPECIAL FORCES SNIPER TEAM

Goldstein and Peters grimaced at the sound of the first explosion. They recognized the sound.

"These bad boys are serious!" Peters exclaimed as the second blast detonated even closer to their position.

Peters wrenched at the burning sensation in his arm from a grenade fragment sticking out of his bicep. He swore under his breath and rolled on his side. He knew he had to stop the bleeding, but that would have to wait.

The four guards continued firing as the caravan sped toward the intersection. Goldstein's team crouched close to the ground, trying to avoid shrapnel.

"They're at six o'clock, four of 'em, two on each side, forty yards from my position," Salinas reported as he acquired one of them in his crosshairs.

"Got 'em. I'll take the ones on the right." Hoffacher started his controlled trigger pull.

The two security guards in the rear dove for cover as the two in front of them collapsed from the sniper rounds that ripped through their bodies. One of the guards fired a burst of .223 rounds from his M-4 toward Salinas's position, quickly followed by a round from the attached M-203 grenade launcher. Salinas tucked his head closer to the ground at the sound of the explosions that hit less than thirty feet in front of him.

Goldstein heard the sound of the remaining Suburbans skidding through the intersection and knew that their attack had been thwarted. He was keenly disappointed that his men had not contained the situation as he keyed his mic to advise the Alpha units of the situation.

Both snipers aggressively searched for the two additional guards who had taken cover positions after they realized their vulnerability to the snipers' fire. Salinas steadied his weapon as the target appeared in his scope. The guard's head slowly inched its way around the tree, lining up nicely in his crosshairs. The sound of two 40mm explosions near the intersection caused the guard to jerk his head in that direction, completing Salinas's sight picture.

Salinas pulled the trigger a split second before the guard began to move toward the tree cover. The round hit him squarely in the center of his forehead, tearing a jagged, three-inch exit wound at the base of his skull. The other guard's face was a mask of terror as panic overtook him and he ran blindly into the open. Hoffacer led him about a sixteenth of an inch in his scope, then pulled his trigger twice, dropping him less than six feet from his dead companion.

"Lieutenant, we're clear back here, all four neutralized," Salinas radioed.

"Copy. Aznack and Lovazzo, you two still with us?" Goldstein queried, checking on the rest of his team.

"Yeah, we're fine. We were pinned down and they went through fast before we could fire." Aznack reported, brushing off the dirt and gravel from his clothing.

"Alright. Let's confirm the hits. I do not want any more surprises. We need to clear out of here in five minutes. We've had enough action for one day and I do not plan to wait for the next wave of the cartel cavalry," Goldstein ordered as he watched the road to ensure the caravan did not attempt to double back for a surprise attack.

CARTEL REINFORCEMENTS

"Get them!" Joaquin screamed over his cell phone.

"No! It is a stall tactic. We must get to the airport. Keep going!" Roberto ordered. Now was not the time to stay and fight.

COMBINED U.S. RESCUE TEAM/OLD AIR STRIP

Baker and his team saw the Troopers as they sped onto the airstrip. He ran out to the field to direct Ward and his team to his location. Both vehicles came to a screeching halt and Ward jumped out.

"You heard they're about ten minutes behind you?" Baker asked.

"Yeah."

"My men are guarding the entrance to the strip," Baker said loudly, trying to project his voice over the roar of the Gulf Stream engines.

"What the hell is that doing in the middle of the strip?" Ward snapped, looking at the charred remains of one of the cartel vehicles.

"We had to wait until you got here. We need your vehicle to push the damn thing to the side so the plane can lift off," Baker responded.

"Let's get it done." Ward was mindful of every second they were losing. "Connor!" Ward yelled as he jumped out of the vehicle, assessing the situation. "Push this piece of shit off the runway."

"No problem!" Connor responded as he slid over to the driver's seat. "Carlos, go to the plane now! We've got this covered," Connor ordered.

Carlos jumped out of the back seat and headed for the jet as Connor drove toward the wreckage.

Connor felt his phone vibrate, recognizing the number. "Ma'am, I'm real busy right now trying to avoid a firefight at the airstrip."

"Understood, Jack. Got the package?" Bancroft asked.

"No!"

"Any chance of recovering?"

"Probably not, hostiles have it," Connor was brief and ready to hang up as he stepped on the accelerator.

"If there's any chance, let me know. Jack, your phone is the only phone that has a special feature on it. We can detonate it from here using your phone, only if you are within 50 yards. It could save a lot of lives. Good luck, Jack."

"Baker, we're going to rig our vehicles with C-4 as soon as the plane clears the area. I want them to think the entire rescue team left on the plane. Tell your men, no shots fired after the plane lifts off...only in self-defense. Copy?" Ward ordered.

"Yes sir!"

"Keep your men in the brush on the west side of the entrance for cover in case they get here before the plane takes off. My men will rig the vehicles and join you afterwards. I don't want to split forces. Use freq four on the radio. Let's move!" Ward barked as Baker flashed the thumbs-up signal.

"Be careful, Marine," Connor called from the moving vehicle. Baker nodded, then ran toward the men.

"Thank God! They're pushing that heap off the runway." The pilot surveyed the air strip from one of the Gulf Stream's small side windows.

"Good," Winston replied, clearly relieved as he went to the back of the plane, preparing to lift off.

"Frank and Joe, you two rig your vehicle with C-4 and drive it back in that south corner away from the entrance. Then, hook up with the Marines on the west side of the runway," Ward shouted to his men.

"Got it!" Jackson replied as he and McDonald jumped back into the Trooper and gunned the engine.

"Dolinski, you and Gallo help Connor push this debris off the runway," Ward yelled.

Connor revved the Trooper's engine, then gingerly accelerated as he made contact with the burned vehicle. The engine revved high and loud, but the charred vehicle barely moved. Dolinski and Gallo saw the problem and started pushing the wreck. The Trooper's tires went into a stationary spin, laying black tracks on the runway. Connor let up off the accelerator, then floored it. The tires gripped the pavement and the wrecked heap started to move, gaining momentum. Just as it cleared the runway, the Trooper spun loose, causing the heap to lunge forward. Connor saw Gallo go down as Dolinski jumped clear. He slammed on the brakes, jumped out and ran toward them. His felt physically ill when he saw Gallo lying on his back, motionless. As Connor fell to his knees beside him, Gallo sat up and wiped the dirt from his palms onto his pants.

"You okay?" Connor asked in relief as he helped him to his feet.

"Yeah, the damn thing almost ran over my foot," Gallo replied in frustration as he quickly placed a detonator on the small parcel of C-4.

"They're coming," one of the team radioed.

"We're out of here, be careful." Connor slapped Gallo on the shoulder.

"It's been my pleasure, Agent Connor." Gallo dropped the explosive into the Trooper and sprinted off the runway as Connor ran straight for the Gulf Stream, leaping up the steps two at a time.

"Go!" Winston yelled, locking the hatch as soon as Connor got onboard. The plane jolted forward, forcing Connor off balance. He fell backwards onto the floor.

"We got an incoming chopper!" one of Marines radioed frantically.

Ward was shocked that he hadn't heard it, but the Gulf Stream's engine was so loud, it had drowned out the chopper noise. The plane's wheels were just leaving the pavement as the chopper swooped in toward the runway in hot pursuit.

"Everybody in the bush, take cover!" Ward radioed.

"Miguel, incoming chopper!" Connor yelled to the pilot as he heard the transmission from the tactical net he was still wearing.

The Gulf Stream had climbed less than a hundred feet when the pilot, at full throttle, banked hard right. The chopper pilot flew past the plane's tail with only inches to spare. A cartel guard fired a burst of .50 cal rounds and one round pierced the jet's tail as it streaked upwards. The chopper pilot tried to correct his direction, but he could not match the small plane's airspeed. Uttering a stream of Spanish profanities, he reversed direction and increased his speed as he flew toward the vehicle at the end of the runway. The plane may have escaped, but the vehicle would not. He would stop any others from using it for their escape.

Ward held his breath as he watched the near miss, then keyed his mic, "Light it up!"

A second later, the C-4 detonated and the Trooper exploded in a pyrotechnic display that sent thousands of flaming-hot metal fragments airborne right into the oncoming chopper. The timing could not have been better. The chopper ignited with an ear-splitting blast into a huge fireball and billowing smoke. Bits of fuselage rained onto the ground, burning small craters into the airstrip and igniting a small brush fire along the end of the runway.

Ward turned toward the sound of screeching tires as the cartel's caravan roared onto the airstrip.

CARTEL REINFORCEMENTS

"Over there!" Jorge pointed as he commanded his driver, who immediately broke from the caravan and sped in the direction of the lone remaining Trooper.

Roberto felt a wave a panic as he screamed into the radio, "Jorge, stop! Stay away!"

COMBINED U.S. RESCUE TEAM/OLD AIR STRIP

"Now," Ward radioed. A second explosion ripped through the vehicle with the force of ten grenades.

All the bulletproofing technology in the world could not have spared the speeding Suburban from instant annihilation. The shockwave from the blast sent the Suburbans in the caravan spinning out of control, crashing into each other in chaos.

CARTEL REINFORCEMENTS

"Jorge!" Joaquin yelled in anguish. He continued to scream Jorge's name as the vehicle went up in flames and burned out of control. In a fraction of a second he saw Jorge materialize from the hollow smoke, running from the flames, clenching the package in his hands.

"Jorge is alive!" Joaquin screamed with relief.

The Gulf Stream encountered slight turbulence from the blast, but only for a few seconds. Connor starred down at the smoke and flames and watched until they were out of sight.

"Bastards," Roberto swore to himself, searching the sky, eyeing the tail of the jet, knowing that the Americans had made their escape.

COMBINED U.S. RESCUE TEAM/OLD AIR STRIP
The Marines and Ward's team lay silently in the brush under the hot sun waiting for the hostiles to leave.

Ward mentally swore to himself, observing Jorge. "Connor, are you still up on this freq?" Ward transmitted.

Connor heard the faint transmission in his radio. "Go ahead, Alpha-1."

"I got a visual on the package."

Connor heard the word "package" and then the transmission stopped. "Turn the plane around now back to airstrip!" Connor yelled at the pilot. "Alpha-1 is trying to contact us."

The pilot pulled the aircraft hard right as Connor tried to reestablish radio contact.

CARTEL REINFORCEMENTS
"Roberto, I want Carlos' head, no matter what it takes. Do you understand?" Joaquin yelled at the top of this lungs, trying to avoid inhaling the black smoke from the two burning Suburbans.

CIA AIRCRAFT
"Connor, one of the Gustos is holding your package. Do you want direct action? Over."

"Stand by, Alpha-1." Connor hit the preset number for Bancroft.

"Ma'am, the rescue was successful, but we did not get the package. We're airborne now. The SF teams on the ground have a visual on the package being held by one of the main targets at the airstrip. Do you want SF to engage them?" Connor asked.

"How much time do we have Jack?"

"I'd say five minutes max before they depart."

"We don't have to worry about the 50 yards from the air, just fly over it. Stand by Jack." The director reached to her secure phone and dialed the NEST Director.

Carlos, oblivious to Connor's conversation, kept on thanking Winston profusely for rescuing him.

"Hey bud, you did all the work, not me," Winston replied. Carlos looked baffled.

"The coin I gave you was a tracking device."

"But I don't have that coin, Jorge took it from me in Cabo."

"What did he do with it?" Connor interrupted.

"He put in his pocket."

Connor instantly keyed his radio, "Can you ID the individual holding the package?"

"It's one of the Gusto brothers…it looks like Jorge."

"Stand by. Gerald, check the computer to see if the GPS is still active."

"On it!"

"Ma'am, we've got something else. I believe Jorge is in possession of our GPS tracking device. We're checking right now for the coordinates."

"Jack, I got it! It's latitude 4° 35' N and longitude 74° 4' W," Winston interrupted.

"Ma'am, he's got it. Here are the coordinates!"

Bancroft switched to the other phone. "Derek, here are the coordinates. Our target is holding the package. You've got your minute, but not much longer. You're good to go."

"You're on speaker." The NEST Director jumped up from his desk, rushed to the nearby conference table and hit the resume button on his classified laptop. The window appeared as the barcode flashed across the screen. His fingers raced along the keyboard, initiated the fire sequence. He paused before inputting the coordinates, mindful of the seconds ticking away.

CARTEL REINFORCEMENTS

"Jorge, are you all right?" His brother yelled from the other side of the burning vehicle.

Jorge reached up and felt blood on the tip of his nose. He rolled his shoulders in pain.

"Yeah." He gingerly reached into his pocket, retrieving his cell phone, when he noticed that the coin that he had taken from Carlos had fallen on the ground next to his feet. Enraged, he stared at the coin and reached down to pick it up.

CIA AIRCRAFT

"Jack, we've got movement. I think they might be leaving, over." Ward's voice cracked in Connor's ear.

"Ma'am, we've got movement," Connor related.

"Derek, time's running out," Bancroft warned switching phone lines.

Ten miles up in the stratosphere, the new prototype R-2 satellite started shifting to the east, initiating the firing sequence.

CARTEL REINFORCEMENTS

"Jorge, bring the package over here and let's get the hell out of here," Joaquin yelled.

NEST HQ, WASHINGTON, DC

Schmidt inputted the final coordinates and tapped the enter key.

CARTEL REINFORCEMENTS

"That son of a bitch!" Jorge swore, clenching the coin in his hand envisioning choking Carlos. He cocked his arm to throw it as far as he could into the tree line.

"They're moving now..." Before Ward could finish the radio transmission, he saw some type of light beam a second before the explosion. He cringed from the blast.

"What the fuck?" Ward whispered to himself, wondering what he just saw.

Joaquin slowly stood up, disoriented. He yelled out, "Jorge!" A twenty-foot crater now occupied the spot where his brother had stood, seconds ago.

COMBINED U.S. RESCUE TEAM/OLD AIR STRIP

"Jack...target, package...eliminated." Winston's voice echoed over the radio net.

CIA AIRCRAFT

"Copy that," Connor transmitted, clenching his fists.

"Ma'am, whatever you did...the package and target have been eliminated."

"Derek, you did it, mission accomplished." Bancroft reported with a sigh of relief.

COMBINED U.S. RESCUE TEAM/OLD AIR STRIP

The Marines and Ward's team lay in the brush under the hot sun, silently observing the carnage sprawled out along the airport. It seemed like an eternity before Ward gave the order over the radio net: "Pack out!"

The two words were exactly what everybody wanted to hear. They slipped away, undetected, as fingers of smoke continued to rise from the airstrip.

CHAPTER 26

MOUNT VERNON, VA

The small cafe was tucked away in the quiet suburb of Mount Vernon. The two high-profile directors sat quietly at a rear booth.

"Sorry for the cloak-and-dagger today, but for a minute there I was sure my secure phone was being intercepted. Turns out it wasn't. This job is making me paranoid, Lynn. It's a little different from the old days," Schmidt said, sipping his latte. He went on in a whisper, "We eliminated one tactical nuke, Lynn. I believe this other package is identical. I'm about ninety percent sure that what we eliminated was ours…but I'd rather be one-hundred percent sure. We need to eliminate the other one the first chance we get. But, if we have any chance to ID it before we destroy it, we should. I would hate to be ten percent wrong. We should make no attempt toward recovery if we can eliminate it. It's too risky, Lynn, believe me. Remember, I was one of its creators. The new system we have can erase this device from the planet without a trace. I'm sure of it now. I just want to make sure it's one of ours and not something they made up. We are back online now, and I believe it will reach the cell in the next twenty-four hours."

"Okay Derek, the first chance we get, we'll do it, and if I can ID it, I will." Bancroft agreed with Schmidt's assessment.

"There might be some collateral damage, but it far outweighs the consequences if we don't. I'm sure of that," Schmidt continued in his low voice.

Bancroft felt the weight of her predicament. She sighed in silent agreement.

BOEING 757

"Sir, we'll be landing in fifteen minutes. Please put your seatback forward," the flight attendant politely instructed.

Connor rubbed his hands over his face. He couldn't believe that he would be home in less than an hour. He had slept the majority of the flight back from Mexico City. The last forty-eight hours had been hell. He was glad that Ryker only had a minor flesh wound. Although Tara's shoulder wound was not life-threatening, she was experiencing partial paralysis in her arm. Connor knew that if Tara didn't fully recover, Ryker would feel responsible for the rest of his life. Medicine couldn't relieve that kind of pain.

Carlos was safely tucked away in a safe house and would be joining his family tomorrow in Texas. Carlos had thanked him over and over for saving his life. His only disappointment was Viper's escape. Given all the circumstances, he wasn't complaining.

Connor dreaded the inevitable onslaught of briefings that awaited him. He thought it was interesting that he was briefing Franklin first thing Monday morning at JTF-5, before he met with his boss or the SAC. Connor wondered if Franklin was working for the agency too.

He was relieved that they had agreed to delay the briefings so that he could spend the weekend with Barrett and recover from the jet lag. He decided not to even think about work, but rather concentrate on the fact he would be seeing her shortly. Connor had attempted to call her, but he had been unable to reach her, which caused him some concern. He had never missed her so much in his life.

The aircraft landed at SFO half an hour early. He hailed a cab and with unusually light traffic he was home by 6:45 p.m. He opened the door, filled with the anticipation of holding her in his arms and feeling her body next to his. The house was quiet and dark and appeared different. He walked in the kitchen and reached for an envelope with his name, recognizing Barrett's handwriting.

As soon as he opened the letter he winced. His worst nightmare had materialized.

"Oh no!" he whispered out loud. Barrett had found his CIA identification badge. He forced himself to read the letter twice as the severity of the situation started taking hold in his mind. He walked around the condo trying to think of what to do, oblivious to the fact that all of Barrett's personal belongings were gone.

Don't contact me, were the only words that kept circling his mind. The ringing of his phone brought momentary relief as he hoped he would be hearing his wife's voice.

"Yes ma'am." Connor responded disappointedly.

"Anything wrong, Jack?" Bancroft asked, detecting something in the tone of his voice.

"Ma'am, Barrett found out I worked for the agency. I forgot that I had an old ID pass that she found. She's gone and she's not answering any of my phone calls."

"You need to find her and discuss this. I'll talk to her, in person, if necessary. We'll get this resolved, Jack."

"Thank you, ma'am, I appreciate that," Connor replied, grateful for her offer. He felt physically sick.

"Jack, right now I need your help. The other package is on the move and I believe it's going to our location near you. Once we ID the location, I'll need you to go there to confirm. Can you do that, Jack?"

"I'll stand by here and wait for your phone call."

"Thanks, and don't worry about Barrett, we'll fix it."

He dropped his head in his hands and felt totally helpless for the first time in a very, very long time.

REDWOOD CITY, CA

Barrett glanced down at her watch. She had a faster pace than yesterday, fueled by the anger. Barrett enjoyed the change of scenery of her new running course and the fresh air from the bay water of the Smith Slough at the tip of Pete's Harbor. She picked up her pace, knowing that the four-mile run was almost over.

The openness of the preserve overlooking the bay was like a metaphor for the new challenges in her life that she was going to embrace. The challenge of her first homicide case and the possible connection between the murder suspect and the FBI terrorist wiretap didn't diminish the rage she felt about Connor's betrayal.

She started to sprint toward the parking lot. Her heavy breathing felt good as she started to walk around the parking lot to cool down.

She stopped momentarily, gazing up at the twilight sky, closing her eyes and deeply inhaling the fresh air.

In a fraction of a second, before she could open her eyes, the van door jerked open as Assad jumped out, striking her in the neck. The only thing she saw was a bright flash before she slid into unconsciousness.

A couple got out of their car in the parking lot. "Did you see that?" The woman exclaimed.

"What?" Her startled husband looked toward the back of the parking lot.

"That guy! He jumped out of that van and attacked that runner! He dragged her back into the van! Oh, my God! What if that's the guy who murdered the college student? He's leaving!" The wife screamed and they both started running toward the van.

Assad accelerated out of the parking lot, screeching the tires as the van slid around the exit and onto the street, heading toward the freeway.

"Call 911!" the woman yelled.

REDWOOD CITY POLICE DISPATCH

A three-second high-pitched beeping sound was heard in every Redwood City police car on patrol.

"Two runners just reported seeing a white male adult, approximately thirty to forty years old, medium height, 150 to 180 lbs, wearing dark clothes, abduct a white female adult runner, height five-six to five-eight, approximately 110 to 125 pounds, approximately same age, wearing running shorts and a white short-sleeved running shirt. Vehicle is a white van, manufacturer unknown, partial plate number 1VC. No further information. Incident occurred at the Smith Slough off the Whipple exit less than 5 minutes ago. The van fled the parking and sped toward the freeway. Possible Redwood Shores murder suspect. All units please respond."

Shit, that's right over here, Officer Randy Hernandez told himself as he heard the call on his police portable scanner as he was driving his personal vehicle to the gym for an evening work-out. Hernandez braked, almost losing control of his vehicle as a driver ahead of him applied his brakes abruptly. Within seconds, Hernandez realized it was the driver a few cars ahead causing the near collision. Hernandez's body stiffened as he saw the white van abruptly cut over two more lanes of traffic, taking the Menlo Park exit. Hernandez shifted over to the fourth lane, maintaining his distance as he took the same exit.

R&B TOWING, MENLO PARK

"Is Assad here yet?" Hakeem demanded angrily.

"Yes, Hakeem. He arrived about ten minutes ago. He is in the warehouse," replied the Jihad guard as Hakeem proceeded directly toward the back.

Assad heard the voices and advancing footsteps as he finished taping Barrett's arms and feet, tying her to a post in a storage shed in the far corner of the warehouse.

"Any problems with the woman?" Hakeem asked.

"No, it was a perfect moment, she never suspected anything."

"Good, she was digging too much. We will dispose of her shortly with the rest of the infidels, but for now she will stay here. The package will arrive any minute. Have you assembled the timing device yet?"

"I am almost done. I just needed one more circuit from the shed," Assad said, feeling a few beads of sweat dribbling down his chest.

"We must move up our timetable. We will strike before tomorrow's sunset."

"I'll be ready," Assad replied, walking toward his work space.

REDWOOD SHORES, CA

Connor's phone rang. This time, he knew exactly who it was.

"Jack, we think the package just arrived at R&B Towing, 13012 Maple Street, Menlo Park. You need to ID the device. Take a picture with your phone, if possible. That's extremely important. You need to be very careful. Once you get there, call me, and we'll keep this line open," Bancroft directed.

"I am leaving now. It should only take me about ten minutes to get there." Connor opened his safe. He quickly disassembled the top receiver group of his Sig and replaced the barrel with a threaded barrel from the safe. He attached the silencer, grabbed two additional magazines and ran down the steps of his condo.

R&B TOWING, MENLO PARK

Assad sealed the last circuit in place as his eyes squinted under the halogen lamp in his workshop.

440

"Assad, can you install the timing device into this briefcase?" Hakeem entered the work space, slowly opened the briefcase and placed it on the bench.

Assad stood for a second, not answering, his attention focused on the words written on the briefcase: *U.S. Portable TACTICAL NUKE*. Assad became nervous and shook his head in agreement. "This should take me two hours," he indicated as he examined the contents of the briefcase.

"Good. I will leave you to yourself. May Allah be with us tonight," Hakeem replied as he walked out of the room.

Damn! Officer Hernandez cursed, gripping his steering wheel as he drove slowly down the industrial area. *This prick has to be here. It's the only street he could've gone down,* he said to himself as he pointed his Maglite flashlight down each driveway.

Hernandez stopped his car when he saw the tail lights and a small section of the back of a van behind the warehouse. He cursed the fact that he did not have his cell phone as he grabbed his off-duty weapon from his gym bag and started across the street toward the building.

He cautiously crept up behind the white van, observing that the first two letters of the license plate were 1Y, not 1V. He knew from experience that numbers and letters were easily mistaken in traumatic situations. He proceeded carefully. Noticing that the lights were on in the warehouse, he quietly approached the back door of the building.

"You have arrived. The address is on the left," the voice on the GPS advised. Connor slowed and parked about two hundred feet behind a pickup truck. He answered his cell phone as it vibrated on his belt.

"Ma'am, I just arrived at the location," Connor transmitted from his earpiece.

"Jack, listen carefully. Don't touch or take anything out of the building, just report what you see. The device is similar to the one we destroyed in Bogota. Punch in this code on your phone, it will act like a GPS device. We just sent you a new app to your phone. You don't need to see the device now. You only need to get within 50 feet of it, but you still need to go inside. Do you see the green and the red dot yet?"

"Yes ma'am."

"Just follow the green dot to the red dot. Once you're in range, your phone will vibrate and send us a signal. That's all we need. You've got 5 minutes to get out, then the device and building will be destroyed. Understand?" Bancroft ordered.

"Yes." Connor knew better than to debate the situation.

Hernandez opened the back door slightly to peek inside the warehouse.

POP...POP... The muffled sounds could be barely heard from the Jihad guard's semi- automatic pistol. Hernandez felt the body-blow as the force of the bullet struck his back, slamming him into the door. A second round instantaneously sliced the side of his neck, lodging in the door frame and shattering splinters into his face.

The force of the two rounds caused his body to bounce off the door and violently spin around, knocking a garbage can onto its side as he collapsed on the cement.

The Jihad guard automatically redirected his weapon as the side door flung open.

"Don't point that at me, you fool! Go see if there's anybody else around the building!" Assad demanded, staring at the body. He dragged the body inside the warehouse, noticing the police badge on a chain around the dead man's neck.

Connor heard the suspicious noise and drew his Sig 9mm as he proceeded along the building. The Jihad guard appeared from around the corner and was startled by the advancing shadow. POP...he fired a single round at the intruder...it missed its mark. Connor double-tapped and two silenced rounds from his Sig struck the guard in the chest, knocking him backwards. Connor ran to the body. He picked up the weapon and cleared it, took the magazine out and tossed it as he continued toward the back door.

"One target down, ma'am."

"Copy." Bancroft minimized conversation, understanding the hot tactical situation.

"I'm in the warehouse now," Connor reported, staring at a blood trail leading into the warehouse as he repositioned himself next to several crates stacked next to a tow truck.

Assad opened the shed door and pushed the limp body inside.

"What happened?" another guard asked as Assad closed the door.

"Go tell Hakeem we just killed a policeman outside the warehouse."

Barrett's eyes opened after the door shut. She tried to scream, but her mouth was duct taped shut. Her lungs seared with pain as she made the effort. She recoiled in horror as she recognized Hernandez's face and frantically shook her hands and body, desperately trying to free herself as his blood slow crawled across the floor.

Connor remained still, crouched behind the tow truck, as he observed Assad briskly walking into another office on the other side of the warehouse. As Connor started to reposition himself, he noticed another individual entering the office. Connor stood up and ran toward the corner of the office.

He peeked in the side window, observed two men arguing and noticed an open briefcase filled with electronics on the bench table in front of them. Connor silently gasped as he read the faint white lettering written on the side of the briefcase: *U.S. Portable TACTICAL NUKE*. He quickly snapped a photo with his phone at the same time his phone vibrated.

"Ma'am, the briefcase…it's a TAC NUKE. Photo is on the way," Connor cautiously backed away from the window and pressed *Send*.

The photo arrived in an instant. Bancroft glanced at it and said tersely, "Jack, get out now! You've got less than five minutes."

"Copy." He hit the button on his Ironman and the stopwatch began counting. Connor ran toward the exit but stopped abruptly and hid behind the tow truck after hearing footsteps. Another Jihad guard appeared by the exit. Connor glanced at his stopwatch. Four minutes, fifty seconds…and counting.

"Jack, are you clear yet?" Bancroft demanded.

"Almost." Connor's head turned at the sound of a muffled female voice crying in the other shed where the blood trail ended. It was out of sight of the guard.

He rushed over and pulled the door open. His heart thudded in instant terror as he saw Barrett frantically trying to break free and Hernandez lying in a bloody heap on the floor. Without hesitation, Connor flicked open his tactical knife and cut the tape from Barrett's hands and mouth.

She jumped up and gasped, as her eyes popped open. Connor spun around low, knocking her to the floor. The Jihad guard flinched and discharged his weapon at Connor's movement. The two silenced weapons barely made a sound. Connor's round hit its mark as the guard collapsed. The guard's round narrowly missed them.

"Barrett! What are you doing here, are you ok?

Barrett nodded yes, feeling intense relief at the sight of Connor.

"We have to leave now. Just stay behind me, let's go!" Connor whispered harshly as they rushed out.

"Randy, what about Randy?" Barrett was frantic.

"He's gone."

"I saw him move Jack. He's still alive!"

"Ok, listen, my car is across the street. Get in there and put your head down. This building is going to blow up in a few minutes."

"What!"

"I said go!" He jammed his keys into her hand.

Connor didn't wait for a response. He looked at his stopwatch as he ran back to the shed. He had 3 minutes and 14 seconds.

"Connor, are you clear? Jack, are you clear? Time is short." Connor heard the voice in his earpiece. "Standby."

Bancroft stood in her office expecting the worst as tension mounted.

"Randy!" Connor whispered into his ear, rolling him over. Miraculously, Hernandez coughed at the sound of Connor's voice. Connor immediately grabbed him and yanked him to his feet as they staggered out of the shed.

"Randy, let's go, you can make it. Walk, walk, walk!" Connor repeated as they approached the exit. He heard voices rapidly getting louder as a guard with a machine gun slipped on the blood, at the same time pulling the trigger.

An automatic short burst of silenced rounds ricocheted off the floor onto walls, breaking glass. Assad jerked while installing the device. Hakeem glared at Assad with fury as he barreled out of the office.

Connor turned around at the sound of rounds ricocheting and observed another guard firing in his direction. One of the rounds hit

Hernandez and he slumped to the floor. Connor, unable to hold the dead weight, let the body fall as he fired at the closest threat.

At that moment, Hakeem entered the area. For a split-second, Connor exchanged eye contact, knowing that time had run out as he pushed the exit door open and started sprinting down the driveway.

Hakeem immediately recognized the panic in that stare. "Assad!" he yelled as he ran back to the office, knowing that they had to leave immediately.

Connor reached the street, running straight for his car, anticipating the explosion. Barrett saw Connor running toward her and unlocked the car door and turned on the ignition. Connor jumped in, slamming the door behind him, almost shutting the door on his foot. He reached down, jamming the car in reverse as he rapidly accelerated backwards.

For a split second he saw a faint laser flash in the sky as the building exploded. He jerked his wheel to the left, throwing the Mustang in a 180-degree spin. The shockwave of the explosion surged the Mustang sideways. Connor jerked the steering wheel in the opposite direction to over correct for slide and sped down the street. By the time the debris fell to the street, Connor's vehicle was a block away.

BOGOTÁ, COLOMBIA

The short row of votive candles flickered, providing scant light from their perch on top of the ornate rosewood casket, the finest that money could buy. Joaquin knelt beside what was left of his brother's remains in the small, dark room, alone with his grief and rage.

It had taken six men to carry the coffin down the stairs into the wine cellar.

Joaquin dropped his head and held his face in his hands, distraught and inconsolable. He wouldn't let anyone near the body. He refused to let them put Jorge into the cold, hard ground.

Above him, a small gray mouse scurried unnoticed along the ledge at the top of the stone wall.

"No!" Joaquin screamed as he beat his fists against the casket, his eyes bloodshot and swollen.

445

The mouse darted into a crevice and cowered there. Joaquin's throat was raw from screaming. He picked up the bottle of whiskey from the floor and drained it. The sour bitterness made his eyes water and renewed his rage.

"Jorge! Jorge, my brother! I will not rest until the bastards who did this are brought before me! I will torture them until they weep in pain! They will pray for death, my brother, they will pray, but death will not come to them! I swear it! I swear it, my brother. I swear it on our mother's grave!" he ranted, his words echoing throughout the cellar.

He threw his head back and looked toward the ceiling as the liquor finally dulled his rage. Then, it dawned on him…a revelation from hell. A half-smile began to form on his lips as he stood and steadied himself, then walked toward the stairs.

As the door closed behind him, the candles flickered, then burned out. The mouse frantically raced along the ledge in the darkness, searching for somewhere to hide.

EXECUTIVE BUILDING, WASHINGTON D.C.

Zif hung up the phone as he stared out his bulletproof glass window, gazing at the Washington Monument in the northwest corner of the Executive Office Building. He was filled with sense of dread.

The Jihad-7, a newly formed radical terrorist group…working with the Bogotá Cartel? Why was Jihad-7 planning a meeting with the notorious heroin drug lord, General Sun? Zif focused on the Washington Monument, wondering how the country's forefathers would respond to this threat. The humid heat waves from the dog days in August were so thick, Zif envisioned the monument already in flames.

CABO SAN LUCAS

The damp basement was twenty degrees cooler than the ground level. The property was leased by a French-based company that was a cover for the elite counterterrorist unit of the Russian FSB. Two men sat in the dimly lit room, staring at one another, contemplating their next course of action.

"Ivan, I can't believe you got wrapped up with this woman. You almost jeopardized our operation?" Alexandrov finally broke the silence. "There are certain factions in Moscow that know you exist and are trying to hunt you down. What were you thinking, Comrade?" Alexandrov shook his head in disapproval.

"I'm a man, she's a woman. I have my reasons," Viper retorted.

"Reasons! Your plan to fake your death and kill a few CIA agents in Panama may have fooled the Americans, but not the zealots in Moscow. You forget they know your capabilities Ivan."

"There's a leak in the cartel, which concerns me more than the power whores in Moscow," Viper barked back.

"Well, you'd better be concerned with those whores. You're here now, aren't you...in cuffs? You'll never finish your mission if you keep this up. You killed two of my men in Paris."

"Those two?" Viper was shocked.

"Unfortunately yes, we were in the area but that's too complicated to explain right now! Fortunately we were able to recover the bodies before the police or anyone saw them. I had to kill two police officers when we grabbed you. That's very sloppy work. I'm not supposed to be anywhere near you. My assignment is just as difficult as yours! You're making this difficult for me with my superior," Alexandrov snapped.

"Aren't you supposed to watch my back?"

"Not if you continue to be a liability to me," Alexandrov sighed. "This is not the appropriate time to debate this issue. We don't have much time before my team returns. We have to come up with a plan that is plausible and one that will not raise any suspicions concerning your escape."

"Yes, colonel, we do. I'll need a gun and the keys to the vehicle."

"Unlock yourself first." Alexandrov tossed a handcuff key to Viper. "We need to go upstairs and stage a fight and you need to get out of here before the troops come back. The last thing I need is for you to kill any more of my men." Alexandrov handed him a 9mm.

Viper stood up, walking to the table. As Alexandrov turned, he felt a sharp pain to the side of his head as he collapsed onto the floor.

"Rest peacefully, Comrade. I'll be more careful in the future," Viper responded sarcastically as he walked up the stairs.

MENLO PARK, CA

The last place Connor thought he would be spending his first anniversary was in Barrett's new apartment in Menlo Park. Connor looked at his wife, sleeping in her own bed. As he walked back into the living room, he wondered how their marriage was going to survive. *At least Barrett listened to my explanation without throwing me out of the apartment.* That was one positive step in the right direction, he reassured himself, but didn't feel any reassurance at all.

For the first time, Connor reflected on the last few days as he clenched his fists and tried to stop his hands from shaking. It was unfathomable that his wife had been kidnapped by terrorists and that he had defused two nuclear devices in the past 24 hours. *What am I involved in with this undercover assignment with DEA? His thoughts tortured him.*

The combination of tiredness and adrenaline meltdown was starting to take a toll on his mind. He closed his eyes and started a breathing exercise he had learned from his martial arts grandmaster. He started inhaling, counting to eight, taking long, deep breaths to clear his mind. As he exhaled, he reversed his count. Just as he started to get his heart rate under control, he felt his phone vibrating. Recognizing Bancroft's number, he reached down and turned the phone off. He'd done enough for one night. Whatever it was, it would have to wait.

In the second book, CIA agent Jack Connor continues his assignment with DEA as his true mission starts to unravel regarding the secrecy of his assignment. Bancroft tries to derail the hidden conspiracy within the top echelon of the executive branch, soliciting help from Zif. Joaquin Gusto plots swift revenge, targeting a top US official. Connor's betrayal forces Barrett to make a dramatic change in her life and their relationship. Tara's dream of becoming a model is crushed as she plots her revenge. Ryker recovers from his wounds and questions his desire to be a DEA agent. Viper is in semi-retirement but the CIA continues to hunt him down. Connor battles General Sun, the notorious heroin warlord, and his ruthless army of Triad soldiers and assassins who team up with Jihad-7, a radical terrorist group. They pool resources when they discover the third missing portable prototype nuclear device. Jihad-7's brilliant scientist, "the Engineer," is empowered to create another timing device to detonate the nuclear prototype. Raven continues his treachery as he pilfers information from DEA and provides it to the Bogotá Cartel. Radcliff and his band of mercenaries profit in the drug trade as DEA inches closer to their operation. Connor must stop General Sun and the terrorists from detonating the other nuclear weapon. The secret plot within the Russian Security Service that threatens world peace is discovered. Connor must muster all of his strength and wit as he travels to the Philippines, Bangkok, and Hawaii to unravel the diabolical plot and battle the biggest national security threat in U.S. history.

Alphabetical Character List

Mohammed Abdul ----- Leader, Jihad-7 terrorist organization

Alexandro ----- Bogotá Cartel pilot

Vladimir Alexandrov ----- Colonel, Federation Security Service of Russian Federation (FSB), Alpha Group, counter terrorist unit

Angel ----- Bogotá Cartel housekeeping

Antonio ----- Assistant Security Head, Bogotá Cartel ranch

Arrowhead ----- CIA Operation codename for Jack Connor

Assad ----- Jihad-7 terrorist member

Aznack ----- U. S. Special Forces Army/Delta Force U.S. Embassy Bogotá

Lynn Bancroft ----- Director, Central Intelligence Agency (CIA)

Bernie Beauort ----- Ex-U.S. Army Airborne/mercenary

Emma Brown ----- Executive Assistant to CIA Director

Razor Byrd ----- Ex-U.S. Army Airborne/mercenary

Caesar ----- Restaurant Manager, Mexico City

El Capitan ----- Javier Mora Police Captain, Cabo San Lucas

Bill Cartwright ----- Group Supervisor, (GS) DEA San Francisco Division

Mary Cartwright ----- Deceased, U.S. Assistant Attorney Miami/Bill Cartwright's Daughter/Jason Steiner's wife

Carol Cartwright ----- Bill Cartwright's wife

Henry Chan ----- DEA Special Agent, San Francisco, CA

Chico ----- Bogotá Cartel bodyguard

Barrett Connor ----- Homicide prosecutor, San Mateo County District Attorney's (DA) Office, Jack Connor's wife

Jack Connor ----- CIA Case Officer, Special Operations Group (SOG) undercover as a DEA Special Agent

Mike Connor ----- Jack Connor's father

Lucas Crenshaw ----- DEA Special Agent in Charge, Washington, DC

Allison Cromwell ----- First Lady of the United States

Russell Cromwell ----- President of the United States

Diego Cuevas ----- Corrupt Mexican business tycoon

Ron Decker ----- Chief Petty Officer, U.S. Navy SEAL, TAD Naval Postgraduate School, Monterey, CA

Jacques Devinure ----- a.k.a. Viper

Fernando Dias ----- Bogotá Cartel bodyguard/hitman

Manuel Dias ----- Bogotá Cartel bodyguard/hitman

Big Dog ----- Drug Dealer Washington, DC

Mark Doliniski ----- Sergeant U.S. Army Special Forces/Delta Force U.S. Embassy Bogotá

Gino Domingo ----- DEA Special Agent in Charge, Miami, FL

Pat Doolittle ----- a.k.a. Patcher, Ex-U.S. Army Ranger-medic/mercenary

Andrew Drum ----- Ex-U.S. Army Ranger/mercenary

Engineer ----- Unknown Jihad-7 terrorist

Francisco Felix ----- Head transportation cell Mexico City for Bogotá Cartel

Ricardo Felix ----- Drug Trafficker/rival cousin to Francisco Felix

Sal Felix ----- Ricardo Felix's brother

Bobby Fields ----- Ex-U.S. Army Ranger/mercenary

Max Finder ----- Ex-U.S. Army Ranger explosive ordinance tech/mercenary

Matt Finder ----- Ex-Miami Police Officer/mercenary

Robert Fernandez ----- CIA Station Chief, U.S. Embassy in Mexico City

Fluntes ----- Sergeant, U.S. Marine Corps, Force Recon

Tony Franklin ----- DEA Supervisor/JTF-5 representative Coast Guard Island Alameda, CA

Dick Freman ----- DEA Resident Agent in Charge, Monterey, CA

Robert Fuerte ----- Security Chief, Bogotá Cartel

Gallo ----- Sergeant U.S. Army Special Forces/Delta Force U.S. Embassy Bogotá

Pedro Garcia ----- Head of Transportation, Bogotá Cartel

Goldstein Elton ----- Lieutenant U.S. Army Special Forces/Delta Force, U.S. Embassy Bogotá

Hector Gomez ----- Lieutenant U.S. Navy SEAL, TAD Naval Postgraduate School, Monterey CA

Phil Goodman ----- CIA Security Officer, Director's bodyguard

Mother Goose ----- CIA's operational codename for CIA Director

Trace Griswold ----- Ex-U.S. Army Ranger/mercenary

Joaquin Gusto ----- Head, Bogotá Cartel

Jorge Gusto ----- Bogotá Cartel, council member, Joaquin's brother

Julio Gusto ----- Bogotá Cartel, council member, Joaquin's brother

Rafael Guzman ----- CIA Case Officer, Costa Rica

William Hacker ----- Colonel, U.S. Marine Corps Provost Marshall Quantico, VA

Hakeen -----Head of local cell, Jihad-7 terrorist organization

Karl Hans ----- a.k.a. Viper

Joe Hatfield ----- Lieutenant Commander., U.S. Navy SEAL, TAD to Naval Postgraduate School, Monterey, CA

Hugh Heist ----- CIA Assistant Station Chief, U.S. Embassy Bogotá

Hank Henderson ----- U.S. Attorney General

Maggie Henderson ----- Hank Henderson's wife

Henry ----- Limousine driver, London

Alfred Herman ----- a.k.a. Viper

Randy Hernandez ----- Redwood City Police Officer

Eric Hickson ----- Ex-U.S. Army Airborne/mercenary

Stephen Higgins ----- Fictitious name used by Bogotá Cartel

Dominic Hilarus ----- DEA Special Agent previously tortured

Hoffacer ----- Sergeant U.S. Special Forces Army/Delta Force U.S. Embassy Bogotá

Hoshi ----- Victoria Secret model

Doug Houser ----- Victoria's Secret photographer

Francis Hunt ----- DEA Special Agent/Class Coordinator DEA Academy, Quantico, VA

Bill Huntington ----- FBI Director

Igor Ivanovich ----- Russian Vice Defense Minister

Jamal ----- 14th Street gang member, Washington, DC

Hal Jarcowski ----- Admiral U.S. Navy

Agent Jansen ----- FBI Special Agent previously imprisoned

Jackson ----- Sergeant U.S. Special Forces/Delta Force U.S. Embassy, Bogotá

Joan ----- United Airlines flight attendant

Devon Jones ----- Sergeant U.S. Marine Corps, Force Recon

Cade Jenkins ----- DEA Special Agent, San Francisco, CA

Juan ----- Security Manager, Bogotá Cartel ranch

Minister Kellman ----- Israeli Interior Minister previously assassinated

Black Knight ----- CIA's codename for Viper

Lester ----- Bogotá Cartel submarine crew member

Lopez ----- Mexico Attorney General

Michelle Logan ----- FBI Special Agent, San Francisco, CA

Lovazzo ----- Sergeant U.S. Army Special Forces/Delta Force U.S Embassy, Bogotá

Lucy ----- Secretary to NSA

François Marcel ----- French vineyard owner

Jules Marcel ----- Francois' wife/French vineyard owner

Maria ----- Housekeeping Staff Bogotá Cartel, CIA confidential informant codename Striker

Eduardo Marquez ----- DEA Special Agent previously killed

Mary ----- DEA SFFD SAC's secretary

Match ----- CIA Operation codename for Hugh Heist

Mateo ----- Bogotá Cartel bodyguard

George Marconi ----- DEA Special Agent in Charge, San Francisco, CA

Joe McDonald ----- Sergeant U.S. Army Special Forces/Delta Force U.S. Embassy Bogotá

Sam McMillan ----- CIA Station Chief, Costa Rica

Mendez ----- Sergeant U.S. Army Special Forces/Delta Force U.S. Embassy Bogotá

José Mendoza ----- East Coast Lieutenant, Bogotá Cartel

Enrique Molina ----- Head of Asia distribution, Bogotá Cartel

Molly ----- DEA GS Bill Cartwright's secretary

Javier Mora ----- a.k.a. El Capitan, Cabo San Lucas Police Captain

Joseph O'Leary ----- DEA Administrator

Michael O'Leary ----- DEA Chief Inspector, Office of Personnel Responsibility Washington, DC

Carlos Padilla ----- Director of Security, Felix Drug transportation cell and DEA/CIA confidential informant

Tara Parks ----- Airlines flight attendant/Victoria Secret model

Pedro ----- Security guard, Bogotá Cartel

Pepe ----- CIA field operative, Bogotá

Miguel Perez ----- CIA pilot

Peters ----- Sergeant U.S. Special Forces Army/Delta Force U.S. Embassy, Bogotá

Posadus ----- Francisco's drug cartel second in command

Nick Radcliff ----- Ex-U.S. Army Ranger/head mercenary

Franco Ramirez ----- Bogotá Cartel accountant

Raven ----- Codename informant for Bogotá Cartel, U.S. Assistant Attorney Jason Steiner, San Francisco, CA

Mr. Red ----- Special Agent instructor, DEA Academy

Richie ----- 14th Street gang member, Washington, DC

Rocky ----- Sergeant U.S. Marine Corps, Force Recon

Roland ----- Fireman Redwood City, CA

Rosa ----- Bogotá Cartel housekeeping staff

Dean Roseberg ----- American medical doctor

Ruiz ----- Sergeant U.S. Marine Corps, Force Recon

Alex Ryker ----- DEA Special Agent, San Francisco, CA

Ricardo Salinas ----- Sergeant U.S. Special Forces/Delta Force U.S. Embassy Bogotá

Jerome Samuel ----- DEA Special Agent, Washington, DC

Juan Sanchez ----- Asia financial officer, Bogotá Cartel, CIA informant/witness protection

Sid Santiago ----- Petty Officer First Class (PO-1) U.S. Navy SEAL Team 5

Derek Schmidt ----- Director Nuclear Emergency Support Team (NEST)

Admid Shiriff ----- Father of murdered daughter

Simi Shiriff ----- Murder victim

Payton Simmons ----- PO-1 U.S. Navy SEAL, TAD to Naval Postgraduate School, Monterey, CA

Ray Smith ----- Sergeant U.S. Marine Corps, Force Recon

Smittie ----- Southern Pacific railroad conductor

Steel ----- Chief Petty Officer (CPO), U.S. Coast Guard Monterey, CA

Jason Steiner ----- a.k.a. Raven CI for Bogotá Cartel, Assistant U.S. Attorney San Francisco, CA

Greg Stevens ----- Senior Intelligent Analyst CIA Headquarters

A.J. Stewart ----- Special Agent, U.S. Immigration and Customs Enforcement (ICE) Oakland, CA

Striker ----- CIA's codename for Maria, Bogotá Cartel Housekeeper

Hans Studgard ----- a.k.a. Viper

General Sun ----- Heroin warlord, Thailand

General Tamir ----- Israeli General previously assassinated

Gil Thomas ----- DEA Special Agent, U.S. Embassy, Mexico City

Frank Tito ----- DEA Country Attaché, U.S. Embassy, Mexico City

Ricardo Tomales ----- CIA Case Officer, U.S. Embassy, Bogotá

Viper ----- Bogotá Cartel Assassin, a.k.a.'s, Ivan Volkov, Heinz Von Berg, Jacques Devinuer, Black Knight, Hans Studgard, Karl Hanns, Alfred Herman

Ivan Volkov ----- a.k.a. Viper, Former Russian Special Forces (SPETSNAZ) Lieutenant Soviet Military Intelligence (GRU) and FBS Counterterrorist Officer

Heinz Von Berg ----- a.k.a. Viper

Jason Ward ----- Captain U.S. Army Special Forces/Delta Force U.S. Embassy Bogotá

Ron Williams ----- DEA Special Agent, Washington, DC

Gerald Winston ----- CIA Case Officer, Cabo San Lucas, a.k.a. Herman

Louisa Winston ----- CIA Case Officer, Cabo San Lucas/wife of Gerald

Sean Young ----- Victoria's Secret photographer

Jordan Zif ----- National Security Advisor

Acronym/Glossary

Alpha Group ----- Russia's Spetznaz Special Forces Army Elite Counter Terrorist Group under the command of the FSB equivalent to U.S. Army Special Forces, Delta Force/U.S. Navy SEAL Team 6

DCI ----- Director of CIA

FSB ----- Russian Internal State Security, Counterintelligence and Antiterrorist Operation for Russia-formerly KGB

Charlie Barracks ----- Top-Secret U.S. Marshal safe house, Quantico, VA

CI ----- Confidential Informant

CO ----- Commanding Officer

Code Blue ----- U.S. Marshal's codename for under attack

Code Red ----- CIA's codeword for death of a U.S. high-ranking government official or CIA official killed in action

Code Yellow ----- CIA's codeword for immediate rescue mission in the field

COS ----- Chief of Station, CIA's highest ranking official operating at a U.S. foreign embassy

DARPA ----- Defense Advanced Research Projects Agency

Dragon ----- CIA's code word for Bogotá Cartel bodyguards

The Farm ----- CIA's Training Academy, Camp Peary, Williamsburg, VA

GS ----- Group Supervisor, DEA first-line Special Agent Supervisor

HRT ----- Hostage Rescue Team

LEO ----- Law Enforcement Officer

LAW ----- U.S. military term for Light Antitank Weapon

Merlin ----- CIA's classified email system

Mikes ----- Military/NATO phonetic slang for minutes

M-203 ----- U.S. military M-16 or M-4 assault rifle fitted with a 40 mm grenade launcher.

NEST ----- Nuclear Emergency Support Team, U.S. Department of Energy

NOFORN ----- No Foreign Dissemination, U.S. classified documents

NOOC ----- U.S. Navy Oceanographic Operations Command

NUC ----- Nuclear Device

NSA ----- National Security Agency, also a separate entity, National Security Advisor (Assistant to the President for National Security Affairs)

Ocean Stalkers ----- Classified Underwater Surveillance Unit with NOOC

OJT ----- On-the-job training

OPS ----- Operations

Pressure Check ----- A procedure by applying pressure to the upper slide of a semiautomatic pistol to see if a round is in the chamber

RSO ----- Regional Security Officer, U.S. State Department Special Agent responsibility for security at U.S. embassies overseas

SAC ----- Special Agent in Charge, DEA/FBI/ICE etc. normally highest ranking Special Agent of U.S. law enforcement field offices throughout the U.S.

Secure SCIFF ----- A room at an office or building that is impregnable to electronic eavesdropping

SCIFF ----- Pronounced "Skiff"-US Department of Defense Sensitive Compartmented Information Facility

Shin Bet ----- Israel Security Agency equivalent to the FBI

Simunitions ----- Training plastic bullet round filled with paint used during tactical training

Spetsnaz ----- Russian Army Special Forces Troops

SOCOM ----- U.S. Special Operations Command

Station Chief ----- Another description/CIA's highest ranking official operating at a U.S. foreign embassy

STE ----- Secure Terminal Equipment-U.S. government encrypted telephone communication system

TAD ----- U.S. Defense Department's abbreviation for personnel temporary additional duty/training assignments

Top Secret ----- Highest U.S. classified documents

UC ----- Undercover

Wire Room ----- U.S. law enforcement control property where authorized telephone intercepts are conducted on suspected criminals and terrorists

Made in the USA
Columbia, SC
30 May 2022

61107716R00278